SEARCHING *for* SHEILA

A NOVEL

SILE O'MURPHY

Searching for Sheila

SEARCHING FOR SHEILA

Originally published by Create Space Publishing
in the United States of America

Copyright © Síle O'Murphy 2017
All rights reserved

ISBN # 978 – 1978401075
Library of Congress Control Number: 2017918708
CreateSpace Independent Publishing Platform, North Charleston, SC

The right of Síle O'Murphy to be identified as the author of this work has been asserted in accordance with sections 77 and 78 of the Copyright Designs and Patents Act 1988.

In this work of fiction, the characters, places and events are either the product of the author's imagination or they are used entirely fictitiously. Any apparent similarity to real persons or places is purely a coincidence and a figment of the author's imagination.

This book is sold subject to the condition that it shall not, by way of trade or otherwise, be lent, re-sold, hired out or otherwise circulated in any form of binding or cover other than that in which it is published and without a similar condition including this condition being imposed on the subsequent purchaser. No part of this book may be reproduced in any form or by any electronic or mechanical means, without permission in writing from the copyright owner.

Front cover and book design by: Shelagh Geraghty Mullen
Website: shecooksdesign.com

Follow Síle O'Murphy on Facebook
@sileomurphy on Twitter
sileomurphy on Instagram

for Sophia

Acknowledgements

Thank you to my friend and editor, Sally Ann McGrath, for working so many hours on this project, your patience knows no bounds. Thank you Shelagh Geraghty Mullen for the beautiful cover, you can certainly judge a book by its cover now.

Thank you to all the people who helped me with my book; your comments, suggestions, guidance and support was invaluable. Thank you so much; Angela and Mark, the nicest people I know, I'd need a few pages to thank them for everything they do, especially Angela who was practically my publisher. Thank you for your input, influence and your help; Monica, Lauren, William, Justin, Christine, Michael, Yvonne, Maura, Mary, Mads, Carol, Tony, Mattie, Lucy and Paddymack. Thank you to Ash and Alwyn for helping me with the audio book, I am so appreciative.

Thank you to Shelagh, Sheila and Shelagh and all of my lifelong friends who have influenced me and helped shape who I am today.

Thank you to the love of my life, the inspiration of my writing, my heart and soul, my beautiful, intelligent, wicked funny daughter Sophia. And to Christian, for taking such good care of her.

To my mother for countless reasons; for her love for me and her love of reading which inspired me, and for her birthplace in Ireland that has called me home.

Thank you.

SEARCHING *for* SHEILA

A NOVEL

SILE O'MURPHY

Chapter One

The sun was illuminating the row of bold coloured buildings perched on the patchwork hill in Allihies, West Cork. The cloudless sky was a brilliant blue, the sea a rich aqua, bursting with frothy whitecaps. Waves barrelled down onto the jagged rocks, sending a cloud of fine mist into the air. Through the sea spray, a rainbow hovered over the cliff's edge and dissipated into the water. A gentle breeze came in from the sea, carrying with it the smells of fish, seaweed and salt. In the small village, aromas of turf and wood burning from previous chilly nights hung in the air. The smells of the sea and land converged in the village of Allihies, intertwined as the lives that have lived there for centuries.

Aelish was twirling around in circles down the village road. Her long straight blonde hair followed her loops, as did her plaid uniform skirt that reached her ankles. She raised her arms high into the air and screamed, 'It's a glorious day! I can't wait to get the hell out of here forever!' Maeve looked at Aelish and shook her head, then she looked down her narrow village road, lined with the multicoloured buildings; searching for peering eyes, thinking Aelish was making a spectacle of herself, but the road was empty. Aelish kept prancing around, yelling, 'Woo hoo!'

Maeve looked at Aelish and said, 'We've three months before leaving here, Aye, and that'll be too soon for me.'

Aelish was exasperated, 'Ah Maeve, you should be so excited! The world is waiting for us. We can do whatever we want after school! I can't wait to live in Dublin. I can't wait to get the hell out of here! If I get into DCU, when I'm finished, I'm going to New York. I'm going to be a fashion designer making dresses, and I'm going to have a wardrobe full of couture clothing. Or, I'm going to be an actress and move to Los Angeles. Or, I'm going to be a singer and live all over the world! I'm going to have a ton of money and buy whatever I want. It's exciting, Maeve! I don't know how I'm ever going to get through the next three months, I want to get out of here now, I'm so done with this place. I want to be freeeeeee!' She continued to twirl herself around in circles down the middle of the road leaving the village towards the rolling green hills.

    Maeve walked slowly as she looked down the road at their small village, looking forlorn. She didn't say anything for a while as Aelish skipped and twirled, throwing her arms in the air, hooting and hollering about her impending freedom. Maeve had a subtle habit when she was deep in thought. She twirled her index finger and her thumb around a lock of her long, curly auburn hair and tapped the end of the lock, over and over again.

    Aelish saw this and said, 'Ah for God's sake, Maeve, what is it? You only do that when you're worried, upset, annoyed, or whatever! What are you on about? What could possibly be wrong? This is the happiest time of our lives! You should be over the moon! School's nearly over! We'll never have to wear these wretched uniforms ever again thanks be ta God! We're going to be free! We can do whatever we want very soon! Maeve! What is it?' Aelish stopped dancing around, tilted her head and looked at Maeve.

    Maeve had tears welling up in her eyes, 'Ah, you wouldn't understand Aye. I don't want to go away to university, I don't want everything to change, I like everything just the way it is right now, I love it here, I don't want to go, I don't want to go anywhere.' Maeve slowly looked off to the distance; up to the rocky mountainous terrain, then down the green hills to their village nestled below. She looked at the cluster of coloured buildings bathed in sunlight, hugging the lone road. Countless visions of her childhood flashed through her mind. She looked out to the sea, her eyes glistening with tears, and continued, 'This is my home, this is my village, everything I want in the world is right here, I don't want to leave.'

Aelish rolled her eyes as she looked up to the sky and stretched her arms above her head, exclaiming, 'That is such a crock of shite Maeve! Me da would say you're away with the fairies so you are! He'd say you're talking flapdoodle gobbledygook nonsense. This place will be here forever, it's not going anywhere! For Christ's sake, you're only going to bloody Cork! It's only an hour's drive from here!'

Maeve half smiled, 'I know, I know, I'm going, I didn't say I wasn't going, I just said I don't *want* to go. Sure, I'll be going to UCC if I get in, that's what I'm meant to do, everyone in my family has gone. They go, they graduate, they get boring jobs, they get married, they have kids, and they're never truly happy because all they do is just work, work, work. I want to skip the university part, get married, have kids and live happily ever after right here in Allihies!'

Aelish shook her head in disbelief, 'Ah my God, that sounds like a positively horribly boring life to me, I'll vomit then fall asleep listening to this rubbish.'

In the distance, they heard music; it sounded like the song, "Wild Rover" with people yelling along with the song like drunken tourists do in pubs. They saw a red car driving up the winding road on the far side of the village. The car was rapidly getting closer towards them; the music got louder. The people in the car were screaming the song. As the car approached, tearing through the village, the girls jumped to the side of the road with their eyebrows raised, and watched as the car zipped past them. A gust of wind blew as the car screeched around the bend in the road. Small pieces of paper flew out of the car onto the road where they stood.

Aelish yelled, 'Jesus Christ! Slow down!' As she followed the path of the car she gave them the finger with both of her hands high in the air, hoping they'd see her through their rearview mirror. As Aelish was busy yelling and chasing after the car, swearing and giving them the finger, Maeve was picking up the little bits of paper that had flown out of the window, shaking her head. As she looked at the pieces of paper, she noticed one of them had a signature on it. Aelish came running back and looked over Maeve's shoulder. She squealed, 'EEJITS! They throw things out of their car window that have their names on it? We should track them down and report them to Mrs. Tierney of Tidy Towns!'

Maeve was unfolding the bit of litter that had the signature on it. 'Aelish I don't think they littered on purpose, they were putting the windows down in the back of the car, the wind was blowing and the papers just flew out, I saw it.'

Aelish was still peering over Maeve's shoulder, 'Let me see that.' She reached around and took the signed piece of paper out of Maeve's hands. Flipping over the paper, she squealed, 'Ha! It's a lottery ticket. That would serve them right if it was a winner, littering like that! Let's see, what does it say here: 'Sheila Murphy, litterbug, but I'm a lottery winner!'

Maeve took back the ticket and said, 'Highly unlikely, it's probably already been drawn.' Maeve looked at the ticket; the date was for that evening's draw. She stuffed the papers into the side pocket of her uniform skirt and said, 'Come on, let's go.'

Aelish said, 'Hang on, has it passed?'

Maeve shook her head, 'No, it's tonight's draw, I'll check it later, come on, let's go.'

They continued to walk up the road leaving the village, onto the grass path that led up into the hills of the old abandoned copper mine. As Maeve led the way up the hill, she started to hum the tune of "Wild Rover."

Aelish stopped and looked back down to where the car sped off and yelled, 'Eejits!' She ran and caught up to Maeve, hooked her arm and loudly began singing,

'I've been a Wild Rover for many a year!'

Maeve laughed and joined in singing as they marched up the hill arm in arm, singing as loudly as they could,

'And I spent all me money on whiskey and beer!
And now I'm returning with gold in great store!
And I never will play the Wild Rover no more!
And it's no nay never! (clap clap clap clap)
No nay never no more! (clap clap)
Will I play the Wild Rover! (clap)
No never no more!'

The two of them collapsed with laughter on the grass hill overlooking their village. The girls were identical in their uniforms; maroon jumpers with white Peter Pan collars, very long, plaid maroon and navy skirts, with thin green stripes that were as brilliant as the green grass that surrounded them. As they sat on the hill, they looked around at the rolling green patchwork hills in the distance. They stared out into the vast Atlantic Ocean, quiet in thought for a moment. Aelish reached into her pocket and pulled out a crumpled tissue. She opened it and said to Maeve, 'I only have four.'

Maeve didn't mind, 'Where'd you get them from?'

As Aelish opened the tissue to reveal four cigarettes, she said, 'From me ma again, she thinks she's smoking more than usual. When she's had a bit of wine, she loses track of how many cigarettes she's had. I take one after she's had one, then another one after that, she never notices.'

Maeve snickered, 'As far as you know, Aye, she probably knows you nick them, she's not thick you know.'

Aelish pulled out a lighter from her uniform pocket and lit Maeve's and then her own cigarette. They both sat there and looked out to the sea. Aelish exhaled her drag and looked around, 'You know this will always be here, right Maeve? This has all been here since the beginning of time, it's not going anywhere, sure it's not.'

Maeve kept looking out into the distance smoking her cigarette, 'I know, I get it, I just like it here 'tis all. It's just not going to be the same, I don't like change.'

Aelish put her arm around Maeve, 'Ah Maeve, you're right, it's not going to be the same, it's going to be better! Change is good! Me da always said, when things in life change, you simply find another way. The greatest thing? We won't have our parents telling us what to do any longer, we'll be able to create our own lives, it's exciting! I don't know what this rubbish is of you just wanting to get married and have kids, you've never even dated anyone, ever! Besides, you gotta have your own life, otherwise those kids would drive you crazy, I see that with me ma, I think she's gone mad with my brother.'

Maeve questioned, 'Your *brother*? Neither you or Owen are model children, you know that Aye, poor Siobhan. I reckon your life plan isn't so solid either, you can't draw more than stick people, so I'm not sure what sort of a fashion designer you'd be. You've never been in a play, so I doubt you could be an actress. And to be perfectly honest, your voice is shrill, so you should never sing for the sake of others.'

Aelish stuck her cigarette in her mouth and shoved Maeve, pushed her down on the grass and sat on top of her.

Maeve yelled from beneath, 'I'm just messing with you! Get off me!'

The bits of paper fell out of Maeve's uniform pocket onto the grass.

Aelish got off Maeve and picked up the lottery ticket and said, 'Jesus Maeve, what if?' Maeve took the lottery ticket back and placed it on her school skirt that was sprawled out like a tartan blanket.

'There's a slim chance this is a winner,' she said. 'Everyone plays, nobody wins, no one wins anything in this village. Besides, it's not ours, apparently it's Sheila Murphy's lottery ticket, whoever she is.' Maeve looked at the first set of numbers. They all meant something to her at a brief glance: there was her age, her birthdate, her mam's birthdate, her dad's birthdate, her home address and Aelish's address; she found it all a bit odd. Maeve had an unsettling feeling she couldn't explain--an overall uneasy sense of the impending changes in her life; but she also felt uncomfortable having something that didn't belong to her, something that had the potential of being worth an ungodly sum of money as far as she was concerned . . . what if this *were* a winning lottery ticket?

Then Aelish said, 'Could you imagine if this was a winner? This little piece of paper would change the life of Sheila Murphy, my God, she'd never be the same person again, she'd have no idea what hit her.'

Maeve cut her off, 'Chances are slim to none this is a winning ticket, Aye.'

Aelish looked off, daydreaming, 'Ah, but you never know, Maeve, there's a first time for everything, there's only a few hundred people that live in our village, one of those lucky sods could be a winner. I wonder if she lives in the area?'

Maeve shrugged, 'Ah who knows, you know what they say: you'd have a better chance of getting hit by lightning than winning the lottery. We don't see much lightning in Ireland.'

Aelish cleared her throat, 'You know what else they say Maeve: 'Tis the luck of the Irish, if you're lucky to be Irish, you're lucky enough.'

'Yes,' Maeve agreed, 'and we're lucky enough to live right here in Allihies! Amazing things happen in Allihies!'

Aelish rolled her eyes, 'Ah stop! Nothing ever happens in this boring place. It's the same thing day after day, everyone knows everyone, no one has any secrets. It's boring as all hell and I can't wait to get out of here.'

Maeve looked at Aelish, 'Ah, quit yer whinging. It's not that bad here, it's not that boring, and we don't know everyone, we don't know this Sheila Murphy, now do we?' Aelish rolled her eyes.

Aelish asked Maeve, 'Seriously though, what would you do if you won the lottery?'

Maeve replied, 'I'd buy myself a husband and a cute cottage in Allihies. I'd have kids and dogs on a farm and I'd live happily ever after!'

Aelish laid back on the grass, looking up to the sky dreamily, ignoring Maeve's comments, 'I know what I'd do if I won the lottery, I'd buy an island, and huge houses and boats and clothes and shoes. I'd buy another island for me ma, a big house for her and a couple of cars. I'd buy *you* a new car! Jaysus, that clunker your da dumped on you won't last another month! I'd buy so many things, jewellery, electronics, art, whatever's for sale, I'd buy! I'd buy so many things! I'd fill my house to the brim with things!'

Maeve shook her head, 'I reckon that would be a few hundred million. Aye, the Irish lottery rarely gets above five million. Personally, I wouldn't tell anyone that I won. I would give money to needy people, anonymously. I'd like to make a profound difference in someone's life. But, I'm not holding my breath waiting for something like that to happen. I'm actually fine if I never have a lot of money in my life, you can't buy happiness and it seems money causes people more headaches than it's worth to me.'

Aelish yelled, 'I don't know how we're best friends! We have *nothing* in common!'

Maeve responded immediately, 'Ah, but you love me.'

Aelish put her arm around Maeve, 'Ah yes I do, and ye love me too, ye boring ol' bat. Come here, let's take a pic.' She held up her phone and snapped a few photos of the two of them saying, 'Everyone always says no one has more beautiful blue eyes than us, ha Maeve?'

Maeve pushed Aelish away laughing, 'You're the only one that says that, ye mad yoke.' She stood up, brushed off her uniform and said, 'Right, let's go down and visit old man O'Neill.'

As the girls walked down the grassy hill back into their village, they passed an old sign: ALLIHIES VILLAGE – IRELAND TIDY TOWN WINNER - with a blank square below where a year should have been posted, and another blank space below that, and another . . . the village had never won the countrywide competition. The sign had been the bright idea of someone holding a council seat, thinking it would encourage residents to keep Allihies tidy. Mrs. Tierney was good at encouraging all of the residents to keep the village litter free, to plant flowers and to keep fresh paint on all of the buildings, with the hopes of winning someday. She had the entire village in a frenzy every July when the judges would breeze through, ticking points on their clipboards. The rusty old vine covered sign was erected in 1974 with no winning date. It was a grave disappointment to Mrs. Tierney, year after year. When the results came in at the end of September, she would be at O'Neill's pub telling everyone off and giving suggestions of what they could do better for the following year's competition. Everyone agreed to comply with whatever Mrs. Tierney said; they let her rant on, year after year.

Maeve pointed to the sign, 'Proof positive no one ever wins anything in Allihies, our entire village has never won anything!'

As the two girls walked down to O'Neill's pub, the building looked as if it were on fire with the sun illuminating the brilliantly red painted building. It was a stark contrast leaving the blazing sun into the dark pub. Maeve stood inside for a moment as her eyes adjusted, looking around at all the familiar photos on the walls and trinkets behind the bar. Nothing had changed in the pub since she was little, and she found this very comforting. The pub was quite full for a Wednesday evening. They were greeted by everyone inside, from the low tables by the front window where boys from school were sitting, to the bar filled with men from the village. A few of the men at the bar turned around to say hello to the girls.

Mr. O'Neill stood behind the old bar as he pointed at the TV that was tucked in the corner of the low ceiling. He was grumbling about something to do with politics in Dublin to anyone that would listen to him, 'Ah they're a shower of bastards they are, particularly that one, a right bloody muppet he is.' A man at the bar responded, 'Ah, you're too kind, John, that one is pure sleeveen he is, and the other spits venom, so he does, they're all useless jackeens.' The other men chuckled at the bar and mumbled in agreement as they continued to discuss their opinions of politicians.

As the girls walked by the bar, saying hello to everyone, Aelish waved her arms and pointed down to herself and Maeve yelling at Mr. O'Neill, 'We'll have two pints of Orchard

Thieves here Mr. O!' Maeve quickly walked to the back room, embarrassed by Aelish and her boisterous ways.

Mr. O'Neill frowned and walked over to Aelish. He spread his hands on the bar, leaned towards Aelish and said, 'Two pints is it? On a school night? Don't the two of you have some readin' or writin' to do?'

Aelish stopped, put her hands on her hips and declared, 'Not a damn thing, Mr. O'Neill! School's nearly over, you'll be happy to hear that we'll be gone soon, forever! Now give us two pints!'

He glared at her, squinted his eyes and shook his head saying, 'Ah ya have some cheek on ye, missus.' He wouldn't budge to get the drinks. He stood at the bar, staring her down with his eyebrows raised.

'Please!' she squealed. Then he picked up two clean Orchard Thieves glasses and pulled the tap, still looking at her.

Aelish saluted him saying, 'Thanks a mil Mr. O'Neill!' and she skipped back to join Maeve in the back room. Mr. O'Neill smirked, still shaking his head as he watched Aelish skip away. He thought to himself how the season of change was coming again, the kids that grew up in Allihies and left for university, year after year; how some returned, some didn't, and how he missed quite a few along the way. It was simply the cycle of life, constantly changing, people coming and going. He went back to the men at the bar.

One man pointed at the TV and said, 'Would ye look at that gombeen, we have the worst politicians in the world we do. Jaysus, the massive corruption is staggering, I don't know who's worse, the politicians or the bankers. They're all crooked, useless, miserable mugs, the lot of them they are.' The other men at the bar agreed, one murmured, 'Hear, hear.' John nodded and smiled as he cleaned the bar.

When Aelish walked into the back room, she saw Maeve sitting with the village idiot, or so she thought. Maeve was talking to Michael O'Malley, whom Aelish used to like, but he didn't like her, so she decided to dislike him with a vengeance. Everyone called Michael O'Malley 'Moma', which he didn't like. Aelish decided to call him 'Mama' because she thought it was funny.

She walked into the back room and yelled, 'Hi Mama!'

To her disbelief, she heard a loud voice from a small table behind the door, 'Aelish Anne!' It was her mam having tea with her brother. Aelish rolled her eyes, turned around, and walked back out the door to the bar. Their two pints of Orchard Thieves were sitting at the bar on coasters.

Mr. O'Neill nodded to Aelish and said, 'That'll be eight euro.'

Aelish acted shocked, 'Eight euro?! That's a bit steep there, isn't it Mr. O'Neill? Mr. O'Neill smiled and held out his hand towards Aelish and gestured with his fingers for her to pay up.

Aelish looked indignant, 'You should give us our pints for free in celebration of us finishing school soon, Mr. O'Neill, as they say, the hand that gives is the hand that gets.'

Mr. O'Neill smiled, 'You've sure a mouth on ye, lass, I will in my eye, I'd never get anything from the likes of you, now pay up, that'll be eight euro.'

Aelish sighed, 'Okay, okay! Me ma's in the back room, she'll sort you out, thanks Mr. O'Neill!' She picked up the two pints and went to the back room. She walked past her mam and brother and put the pints on the table in front of Maeve and Michael O'Malley and plopped herself down between them on the bench.

Maeve said thanks and Michael stood up, 'I'm gonna head on, see yous at school.' Michael walked away from their table and out the door. Maeve had been used to this behaviour for over a year--Aelish and Michael didn't speak to each other. Maeve subtly tried to keep the peace between the two, 'Okay, *we'll* see you at school then, bye.'

Aelish held up her glass to Maeve and said, 'To endings and new beginnings and getting the hell out of here!'

Maeve smirked, clinked her glass to Aelish's and said, '*Sláinte* my friend.'

Maeve took a sip of her cider and thought about the lottery ticket in her pocket. She slipped her hand into her pocket to make sure it was still there. She thought curiously, what if the lottery ticket was worth a few hundred bucks? They could just cash it in and keep the money, no one would be the wiser, no matter whose ticket it was. She reconsidered and thought if it were a winner, the ticket owner should be found, but no one should know, that should be up to the ticket holder to let anyone know. Maeve stopped her thoughts as Aelish's mam and brother walked over and sat on the little stools facing them, placing their cups of tea on the table.

Maeve stood up and gave them both hugs, 'Hi Siobhan! Hi Owen! Good to see you both.'

Aelish's mam said, 'Ah it's grand to see you too, Maeve, how are you getting on? Are you all set for university?'

Maeve answered reluctantly, 'I'm grand, set to find out anyway; my first choice is UCC, it's hard to believe we're going in three short months.'

Owen chimed in, 'I'd say it'll be three very long months for us listening to this one whinging about how much she wants to get the hell out of here!' Siobhan gave Owen a look, 'Owen stop.'

Aelish interrupted, 'Hey Ma, have you ever heard of Sheila Murphy?' Maeve kicked Aelish under the table, Aelish jumped and looked at Maeve with her mouth open. Owen looked intrigued.

Maeve pretended she was adjusting herself on the bench, leaned towards Aelish and said very quickly and quietly, 'Don't say anything.'

Owen heard the whisper, but Siobhan didn't notice; she answered Maeve's question, 'Yes, she's Martin's widow. Sheila lives just past the Fitzgerald farm, it used to be the old O'Brien farm, you know the one, just outside the village, around the bend by the large rock. I'm sure you've seen her cottage, still thatched, cream colour with a pale green door, you can't miss it. She's been on her own for so many years, keeps to herself, poor thing, always has, no one ever sees her or knows much about her. Why do you ask?'

Aelish didn't know what to say, so Maeve chimed in, 'Oh, a kid at school was asking about her, I think he's a relative, not sure, we were just wondering.'

Siobhan said, 'That's odd, she has no family left, I'm not even sure if she has any friends.' Owen's face was all screwed up, not understanding and finding the whole conversation and the kick under the table strange.

Siobhan took a last sip of her tea and stood up, 'Right then, Owen, finish your tea, I need to get you to the pitch now, let's go. See you ladies later. Aelish, when you get home please feed the dog and clean up the kitchen, all right? Your room is an absolute kip, tidy that as well. Don't forget, it's Thursday tomorrow...'

Aelish was seething; she interrupted, 'I know Ma, it's rubbish day, I know, I'll put the bins out. What *else* can I do for you?'

Maeve kicked her under the table for her sarcastic tone to her mam and said, 'I can help with all that, right, Aye? When I drop her off I can help. Good to see you both, bye Siobhan, bye Owen.' Siobhan smiled and nodded to Owen to walk out the door. Owen picked up his hurling stick and waved it towards the girls as they walked out. Aelish was relieved to see them leave.

She glared at Maeve, 'Why'd you keep kicking me? Who cares if I ask about Sheila Murphy? What's your problem?'

Maeve replied, 'I don't know Aye, I just wanted to see...'

Aelish interrupted her, 'Ah Jaysus, you actually think there's a possibility of that ticket being a winner? Ha ha, you're hilarious!'

Maeve cringed, 'No Aelish, I don't know, I just thought we'd keep it to ourselves for the moment 'tis all.' She stood up and said, 'Come on, let's take our drinks up front and talk to the boys.'

Aelish quickly stood up, 'Now you have some sense on you.' They picked up their drinks, walked to the front of the bar, and joined the conversation with the boys.

It was the usual chatter about sports, which Aelish loved. Maeve's attention was drawn to the TV mounted up in the corner behind the bar. It was the national lottery draw with the tumble machine spitting out the lottery balls for five million euro. The ball was 26. Maeve had looked at the numbers on the ticket and remembered 26 being one of the numbers because that was her birthdate. She sat there looking at the TV screen, slack jawed as she saw the other numbers lined up on the bottom of the screen. She remembered the number 2 because that was her mam's birthdate; 4, her dad's birthdate; 8 was her home address; and 12 was Aelish's home address. She was twirling her hair as she gawked at the TV, in shock and hardly believing that she saw the same numbers on the lottery ticket.

Maeve slowly stood up and said, 'I'll be right back, Aye, I'm going to the ladies,' and she walked off. She went into a stall, took out the lottery ticket from her pocket and looked at the numbers in disbelief. She whispered out loud to herself, '2,

4, 8, 12, 18 and 26, my God…' She leaned against the wall and looked all around, not knowing what to do. They matched--all of the numbers matched. She was holding a piece of paper worth five million euro. She was stunned, even though it wasn't her ticket. She thought of how lucky that old widow Sheila Murphy was; that woman had no idea how her life had just changed this instant. Maeve couldn't believe it; she was a bit shaken up. Her hands were trembling. She didn't want to be responsible for this ticket worth so much money. She wanted to go to Sheila Murphy's house immediately; she wanted to give her the ticket and be done with it. Aelish's mam had told them where Sheila lived; she wanted to go to her house now without delay. She was awestruck staring at the lottery ticket, the winning ticket that would have been trash by the side of the road had they not found it. She put the ticket back into her skirt pocket and slowly walked to the front of the pub where Aelish was sitting at the table, laughing and talking with the boys from school.

Maeve walked up to Aelish looking as if she had just seen a ghost, 'We need to leave.'

Aelish responded, 'No Maeve, we've just ordered a round, don't be daft.'

Maeve looked wide eyed with her eyebrows raised and said again slowly and in a calm voice, 'We need to go'. She walked out.

Aelish knew something was terribly wrong by the look on Maeve's face. Standing, she said, 'Sorry guys, we gotta go, see yous tomorrow!' Maeve was already out the door of the pub, standing in the middle of the road.

Aelish quickly followed Maeve, 'What's your problem Maeve, what happened, what are you on about?'

Maeve slowly turned around to Aelish looking shocked, 'Aelish you're not going to believe this, but that Sheila Murphy won.'

Aelish jerked her head back, 'What?! You're joking!'

Maeve spoke slowly, 'I swear to you. The ticket, Aelish, the signed ticket. That Sheila Murphy won the lottery, all six numbers matched, the bonus number matched. We need to get this ticket over to her immediately, I do not want to be in charge of five million euros with this flimsy little piece of paper. I'm wrecked having this ticket on me worth so much money. I want to bring it over to her right now, this is unnerving.'

Aelish put her hand on Maeve's arm, 'Okay, okay, it's not too late, let's go then. I know exactly where she lives from what me mam said, don't worry Maeve, let's just go and give it to her. I don't know why you're so freaked out, Jaysus, I thought someone died, for Christ's sake.'

They walked to Maeve's car, got in and drove down the road, repeating the directions Siobhan had given them; just outside the village, past Fitzgerald's farm and past the large rock. They saw the cottage down the long road in the distance; the lights were on and smoke billowed from the chimney. She was home. Maeve pulled in slowly and stopped the car in the middle of the bumpy dirt road, took a deep breath and sighed.

Aelish asked, 'Why are you stopping? Let's get on with this.'

'Aelish, I had an odd feeling from the start about this ticket, the last few hours I've been very uneasy. I think I had a premonition that something was going to happen, something monumental, this is so surreal.'

Aelish interrupted, 'You're uneasy about everything these days Maeve, you're mental. Just carry on, let's give the auld one her ticket and be gone.'

Maeve agreed, 'I'm just glad we found it and we *can* pass it on. Look, it's raining! This little piece of paper would have completely disintegrated on that road!'

Aelish replied, 'Maybe she'll give us a reward!' They continued driving down the bumpy old road and reached the cottage. When Maeve turned off the engine and got out of the car, there was dead silence outside. Aelish walked towards the door looking to get out of the misty rain; Maeve stood and looked all around, gazing out to the farm fields, to the old stone walls and the patchwork hill they were on. 'You know this is the view we've been looking at our entire lives, don't you? It's odd how quiet it is here, being away from the sea. It's grand, I wouldn't mind living here and raising a family.'

Aelish responded while she was reaching the door, 'Well then, why don't you tell old Mrs. Murphy here that she should kick off so you can start that boring dream of yours.' Maeve gave her a smirk as she walked towards her.

The girls knocked on the door. It was opened by a naturally beautiful woman, physically fit, with salt and pepper hair pulled into a loose bun, and crystal blue eyes. The woman looked to be in her 70's. She opened the door with a big hello and a warm welcome.

Maeve said, 'Hello, Mrs. Murphy, sorry to bother you.'

She was interrupted, 'Not at all, not at all, c'mere, come in, you're getting drenched, you'll catch your death. Please don't call me Mrs. Murphy, I haven't been called that since my husband passed twenty-five years ago.' The woman ushered the girls into her cottage and continued, 'It's Sheila, please call me Sheila. Now then, who are you two lovely ladies, and to what do I owe this pleasure?' Maeve couldn't help but notice what a warm feeling she had immediately upon meeting this woman and entering her cosy cottage. Although she had never met Sheila before, she felt as if she knew her. The fire was lit, as were a few candles scattered throughout the cottage. The décor was in all warm jewel tones; emerald, maroon and dark brown wood throughout the walls and floors. The entire cottage was soft, comfortable and inviting.

Aelish trailed behind Maeve as they entered the cottage, letting her do the talking.

'We have something of yours, Sheila. While you were driving through Allihies today…'

Sheila interrupted with laughter, 'Twasn't me driving through Allihies today, I can assure you of that. My car's in service, has been all week.'

Maeve cocked her head in question, 'Well then, someone else must have had something of yours that flew out of their car window today.'

Sheila looked puzzled, 'Whatever are you talking about, dear, no one would have anything of mine, and if they did, I'd certainly hope they wouldn't be throwing my belongings out their windows. Now, what are you on about?'

Maeve looked at Aelish, hesitant, but continued, 'It was your lottery ticket.' Again, she was cut off by laughter.

'My *lottery* ticket? I've never had a lottery ticket in my life, I wouldn't even know where to get one. Why don't you girls sit down and I'll make us a cup of tea.'

They sat at the table near the fireplace, just off the kitchen. Sheila put the kettle on and brought cups, saucers and a plate of biscuits, setting everything on the table. She stood there looking at Maeve and Aelish with a concerned look on her face, 'C'mere to me, tell me what's this all about.' The girls looked at each other, confused. Maeve was quiet. *What could this mean?* She was perplexed. She hadn't wanted to tell anyone about this whole situation; her uneasy feeling came back. How could she not be the Sheila Murphy that signed this ticket?

As she twirled her hair in her fingertips, she thought about the next thing she was going to say, but Aelish interrupted her thoughts, 'Sheila, we have a proposition for you!'

Maeve butted in, 'We do *not* have a proposition for her!'

Aelish glared at Maeve, she squinted her eyes and said, 'Wait, I'm confused, how can she not know anything about this?'

'How am I supposed to know?'

'Jaysus, you were in such a rush to come over here.'

'Now what are we to do with it?'

'Christ, I don't know, throw it out o*ur* window?'

Sheila fetched the pot of tea from the kitchen and sat down, 'Now girls, when I get flustered about something, I take a deep breath and I relax myself. If one deep breath doesn't work, I take another. Take a deep breath now, slow down, and start from the beginning.' The girls went back and forth and told their story about their day, how everything had unfolded, ending their story showing the signed lottery ticket to Sheila. She looked at the signature and said it looked nothing like her own; she assured them it wasn't hers.

They all sat in silence for a moment, sipping their tea. Sheila looked off beyond the table, into the rest of her cottage. She had lived there for her entire life, as her father had before her. Having a farm had never been easy for Sheila. She'd had many struggles throughout her life, but she'd always managed to make ends meet. She'd scaled the farm back when Martin died, doing what she could to make money. She'd always had a roof over her head and something to eat, and often thought that was all she needed or wanted. Her thoughts went briefly to how grand it would be to have such a vast sum of money, it would be life changing. These young girls were sitting at her table holding a five million euro ticket with her name on it. It was her name, but it wasn't her. Pretending to be the winner wasn't an option; it was out of the question. One principle had always been more important to Sheila than anything else: to live truthfully and honestly.

Sheila assured them it wasn't hers. Aelish nudged Sheila, saying she could pretend it was hers. Maeve didn't entirely agree with Aelish, but questioned if Sheila would agree to be the Sheila Murphy that was on the ticket. They went back and forth, Aelish nearly begging Sheila to be *this* Sheila Murphy, swearing to secrecy that no one would ever know outside of this room.

Sheila wasn't getting through to the girls the importance of being honest, no matter the cost. She decided to tell the girls a story--a story her husband had told about when he was a soldier for England during World War II. Martin couldn't get any work in Ireland so he'd enlisted in the English Army to help with the war effort abroad. Martin was sent to the front lines in North Africa in 1942 where the fighting was heavy. The German and Italian forces had had some initial success in the area, but then they were defeated, at the expense of Martin's entire troop.

There was a turn of events where things became misconstrued during the last battle Martin fought. The British Army was fighting hand-in-hand with the Indian British Army, the French, American and New Zealand Armies, all fighting against the Germans and Italians. The allies had first managed to gain on the enemy, killing hundreds of German and Italian soldiers. It was Martin's unit that had changed the course of the outcome of this battle; they were the first ones in and they had killed key enemy commanders, the leaders of the German regiment. Martin's unit had then been overrun by enemy troops in a bloody battle. Martin was wounded and all of his fellow servicemen were killed. Martin was hailed a hero, but he wouldn't accept the accolades. He needed to tell the truth; he couldn't live with himself otherwise. He couldn't imagine living a life with any sort of lies; he said it would eat away at his soul.

He explained to everyone that he had actually been scared to death in the desert sands; he wasn't proud. He'd hidden when they were ambushed, and everyone was killed around him. He had carried this with him for the rest of his days. He had chosen to tell the truth, when he could have easily claimed to be a hero, since no one was left alive to say otherwise.

In the end, allies had swept in, rescuing Martin, and ultimately succeeded in swarming the German and Italian troops, taking thousands as prisoners of war. Immediately afterwards, Martin could barely function. He was wounded; he couldn't speak, so others spoke for him, assuming what had happened--they assumed he was a hero. When he was able to speak, he refuted their claims. Martin explained to them that he'd done nothing--he'd frozen. He had to live with the choices he made and the guilt that came with his choices. He could have lied; no one would have known the difference. But he'd told the truth and lived with the shame of his actions. It was his own truth, and that was all that mattered to him, not what others thought. He owned the shame; he took responsibility for his actions--or non-actions--and he was at peace with his decision.

Sheila explained to the girls that this had been an extreme circumstance: life and death and in the throes of a World War. But she told them that was how he'd lived his life in everyday circumstances--honestly and truthfully, not only to others, but to himself as well. Sheila told the girls how much she respected and admired Martin for living his own truth, no matter what. She went on to say that he'd expected the same from people that he allowed into his life. It was obvious to the girls how much Sheila had loved her husband: the look on her face, the sincerity in her eyes, the passion in her voice when she spoke of him.

Carefully, she said to the girls, 'If Martin were here today, he would tell you the same thing I am about to tell you now: you must do the right thing, find the owner of this incredibly large sum of money. Find the Sheila Murphy who purchased this ticket. She is the rightful owner, find her and don't question it, it's simply the right thing to do. Make it your quest.'

She continued to explain to them that they should be wary of people they might encounter along the way. She said although there were many good people in the world, there were many who have no conscience. Money breeds greed and causes blindness. Honesty cleanses the soul, enveloping you with pride. She told them to do the right thing, always.

The girls sat at the table sipping their tea, listening to Sheila.

Aelish chimed in, 'But, if we didn't find this ticket, if we weren't on that road at that exact moment, this ticket would have been lost forever, it would have been rubbish, either blown to bits or dissolved in this rain. I think that was a sign. We were meant to find it, we were meant to keep it!'

Sheila touched Aelish's hand on the table and kept her hand on top of hers as she spoke, 'Ah sure, I'll agree, I think you girls were meant to find this ticket, that is set in stone; but I also believe you were meant to find it within yourselves to do the right thing.'

Aelish couldn't believe it, 'Wouldn't you like to have it? It's five million euros! This could all be yours!'

Sheila responded thoughtfully, 'Of course I'd like to have it, dear, if it were rightfully mine. If I had purchased that lottery ticket, I'd be kicking up my heels this very moment. But I didn't, so I won't be, and it's not an option for me to pose as the winner.' She looked around the interior of her cottage, 'Ah besides, what would I do with all of that money? I quite like my life as it is, I've never been one to embrace change, anyhow.'

Maeve was curious, 'What does this mean? Is there another Sheila Murphy?'

Sheila responded with laughter, 'Ah dear, I don't want to disillusion you, but I've lost track of how many Sheila Murphys I've encountered during my lifetime. I was related to one, and the best of friends with another. Sadly, they've both passed away, God rest them. But that narrows down your search a bit.'

They all chuckled, but the girls had looks of worry on their faces.

Maeve wondered aloud, 'What are we to do?'

Sheila responded in a careful tone, 'The beauty of this life is figuring things out for yourself. Life is like a puzzle, and you are putting the pieces together. Figure things out and be proud of yourself when you do. When things go wrong, it may seem as if the puzzle pieces are strewn about, scattered upon the floor. It's your job to pick up the pieces and put them in a place where it feels comfortable for you. As you girls become adults, you'll learn that you are now in charge of your own puzzles, you are creating them all yourselves. So, as you create the puzzle of your life, as you put all of the pieces together, carefully choose the pieces you put permanently into your work of art, which is your life.'

Aelish was looking at the ceiling, thinking about what Sheila had just said. But she still couldn't grasp everything, 'Why couldn't you just copy the signature, and collect the money, you could give it to us and we could look after it for you?'

Sheila tilted her head to the side with a smile, 'Aelish, on this quest of yours to find this Sheila Murphy, you'll probably come across someone that would take you up on that offer. I assure you it would be a wrong path to take. Not only for your own conscience, but the choice you would be making--to not live honestly and truthfully--would have a consequence in the eyes of the law. If you were caught, it would be fraud, and you'd serve time in prison. Is that the path you'd like to take, and is that a permanent puzzle piece you'd like to place in your life?'

Aelish wouldn't relent, 'How would we ever be caught? No one would need to know!'

Sheila was getting exasperated, 'You can justify everything you do in this life to suit your own needs. You could justify taking this money for a thousand reasons, but the fact remains, it's not your money to take in the first place, it's not yours to make any decision whatsoever. It's not your claim. It's not yours, it's not mine, it's Sheila Murphy's, the Sheila Murphy that signed this ticket. You need to find her, she is the rightful owner.' She continued to bestow her wisdom on the girls, 'I would be careful how you approach this, people act very strangely when it comes to money, especially if they've never had it before in their lives. Money brings out the worst in some people. So, you must be very careful who you tell that you're holding onto a five million euro ticket. Oh, I just had a thought: I have a little something for you to put this ticket in to keep it safe.' She stood up and walked off to the back of the cottage. They could hear wardrobe doors opening and closing, and her muttering where the little bugger could be hiding.

The two girls looked around the living area. There were two framed photos: one looked like Sheila and her husband; the other was of a girl that could have been Sheila, holding two baby girls in white dresses. It looked similar to a photo

Maeve's mam had in their house. Maeve guessed by the photo that her girls would be about the same age as her mam. She didn't see any recent photos of anyone, and wondered to herself if Sheila had any children or grandchildren, or anyone else in her life, for that matter. The house was warm and inviting, but there seemed to be something missing. The girls sat there in silence looking around Sheila's cottage while she was rummaging through the wardrobes and drawers in the bedrooms.

When Sheila returned to the sitting room she was holding a small metal box that looked like a treasure chest, along with an antique key.

'I want you to have this to keep that ticket safe until you find its rightful owner,' she said. Maeve stood up and took the box and the key from Sheila, thanked her and gave her a hug. Sheila hugged her the way Maeve's mam hugged her; it was very warm and strong and genuine, and lasted just a bit longer than the usual hug you get from someone. Maeve felt an immediate connection to Sheila; she felt as though she knew her and took a liking to her immediately.

Maeve didn't want to leave, but it was getting late and they needed to head home. They thanked Sheila for the tea and biscuits and headed for the door. Sheila told them to be careful; she reminded them to choose wisely whom they told about the ticket and to come back if they needed any help whatsoever, or just to visit and have a cup of tea. She told the girls they were always welcome at any time, day or night. The girls thanked her again and left the cottage. As they drove away, they looked back to see Sheila

standing at the doorway of her cottage, waving goodbye until they were no longer in sight.

Maeve and Aelish were silent in the car. They really didn't know what to think. After a few moments, Maeve perked up, 'I know! I'm going to call the Irish lottery office in the morning and just explain this whole situation; they'll take care of it!'

Aelish shrugged, 'That'd be grand, I'm sure they'll know what to do, it's not our problem.' Maeve drove Aelish home, both deep in thought.

As they pulled up in front of her house Aelish put her hands up, 'Ah Jesus, I forgot.' Her mam was pulling out the rubbish bins with their dog by her side. When she saw Maeve's car pull up, Siobhan stood there with her hands on her hips, shaking her head in disappointment. Aelish muttered, 'Ah Jesus, I can't take this any longer.'

Maeve responded thoughtfully, 'Three short months, Aye, you'll be grand, I'll see you in the morning.' Aelish got out of the car and slammed the door. Maeve remembered that she'd mentioned to Siobhan that she'd help Aelish. She cringed, hearing Siobhan yelling at Aelish, she quickly drove away.

Aelish walked towards the house to a barrage of questions, 'Aelish Anne, *where* have you been? You were supposed to be home hours ago, the poor dog was starving! The house is a mess! What's wrong with you, Aelish? You just gallivanting around? Mr. O'Neill called me and told me you walked out on your bill--how dare you, Aelish? You have responsibilities here! While you're under my roof, you will obey my rules and you'll have respect for others. You'd better get into O'Neill's tomorrow and pay for what you owe him and never do that again! And if you ever let your dog go hungry again…'

Aelish walked inside the house not hearing the rest of her mam's barraging. *That woman has no idea the kind of day I've had, she never understands anything about me or my life and I can't wait to get out of here. Ah my God, I can't wait to get out of here, I can't stand it when she yells at me, I feel so out of sorts. My head is spinning.* Then she heard Sheila's voice in her head, *'Take a deep breath, just relax for a moment; if it doesn't work, take another deep breath.'* After a few deep breaths, it worked.

Aelish walked up the stairs towards her bedroom. Her phone rang; it was Maeve; she didn't say hello, she just continued the conversation she'd been having in the car with Aelish. 'Okay, this is what we're going to do, I'll pick you up for school in the morning, we'll go to first class, then we'll leave, we'll go to the back garden or someplace and phone the lottery office and pass this whole thing off to them. So, it'll no longer be our responsibility or our problem, okay?'

Aelish, feeling a sense of relief, yelled, 'Yes! Ah my God, Maeve, I never get stressed about anything and I was feeling stressed about this. I can't believe it! If we can give the winning ticket back to the lottery office and they find the rightful owner, then hallelujah! We'll be done with this and we don't need to go and find another Sheila Murphy! I didn't ask for this headache today and I don't want it, it's doing my head in! Keep the ticket in that metal box, hide it in your room or something, I don't even want to see it again!'

Maeve laughed and agreed, 'Perfect. See you in the morning.'

Aelish hung up the phone with a sigh as she walked past her brother's room; she waved at him as he sat on the floor near his bed with his headphones on, bopping his head to his music. He waved back as she passed by his door. She entered her bedroom, dropped her book bag, collapsed on her bed and fell asleep, still in her uniform.

Chapter Two

Maeve sat in front of Aelish's house for a few moments before she decided to get out of her car and go up to the door. She didn't want to be late for first class. As soon as she arrived on the doorstep, Owen opened the door holding his hurling stick, 'Hello Maeve, what are you up to today?' Maeve responded as she gestured towards her uniform, 'Well, by the looks of things, I'm going to school Owen, how about yourself?' As he stood there in his grey school uniform, he put his hands out, shrugged and smiled, then he asked if he could have a lift to school. Owen wasn't particularly interested in school. He was obsessed with sport, particularly hurling, and making money. Owen liked to keep his blonde hair cropped with extra-long fringe brushed far to the side. He was a tall boy for seventeen, over six feet. Maeve was looking up at him in the doorway and agreed to take him to school on the condition that he would hurry Aelish along. Maeve didn't like being late for anything.

Owen left Maeve at the door and ran upstairs yelling, 'AAAAAEEEELLLIIIIISH!' Then he started banging on her bedroom door. He squished his face in the crack of her door and yelled in a deep voice, 'AAAAAEEEEEEELLLLLLIIIIISH, I am your brother.' All he heard was 'Feck off Owen' muffled into her pillow. He banged on the door again and yelled, 'AELISH! Your lift to school is leaving!'

Aelish jumped up, sat on her bed and looked at her phone. She couldn't believe the time. She looked down at herself, seeing she was still in her full uniform from yesterday, she stood up, brushed herself off, smoothed her skirt, picked up her school bag and opened the door.

'What's your problem, pest? I'm ready to go. Why do you care if we're leaving anyway?' Owen explained that Maeve was giving him a lift to school.

Aelish snapped, 'Since when?'

Owen responded, 'Since when you were still asleep in your uniform, we had a chat and she's driving me to school and she doesn't want to be late, so hurry up!'

Aelish yelled down the stairs, 'Sorry Maeve, I'll be down in a tick!' She brushed her teeth, put on some deodorant and went running down the stairs. Her mam must have gone off to work already, so Aelish made sure the dog was inside, she gave him a treat and ran out to the car. Owen was sitting in the backseat looking at Aelish running out of the house. It reminded her of when they were kids. Owen always wanted to sit in the back, whereas most kids usually bagged the front seat. Aelish would call the back seat just to annoy him, leaving their mam to drive them around like a chauffeur. Owen saw Aelish reaching for the back door handle and he quickly locked it. She laughed, skipped around to the front of the car, plopped herself in the front seat and said, 'Good morning, missus!' Maeve said good morning, put some music on and asked why her brother needed a lift, wondering what had happened to his usual carpool.

'I have no idea.' She looked in the back seat and asked what had happened to the lads. Owen shrugged, put on his headphones and started bopping his head back and forth, playing air guitar on his hurling stick.

They were driving along the road adjacent to the sea. Maeve always loved this drive; she never tired of it and enjoyed the view every time. She knew now they would be at school before the first class bell rang so she didn't see the point in rushing. A car was driving up behind Maeve. She pulled over to let them pass.

Aelish squealed, 'What are you *doing*?' She looked back, recognised the car, opened her window and gave them the finger as they passed. It was Owen's carpool.

'Why the hell didn't he go with them?' She looked in the back seat and yelled, 'What the hell, Owen?' He continued to bop his head to his music, looking vacantly out the window at the vast sea.

'Ah my God, he makes me so livid, the langer.'

Maeve interrupted Aelish and asked if Owen could hear what they were saying.

Aelish responded as she looked in the back seat to Owen, 'Hell no, he plays his music so loud he can't hear his own thoughts!'

Maeve continued, 'Aye, like I said last night, this is what we're going to do. As soon as first class is finished, meet me in the back common, it's usually empty and there's good phone reception out there. We're going to call the lottery office together, give them the ticket and have them sort this out, they can find that Sheila Murphy. It's their problem, not ours.'

Aelish agreed, 'It would be like finding a needle in a haystack if there are that many Sheila Murphys out there as Sheila said last night. You're right, it's not our problem. Okay, I'll see you out back as soon as first class is finished. I might have to go to the loo first, so don't go berserk if I'm not out there immediately.'

Maeve said, 'Ah Aelish, I know that means go and have a cigarette. Who do you think you're talking to? No one ever goes into that back yard, just bring the cigs out there, then we'll make the call. I'll be glad to be done with this! I feel stressed holding on to this multi million euro ticket. I'll be so happy to pass it on!'

Aelish asked, 'Wait, you don't have it with you, do you? It's in that metal box that Sheila gave you, right?'

Maeve said, 'It's safe and sound, don't you worry about it.'

They pulled up to the school and started to get out of the car. Owen took off his headphones and panicked: 'Holy shite, I forgot my paper that's due this morning! Ah Jaysus, I can't go in there without it! Christ Maeve, let me borrow your car to run back and get my paper! I can't handle going into Mr. O'Sullivan's office again! I have my license, let me take your car! I swear I'll be so careful! Please Maeve!'

Maeve threw her keys at Owen and told him to calm down.

Aelish agreed, 'Jesus, Owen, calm the feck down, go on with you for Christ's sake. Come on Maeve, let's go.'

The girls stood in the carpark as Owen drove away to retrieve his paper. They walked across the brilliant green grass that surrounded the long, circular gravel drive that led to the school. Mr. O'Sullivan was standing at the top of the stairs of the grandiose Georgian structure, as he did every single morning, greeting all of the students. He was a man of some stature, 6 foot 5, and carried a staunch front like the school itself, but he was a kind, warm man. Mr. O'Sullivan was looking at his watch as the girls approached the front of the towering, three storey, grey granite stone school.

'Good Morning ladies, well done, even a bit early today. God performs miracles every day, ha ha.'

Aelish laughed a fake laugh, 'Heh heh heh, say, Mr. O'Sullivan, Owen Flanagan is going to be a little late this morning, me ma needed his help with something, he couldn't avoid it.'

Mr. O'Sullivan looked proud, 'Ah, good man that Owen, I'll talk to him when he arrives, that's a good lad, your brother.' Aelish rolled her eyes as she walked past him and entered the school corridor. Mr. O'Sullivan was awkward with the girls; he was just getting used to girls being at the school. It had been an all boys' school since the early 1800's until just recently, when it merged with the girls' school which needed to close, due to lack of enrollment and a dilapidated building that was beyond repair. The girls had just joined the boys over half-term, so everyone was still getting used to the new order.

    Owen was speeding down the road; he knew he would be a bit late but also knew he could get away with it. Mr. O'Sullivan liked him--he was hurling champion for the school, and Mr. O'Sullivan loved his hurling. Owen also knew this would be the only chance he would have. He pulled up in front of Maeve's house, and in a lame attempt to disguise himself, put on a coat and scarf that he found in the back seat. Owen had been to Maeve's house many times over the years, dog sitting. He knew where the spare key was kept outside, and he knew her parents would both be at work; their other kids had long since moved away. Maeve was the youngest and the last one living at home. He was thinking to himself what eejits his sister and Maeve were, willing to give up five million euro. He wouldn't have it, he was going to take matters into his own hands before they gave the ticket to the lottery people. He would find a Sheila Murphy himself.

    He'd first heard Aelish on the phone with Maeve the night before, then confirmed it in the car on the way to school. He didn't care who it was, or how he would find one, but he was determined to find a Sheila Murphy and split the winnings with her. Owen always pretended to listen to music with his headphones on, looking like he was in his own world, but he'd been listening to everyone's conversations over the years, ever since he was a young boy. He always felt the need to hear the goings on, but he didn't want to participate in the conversations. He'd never dreamed his eavesdropping would lead to five million euros. He was quite proud of himself with his plan.

Owen walked up to the largest rock along the footpath in front of Maeve's house where the key was always hidden. It wasn't there. He turned over another rock, and another and another. He went back to the large rock; the key was always under the large rock--where was it? He panicked. He was running out of time to get the ticket in the metal box and rush back to school. He didn't want anyone to see him going into Maeve's house. While he was frantically searching for the key under every rock outside the house, the dogs were barking inside the house and his cell phone went off, beeping a text message. It was Aelish:

You had to help Ma, that's why you're late – Mr. O'Sullivan. He was tempted to write back: *Thanks! Where the hell is Maeve's spare key?* But he just responded: *Thanks.*

He ran up to the door, felt the top ledge and ran his fingers all around the eaves of the overhang surrounding the door. He finally looked under the mat and there it was. He opened the door, calmed the dogs, and ran up to Maeve's bedroom and looked everywhere for the metal box. Being over six feet tall, he laughed when he saw where Maeve had 'hidden' the metal box; it was sitting on top of her wardrobe, pushed back just enough so she couldn't see it. He grabbed the box, not thinking to look for its key, and ran out of the house. He didn't care, he had every intention of smashing the box. He locked up, put the key back under the large rock and sped off back to school. He knew exactly what he was going to do; he had thought of a Sheila Murphy he met a few months ago. He would take care of this and reap the benefits; the girls wouldn't be able to give the ticket back to the lottery people now. How foolish they were--he was quite chuffed with himself that he knew how to handle this situation.

Mr. O'Sullivan was still standing at the large main doors of the school. Owen had gone to this school since he was five years old. The primary school buildings were in the back; smaller, less imposing stone structures, they had originally been the stables of the main house. The secondary school in front was a magnificent Georgian building, commanding the hill upon which it had stood since 1740.

Before the time-watching principal could say anything, Owen approached him, saying, 'I'm sorry, Mr. O'Sullivan, me mam needed help, I couldn't say no.'

Mr. O'Sullivan waved him into school and said, 'Good lad, see you after school for practice!' Owen ran into the school and down the old hallway towards his class, which was already in session. He nearly went into the classroom, but remembered the metal box in his school bag; he wanted to put it into his locker. He ran past his classroom and went into the sports lockers, tucked the metal box under his runners at the bottom of his locker and latched the lock. He would deal with it later.

After first period was finished, the girls went out to the back yard.

Maeve looked at Aelish, 'Let's have a ciggie, then we'll call the lottery people. I have to tell you something first, Aye.' Aelish panicked, *Ah God, what now?*

'I didn't want to tell anyone about this whole thing, Aelish, I just wanted to sort things out for ourselves. I feel like we are, and I'm proud of us. The thing is, I didn't feel safe having that five million euro ticket in my possession, it made me so nervous, so I told my mam everything, but I told her that you and I wanted to work this out ourselves. Anyway, she took the ticket to her work at the bank and put it into a safety deposit box. Now it's safe and we don't even have to think about it until we turn it over to the authorities.'

Aelish looked relieved and said, 'Ah Jaysus, I thought it was going to be something bad. I love your ma, of course that's grand. I didn't know we were keeping everything to ourselves or that we wanted to sort everything out on our own.'

Maeve jumped in, 'You didn't tell anyone, did you?'

Aelish laughed and said, 'Don't be daft, I haven't said a word.'

They finished their cigarettes and dialled the number to the lottery office in Dublin.

'Irish Lottery, Siobhan speaking, how can I help you?'

Maeve said, 'Hello *Siobhan,*' looking at Aelish and smiling because that was her mam's name. 'My name is Maeve Mulligan and I found a signed lottery ticket that turned out to be a winner in last night's draw, it's not mine, and I was just wondering…'

Maeve was interrupted by the lottery agent, 'If you tamper with a ticket in any way, it is rendered invalid. If you read the back of the ticket, it's in bold print: "Forgery is a legal offence and will be prosecuted to the full extent of the law." Whoever the ticket holder is, the signatory must claim the prize from a store clerk up to the amount of 600 euro or they must come to our offices in Dublin for larger amounts, and they must claim the prize within 90 days of issue. If a person does not claim the prize within this time, the money goes back into a general fund which is dispersed throughout the country for good causes which you can read about on our website. Does this answer your question?'

Maeve paused, 'Well, yes it does, but, what if we turned in this winning ticket to your office, would you try to find the person the ticket belongs to?'

The woman was a bit snarky, 'If you read the back of the ticket, it states that the ticket should be treated as regular currency. If you lost a twenty euro note, I don't think anyone would come looking for you. In larger sum winnings, there is a verification process, which includes but is not limited to a questionnaire, interviews and the retrieval of tapes from CCTV cameras from the facility of which the ticket was purchased. Now then, have I answered all of your questions?'

Maeve jumped, 'Yes, thank you very much, bye-bye, bye-bye, bye-bye.' and hung up.

'What just happened?' asked Aelish.

Maeve shook her head, 'She just went on and on about the legal ramifications of any sort of forgery and blah blah blah. What got me was when she said that if no one claims the prize, the money is pretty much lost and if we turned in a ticket with a name clearly on it, they would never look for the person. So, the money would just go back into a general fund for the lottery to do with it what they want. I was thinking, we have 90 days, or 89 now, how hard could it be for us to find this Sheila Murphy? She probably lives around here somewhere. I can't help but think it wouldn't be that difficult to find her, let's just do it, what do you think?'

Aelish looked at Maeve as if she were mad, 'This thing has been driving you crazy! You've been worried and bothered about this, and so have I. What are you thinking? Whatever, Maeve, as long as this doesn't drive you to distraction. Exams are coming up, school is out soon, we can do it I suppose, how hard could it be? Didn't Sheila say she knew of a couple of Sheila Murphys?' Maeve said yes, but she reminded Aelish that they had passed away. Aelish reminded Maeve what else Sheila had said: that she had lost track of how many Sheila Murphys she had come across during her lifetime in Ireland.

Maeve said, 'I bet we can find her! There can't be *that* many Sheila Murphys, now can there be? We should go back to that Sheila's house and find out if she has any more information. Maybe she'll know where we can find the winning Sheila Murphy.'

Aelish agreed, 'She did invite us back anytime, and she did offer to help us, and since she already knows about everything, why not? I feel like we can trust her.' Maeve continued, 'Right then, let's go back to her house after school today.'

The girls walked towards the school from the back yard. Maeve stopped and looked at Aelish, 'I reckon I don't feel as stressed about this any longer. I feel like we can do something about this, we'll find this Sheila Murphy, and like you said, maybe she'll even give us a reward!'

Aelish agreed, 'She had better! Okay, let's do this!'

They walked arm in arm back into the old stone school building. Needing to go to their next classes, they parted ways in the wood lined corridor saying they would see each other in the car park after school.

As they walked in opposite directions down the hallway, Aelish remembered something she didn't want to forget again, so she yelled really loud down the hallway to Maeve, 'I need to go back to O'Neill's today and pay for our drinks from last night!'

Sister Mary Margaret was walking quietly down the hallway minding her own thoughts. Startled by Aelish's yelling, she jumped and grabbed her heart, 'Modulate your voice Miss Flanagan, modulate your voice!' Aelish spun around, surprised herself.

She yelled very loud at the nun, 'Sorry Sister!!' then skipped off down the hallway to her next class.

The speakers were beeping down the halls, signalling the end of the school day. It had once been a melodic tone of real bells, but a speaker system had been installed a few months back, when the girls joined the school. The boys didn't like the new speaker system, nor were they used to the shrill voices in the hallways when the girls invaded their home territory. The boys said the girls couldn't hear the real bells, they weren't loud enough, so they had to install the new speaker system so it could be heard above the shrill of the girls' voices.

Aelish burst out of her last class into the hallway. She dropped her book bag on the floor, raised her arms and yelled, 'Hallelujah! That was the last time I will ever take a religion class in my life! Woo Hoo! Yes!'

Sister Mary Margaret appeared out of nowhere and asked her to come into her office.

Aelish looked up to the ceiling, 'No! Sister, I can't! I have to go! I'm sorry, Sister, I'll take another religion class, I will, I swear!'

Sister Mary Margaret insisted, 'It will only take a moment, come this instant.' Aelish rolled her eyes, picked up her book bag by one strap and followed the nun, dragging her bag behind her on the floor as she imitated the quick steps the nun was taking in front of her. When they reached her office, she sat down and slouched low in the chair opposite the nun's desk. The nun told her to sit up.

Aelish said, 'Sister, I'm sorry, I won't yell down the hallways any longer, I swear I won't, now I really must go.'

Sister Mary Margaret stopped her, 'It's not about that, Aelish, although I would appreciate you keeping that into consideration and stop your incessant yelling. This is about your brother; he came in late today, and he left school early, without permission. I was going to call your mother, but I thought I would check with you first, is he having trouble at home?'

Aelish didn't know what to think. She knew why he'd come in late, but she didn't know why he left school early. 'I don't know, Sister, I'll find out and let you know tomorrow, now I really must go, school is over!'

Aelish left the nun's office and went running down the hall, dodging people along the way. As she made her way down the main hallway she saw Owen's friend Liam in the distance. Liam was Owen's best friend; they were on the hurling team together, but he preferred rugby, and had the build for it. He was strong and stocky and had a mop of long, brown, curly locks that Aelish always thought he was hiding behind.

Aelish ran up to Liam, bending down to look under his hair to meet his eyes, 'Hey Liam, what's going on with your carpool, are you still driving Owen?'

Liam looked confused and uncomfortable, 'Yeah, but he said he had his own lift to and from school for the rest of the week.'

Aelish was confused, 'So, he's not going home with you today?'

Liam said, 'No, he said he was helping his mam, I mean your mam, with something, but we have practice, I don't know, he changes his mind all the time.' Aelish knew her mam was at work; she'd received a text from her saying that she wouldn't be home until six. Aelish wondered what Owen was up to. She thanked Liam and continued running down the main hallway, dodging people as she made her way to the large front doors. She was surprised to see Maeve's car out front in the horseshoe driveway; usually they met in the car park, but she realized she was a bit late after being detained by Sister Mary Margaret.

As Aelish approached the car, she noticed the windows were down. She could hear Maeve saying, 'Honestly, what takes you so long, where have you been?' Aelish thought, Good God, she sounds like my mam. She got into the car and told Maeve about Sister Mary Marching Orders calling her into her office. She told Maeve what Sister Mary Militia had said about Owen.

Maeve chimed in, 'Don't forget Sister Mary Masochist.' They both laughed and drove off.

'Right, let's get you to auld man O'Neill's to sort out your bill.'

Aelish laughed, '*My* bill? It was *our* bill and I forgot to get some money from me ma!'

Maeve smiled, 'Ah, no worries, I'll pay it, then we can go and visit Sheila.'

They pulled up in front of O'Neill's, went inside and sat at the bar. Mr. O'Neill looked surprised to see them--it was only 3 pm.

'How's the form?' he asked. 'Are you here for another pint just out of school, are ye ladies? A bit early for that now, isn't it?'

Maeve smiled at Mr. O'Neill, 'We're here to pay our bill from last night, Mr. O'Neill, we're sorry about the misunderstanding. We thought Aelish's mam was paying for it.'

Mr. O'Neill smiled at the girls, 'Not a bother, I knew you'd be good for it, as you are. Besides, I know where to find ye both.'

Maeve smiled and handed him eight euro, 'Hey, Mr. O'Neill, do you know of *another* Sheila Murphy in the village besides Martin's widow?' Aelish was surprised that Maeve had asked him that so she kicked her under the bar.

'No, I can't say that I do. We did many years ago, the two of them were friends they were, that was a bit confusing. She's passed on though, God rest her. What are you looking for *another* Sheila Murphy for? What's wrong with the widow? She's a lovely woman, that one.'

Maeve hadn't thought this through, 'I think I was thinking of the other one, the friend, I bet that was confusing, the two Sheila Murphys being friends and all.'

Aelish kicked Maeve's leg again as they stood by the bar. Maeve's eyes bugged out.

'Thank you Mr. O'Neill, bye now!'

Aelish walked out first, 'Bye Mr. O'Neill!'

Maeve limped behind her into the road, 'What did you do that for, why'd you keep kicking me?'

Aelish laughed, 'To get you back, and I was wondering what were you thinking? Are we going to go round asking everyone if they know another Sheila Murphy besides the widow? That would be weird and suspicious! We need to think of a plan before we start spouting off to the whole village about us looking for a Sheila Murphy because we're holding her five million euros!'

Maeve knew she was exaggerating, but right, 'Okay, let's go to Sheila's house and hopefully devise a plan. I have a feeling she'll know what to do, or at least she'll help guide us. She seems like a very wise woman, I like her.'

Aelish smiled, 'I like her too, I hope she has those lovely chocolate biscuits again, I'm famished.'

They drove down the sea drive and up over the hills to Sheila's cottage. As they were driving down the road Maeve remembered something.

'I was going to bring her metal box back to her! I thought since we're not using it, I'd return it. I forgot to stop by my house to fetch it!'

Aelish said, 'Bring it to her next time, I have a feeling this isn't going to be our last visit with this Sheila Murphy.'

Chapter Three

Maeve and Aelish drove down the long, bumpy road leading to Sheila's cottage. There was a brilliant green strip of grass streaming down the centre of the dirt road. Potholes filled with water were scattered on each side of the long line of grass. Each pothole looked like a little lake, filled with the reflection of the blue sky. There was no avoiding them, so Maeve just drove through them, splashing the water out of each hole.

Aelish shouted, 'Jesus' with each and every pothole Maeve encountered and drove through.

'Jesus, Jesus, Jesus, Maeve, *Jaysus*, I don't remember this road being this bad yesterday, can't you drive *around* the holes for Christ's sake?' Maeve just shook her head and kept driving down the ill kept road, hoping it wouldn't damage her tyres or the old car's suspension.

Before they'd parked the car in front of the cottage, Sheila was standing outside of her front door, as if she had been expecting them to arrive.

'Hello girls! How's things? I had a feeling I'd see you again! Come in, come in, I'm just making toasted cheese sandwiches, would you like one?'

Aelish was very happy, 'That'd be grand, thanks a mil, I'm famished!'

Maeve agreed, 'Ah thanks, Sheila, I'd love one.'

The three of them sat down at the table, in the same chairs they'd been sitting in the night before. Sheila had the fire going, as usual, with turf glowing like coal in the old wrought iron fireplace.

'I didn't think I was going to see you two again so soon, but I'm glad to see you just the same. c'mere to me, have you any new developments? Tell me everything and don't leave out a thing.'

They both started to talk at the same time.

Maeve said, 'Right, we decided to phone the lottery office.'

Aelish said, 'Ah sure, look it, I fell asleep in my uniform last night, I did.'

Maeve looked at Aelish, confused, 'What does that have to do with anything, Aelish?' Sheila smiled and got up to finish making the sandwiches and to put on the kettle.

Aelish laughed, 'She said tell her everything.' Maeve got up, found cups and saucers in the press and placed them on the table.

'Well then, anyway, Sheila, after Aelish got her good night's sleep in her school uniform, we phoned the lottery office this morning and they pretty much told us the ticket was useless, and if we turned it into them, they would toss it and keep the money, no matter whose name is on it.'

Sheila listened intently and looked at the girls while she was making the sandwiches, 'Go on.'

Aelish finished, 'We've decided to do everything we can to find the rightful owner of the winning lottery ticket and we need your help to find the real Sheila Murphy.'

Sheila laughed, 'I assure you, I'm very real.'

Maeve interjected, 'Would you mind helping us, or at least letting us know of any other Sheila Murphys that you know of?'

Aelish continued, 'We need some sort of a plan to find the rightful owner, would you mind helping us devise a plan?'

Sheila stood smiling at the girls, 'It would be my absolute pleasure.' She went back into the kitchen still talking, 'Now then, did you girls Google Sheila Murphy? I've never Googled myself before, let alone anyone else. There are literally thousands of Sheila Murphys in this country! My God, they're as common as potatoes, so they are!' The girls looked pathetically surprised: they couldn't believe *they* hadn't thought of doing a Google search; and they were surprised to hear just how common the name Sheila Murphy was.

Sheila brought the tea over to the table, 'Now then, this is going back a few years, but I do know of a Sheila O'Leary who married Fergus Murphy about ten years ago, they lived in the Kilgarvan area. The only reason I know this is because An Post delivered packages here on numerous occasions, items that *I* certainly didn't order. The contents were horrid and I demanded they be picked up at once!'

The girls laughed, 'What were they?'

Sheila shook her head, 'That's neither here nor there ... the first time they picked up the box they traced it to Sheila Murphy in Kilgarvan. The next thing I know, she's on the phone ringing me, being quite obnoxious she was, asking if I had taken something from her box, as there were items missing. I couldn't believe the cheek on her! I said to herself, "No I certainly did *not* take anything from your box, dear woman, I didn't want that box, nor the contents of that box, in my house, it was absolute rubbish," and I hung up. My friend Sheila Murphy, God rest her, was actually a distant relative of Fergus. *This* Sheila Murphy in Kilgarvan seemed to be a right obnoxious snit she did. But there you have it, she may be the one you're looking for.'

The girls were laughing, they both thought about the two people in that car speeding through Allihies, how loud and obnoxious they were with their singing, and how crazily they were driving. They agreed, it was probably her--they'd found the winner.

Sheila served the girls their warm toasted cheese sandwiches and crisps. As she put a plate in front of each of them, she said, 'I've been thinking since you left, did you girls happen to get a good look at the car?'

Maeve said, 'Yes'.

Aelish said, 'No'.

Sheila continued, 'I was thinking how miraculous would it be if you two could remember the number plates, the make and model of the car, then the Guards could track her down for you. Can you at least remember what colour the car was?'

Maeve said, 'Red'.

Aelish said, 'Maroon.'

Sheila was trying to think of how she could get the girls to remember.

'Do you remember what kind of car it was?' she asked. They both remained silent.

Maeve remembered one thing, 'It was absolutely for sure a four door! I remember the back window going down, that's when the papers flew out!'

Sheila looked pleased, 'I'm going to give you girls paper and pens, I want you to write down every single thing you remember about that car. Picture yourselves on that road, where you were standing, what you were thinking, how you were feeling, look at the car and write down all of the details you saw but didn't pay attention to at the time, look at the colour, the lights, the number plate, any markings, write everything down while you eat your sandwiches.'

Sheila poured their tea in silence, then she left them with their pens and paper and went off to clean up the kitchen area. The girls were busy writing everything down. Sheila thought how interesting it would be to see if the two of them came up with any of the same details.

Aelish put her pen down first, 'I can't think of anything else.' Maeve was still writing. Aelish looked across the table trying to read what Maeve was writing upside down. Maeve was writing how she was feeling, how she didn't want to leave Allihies.

Aelish pulled the paper away from Maeve and said, 'Jaysus, you're supposed to be writing down things you saw about the car! Would ye look at this.' She read out loud that Maeve was thinking how sad she was to leave Allihies, but, she was certain it was a red car; it had four doors. There was a sticker on the back window that she couldn't make out, but she remembered a rainbow on that sticker. She remembered a blue oval of the Ford logo, but then wondered if it could have been a Kia.

Sheila was impressed, 'Well done. If you girls could close your eyes, look at the number plate on the car. This is very important because it could narrow down your search. It would be miraculous if you could remember the numbers, your search would be over! Can you at least see the letter in the middle of the numbers on the plate? That will tell you what area the car came from, originally anyway, can you see it? Was it a 'D' for Dublin? Was it a 'G' for Galway? Were there two letters? Was there a 'WX' on the number plate for Wexford? 'SO' for Sligo?'

The girls agreed there was only one letter but they couldn't agree which letter it was, but narrowed it down to a 'G' or a 'D'. Then Maeve changed her mind and said she thought it was a 'C' for Cork, but then agreed that she just had Cork on her mind. Neither of them could remember any numbers.

Sheila said, 'Ah, it doesn't matter I suppose, it could have been bought and sold and moved around the country anyway, it was just an idea, but, well done remembering the other details about the car, this may come in handy.'

The girls picked up their cups and plates and brought them into the kitchen, thanking Sheila for the tea and sandwiches and for the information.

'Are you off to Kilgarvan then?'

Aelish quickly replied, 'Yes! Why not? We've found Sheila Murphy, thanks to you Sheila Murphy! We'll go and give her the good news that she's the winner of five million euro!' As Sheila hugged both of them, Maeve didn't want to let go.

Sheila looked into Maeve's eyes, 'Now you girls be careful, don't just give it away, make sure she's the rightful owner before you go handing over that ticket. Ask lots of questions, be sure now. Call into me again and let me know how everything works out.'

The girls got into the car and drove off. Sheila stood at the doorway of her cottage waving goodbye to them until they were out of sight. She smiled and went back inside, thinking how she loved their energy; it had been so many years since she'd had company in her house--she missed the excitement, and the jubilance, especially of these girls. She loved being alone, but now she questioned if she really did. She smiled, hoping they'd come back and visit again soon.

Maeve and Aelish were determined: they would find this Sheila Murphy. They embarked on their drive to Kilgarvan. It was only about an hour and a half away, but they felt as if they were going on a journey.

Aelish was excited, 'Let's stop at the first petrol station, we must get some treats for the road trip. She didn't have those chocolate biscuits! I want some chocolate!'

'Aye, it's not *that* far to Kilgarvan and there isn't a petrol station for at least half an hour.'

Aelish wouldn't give up, 'Stop anyway Maeve, I need chocolate.'

Owen went back after school to go to his hurling practice. He'd skipped classes for no reason, he was just totally bored with school. He loved hurling, but his mind wasn't on the game today. He was thinking about a girl he'd met a few months ago, after a game up north. One of the guys had told him a girl was asking about him--she was asking everyone who the good looking hurling star was. After that game, he had been introduced to her, but he wasn't interested. She was way too made-up for his taste. She wore thick foundation about three shades darker than her skin tone, and severely painted on eyebrows and false eyelashes; it was all too much for him. He remembered her clothes being mismatched, brightly coloured, and skin-tight.

After she had been introduced to him, she wouldn't leave him alone. She kept saying: 'Call me, my name's Sheila, here's my number, I live at the travellers' camp outside of Kenmare.' He had only a vague recollection of what her last name was, but thought it might have been Murphy, or it could have been Murray or Morphy. He thought it very well could have been Murphy because that's the most popular name in Ireland, so the chances were pretty good. He thought, even if it's not, if it's close enough, she could pose as Sheila Murphy and they could reap the benefits of this lottery win.

After practice Owen asked Liam to drive him to the travellers' settlement. Liam was surprised.

'What the hell Owen? Have you gone mad? Are you mental? Why the hell would I drive you into that war zone?'

Owen explained there was a girl there that he wanted to see.

Liam continued, 'Honestly, are you bleedin' mad? No one goes into those places unless you *are* a traveller! Jesus, Owen, they all have guns, the guards won't even go in there, are you mad? And a girl? You know you'd never be allowed to see one of their girls anyway. They stick with their own kind and you know it. Anything else is just asking for trouble, what are you on about?'

Owen was persistent, 'It was a girl I met a few months back, her name was Sheila, I want to find her, I don't know her last name but I want to look for her, it might be Sheila Murphy, Murray, Morphy, it's really important, Liam.' Liam was still looking at him as if he were mad, but the two of them always did whatever the other wanted.

'I'm not driving you *into* their settlement Owen, that's a death wish, but if it's that important to you, I'll drive you over to Kenmare; my cousin works at a local pub, he knows some of the travellers, he may know something.'

That made Owen feel better; he patted Liam on the back, and said, 'Good man, that's it then, that'll be grand, let's go.'

They drove for half an hour. Liam slowed the car as they approached a petrol station.

'I need to stop for petrol.'

Owen immediately bent over and opened his athletic bag at his feet, looking for his wallet.

Liam knew what he was doing, 'Ah, you can forget that, you can get our pints later.'

Owen sat up as they were pulling into the petrol station. He looked out the windscreen and saw Maeve's car in the car park and he ducked back down near his feet saying, 'Ah Jesus.' Owen's head was spinning. All he could think about was how he hadn't thought this whole thing through; he imagined his sister going absolutely ballistic and freaking out, so he panicked.

He shouted, 'Don't pull in here!' Liam jerked his head back and looked down at Owen with his head practically inside his athletic bag. Owen continued his panic, 'Christ Liam, go to another petrol station! Get out of here!'

Liam had no idea what was going on, but he listened to Owen and bypassed the petrol pumps and continued through the station, intending to make a u-turn to exit. Liam figured he'd get an explanation out of Owen soon enough. He sensed the urgency and tried to exit.

As he was driving back around to exit the petrol station, they heard a shrill voice outside. Owen knew that voice; it went right through him. With his head still down near his bag, he needed to think quickly.

He jumped up and shouted at Liam, 'Christ, it's too late, just tell her we're going to visit your cousin, that's it, say nothing more. We are just going to visit your cousin!'

The shrill voice got louder as she ran towards the car, 'LIAM McGUIRE!' Then she started banging on his window, 'What the hell are you two doing way out here?'

Liam put his window down, 'Well hello Aelish, we're visiting my cousin in Kenmare. What are you doing all the way out here?' Aelish stomped around the car to the passenger side and banged on that window.

As her brother put his window down, she said, 'What are you doing, pest? You have school tomorrow, what the hell are you doing in whatever the hell this town is called in the middle of nowhere? And why are you going to see Liam's cousin in Kenmare on a school night? What the hell, Owen? What are you up to? You're up to something! Why did you leave school today? Sister Mary Margaret is on to you, and Ma's next! Get out of that car at once! What are you two up to? Some sort of drug run or something? Get out!'

Owen got out of the car as it sat in the way of cars entering and exiting the petrol station. Liam, thinking this might take a while, pulled over and parked the car in the car park.

Owen slammed the door, 'Jesus, Aelish, calm down, I'm not twelve and you're not my mam, so back off!'

Aelish was fuming, 'Ah my GOD, *are* you getting drugs from Liam's cousin? Is that it? Ah Jaysus, I keep so much from Ma, but I'm not keeping this, not anymore! Christ, Owen!'

Owen laughed, stopping her mid-sentence, 'Yeah, Aelish, we're getting drugs from Liam's cousin, for fecks sake, you caught me, now why don't you go on about your business and I'll mind mine. If you noticed, I didn't ask you what *you* are doing all the way out here. Why don't you do your thing, and I'll do mine. You don't have to look after me any longer Aelish; I'm no longer your responsibility.'

This was a new reaction from Owen; Aelish was confused and didn't know how to respond.

'Whatever, Owen, I'm not covering for you any longer. In fact, you'll be in Sister Militant's office tomorrow morning; I'll have nothing more to do with it, or you. I'm simply not covering for you any longer.' Aelish walked away, towards the petrol station where Maeve was just walking out. She snapped at Maeve, 'I'll be back, I'm buying a pack of cigarettes.'

Maeve was surprised, 'What? They're ten euro a pack!'

'I know. I'm getting loads of chocolate and cigarettes and maybe even some booze!' Maeve had no idea what had just happened. Then she saw Owen getting into Liam's car, she stood and watched them as they drove off.

When Maeve and Aelish were back in the car, Aelish was visibly upset, 'I can't wait to get out of here, Maeve, I can't be responsible for him any longer. It's been almost a whole year now since Da died, it's been a year of hell for me coddling him and covering for him, I can't do it any longer, I need to get out of here, I need to get out of Allihies.'

'Ah Aye, I'm sorry, I don't know what just happened, but you can't smoke in my car.'

Aelish threw the pack on the floor, 'Could you pull over then?' Maeve pulled over down the road from the petrol station. She pulled up by a stone wall overlooking the Kenmare Bay. The girls sat on the wall and smoked their cigarettes in silence.

Aelish looked around, 'Where the hell are we?' She looked down the side of the road just beyond the car; there was a sign that looked homemade: PLEASE KEEP DIRREENCALLAUGH LITTER FREE.

Aelish was squinting at the sign, 'I can't say I know Dirreencallaugh, not sure I can even pronounce it. I'd say we're in the back arse of nowhere.'

Maeve tried to calm her, 'I know where we are Aye, we're grand.'

Aelish was avoiding any further discussion about her brother; she tried to shake it off and change the subject:

'Ah sure it's a lovely day, not a cloud in the sky now is there. We seem to be getting some pleasant weather lately, wouldn't you say? I bet you think it has something to do with global warming, ha Maeve? You're probably right.'

Maeve knew when to leave Aelish alone, 'Yeah Aye, let's get going, shall we?' They got back into the car and continued the drive to Kilgarvan.

Maeve continued, 'You know we have no idea where these Murphys live, but Kilgarvan is a small village . . . I'm sure it won't be difficult to find them. A pub's probably our best bet, someone's bound to know them, as they do.'

Aelish was a bit quiet but agreed, 'Yep, let's go to a pub and have a pint.' She didn't care much for the quest they were on; her thoughts were consumed with the annoyance of Owen.

The girls drove into Kilgarvan and picked what seemed to be a popular pub with all sorts of signs and flags out front, and cascading, colourful baskets of flowers.

They walked into the pub and were greeted by a few people sitting at the bar and by the barman himself.

'Ladies, welcome, what can I get you?'

Maeve quickly answered before Aelish had a chance, 'One lime soda and one ginger ale and bitters, please.'

Aelish rolled her eyes, 'I guess I'm not getting that pint.'

Maeve looked at Aelish, 'Let's just do what we came out here to do and be gone.' Their drinks were presented.

'That'll be six euro.'

Maeve handed over the money to the barman and asked, 'Would you happen to know where Sheila and Fergus Murphy live?'

The barman shrugged and shook his head, 'Can't say that I do.'

A man sitting at the bar chimed in, 'Not far from here, no it's not, I worked with Fergus, he and the missus live up the road, just at the top of the village, ye turn left past the house that sells wood stuff, down that road past the dairy farm on your right, you can't miss it, it's one of those monsters they built during the Celtic Tiger. It's a huge house, so it is, horrible, it doesn't fit in here. No it doesn't, you'll see, you'll agree, mark my words. They have four kids but they don't need a house that big, you could fit three families in there, so you could.'

Maeve thanked the man and the barman and took their drinks to a small table away from the bar, looking around thinking.

'Aelish, we need to think of a plan, we can't just walk up to this woman's house and say, hey, we have your lottery ticket that's worth five million euro, here you go, bye! There's a slight possibility it may not be her, so, we need to think of a reason why we're paying her a visit. What's a good reason?' Aelish thought for a moment; she sipped her drink, made a face and pushed the drink toward Maeve.

Maeve switched their drinks and continued, 'Let's just say we're working on a school project and we have a few questions for her, we're in full uniform, that'll work.'

Aelish was still thinking, took a sip of the other drink and pushed it away, saying, 'I have an idea, let's get a pint of Orchard Thieves and we can split it.' Maeve shook her head.

Aelish looked up to the ceiling, 'Okay then, this is what we're going to do, we'll go to the door with pad and pen in hand and we'll say we've got a questionnaire that will only take a moment of her time for a school project.'

Maeve said, 'That's what I'm just after saying, Aye.'

Aelish raised her eyebrows, 'Ah yes, but your plan had holes in it. I made it foolproof by adding the pen and paper bit. Then, right after we leave her house, we'll go to a pub for a bit of cider.'

Maeve agreed, but said it would have to be in Allihies, she wouldn't make that drive back on a half pint of anything. Aelish agreed as they left to find the large, apparently ugly, Murphy house. They discussed the directions as they walked out the door of the pub. The man who had originally given them the directions, shouted them out again before they exited the pub, making sure they got all the details. They thanked him.

The girls drove out of town into the country following the directions, as they talked over their plan.

Maeve was looking for a more solid approach, 'What is the project we are writing about, what questions will we ask her? We should have a few prepared questions. Get a pad out, let's write some questions down before we get there.' Aelish sat quietly thinking, then rummaged through her book bag for a notebook and a pen.

She thought for a moment and proclaimed, 'As we are embarking on the road to our future, we are interviewing people about where they were mentally at this point in their lives.'

Maeve was interested, 'Go on.'

Aelish continued, 'We are going door to door asking three questions, going back to the time you left secondary school. But now I can't think of what the three questions should be.'

Maeve thought quietly for a moment and came up with questions to ask.

'One: "Do you wish you'd done anything differently when you finished secondary school, or are you happy with the path that you chose?" Two: "Did you move away from the town where you were raised?" Three: "Do you wish you'd married and had children sooner than you did?"'

Aelish laughed, 'Ah, those aren't pointed questions of what's going on in your head at the moment now, are they, Maeve?' Nevertheless, she agreed to the questions and wrote them down; she didn't care what the questions were, they were just to find out if this woman had bought the winning lottery ticket or not.

Maeve and Aelish followed the directions the man had given them at the pub, they were spot on. His description of the house was accurate as well: it *was* huge, it *was* ugly, and it didn't fit into the Irish countryside. It was an oversized, wooden, white, box shaped house with light beige trim. There was no character; it was just really big and ugly. They gasped when they pulled into the long horseshoe driveway. There was a red car parked to the right of the driveway near the three-car garage. Maeve stopped the car.

'Oh wow,' she said, stunned, 'We really found her, this is weird. It's fantastic, I can't believe Sheila knew, we never would have found her if it weren't for Sheila.' They parked their car off to the left side of the drive, in front of the house. Two ladies came out of the house with cleaning supplies in hand. They said hello as they passed each other. Maeve led the way and rang the bell. A bleach blonde haired woman answered the door all dressed up in very high heels. She was wearing a very colourful, patterned dress with a plunging neckline, and she had a full face of overdone makeup. Aelish took over with pen and paper in hand.

'Hello, my name is Aelish Flanagan, and this is my colleague Maeve Mulligan.' As Aelish gestured towards her friend and looked at her, Maeve raised her eyebrows and silently mouthed out the word '*colleague*?' Aelish continued, 'I'm terribly sorry, it looks as though you're about to go out, we only have three questions that will take but a minute, it's for a school project that we need to complete before tomorrow morning.'

The woman opened the door wide, 'I'm not going anywhere at all! Come in! I dress up every single day, you just never know what the day will bring and I'm ready for anything I tell you. I believe in spontaneity, it's the spice of life! I also believe whiskey is the spice of spontaneity, but that's a whole other story. Now you girls come in, let me take a picture of you!' Maeve looked wide eyed at Aelish as the woman took a quick photo of the girls, then walked away from them into the house. Aelish twirled her finger near her temple while Maeve tried not to laugh.

Aelish looked around the huge house in amazement, 'So, this is your house?'

The woman spun around in delight, 'Yes, it's all mine.'

Aelish felt she should be writing something down, 'Can I have your name please?' she asked.

The woman waved them towards the sofas as they walked into the front sitting room. She continued on to look out of the front window as she answered Aelish's question, 'My name is Sheila O'Leary Murphy and I will make us a cup of tea, you girls sit down, I'll be just a minute.' She left the girls sitting on the sofa in the large, sunny room overlooking the front drive.

The house was filled with all sorts of statues, figurines, vases, and garish paintings stacked two and three deep on every wall. Maeve looked at the crowded walls with a grimace of distaste on her face. Aelish was looking around the room with her mouth hanging open, looking at all of the items on every table and shelf.

Maeve whispered, 'They don't seem like they're hurting for money, or garishness.'

Aelish leaned towards Maeve and whispered harshly, 'Don't be judgmental, Maeve, it's unlike you. I think it's fabulously interesting, will you just look at all of this shite!'

The woman came back with a tray holding three mugs with tea bags inside, and a box of biscuits. She placed the tray on the table in front of the girls and went to the window looking down the driveway again before sitting down.

'So, what are your questions? Oh wait, I want to take a photo of us having tea first, I haven't posted anything for hours!' The woman looked around, removed the tray she'd brought in for them and replaced it with a silver tray holding a proper tea set. She placed a vase full of flowers on the table, and staged the tea set. She handed the girls empty, beautiful china cups and said, 'Take sips of your tea for the photo!' She sat down between Maeve and Aelish and took a few selfies as the girls tried to contain their laughter.

After she had taken the photos she took their cups, 'Let me take these away before you break them, they're worth a fortune.' She replaced the tea set with the other tray holding the mugs and sat down in the chair across the room from them. She continued to look out the front window.

Maeve cleared her throat, 'Right then, our first question is about after you finished secondary school: Are you happy with the path that you chose to bring you to where you are today?'

The woman laughed as she looked at her phone, 'Don't I look like I'm happy with the choices I've made with my life? Look at my house, isn't it fabulous?' Aelish nodded and smiled. The woman continued, 'Don't look too closely at this room, I'm having this whole downstairs ripped up and redone starting next week!'

Maeve looked perplexed, 'Why? What's wrong with everything the way it is right now?'

Sheila got up and walked over to look out the front window again, 'Oh you wouldn't understand, everything needs to be changed, upgraded, new, fresh, you'll get it when you're older. I like everything new, I've redone this house three times in ten years.' She stood at the window looking at her phone while saying, 'What are your other questions?'

Aelish was curious, 'What did you study in school and what was your career when you finished?'

Sheila sat down in the chair and responded, 'I went to university and met my husband; we married and I never had a career, I had kids instead.'

Aelish raised her eyebrows and smiled; looking interested, she asked, 'What do you do with your days?'

The woman shrugged, 'I go to the health club every morning, I shop, I lunch with girlfriends, I go and have drinks at night with my friends, my husband works, the kids go to school, I post things on Facebook, I do Instagram, I have

Twitter followers, I do what I want--isn't that what everybody does? If they don't, I'm sure it's what they *want* to do.' She stopped talking as soon as she heard a van engine coming down the driveway. She leapt up from the chair and ran to the front door yelling, 'God bless Amazon! Ah I love the driver, wait 'til you girls see how cute this driver is, he's *gorgeous*.'

She flung the door open and ran, shouting and waving, 'Hello Justin! What do you have for Sheila O'Leary today, handsome?' Maeve and Aelish jumped up from the sofa to look out the front window. They watched the woman run in her high heels, nearly tripping, towards the delivery van, waving her hands in the air. She took the box from the man and took a photo of him, then took a selfie of the two of them. Maeve and Aelish stood watching with their mouths open. When the woman headed back to the house with box in hand, the girls scurried to sit back on the sofa.

When Sheila returned inside, Aelish asked her point blank 'Is your name Sheila Murphy or Sheila O'Leary?'

Sheila responded, 'It's both, I was born O'Leary, I married Murphy. I never gave up my *real* name, I use both names because I have to.' She continued looking at her phone and said, 'Give me a second, I just have to post this quickly.'

Aelish pressed on, 'You look so familiar to me, were you driving in Allihies a couple of days ago in that red car of yours in the drive?' Maeve was hopeful this would answer their question.

Sheila responded, 'Why would I be driving in Allihies on any given day, and in what red car? If you asked me if I was in Dublin a couple of days ago, I'd have said yes, and I was in my blue BMW.'

Aelish wanted to make absolutely sure, 'So, when you sign something, do you sign it Sheila O'Leary, or do you sign Sheila Murphy?'

The woman answered, 'Usually Sheila O'Leary, more often than not, why do you ask? Are these still your questions for your school project?'

Aelish really wanted to make sure and be done with this, 'Yes, we have one more question for you, do you play the lottery, or have you played the lottery within the last week?'

Sheila looked a bit confused, 'No I don't, and no I didn't.'

Maeve wasn't going to interfere with Aelish's questioning, but she thought she was getting a bit obvious and it was making her nervous. She interjected, 'We are also taking a survey of dietary habits: Do you drink Coke or Pepsi?'

The woman answered, 'Coke if it's with my whiskey. Pepsi with me rum.'

Aelish rolled her eyes and wasn't having any more of this; as she stood up she said, 'That's it then, thank you very much, we need to move on with our questionnaire to the next house, thank you for your time.' They headed towards the door and said goodbye. Sheila didn't walk them to the door. She picked up the box and started to open it, glancing towards them as they walked outside.

When they reached the driveway, they noticed that the red car was gone. They were relieved to find out this was not the Sheila Murphy they were looking for. They looked at each other and grinned, got into the car, and buckled their seatbelts.

Maeve sighed, 'Wow, that was interesting.'

Aelish looked at her with her eyebrows raised, 'Is that what you want to do with your life, Maeve? Is it? You want to skip school, have no career, get married, have kids and spend your husband's money and shop all day long for loads of CRAP?'

Maeve looked surprised, 'Is that what *I* want? I question you, is that what *you* want? Loading up your big house full of stuff, having a wardrobe the size of a room! That looks to me like that's what *you're* looking for, Aye.'

Aelish was surprised, 'I wouldn't want to be anything even remotely similar to that woman! Ah, the amount of shite she had! It was a gas looking at all that crap. But I felt gross just being in there, talking to her. That was one wretched, one-dimensional, unhappy, unsatisfied wagon as far as I'm concerned!'

Maeve agreed, 'Honestly, I wouldn't want any of that, I wouldn't touch that life with a barge pole, it seemed so empty and meaningless. It seems she just buys things all day long, she posts prefabricated rubbish, and gets all dressed up every day for a delivery driver? That was horrid.'

Aelish agreed, 'Ah, I'll give her that one though, yer man the delivery driver was cute, you have to admit.'

Maeve drove away from the house shaking her head, saying, 'Thank God she wasn't the winner. Can you imagine?'

Aelish agreed, 'That cow would have had that money spent in a day and wouldn't have done a good thing for anyone but herself. And, I reckon she wouldn't have given us a reward for finding the damn ticket!' They both fell silent. They still had a ticket worth five million euros to contend with; they needed to find the rightful owner. Maeve stopped the car just before she exited the long driveway and looked at Aelish.

Aelish asked, 'What is it?'

Maeve responded, 'Just thinking of our next move, 'tis all. We have some researching to do, and some searching to do. I could use that pint now, let's head into O'Neill's.'

Aelish agreed, 'Let's stop off at your house and get out of these uniforms first.

The girls drove back to Allihies. They pulled up to Maeve's house, no lights were on; she remembered her parents were out for dinner.

'Come on then, let's get you some clothes so you can get out of that wretched uniform you're always whinging about.' She walked up to the house and lifted up the front door mat to find her spare key gone.

'That's odd, I put the key back here this morning.'

Aelish helped look for it, turning over the big rock on the foot path; she picked up the key.

'Maeve, it's here where you always keep it.'

Maeve disagreed, 'I've been leaving it up here under the mat for a while now; strange, I don't know how it got down there, but thanks.'

The girls went inside the house and upstairs to Maeve's bedroom. Aelish rummaged through Maeve's wardrobe to find something to wear. She threw on a jumper and some jeans saying, 'Okay, let's go and have a pint. Let's have some fun and worry about this whole thing tomorrow, what do you say?'

Maeve smiled, 'Sounds good, but just for one, we still have a bit of school left you know. I'd like to go to Sheila's after school tomorrow, we have some planning and researching to do, I think she'll be very helpful.'

Aelish said, 'Well she hasn't been all that helpful so far, with her not being the right Sheila Murphy to start, then directing us to another wrong Sheila Murphy, but we could return that old metal box to her since we're not using it.'

Maeve walked over to her desk, picked up the chair and brought it over to her wardrobe, 'Thanks for reminding me, we'll take it back to her tomorrow.' She climbed up onto the chair, reached up and looked on top of the wardrobe, then gasped.

Aelish turned and looked up at Maeve, 'What is it?'

Maeve looked down at Aelish and slowly looked around the room. 'Ah Aye, we have a problem.'

Chapter Four

Owen and Liam arrived at The Horseshoe pub in Kenmare. Liam's cousin Rory was behind the bar, leaning close to a girl as she was stacking glasses. He looked up and saw his little cousin walk in the door.

'Jaysus, look what the cat dragged in!'

Liam hadn't seen Rory in a while, 'Hey Rory, how's things?'

Rory was wondering what his cousin was doing in his pub so far from home. 'What can I do for you lads, are ye out on the lash on a school night are ye there, Liam? Ha? On the sesh are ye, lads?'

Liam responded, 'Ah, no, Owen here is looking for a girl.'

Rory smiled, looking curious, 'Are ye now? Is it any girl you're looking for, or is it a particular girl?'

Owen looked a bit embarrassed, 'It's a girl that lives in this area, she might be a traveller.'

Rory looked at Owen and raised his eyebrows, 'Is it? And what do you plan to do when ye find this girl, ha? Are you going to march into her camp and whisk her away from her family are ye there, ye nob?'

Owen looked wide-eyed at Liam for help and stuttered, 'It's not like that, it's just that she was asking about me a few months back, and I just thought…'

Rory didn't care about the details. 'I'm just winding you up, I don't give a lump what you mugs are up to. Does she have a name? I may know her.'

Owen stumbled, 'It's Sheila, Sheila Murorphyer.'

Rory's face was inquisitive, 'What the hell kind of name is that?'

Liam interjected, 'He's not so sure of her last name, it might be Murphy or Murray or Morphy.'

A man at the bar was listening to their conversation and chimed in, 'Sheila Murphy works at the Centra, just a few shops down from here, are ye the father?'

Owen looked shocked, 'What? No! What?'

The guy laughed, 'Ah, that's all right, rumour has it she doesn't know herself. Jaysus, I wouldn't touch that one with a barge pole.'

Rory interjected, 'Ah now, a gossip's mouth is the devil's postbag.'

Owen glared at Liam and started walking quickly towards the door, 'Come on, let's get out of here.' Owen was out the door and Liam followed.

'That's it? Barely a hello?' said Rory, surprised, 'Not even a goodbye?'

Liam looked back, 'Sorry Rory, see you soon.'

Rory yelled back, 'You're a chancer if you go into that camp little cousin, don't be an eejit!'

Liam walked out of the pub, joining Owen on the footpath. 'Are you mad? What have you done, Owen? When are you going to tell me what this is all about? Did you have something to do with that? With her?'

Owen laughed, 'Ah Jaysus, Liam, it's nothing like that, look it, let's go down to the Centra and see if it's the same girl I met. Just act normal like we're up to nothing.'

Liam was perplexed, 'How would I know we're up to nothing ye langer, I don't know what we're up to at all Owen, this is mad, you're mad.'

They walked down the footpath and entered the convenience store. They saw a girl behind the counter; she did look familiar to Owen. She had so much makeup on she looked orange, with black eyes, big, drawn-on eyebrows and fake eyelashes--and she was visibly pregnant. The two boys walked up to the counter; Owen picked up a candy bar and handed it to the girl. He saw her nametag, "Sheila". She was chomping on gum and had a surly look on her face. She looked at Owen with no obvious memory of meeting him, and snapped her gum, 'One fifty.'

Owen fumbled, feeling the outside of his trouser pockets for money. She immediately grew impatient, 'There's a queue of people behind you.' It was Liam standing alone.

Liam spoke up, 'Ah no, that's okay, I'm with him, no hurry.' Owen looked at Liam in a panic, obviously not finding any money in his pockets. Liam reached in front of Owen and handed the cashier the one euro fifty. He felt like he needed to say something to the girl, so he announced, 'I like your shirt.'

'It's a goddamn polyester uniform, what do you want?'

Liam wanted to get out of there, 'Nothing, nothing, come on let's go.' He pulled on Owen's jumper, tugging him towards the door. Owen didn't know what to do; it *was* the same girl he had met months prior, but he couldn't do it. He couldn't imagine getting involved with her whatsoever about anything. He was pulled outside by Liam.

As they got outside the store, Liam quit pulling Owen and shoved him nearly into the road yelling, 'Jesus, Owen, what the hell? Was that her? The girl of your dreams? Seemed like a nightmare to me! Holy hell, the tide wouldn't take her out! Are you going to tell me what this is all about now?'

Owen was disappointed; he'd thought he had everything figured out. He wasn't sure if he should tell Liam the whole story.

'I'll tell you on the drive back. Let's go and have a pint at O'Neill's, I'm buying.'

Liam laughed, 'With what? All that money in those pockets?' They got into Liam's car and headed back towards Allihies. They were both quiet for a good portion of the drive.

'Are you going to tell me what's going on or not, Owen?'

'Yeah, yeah, let's go have that pint, I'll tell you. I'm still a bit shook up about all that.'

Liam looked at Owen, worried--that didn't sound like him at all, talking like that, 'Jesus, what is it, Owen?'

Owen looked very serious, and spoke slowly, 'Ah there was something about that girl though, you have to admit Liam, there was something there, she had a face on her so she did, she had a face of a bulldog licking piss off a nettle.'

Liam burst out laughing, 'That's brutal, you had me worried about you there for a minute, ye tosser.'

Owen laughed, 'Ah, it's all grand, stop by my house first, then let's go to O'Neill's.'

The boys pulled up in front of Owen's house. As Owen got out of the car, he told Liam he'd be just a minute and left him for a change of clothes. Owen walked up to the house feeling a bit defeated. His day hadn't gone as he'd imagined. He thought he would have found this girl willing to act like the Sheila Murphy whose name was on a winning lottery ticket and he'd be an instant millionaire; they would have split the profits. As he walked into the house and slowly up the stairs to his room, he started to think about Aelish and Maeve and how he probably should have left the whole thing alone and let them deal with it. He needed to return the box before they discovered it was gone, and forget the whole thing. Then he remembered--he'd left the box in his locker at school.

His mam was upstairs in her room, 'Owen, is that you? How's things?'

Owen yelled towards her room, 'Grand, Ma, I'm going out with Liam, see you later.' He dropped his uniform on the floor, put on jeans and a shirt and started to leave, 'Ma, can I have some money?'

She came out of her room, 'I will this time, but only if you promise to talk to Mr. O'Neill when you go in there tonight, Owen, ask him if he needs any help, I'm not an ATM machine, you need to stop asking me for money. You're at O'Neill's so much they may as well pay you, not ask John if he needs help Owen.'

He'd heard this before from his mam, 'What makes you think I'm going into O'Neill's Ma, ha?'

She didn't feel the need to answer that question. She walked towards Owen with a blank look on her face, 'Just ask Mr. O'Neill, Owen. Here's a tenner. Tell Liam I said hello.' Owen took the money and kissed her on her cheek, 'Will do. Thanks Ma.'

Aelish looked up at Maeve standing on the chair in front of her wardrobe, 'What is it Maeve? What's the problem?'

Maeve took another look at the empty space on top, where she'd placed the metal box. Only the antique key remained. 'It's gone, Aye, I put the metal box up here and now it's gone.'

Aelish shook her head, 'What do you mean, gone? Are you sure you didn't put it somewhere else? You seem to be doing a bit of that today.'

Maeve jumped down from the chair and carried it back over to the desk and stood there thinking for a moment. 'Aelish, it's gone, someone took it and I think I know who it was.'

Aelish looked confused, 'What are you on about?'

Maeve stood there shaking her head, 'This morning, I left my key under the front mat. Owen took my car to fetch his 'paper'. He must have been listening to our conversation in the car, Aye.'

Aelish started to freak out, 'Ah my God, he wouldn't! He couldn't! What's he thinking?'

Maeve looked worried, 'What's he done? Who has he told? What's he planning to do?'

Aelish was visibly angry, 'Thank God he can't do anything with an empty box, but what could he be up to? Ah my God, he's a thieving maggot!'

Maeve calmed her down, 'Let's think for a moment, since there's no harm in losing the ticket--that's safe with me mam--let's just see what he does. Can you imagine him telling anyone he had a winning lottery ticket with no proof? He'd be laughed out of the village. I say we sit tight, let's see what that little bugger brother of yours does.'

Aelish said, 'Let's just go to O'Neill's, this has turned into another annoying day as far as I'm concerned.'

Maeve smiled and started to walk towards the door, 'Ah sure look it, it's all in how you look at things, isn't it? This could either be annoying, or it could be an adventure, it's a puzzle to piece together. What do we have to lose? Let's at least enjoy the search, ha? We can look at this as a treasure hunt, right? Come on then, freshen up your face, paint a smile on it and let's go and have a chat with the boys at O'Neill's.'

Aelish looked in the mirror, 'What the hell's wrong with my face?'

Maeve laughed, 'It's what me mam always says, your face is fine. Come on, let's go.' The girls walked out the front door. Maeve went under the mat to retrieve her key to lock up the door, 'I'm not leaving my key out here any longer, can't trust anyone in this village.'

Aelish laughed, 'Ah, we'll sort that thieving maggot.'

Maeve said firmly, 'Make sure you don't let on, Aye, he can't know we know anything, let's just see what he does.' They got into Maeve's car and drove into the village to O'Neill's pub.

Michael O'Malley was walking into O'Neill's at the same time Maeve and Aelish arrived.

Aelish yelled, 'Hi Moma!'

Michael walked up very close to Aelish and looked her in the eyes: 'It's *Michael*, Aelish. I prefer to be called Michael.'

Aelish was surprised, taken aback that he actually acknowledged her at all. She raised her eyebrows and stuttered, 'Wa, what, whatever you say.'

Michael opened the pub door and gestured for the girls to enter. The girls walked in.

Maeve was laughing as she put her arm around Aelish, 'Cat got your tongue, missus? I don't think I've ever seen you flustered like that. That was interesting, I'd say he's chancing his arm with you.'

Aelish looked smug, she wriggled away from Maeve and said, 'It's nothing.'

Maeve laughed, 'Ah, there's a lid for every pot, Aye, you never know.'

Aelish snapped, 'Ah stop, nothing will ever happen between us, that's for bloody sure.'

The girls walked up to the bar. Aelish was happy to be there, 'Hiya Mr. O'Neill! I'll have a pint of Orchard Thieves, maybe two.' She looked at Maeve who smiled in agreement. As Maeve looked down the length of the bar, seeing all the familiar faces, she stopped at a man she didn't recognise. He looked to be 19 or 20 years old, very good looking as far as Maeve was concerned. She backed up and looked down the other side of the bar to have a look at him fully, sitting on the bar stool. He was dressed in a shirt and blazer, jeans and cowboy boots--fancy cowboy boots: she thought they could have been alligator or snake skin. Her eyes went slowly back up to his face and she found he had been watching her looking at him. She grabbed Aelish and shoved her to block the line of vision between her and the young man. She whispered harshly to Aelish, 'Don't look now, but, look at that guy down at the end of the bar with the dark hair, he's *gorgeous*.'

Aelish started to turn to look down the bar. Maeve grabbed her with both hands and turned her back around, 'I said don't look!' She moved Aelish aside slightly and peered around her to have another look, her mouth hanging open, 'Ah, would ya look at the head on him.'

Aelish looked impatient, tilting her head to Maeve, 'Jesus, Maeve, look at you! Close your mouth or the birds will start nesting in it. Don't lose the plot, he can't be *that* good looking.'

Maeve let go of Aelish, 'Ah sure he is, see for yourself, he is.' Aelish looked down the bar and saw the guy looking in their direction.

She turned back to Maeve and shrugged, 'Ya, he's cute enough. He looked like he was looking right through me to you, why don't you just go and talk to him.'

Maeve hissed, 'I'm not going to go and *talk* to him, *you* go and talk to him!'

Aelish laughed, 'I don't have the slightest notion to talk to him, you ninny.' Maeve leaned forward, slowly looking down the length of the bar, and found him looking at her again. He then turned his attention to Mr. O'Neill, who started talking to him.

Maeve wanted to hear their conversation, so she moved down towards the end of the bar, pretending she was looking for a place to sit. She caught part of the conversation the young man was having with Mr. O'Neill. It was clearly an American accent:

'I know you probably get this a lot from fanatical Americans looking for their long-lost relatives in Ireland, but, it's not like that, he's not a relative of mine.'

Mr. O'Neill looked at the guy and responded, 'I'm sorry to tell you, but Martin Murphy died many years ago, and that's all I know.'

Maeve's ears perked up, she gestured towards Aelish to get closer and whispered, 'Did you hear that? Why is this American looking for Sheila's dead husband? This ought to be interesting, let's find out.'

As the girls waited for their pints, a bar stool opened up next to the American. Maeve quickly sat down, Aelish stood next to her. Maeve and the man looked at each other.

Maeve spoke up, 'Hiya, you from the States?'

The man smiled, 'Yes, I am, are you from Ireland?'

Maeve laughed, 'Yes, a lot of us are here. What brings you to Allihies then?'

Aelish, bored and not interested in watching Maeve flirt with this man, muttered, 'I'll be back.' She took her pint and went to the back room.

'That's Aelish, she'll be back if she doesn't find anyone else to talk to. I'm Maeve, by the way.'

Maeve put out her hand, and he took it, saying, 'I'm Patrick, Patrick McGettigan.' Maeve had an immediate feeling of a mixture of panic and excitement when he touched her hand; he had a nice firm grip. She felt a flutter in her stomach, something she'd never felt before. She was immediately attracted to him. Trying hard to keep her composure, she said, 'Pleasure to meet you Patrick, how long are you on holiday?' He was so good looking, she had a difficult time listening to what he was saying. Her thoughts seemed louder than his talking: *He is so good looking, his touch gave me a spark, look at his green eyes, ah my God, look at those eyes.* Maeve couldn't believe she'd missed what he'd been saying. Patrick was finishing his sentence, 'And so, I've been taking this year off as a gap year, and I'll be starting college in the fall.'

Maeve panicked; she'd missed most of what he'd said. She was disappointed in herself. *Okay, get a grip, snap out of it Maeve, think of something that won't make it obvious you weren't listening at all, for the love of God.* She said, 'So, what's the exact date you'll be going back to the States then, have you a return ticket?'

Patrick smiled, 'Yes of course I do, they wouldn't let me into your country otherwise, I fly back in about three months, August 26th to be exact. I plan to do a lot of travelling around Ireland and maybe Northern Ireland as well, but I wanted to find something down here first.'

Maeve remembered what she'd overheard, but didn't want to let on. 'What are you looking to find in Allihies?'

Patrick looked a bit disappointed, 'I wanted to find a man that I thought would be here, he'd be in his 90's now. But, I sadly just found out that he died a long time ago, so I missed out on meeting him, which is such a bummer. Now I'm just going to hang out around here for a bit, stay at the hostel, and head out in a week or two.'

Maeve wanted more details. 'Who was this man you were looking for and why were you looking for him? Is he a relative of yours?'

Patrick laughed, 'No, no long-lost relatives, it's not like that, it's a long story.'

Maeve really wanted to know, since it involved Sheila, so she pressed, 'I'm not going anywhere if you'd like to tell me this long story of yours.'

Patrick looked at her, smiled, and took a deep breath, 'If you want to hear it, I'll tell it.' Maeve smiled and nodded, she looked intently while he spoke and she prevented herself from daydreaming. Patrick continued, 'My grandmother passed away not too long ago, I was really close to her. I was named after her husband, my grandfather, she always referred to him as my Grandpops, I never got to meet him. His name was Patrick, but everyone called him Paddy, he was born somewhere in Ireland. Anyway, my Grandmother and I talked about everything, but she would never talk about World War II. I heard she lived through some terrible bombings in London, then she escaped to America. If you asked her any questions though, she would change the subject.' He paused and took a sip of his pint.

Maeve felt bad, 'I'm sorry for the loss of your grandmother.'

'Thanks, it's been a few months, it's getting a bit easier.' He continued, 'Anyway, I helped clear out her home afterwards, and I came across a stack of letters my Grandpops sent to my Grandma during the war. It was early on in their marriage, just after my dad was born. My grandfather was stationed in Africa and wrote to my Grandmother every single day, it was crazy. My Grandma kept all of his letters; they were all in a small chest, stacked, bound and wrapped in red ribbons. It took me forever to read through all of the letters, but I did.'

Maeve smiled, 'That's sweet; I bet he was a lovely man.'

Patrick looked sad and stood up, 'Yep, and she was a lovely woman. If you'll excuse me, I have to go to the restroom.' He stood next to his bar stool and looked around, not knowing where to go.

Maeve looked at him for a moment, then said, 'Ah, yes of course, the loo, the jacks, straight down towards the back on your left, you can't miss it, it's the one with a man on the door.' She cringed at what she'd said. He smiled, excused himself and went off.

Maeve sat still, thinking what a dream he was--he seemed so sweet and incredibly good looking. She couldn't believe he was looking for Sheila's husband. She couldn't wait to hear the rest of the story. Maeve didn't want to let on that she knew Sheila; she wanted to get more information out of him first. She also realized Mr. O'Neill felt the same way: when she overheard him telling Patrick that Martin was gone, he wouldn't give any information about Sheila--no one would, with her living out there on her own. *I'll just find out everything I can now, and let Sheila know later.* She was looking forward to seeing Sheila again.

Patrick returned, saying, 'Sorry about that, where was I?'

Maeve was so attracted to this man, she couldn't believe how nervous and flustered she was in his presence. 'No worries, you were saying how you found letters from your grandad to your gran and you read them all.'

Patrick half smiled; he had a sadness in his eyes. 'Yep, I read them all. There were a few things I wish I hadn't read, very private things between my grandparents, but it was all good. The interesting thing was, my Grandpops kept mentioning in nearly every single letter about his best friend, Martin Murphy. They were amazing stories--I just wanted to find the man and find out more. I didn't know my grandfather; I was looking for this man that knew my grandpops and maybe find out something about him. It was such a loss with my grandmother's death, I guess I wanted to find out more about her life, about their lives, things I never knew, I don't know, I was just looking for pieces of her, I guess.' Maeve hung on his every word, enamoured.

She wanted to slap herself and snap out of it; she knew she couldn't let on, and silently begged herself to act normal. She wanted to know more. 'Did you say you're staying at the local hostel? I can see if I can find out anything for you, and I could leave the information for you there.'

Patrick looked at her happily, 'That would be so great, everyone is so helpful and friendly in Ireland, it's so nice.'

Just then Mr. O'Neill walked in front of them from behind the bar. Patrick leaned towards Maeve in a whispered tone, 'Well, *almost* everyone I've met in Ireland has been friendly and helpful.'

Maeve touched his arm a bit, feeling a tingling sensation, 'Ah, don't mind him, his bark is worse than his bite.' She couldn't tell if the attraction was mutual, so she didn't want to embarrass herself, if she hadn't already. She felt the need to leave before she made a fool of herself. 'I promise I'll find out something and be in contact with you by the weekend. I'm going now to join my friends in the back room, it was a pleasure meeting you and talking to you.'

Patrick stood up as she was leaving, 'It was nice meeting you as well, Maeve, is it?'

She held out her hand, 'Yes, it was nice to meet you, Patrick.' They shook hands. Maeve didn't want to let go.

She walked into the back room of the bar to a surprise: Aelish and Michael O'Malley sitting next to each other and actually talking to each other in a civilized manner. Maeve thought, what a strange day this was; she was curious how this had come about.

'Well, look at you two, what's going on here?'

Aelish seemed subdued, 'Michael and I have decided to call a truce.'

Maeve raised her eyebrows, 'Shall I leave you two?'

Michael stood up, 'Don't be ridiculous, sit. I thought . . . all of us are going off to college soon, best to bury the hatchets before we leave. Can I get you two a pint?'

Aelish jumped in, 'Yes please!' Maeve was reluctant and paused. Aelish wouldn't have it, 'Two please!' Michael agreed and left the room.

Maeve sat down, 'Aye, you're not going to believe this, that American, his grandfather was Sheila's husband's best friend! I didn't want to let on that we knew Sheila or where she lives, I want to check with her first, then we can go back to Patrick and we could organise them to meet!'

Aelish rolled her eyes, 'Maeve, aren't we doing enough things at the moment? We already have a bit of a search on our hands, you want to help someone else find what they're looking for as well?'

Maeve wouldn't let up, 'Absolutely! I'm going to help him find what he's looking for, it's no effort at all, besides, I think he's gorgeous!'

'Yeah, I saw you looking at him all googly-eyed, the Yank. When does he go back?'

Maeve looked dreamily at the ceiling, 'Not for nearly three months!'

Aelish laughed, 'That's great, but let's go back to Sheila's tomorrow and see if she can help us with our original quest of searching for Sheila, the winner, the lottery winner. Remember that task we took on?'

Maeve pushed Aelish, 'Yes, I remember and I still want to find her and of course we will. Nothing wrong with a little distraction. Speaking of distraction, this is an interesting development between you two.'

Michael walked in with two pints in his hands and placed them in front of the girls on the small table, 'I'm off now, enjoy, see you later.'

Aelish didn't care, 'Thanks, *Michael*.' She'd agreed to call him that from now on as part of their truce. As Michael was walking out the door, the girls clinked their glasses. Aelish said, 'Here's to new things, whatever they may be.' They took their first sips, delving into their pints just as Owen and Liam walked into the back room. Aelish nearly spat up her sip. Maeve nudged her with her elbow, reminding her to act normal.

Aelish sat up, 'What's the *craic*, pest?'

Owen looked at Aelish, 'Nothing, what's up with you?'

Aelish was thinking how she was going to enjoy this. 'Nothing, we're just having a pint and a chat about all sorts of things. So, did you get your load of drugs from your cousin in Kenmare, did ya Liam?' Liam looked worried, shaking his head and backing away from Aelish.

Owen looked annoyed, 'No, Aelish, we didn't go and get drugs, it was just Liam wanted to see his cousin is all.'

Aelish really wanted to play with this, '*Really*, Liam? Are you close with that cousin of yours? Long drive to say hello I'd say, does he not have a phone, does he not?'

Maeve wasn't liking this, 'Why don't you boys get yourself a drink and join us.'

Owen wasn't having it, 'No, we have to go and meet someone.'

Aelish wouldn't let up, 'Are ye now? Meeting another cousin of Liam's are ye?'

Owen tapped Liam on the back, 'Let's go.' Liam shrugged and followed Owen, still not knowing what was going on.

Liam looked at Owen, 'Okay, you said you were going to let me know what's going on, now let me know what's going on, everyone seems to be acting a bit odd.' Owen couldn't think of what to say; he didn't want to tell Liam the whole story; he decided he didn't want to be involved with his sister's search; he just wanted to return the metal box he'd taken.

'Listen,' he said, 'we need to go to school and get something out of my locker. I need to return something I took before anyone finds out.'

Liam was shaking his head, 'What? You stole something from someone and now you want to return it? It's at school? Have you gone completely bonkers? The school is locked up and they have alarms. What the hell are you on about?'

Owen was determined, 'I'll tell you in the car, let's go, this is important.' Liam went along with it, as usual. They got into his car and started driving towards their school. Liam continued, 'And what if alarms go off, then what, Owen?'

Owen laughed, 'I doubt they have an alarm system, maybe they do now with all the upgrades since they let the girls in. But, even if an alarm goes off? Who cares? You hear alarms going off all the time with people's houses and cars and businesses, no one pays any attention to them and the guards never come.'

They pulled into the car park in front of their school. Liam parked the car under a tree near the front gates, thinking they might need to exit quickly. They both got out of the car, not discussing any sort of plan. Owen started to walk fast in front of Liam, around the left side of the main building towards the back, where the locker rooms were. Liam had given up hope of finding out any information at this point. He decided to just help Owen get whatever he came for and get out of there. Owen was walking alongside the large grey granite stone building under the tall windows where the sills were six feet from the ground. He was scanning his eyes as he walked along the grass to see if he could find an open window. Ahead, he spotted one of the tall, narrow windows slightly open--he thought it was either the girls' toilets or their locker room. Standing beneath the open window, he whispered, 'Give me a boost.' Liam obliged, bending over and clasping his hands together. Owen put one foot into Liam's hands and hoisted himself up to the open window, opening it further so he could squeeze in.

Liam stood outside, waiting to hear some alarm go off, but he heard nothing. He leaned up against the old stone building and waited. Owen jumped in, causing an echo in the empty room as he landed on the marble floors; he looked around the girls' locker room. It was pitch black. He fumbled for his phone and turned on the torch. Owen ran through the locker room, out into the dark hallway, into the boy's locker room and to his locker. He quickly opened his locker, retrieved the metal box, and ran. His heart was beating fast; he wasn't sure if he would get caught. He ran back through the girl's locker room, reached the window, looked out to Liam below and whispered, 'Catch me.'

Liam hissed loudly, 'Like hell I'm going to catch you!'

Owen started out of the window saying, 'I'm going to jump, catch me!'

'Jesus Owen, just climb out the way you climbed in!'

Owen laughed, 'I was just messing with you.' He turned around and slid down the wall backwards and jumped the last bit to the ground. Liam did try to break Owen's fall, with a loud grunt, they both ended up on the ground, laughing. As they scrambled to their feet and started to run along the side of the building, a light turned on as they ran past the rectory; then they heard a door slam.

Owen whispered loudly, 'Ah Christ, keep running, follow the line of trees, Jesus, leg it, Liam!' Their hearts were pounding. They made it to the car and jumped in.

Owen said, 'Don't turn on the lights.'

Liam started the car and started to drive out the gates, 'Ya, I'm going to turn the lights on, and I'm going to honk the horn and ask Sister if she'd like a lift.'

Owen looked back and saw Sister Mary Margaret standing in front of the rectory building and said, 'Just get the hell out of here.'

Liam's heart was racing, 'Did anyone see us?'

Owen looked back down the road to the tiny figure of Sister Mary Margaret, still standing in front of the rectory looking at the car drive away.

He responded, 'Na, I don't see anyone, you're grand, it must have been one of those automatic lights. Now, we need to get this thing back into Maeve's bedroom, this might be a bit tricky.'

Liam was about to lose his mind, 'So, that's it? You stole that box from Maeve and now you're returning it?'

Owen laughed, 'Ah yeah, it's nothing, I just took it out of Maeve's bedroom and I shouldn't have. I want to return it before she notices it's gone, before they get back from O'Neill's.'

Liam didn't understand, 'What's in it?'

Owen held the box up and turned it around, looking at all sides, 'I dunno, I forgot to get the key.'

Liam looked at him in disbelief, 'You don't know? Jaysus, then why'd you go and take it in the first place then, ye pox?'

Owen shrugged, 'I just heard Maeve and Aelish talking about something special in the box, so I took it.'

'So, ye stole the box from Maeve, then we break into school to get it, now we're going to break into Maeve's house to return it and you don't even know what's in it? Bollocks. How'd you get it in the first place, did ye break into the Mulligans'?'

Owen chuckled, 'I didn't break into Maeve's house, I used the key. If no one's there, I could do that again. But, if someone's home, I'll just sneak in and put it back in her room.'

Liam was shaking his head, 'What if *Maeve* is home, ye langer?'

Owen hadn't thought of that, 'I don't know. Just go to her house anyway, I bet she won't be home yet and I can just return it, no harm, no foul.'

Liam was shaking his head, 'It would be easier if you just gave it back to her at school tomorrow and apologised.'

Owen laughed, 'That's not going to happen, just go.'

Liam pulled up in front of Maeve's house. The lights were on; two cars were in front--the parents were home; Maeve was not.

Owen was happy, 'Perfect! I'll just climb up the back of her house and into her window.'

Liam was fed up, 'Jesus Owen, you think she just left her bedroom window wide open for you?'

Owen gestured for him to pull over a bit further from the house; shaking the box in front of Liam, he said, 'I'll be back without this box.' He got out of the car, walked to the back of the house and saw Maeve's parents in the kitchen; he ducked and crawled under the kitchen windows, and looked up, only to see Maeve's window closed. The dogs started to bark inside the house. As Owen ran to the front, he heard the sliding back door open and the two dogs came charging out, barking and sniffing around the back garden.

As he reached the front of the house, he looked under the rocks for the key, but remembered it was under the mat. He looked under the mat to find the key gone. Frantically he tried the door handle; to his relief, it was unlocked. Knowing Maeve's parents were in the kitchen, he quietly opened the door and snuck upstairs. He entered Maeve's room and placed the box on top of her wardrobe. Quickly and quietly he snuck back downstairs. The dogs were still barking outside, but then he heard the back sliding door open and close just as he reached the front door. The dogs were now barking and running on the kitchen floor as if it were ice, skidding, barely able to gain traction. Maeve's parents didn't know what to make of their dogs' behaviour. The dogs made it to the front door just as it was closing, barking like mad but wagging their tails; they knew Owen--he always played with them and gave them treats when he looked after them. Maeve's parents came towards the front of the house wondering what was going on. The dogs stopped barking and just whined a bit, looking at the door as they wagged their tails.

Owen ran to Liam's car, quite proud of himself. He got in and sighed, 'That was brilliant! Thanks Liam! That's done and dusted like it never happened, now let's go back to O'Neill's.' Liam wasn't going to ask again what was going on--he was tired of it. He drove back to O'Neill's in silence. While he was parking the car in front, he saw Maeve and Aelish walking out of the pub door.

Owen stopped Liam from getting out of the car, 'Let's wait 'til they leave, I don't want to run into that again.' They didn't notice that they'd parked right next to Maeve's car.

Aelish walked up to Liam's car yelling, 'What are you two *doing?*'

Liam responded, yelling very deliberately, 'I don't *know!*'

Owen gave Liam a swat, 'Take it easy.'

Owen opened his car door, 'We're all just coming and going now aren't we Aye, so off you go then.' Aelish shook her head and got into Maeve's car.

They arrived at Maeve's house. 'Come in for a minute, I'm sure me ma has something to eat.' Maeve parked the car and started digging in her book bag for her house key. 'This is a pain this, I prefer just leaving it under the mat.'

Aelish said, 'We never bother locking our doors at all, we haven't got anything anyone would want.'

Maeve laughed, 'We just started locking ours recently, Da said he didn't want anyone taking the dogs.'

The dogs, hearing Maeve outside the door, were barking like crazy and wagging their tails. Maeve opened the door to find both of her parents and the dogs just inside the door, 'What's this?'

Her Dad spoke up, 'The dogs are going mad, were you just here a few minutes ago and then left?'

Maeve didn't know what he was talking about, 'No, I've just arrived.' Both her mam and dad started walking back to the kitchen. Her dad was muttering, 'Not sure what their problem is, they've been barking like mad all night long, for Christ's sake.'

Maeve's mam looked at her dad, 'It really hasn't been all night long now, has it, Jack?' Jack walked back to the kitchen.

Aelish came in behind Maeve, 'Hi Mary! Hi Jack! How's things?'

Mary gave Aelish a big hug, 'Everything's grand, Aelish, how are you getting on, okay? You girls hungry? Come on back, let's get you something to eat.'

Aelish was happy, 'I'd love anything you have Mary, it's always the best!'

Jack sat back in front of the television saying, 'If I can't get through one episode of Father Ted without being interrupted, I'll start acting like Father Jack, I will.'

Mary smiled then looked at the girls in an inquisitive way, 'So, tell us, how's the treasure hunt coming along?' Maeve looked over at her dad. Mary continued, 'Ah, don't worry, I didn't say a word, your secret and your ticket are safe with me. So, any luck?'

Maeve looked at Aelish and said to her mam, 'No, not much luck, we found another one, turned out she wasn't the winner either. We were glad about that one though, a right cow she was!'

Her mam looked surprised, 'That doesn't sound like you, Maeve Marie.'

Aelish chimed in, 'She was a cow!' Mary painfully smiled at Aelish.

Aelish put her arm around Mary and laughed, 'I'm the best influence, I am! Your daughter wouldn't be nearly the woman she is today without my guidance over the years! Hey Mary, you wouldn't happen to know of *another* Sheila Murphy now, would ye?'

Mary laughed, 'I think you'd be hard pressed to find someone in Ireland who *didn't* know a Sheila Murphy. I'm afraid the only one I know of personally is Martin's widow, but I've heard of a few others over the years, there are quite a few in County Cork alone.' That didn't sit well with the girls.

Maeve looked worried, 'A *few*, *quite a few*? How many are there? Are we wasting our time Ma? How will we ever find the right one?'

Mary looked at both of the girls, 'You girls are out of school soon, you'll have nothing but time on your hands. You'll find her. Now then, I've something for you, I took the liberty of having a look myself, I had a bit of extra time at work and did a little research for you girls. Mind you, it's something we'll keep between the three of us, but, I had a look at bank records and I found a couple of Sheila Murphys in the area for you.'

Maeve looked shocked, 'That's great Mam! Come on then, give us everything you know!'

Mary looked in the other room at Jack, engrossed in his TV show. 'I need to feed your father, then we'll go into the office after dinner and I'll show you what I've found. Now let's get you girls something to eat.'

Aelish touched Maeve's arm and leaned towards her, 'Why is it you don't want your da to know?'

Both Mary and Maeve laughed, 'If you told me da, the entire village and the counties surrounding us would know, especially after a pint or two.'

Mary agreed, 'I think it's best he doesn't know just yet, let's just see what you girls come up with first. Now sit down, let's eat.'

Chapter Five

Owen and Liam were sitting at the bar at O'Neill's. Owen remembered what his mam had said, 'Hey Mr. O'Neill, do ye need any help here, do you?'

Mr. O'Neill smiled, 'And what sort of help are ye capable of there, Owen?' Liam was laughing because he knew Owen had a reputation of being a bit lazy.

'I dunno, I could tidy up this place a bit, it could use it.'

Mr. O'Neill laughed--he kept the place perfectly clean. 'I tell you what Owen, you come here first thing Saturday morning, around 10 o'clock, I have a little construction project you can do, how does that suit?'

Owen smiled, thinking how happy his mam would be. 'That's grand, see you then, then. Hey, could you give us a couple of pints here Mr. O'Neill, the two of us put in a good day's work today, we did.'

Mr. O'Neill chuckled, 'My arse you did. What'll it be, lads?' They both agreed to Carlsberg. Mr. O'Neill went to fetch their pints. Patrick McGettigan was sitting at the bar, listening to their conversation; they all made eye contact and nodded hello to each other.

Patrick spoke up, 'If you need any help with that construction project Saturday morning, I'd be happy to help, no need to pay me.' Owen's eyes lit up; he glanced over to make sure Mr. O'Neill hadn't heard what the Yank said.

'That's brilliant! Meet me here Saturday morning at 10 then, out front, don't come in, and don't tell Mr. O'Neill, I'll come out and get you.' Owen immediately had a plan. He thought he would have this dumb American do all the work for him since he'd offered to work for free. He couldn't believe his luck. What a genius he was! Everything always worked out for him. 'Sounds like you're from the States, what part?'

Patrick was happy to talk to anyone. 'Born in Chicago…'

Owen cut him off, 'We have *loads* of relatives over there, I'm going to visit as soon as I have enough money. I want to go to New York.'

Liam laughed, 'What Irish person doesn't want to go to New York?'

Owen pushed Liam off his bar stool, 'I reckon you'd like to go as well, Liam, if you had the money!'

Liam pushed Owen, nearly knocking him off his stool, 'If I had the money? I've more money than you, ye tosser. I've some relatives in Chicago myself, me da's always going on about the McGuires in Chicago, goes back generations when they left Ireland, but we're related to *all* the McGuires in Chicago, so he says.

Patrick assumed the two were around 17 years old, 'Are you guys still in High School?'

The boys laughed; Liam said, 'Yeah, but we call it Secondary School here, one more year.'

Patrick was a bit confused, 'What's the drinking age here?'

The boys laughed again and Owen said, 'It's 18.' Then he whispered, 'To be honest, Mr. O'Neill thinks we're 18, as he thought Aelish was 18 before she was, it was me da, he was a chancer, he told Mr. O'Neill every year we were a year older than we were he did, he figured it would give us a head start, an extra year of fun. They all know we'd find cans somewhere, somehow, so why not have it here where they can keep an eye on us? Auld man O'Neill will let us have a pint or two, but he won't let us get pissed, we do that on our own up in the hills.'

Patrick lifted his glass, 'Here's to underage drinking, you wouldn't get away with that in America, it's 21 in every state and it's heavily enforced, you have to prove you're 21.'

The boys couldn't believe it. Owen said, 'Hell if I'm going there anytime soon, then!'

Mr. O'Neill came back with their pints, 'That's it for you lads tonight, drink up and be gone with you.'

Maeve started to clean up the plates from the table and signalled to Aelish to give her a hand. Aelish got up and started clearing the table with Maeve, 'I'll clear, you clean.' Jack went back to the TV, putting in another DVD of Father Ted. Mary went off to her office.

Maeve said, 'Aye, let's *both* clear and *both* clean and get it done quicker and find out what Ma's got in the office for us. I'm glad she's helping, this seems a daunting task if there are *so* many Sheila Murphys in Ireland. I don't know if we'll ever be able to find this woman on our own. Sounds to me like we're going to be looking for a needle in a haystack.'

Aelish agreed, 'Come on then, hurry up, you're gabbing on while you could be working, now load the dishwasher, let's go and find out what yer mam found.'

The girls quickly cleaned up the kitchen and joined Maeve's mam in the office, 'What did you find, Ma? How many Sheila Murphys are we talking about?'

Mary was sorting through papers on her desk, 'There are quite a few in Ireland, but I've narrowed it down to a couple in this area; one lives in Bantry, which is just over an hour's drive from here, and there's another one in Clonakilty, which is about a two hour drive from here. Now, through a little research and asking a few stealthy questions, I found out the Sheila Murphy in Clonakilty is actually a cousin of a person, a 'girl' at your school.' The girls perked up a bit.

Aelish was excited, 'Great! What's her name, we'll talk to her tomorrow!'

Mary smirked, 'It's a cousin of Sister Mary Margaret's.'

The girls looked deflated, especially Aelish, 'Noooo! I don't know how we could ask her any questions without her becoming suspicious or finding out exactly what we're up to, she is *so* nosey, and *so* pernickety!'

Maeve didn't agree, 'Ah, it'll be grand, we'll figure something out, Aye, she wanted to talk to you about your brother, didn't she? There's your chance!'

Aelish wasn't happy about that, 'I wasn't going to talk to her about anything of the sort, I've washed my hands of him!'

Maeve touched her arm, 'Don't give up on your little brother just yet, we may need that thieving maggot to help us with our search.'

Mary looked cross, 'Maeve!'

Maeve continued, 'Okay, Ma, did you find out anything about the Sheila Murphy in Bantry?'

Mary nodded, 'I didn't find out anything personal, but I managed to get an address from her account. Keep it hush hush, girls, you know I really shouldn't give out personal banking info to anyone, so mum's the word on all this.'

The girls smiled, Maeve made a gesture as if she were zipping her lips and tossing the key.

Aelish said, 'If we get a reward we'll give you a bit of it, Mrs. Mulligan!' That seemed to be the only thing keeping Aelish going on with the search, the possibility of getting a reward. Maeve thought it was exciting, like a treasure hunt, finding out these little clues along the way.

Aelish said, 'What's it going to be this time? Another school project we need answers to?'

Maeve thought for a moment, 'I think I have a more brilliant idea, we're going to go and visit Sheila first.'

'Old Sheila?' Aelish asked.

Maeve looked displeased, 'Wise Sheila is a better name for her.'

Aelish laughed, 'As opposed to cow Sheila, the wretched one.'

Mary was amused with the girls, 'Ah, you girls are doing just fine, you'll have to keep them all straight now, and don't let on what you're doing to just anyone, otherwise we'll have everyone knocking our door down wanting to help, for the hopes of getting a reward like Aelish here. Now then, I'm going to go and sort your da out with dessert, I wasn't expecting you girls, so I only have two tarts, unless of course you'd like me to split them up.'

Maeve smiled, 'Don't be silly, you go and enjoy it with Da, we'll see you later.'

She gave her a kiss on the cheek, 'Thanks for your help, Ma.' Mary left to join Jack in the sitting room; as he caught a glimpse of her coming in, he patted the sofa next to him.

Maeve and Aelish now had a new sense of direction. Maeve said, 'You know what? We'll just search one at a time, we'll find this Sheila Murphy and hopefully get that reward of yours.'

Aelish was a bit more sceptical, 'I'm not handing over that ticket *unless* we get a reward!'

Maeve looked Aelish in the eyes, 'That sounds a bit like blackmail or extortion to me, it's a good thing my mam has the ticket.'

Aelish didn't agree, 'It sounds to me like it would be a finder's fee and just negotiating some sort of contract, 'tis all.'

Maeve laughed, 'Yeah, a contract you are conjuring up in your head! I'm sure we'll sort something out, let's just find her first and see what happens.'

Aelish looked at the time; it was after 9pm, 'I need to head home, Maeve, would you mind giving me a lift?'

Maeve got up, 'Not a bother, let's go, we'll sort our details out tomorrow.'

The girls left the office and walked through the kitchen. Aelish called towards the sitting room, 'Bye Mary! Bye Jack! Thanks for dinner! See yous later!' As they started to walk towards the front door, she said, 'Ah Maeve, I forgot my things in your room.'

Maeve turned around, 'I'll get it, I want to get a jumper anyway.'

Aelish followed her, 'I'll come up, I threw my stuff everywhere.'

They entered her bedroom. As Maeve walked over to her desk to get her jumper that was on her chair, she looked up at the wardrobe and laughed, 'Ah, would you look at that, your brother was here again.'

Aelish walked over and looked up at the top of the wardrobe to see the metal box, 'Ah Jaysus, you're *joking*! What is that eejit up to? Why do you suppose he returned it, did he find it empty, or did he grow a conscience?' Maeve dragged the chair over to the wardrobe and reached up to fetch the metal box. She stood on the chair and looked at Aelish confused.

'Strange, it doesn't look like he tried to break into it at all, and he didn't have the key. I have no idea what he's up to, but we'll find out. Let's have a think about this and talk about it tomorrow.'

Aelish agreed, 'I'd like to punch him is what I'd like to do, but, you're always a bit more diplomatic than me.' She gathered her things, and shoved as much as she could into her book bag.

Maeve said, 'Right, let's get you home.'

They went off into Maeve's car and she drove Aelish home. 'See you in the morning; don't make me get out of my car, okay? Just be ready for once.' Aelish agreed. As she walked into her house and up the stairs, she could hear Owen in his room tapping a pencil on paper over and over again.

'Hey pest, what are you up to?'

Owen removed his headphones, 'What?'

Aelish laughed and spoke slowly, 'Hey. Pest. What. Are. You. Up. To?'

Owen didn't seem amused, 'Homework, what does it look like?' He looked back at his paper and continued tapping his pencil.

Aelish still hadn't figured out how she was going to work him. 'Hey Owen, do you need a lift to school in the morning again?'

Owen looked around thinking about what to say, 'No, I got that all sorted out, my carpool is grand, thanks.'

Aelish didn't want to let it go, 'What was wrong with your carpool in the first place?'

Owen was getting annoyed, 'Nothing Aelish, I just messed up, leave me to my homework now, will ye?' She decided to leave it--she would deal with him later.

In the morning, Maeve was on time as usual. Aelish, surprisingly, was in front of her house when Maeve pulled up. Maeve was shocked; she put her window down as she pulled up.

'Are you all right? Did something happen? Why are you out front?'

Aelish got into the car, 'I don't know, I woke up early hearing some noises. I know, it's a miracle.'

Maeve looked at the house, 'No Owen today? Is his carpool back on track?'

Aelish chuckled, 'Yeah, he got the information he was looking for, so I'm sure he's back in his carpool now. Who knows what he's up to, but we do need to find out.'

Maeve agreed, 'We will, I don't think he'll be a bother, we could use him to help us get some information, so we could.'

Aelish didn't know what Maeve was talking about, 'What do you mean?'

Maeve thought about Sister Mary Margaret, 'You said Owen is in a bit of trouble with Sister Mary Martyr? Well, we know what she thinks of him, he can go into her office and ask all sorts of dumb questions and she wouldn't be phased because of how scatterbrained she thinks he is, so, we'll have him ask her about this cousin of hers, Sheila Murphy in Clonakilty that my mam mentioned, he can help get the information we need to either find her, or take her off the list, what do you say?'

Aelish was up for anything, 'Sounds good to me, but wait. Let's go back and *make* him drive with us to school, let's tell him off! He's busted and I can't wait to bust him to his face!'

Maeve agreed and quickly turned the car around, 'Okay, we do need to sort him out, let's do it now.' When they arrived back at Aelish's house, she jumped out of the car, ran into the house and up to Owen's room but she found it empty. She went downstairs shouting his name. He was gone. Aelish was bothered not knowing what he was up to and not having control over him as she once had. She went back out to the car annoyed, 'The thieving maggot's gone already. Who knows what he's up to, but he better be at school.'

Owen had received a phone call earlier that morning; Mr. O'Sullivan told him he was in front of his house and he was going to give him a lift to school. Owen and Mr. O'Sullivan drove to school in silence. Owen knew it probably had something to do with Sister Mary Margaret seeing him and Liam leaving the school last night.

Mr. O'Sullivan spoke up as they pulled into the school carpark, 'There have been some allegations, Owen. I want you to come into my office and sit tight, we'll sort this out, come on then.'

Owen followed Mr. O'Sullivan as he unlocked the large wooden doors of the school. They walked down the quiet corridors, their footsteps echoing in the absence of students. As soon as Owen sat down in Mr. O'Sullivan's office he heard Liam's voice outside the door, along with Sister Mary Margaret's. Owen wasn't bothered--he would just deny everything, and he hoped Liam would do the same.

Sister Mary Margaret snapped, 'You stay put, ye hooligan!'

She marched into Mr. O'Sullivan's office, 'Do you know why ye're here, Mr. Flanagan?'

Owen shrugged, 'Can't say that I do, Sister.'

He watched as the nun folded her arms, visibly angry, 'Ah you and yer shenanigans . . . I saw you, Owen. I saw you and Liam leaving the school grounds last night. I also found the window wide open to the girls' locker room. What in God's name were you two doing in the girls' locker room? You disgusting, dirty minded mongrels! What were you hooligans doing?'

Owen tried not to laugh, 'I wasn't here last night, I don't know what you're on about.' She pressed a bit further. Owen denied everything. Eventually she gave up. Mr. O'Sullivan said nothing.

Liam was called into the office as Owen was dismissed. As they passed each other in the doorway, Owen whispered sharply, 'Deny everything.' Liam nodded in agreement. All the same questions were posed to Liam; he acted like he didn't know what they were talking about and eventually they gave up and let him go.

Owen was waiting outside the door for Liam. The two of them were laughing. Owen said, 'I think she thought we were after the girl's knickers or something, it was a bit awkward that was.'

Liam agreed, 'It was funny, I just denied it and I kept denying it, funny watching her get all worked up.'

Owen shrugged it off, 'That's the end of that then, now it's as if nothing happened at all.'

Liam seemed satisfied, 'So, you put the box back in Maeve's room and she didn't notice it was gone?'

'Not a clue, like I said, it's as if nothing happened. I'm good as gold, right as rain I am.'

Chapter Six

Maeve and Aelish arrived at school and were surprised to see that Mr. O'Sullivan was not at the front entrance greeting all of the students. They walked into school to find Owen and Liam running down the hallway, laughing.

Aelish was annoyed at everything Owen did lately. She looked at Maeve, 'What was that plan you had in mind?'

Maeve put her hand on Aelish's back and said, 'Don't worry, we'll take care of him.' They went off to their first class. Maeve walked down one hallway and Aelish turned down another and practically ran right into Sister Mary Margaret. Aelish twirled around to walk in the opposite direction but the nun wouldn't have it.

'Aelish, please follow me to my office.'

Aelish rolled her eyes, 'But Sister, I can't be late for first class!'

Sister Mary Margaret gestured down the hallway, 'I've taken care of that, now follow me.' Aelish dropped her book bag, dragged it on the floor and shuffled her feet.

The nun was not amused, 'Pick up your bag at once, don't drag your feet, come along now.' They entered the nun's office. Aelish sat down and slouched in the chair. The nun raised her hand in front of Aelish, 'Sit up straight. Tell me what's going on with your brother.'

'I have *no* idea Sister.'

The nun pressed on, 'I have reason to believe your brother broke into the school last night and was rummaging through the girls' locker room.'

Aelish tried not to laugh, 'Really? What do you suppose he was looking for, some smelly knickers?'

The nun's eyes widened, then she squinted, looked down and wrote something as she said slowly and directly, 'That will get you detention, Ms. Flanagan. I know you find yourself amusing, but I do not. I was giving a courtesy to your mother by not bothering her with any of this recent nonsense with your brother. Now, are you going to be cooperative, or shall I phone your mother?'

Aelish's thoughts took a spin. She thought of her mam and what she'd been through since her dad's death, and the long hours she worked. Aelish didn't want her mam to worry about anything to do with her or her brother.

'I apologize Sister, I really don't know what's going on with my brother, but I intend to talk to him today. Then I'll come back to you, how does that sound?'

The nun seemed somewhat satisfied, 'All right then, come back to me by the end of the day, I would like some explanation. If I'm not satisfied with what you find out, I will then go to your mother.' Aelish agreed and left her office. She wanted to find Owen right then, but she needed to go to class.

Owen and Liam were in English class, still laughing about not getting caught breaking into the school the night before.

Owen was thrilled, 'Ah, we could do no wrong in Mr. O'Sully's eyes, you know that. He'd be nowhere in the hurling world if it weren't for us.'

Liam disagreed, 'If it weren't for *you*.'

Owen agreed, 'Yeah, I'm the best, I can do no wrong! Jaysus, I can do no right in my sister's eyes though.'

Liam didn't look surprised, 'Well, ye *did* break into her friend's house and steal a box of something, and then you *did* break into school, and you *are* a langer…' The boys were interrupted by the teacher pounding on the desk with a wooden stick to have quiet.

Aelish burst out of her class into the hallway, on a mission to find Maeve and make a plan of how to deal with her brother, and to discuss how they could use him for their mission. She ran down the hallway to Maeve's class, and fought her way in as everyone was coming out. Maeve was still sitting at her desk packing up her school bag.

Aelish sat in the empty desk next to Maeve's, 'Sister Mary Maggot dragged me into her office before first class. Apparently, that shite Owen and his servant Liam broke into the school last night! Into the girl's locker room, the pervs! He's getting worse, I don't know what he's up to, but we need to sort him out. I need to confront him about everything before he gets out of hand. And I don't want my mam bothered with any of this nonsense.'

Maeve finished packing up her things, 'Right. We'll have a chat with him straight away during this break, I've seen where he and his friends go to that back area by the primary school.'

Aelish, happy and determined, ran out of the classroom, and down the hallway to the back entrance of the school, not waiting for Maeve. She could hear her in the distance: 'Wait for me! Don't say anything stupid in front of anyone else! Wait for me!'

Aelish reached the back doors and Maeve caught up, 'Leave it to me Aelish, you're bound to say something that will set you two off, I'd like to prevent a row.' They found the boys walking on the footpath towards the back yard, and walked quickly to catch up to them.

'Owen, can we have a word?'

Owen looked back at Maeve and his sister, 'What is it?'

Maeve couldn't think of anything to say because she really hadn't thought the whole thing out, 'It's your mam, Owen, can we have a word?' That spun Owen on his heels, he told his friends he would see them later and quickly walked back to Maeve and Aelish. Anything about his mam came first.

'What is it? Did something happen?'

'Come with us so we can have a word in private.' Maeve led the way back into school and went into the first empty classroom. She pulled Owen by his jumper into the classroom and told him to sit down.

He was worried something terrible had happened to his mam, 'Ah Jesus, what is it?' Aelish was about to say something. Maeve looked at Aelish and gestured for her to be quiet and sit down by putting her finger to her lips and pointed to an empty desk. Aelish sat down. Owen was visibly worried.

Maeve snapped, 'Sit! yer mam is *fine* Owen.' Maeve stood before them pacing back and forth, then she slammed her hands on the desk in front of Owen which made him jump, 'I know what you've been up to Owen Flanagan, I know everything you've been doing, and I mean *everything*, you little thief.'

Owen could feel his face filling with heat; he'd gone scarlet. He'd been caught, but he was still worried about his mam, 'What's this have to do with Ma? Is she okay?'

Aelish jumped in and slammed her hand on the desk in front of Owen as Maeve had done. Aelish yelled, 'Shut up, ye thieving maggot, she's fine, now you listen to Maeve before you get yourself into a whole hell of a lot more trouble than you're already in!' Maeve almost started to laugh but kept her composure. She was enjoying this.

She slammed on the desk in front of Owen again, even harder this time, 'Listen up you little criminal, you've been caught red handed and you're going to pay for it. I know how much you like your money with your odd jobs. It's all going to end, right here and now if you don't do everything I'm about to tell you to do. You'll never walk another dog in this village, you little thief. I know you took that box of mine, and I know you brought it back. I want you to tell me *exactly* what you know, what you did, who you told, and what you planned to do, or you're finished, your life as you know it is *over*!' She slammed on the desk again because she felt it was so out of character for herself; she was enjoying this.

Owen was acting tough, 'I didn't do a thing, you nutter.'

Maeve squinted at Owen, slammed her hand on his desk again, then turned, took the empty desk next to him, and flipped it on its side, yelling, 'Tell me everything *now* you thieving maggot!'

Owen was shocked, 'Jesus Maeve! Okay! For Christ's sake! I'll tell you! Calm down!'

Maeve leaned close towards Owen, 'Don't leave out a single thing, you little vermin, leave out one detail and you're ruined.' Aelish was picking up the overturned desk with her mouth hanging open trying not to laugh. This wasn't the Maeve she knew; she felt like she was watching her crazy self, not her calm friend. Maeve was in Owen's face yelling, 'Out with it now Owen, we haven't all day!'

Owen looked worried about Maeve. He looked at his sister, who just glared at him with her eyebrows raised and said, 'You heard her! Out with it!'

Owen looked concerned, 'Okay, okay, Jesus, I made a mistake. I heard you two talking about the ticket you found, I heard you saying you were just going to give it back to the lottery office and I thought that was incredibly stupid. I thought I would find a Sheila Murphy myself, I was going to find any Sheila Murphy that would agree to pose as the winner. I thought I knew of one, but it turned out she was a nightmare, so I did nothing, I swear to you. I left the box at school, and wanted to return it before you noticed it was gone, but it seems you noticed. That's it.'

Maeve wasn't satisfied. She leaned over the desk in Owen's face, 'Did you tell anyone about the winning ticket?'

Owen backed his head away from her, 'No, I didn't tell anyone, I didn't even tell Liam.'

Aelish laughed a fake laugh, 'Yeah, right.'

Maeve was squinting at Owen, 'I don't believe that either, he knows everything that goes on with you.'

Owen looked serious, 'I swear to you on Da's grave he doesn't know, he knows it was something, something in that box was important, I mentioned money or something, he doesn't know it was a lottery ticket.' The girls felt a bit more satisfied.

Maeve, thinking about how they could use Owen to help them, said, 'Listen, this is what you're going to do, you little thief. You're going to go into Sister Mary Muck Face's office and tell her you're a little perv and you need help. Tell her your hormones are going crazy with all of these girls suddenly in your school. You need to get away. You tell her you want to go to Clonakilty. You ask her if she knows of anyone that lives in Clonakilty, you need to get away this weekend, you need someplace to stay, that's what you're going to do, you got that?'

Owen's face was all screwed up, 'What the hell are you on about?'

Maeve wasn't finished, 'Listen to me, you thieving rodent, you're going to get to that nun's cousin's house in Clonakilty, her name is Sheila Murphy, you got that? We're going to put you to work to help us find this Sheila Murphy! It could be her, and you're going to find out.'

Owen was getting annoyed, 'You're mad! This is exactly why…'

Maeve wouldn't have it, 'You have no say in this Owen Flanagan, you will do as I say or your life is ruined. You go into that nun's office and you tell her your hormones are raging, you can barely help yourself, you were sniffing through the girl's locker room, you need help and you really do need to get away. What you're going to do is find out if Sister Mary Margaret's cousin in Clonakilty is the Sheila Murphy we are looking for, you got that?'

Owen stood up, 'This is insane.' He walked towards the door of the classroom, 'I'll go and talk to her, I'll go now, I'll find out something one way or another.' Owen walked out of the classroom and down the hall.

Aelish stood up and gave Maeve a hug, 'You were brilliant! I've never seen you stand up to anyone like that before, Maeve! That was fantastic! Now, we have that little shite working for us, we've got him right where we need him.' Aelish was holding out the palm of her hand.

Maeve laughed and slapped her hand down, 'We'll see how he does.'

Owen was walking down the hallway thinking how ridiculous those two were. He was sorry he'd got himself involved at all. He wanted nothing to do with his sister or their little search. At the same time, he thought he might have a bit of fun with this. There wasn't a chance in hell he was going to admit that he broke into the school last night; he also had no intention of going to Clonakilty. He knocked on Sister Mary Margaret's office door. She was at her desk, on the phone; she looked up and gestured for Owen to come into her office and sit down as she finished her conversation.

'Yes, thank you very much, I'll be in touch. Bye-bye, bye-bye, bye.' She hung up the phone and looked at Owen, 'What can I help you with, Mr. Flanagan?' Owen pretended he was nervous. He had a plan to make the nun feel uncomfortable so he could get the information out of her more quickly; he didn't want to be in a conversation with her any longer than necessary.

'Sister, I'm sorry, I'm having a bit of a problem. Ever since the girls came into our school I feel like my hormones have been going crazy and I don't know what to do. I didn't break into the girls' locker room last night, but ever since you mentioned it, I can't stop thinking about it and I want to, I want to go into their locker room and smell their clothing. It's been really hard on me, Sister. I mean, ever since the girls were let into our school, it's been really hard on me.' The nun had a look of disgust on her face but didn't say anything. Owen continued, 'I need help Sister. I need to get away, I need to get away this weekend. Do you know anyone that lives in Clonakilty? I need to go there this weekend but I need a place to stay.'

The nun looked more disgusted, 'No I don't know anyone in Clonakilty and you can't run away from your problems, Owen Flanagan, you must face them and you will face them through guidance, counselling and prayer. We can start a program with you immediately. I will get Father O'Shaughnessy involved--this is very serious.'

Owen panicked; he would have nothing to do with that, 'Sister, don't you have a cousin named Sheila Murphy? Couldn't I go and visit her, and stay with her in Clonakilty?'

Sister Mary Margaret, outraged, stood up. 'How in *God's* name in heaven above do you know about my cousin Sheila Murphy? And *why* in God's good grace are you asking me about her and why on earth would I allow you, a hormonally raging degenerate, to even set eyes on my cousin in Clonakilty, let alone *stay* with her? This is an outrage. I want to know this instant how you know of my cousin Sheila Murphy!'

Owen really started to panic, 'Sister, I'm sorry, someone from the village saw her last week as she was driving through Allihies, you know how everyone knows everyone everywhere around here, I just heard she lived…'

He was cut off by the angry nun, 'Ah yes, everyone knows everyone, and everyone knows everyone's business. I'm so tired of people meddling! That cousin of mine was certainly *not* in Allihies this week, last week or four weeks prior to that! Whoever told you this nonsense probably knows this. The gossip of some people is atrocious, I tell you it is. My cousin is in the safety of the sisters' home at Clonakilty Care Rehab Facility where she's been for nearly a month now. That should put an end to her antics and more so of people talking gossiping nonsense. I can tell you one thing, if I put you in the care of the nuns down there, they'd sort you out in fifteen minutes with your nasty problems. Now, I want you to get a hold of yourself, stop your sick and perverted thoughts, go to confession, and concentrate on your studies for the love of God! If I hear so much as a peep out of you, or any further antics, I *will* send you to Clonakilty, to the rehab facility, they'd be happy to lock you up for a month! Trust me, you wouldn't be the same person after that, so I suggest you stay out of trouble from this point on. I would appreciate it if you wouldn't mention the name of my cousin to me or to anyone else again. Is that understood? I should think so. Now, you leave my office at once, go to class, I want to hear *nothing* from you or about you until the end of term. God will strike you down if you cross me again.'

Owen didn't feel the need to say anything else; he stood up, gave her a salute and left her office. He felt he'd handled Sister

Mary Margaret very well and felt exonerated and relieved that was over. He was pleased with himself and hadn't admitted to anything he didn't want to.

Not bothering to find Maeve or Aelish to tell them anything, he went to his next class. During his maths class, there was a knock on the classroom door. It was Maeve. When he saw her talk to the teacher he rolled his eyes and said out loud, 'Jaysus, what now.'

The teacher looked at Owen, 'Mr. Flanagan, your presence is requested, come here, make it quick.' Owen reluctantly went to the front of the room; Maeve led the way to the door and Owen followed. Once in the hallway she pushed Owen against the wall.

'What happened in Sister Mary Margaret's office?'

Owen laughed, 'Yeah Maeve, her cousin is not who you're looking for, she's been locked up in rehab for the last month.'

Maeve looked surprised and impressed with the information he'd found out, 'Really? You sure? You're positive?' Owen nodded and started to walk back into his classroom. Maeve smiled, 'Well done, Owen, we'll strike her off our list then. Carry on.' Maeve walked away, leaving Owen watching her walk down the hallway shaking his head and thinking she was nuts.

Maeve was happy with the information; it had saved her a trip to Clonakilty. Her thoughts now went towards Bantry, the Sheila Murphy in Bantry they knew nothing about except for her address. She was planning to tick each one of these Sheila Murphys off the list in her head, and just keep going on, no matter what it took. Maeve felt like she was on a mission and she didn't feel stressed about it; rather she felt excited and liberated, like she had a purpose and a goal, and three months to achieve it. She was looking forward to a visit with wise Sheila again, she was certain she would have another lead, or another Sheila Murphy to track down. Aelish didn't yet know it, but they were going to go and visit Sheila after school today.

Maeve was surprised to see Aelish coming out of school immediately after last class, walking quickly towards the front entrance of the school to meet up with her.

'How's it? Have you seen Owen since your interrogation this morning, you battleaxe?'

Maeve laughed, 'That was pretty funny, I didn't know I had that in me.'

Aelish put her arm around Maeve, 'I hope I haven't been a bad influence on you over the years, there, Maeve.'

Maeve pushed her away, 'Ah no ye haven't Aye, you've been a good influence on me, God knows if it wasn't for you I would have taken a different path in my life, I would have become a nun, so you saved me!'

Aelish laughed, 'A nun is it? I could hardly see you being a nun, although you did show that side of you this morning. So, did he go and talk to Sister M?'

Maeve smiled, 'Yes he did and he got her all flustered telling her his hormones have been working overtime with all these girls in school all of a sudden. Anyway, she spilled her guts about her cousin and told him that Sheila Murphy was in rehab in Clonakilty, she's been in there for the last month, so she wasn't anywhere near Allihies last week.'

Aelish laughed, 'Jaysus, I'd love to hear more about that one! Ah well, we can scratch her off the list then, ha?'

Maeve agreed, 'Speaking of lists, I thought we'd pop over to Sheila's house now, see if she's come up with anyone else.'

Aelish looked disappointed, 'Ah Maeve, I can't, me ma is picking me up at the house, she's left work early to fetch me at home to pick up a few things, it's Da's one year anniversary tomorrow.'

Maeve looked in pain, 'God, it's tomorrow, I'm sorry Aye, that's gotta be hard.'

Aelish put her arm around Maeve, 'It's okay, it's been a hard year, but the year is over tomorrow. I don't know why, but it's actually a bit of relief being done with the year, being done with all the 'firsts', you know: the first Father's Day without him, the first Christmas without him. I dunno if it's easier because a year has gone by, or because all the 'firsts' have all gone now.'

Maeve looked sympathetic, 'It's probably a bit of both, Aye. Okay, I'll drop you at home, then I'm going to go and see Sheila and I'll check in with you a bit later, how does that sound?'

Aelish agreed, 'Sounds good to me.' They got into Maeve's car. The drive was quiet to Aelish's house. Wanting to break the deep thoughts for a moment, Maeve said, 'Hey, that was a gas this morning scaring the bejesus out of Owen, ha?'

Aelish laughed, 'Ya, you scared *me* a bit, you were a bit psycho, so you were. Slamming your hands on the desk making him jump, and Jaysus, throwing that desk on its side? I don't know what's got into you, but it was hilarious!' They both laughed.

Maeve said, 'Well, it worked; he got us information that we needed. I think he may be useful to us, Aye, he's going to help us in this venture, whether he wants to or not.'

Aelish chuckled, 'Yeah, well at least he'll be good for something.' They pulled up in front of Aelish's house.

Maeve gave Aelish a hug, 'Call me if you need anything.'

Aelish hugged her back, 'Will do, thanks, see you later. Bye!' She got out of the car and walked up to her house.

Maeve sat there for a moment thinking about that day a year ago, one year ago tomorrow . . . it didn't seem like it had been an entire year already, it seemed like it was just a few weeks ago that she'd been sitting out in front of her house, picking her up for school, when Aelish slowly came out to tell her the horrible news of finding her dad dead in the house; it was a devastating blow. She remembered the last time she had seen Mr. Flanagan alive was that night before he died. Maeve dropped Aelish home that evening, and as she drove away from Aelish's house, her dad was walking down the road towards their house. He was singing very loudly as he walked down the middle of the road:

'Looooow liiiiiie, the fields of Athenrrrrryeeee!
Where once we watched the small free birds fly!
Our love was on the wing.
We had dreams and songs to sing.
It's so lonely round the fields of
Athenrrrryeeee!'

Maeve remembered stopping to ask him if he needed a lift. 'Hiya Mr. Flanagan, would you like a lift home?'

He smiled, barely able to focus on Maeve, 'Do I loooook like a need a lift home? Tanks but no tanks just the same, you get yourself home there, missus.' He continued to walk towards his house and resumed singing 'The Fields of Athenry'.

She waved him off, 'Okay, g'bye Mr. Flanagan!' It was hard to believe that was a year ago, and that he was gone.

Chapter Seven

Maeve couldn't wait to see Sheila again. As she drove down the bumpy dirt road towards the cottage, she saw her in her front garden tending to her plants. Sheila looked up, saw Maeve and smiled; she stood up slowly and stretched a bit, standing there in her apron and gloves. She waved at Maeve and started to walk towards her car. Maeve smiled, thinking what a nice feeling she had whenever she saw Sheila. She got out of her car to a big hug, lasting a little longer than the last time.

Sheila was equally happy to see Maeve, 'C'mere to me and tell me what you know,' she said. Maeve smiled. She wasn't close to her grandmother; she guessed if she were, this is what it would feel like. Sheila took Maeve's hand and guided her into her cottage, 'I was hoping you'd come back, I have a bit of news for you, let's go and have a cup of tea.'

As she followed, Maeve said, 'I have a bit of news for you myself.'

Sheila laughed, 'Well, I have a feeling this is going to be a very good cup of tea indeed.'

Maeve walked into Sheila's kitchen and immediately put the kettle on. Sheila loved how she made herself at home. 'Thank you, dear! I'll get some biscuits, why don't you sit down.'

Maeve brought two cups and spoons to the table and sat down; Sheila followed with milk and a plate of biscuits. Looking at Maeve she said, 'C'mere, how's things, anything strange?'

Maeve smiled, 'Everything's grand, we found two more Sheila Murphys; one in Clonakilty who seems to have been locked up in a rehab facility for the last month, and the other one is in Bantry; we have a home address for that one, but we haven't pursued anything just yet.'

Sheila was pleased to hear they were making progress. 'Well done you,' she said. 'Now, I've done a bit of researching myself and I may have a couple of strong leads towards a Sheila Murphy or two. I phoned the Seaview Guest House in Allihies and asked Angela down there if any of my relatives, you know, the Murphys from Cork, if any of them stayed in her B&B this past week. She checked her reservation book and said they hadn't, no Murphys this week. That got me started, I called all the B&B's in the area. I thought maybe someone might have hosted Sheila Murphy in the area the day she breezed through Allihies.'

Maeve was impressed, 'That was a great idea, so, any luck?'

Sheila put her hand on Maeve's, 'I may have a lead, but it got me thinking, I could be of good use to you girls, I can be used as the decoy in finding the winning Sheila Murphy. It can be under the guise of me looking for my cousin Sheila Murphy, no one will know that my real cousin Sheila Murphy has since died, God rest her. But no one would question why I'm looking, I'm just an old lady looking for my lost cousin-- who wouldn't want to help me?'

Maeve loved it, 'Grand idea, we'll just keep looking until we find her,' she said, 'Well done! Now, speaking of looking for someone, I have some news for you. I met a boy at O'Neill's pub, he's visiting here from America, apparently his grandfather knew your husband, he was looking for him.'

This surprised Sheila, 'What's this? Who is it? Did you get his name?'

Maeve was excited, 'Yes, his name is the same as his grandfather's, it's Patrick McGettigan.'

Sheila sat back with knowing smile on her face, 'Paddy. Oh, Martin loved his dear friend Paddy McGettigan, God rest him. Where is this boy Maeve, where is this American?'

Maeve was glad Sheila was interested; it gave her a reason to see Patrick again, 'I know where to find him, would you mind if I brought him 'round?'

Sheila was delighted, 'Yes of course dear, that would be lovely. I'll go searching for a few old photos. I know we have one or two of Paddy--I only ever heard good things about him, you know, he was a good man according to Martin, such a dear friend of his, he was.'

Maeve was excited to go and find Patrick at his hostel; she wanted to leave that moment. It was all she could think about, seeing that good looking guy again.

Sheila, sensing this, asked, 'Maeve dear, is his grandson your age?' Maeve quickly nodded. Sheila continued, 'I suspected so. If he's half as good looking as his grandad, he's good looking enough.' Maeve nodded feverishly with a smile, 'Ah Sheila, he's *gorgeous!*' Sheila saw the sparkle in Maeve's eyes, 'Now dear, slow down your thinking. Don't put all your attention towards this fella, or any other for that matter, you have your own agenda, your life, don't forget that. We'll get back to that dreamboat of yours; I haven't finished telling you about my Sheila search. I do have a few that must be explored.'

Maeve preferred to talk more about the dreamboat, but she shifted her focus to the task at hand, 'Grand! What did you find?'

Sheila poured them a cup of tea, 'Now then, you know Cork County is riddled with Murphys, you can't throw a coin and not hit one, no you can't. You also know that Sheila is a pretty popular girl's name in Ireland, especially back in the 40's through the 60's. Put those two names together and we have our work cut out for us, we do. As I've mentioned, I've come across quite a few Sheila Murphys in my lifetime, especially since I got married. Anyway, I had a fairly common name to start, being Sheila O'Brien as it was, but I found out shortly after getting married and changing my name to Murphy that I was joining one of many, many Sheila Murphys in Ireland, including Martin's cousin, who I was close to. Also, my dear friend from childhood, Shelagh Delaney, she also married a Murphy, it was all quite confusing really. Over the years I came across quite a few more. I'm never surprised to come across another Sheila Murphy. Now then, we need to find the one who was driving through Allihies last week, and which one of them purchased that lottery ticket. I have every confidence that we can, and we will find her.'

Sheila continued on about her findings, 'Now then, I have located a couple of Sheila Murphys that seem worth investigating; if we go traipsing around the country we may as well make good use of our time and make our trip worthwhile. We can certainly open up the search by using me as an excuse; ask your da, ask anyone if they know a Sheila Murphy--let's broaden the search.'

Maeve was so excited that Sheila wanted to be part of this, she said, 'Will do, now go on, you said you found a couple of leads, who's the other one then?'

Sheila looked down at a piece of paper on her table, 'The other one I found lives out in Crookhaven, now that's about a two hour drive from here, it's clear at the tip of the Mizen Head Peninsula. That one may very well be another cousin of Martin's, ah but who knows, there are so many of them, Murphys are as common as potatoes, so they are.' She continued, 'I also found one that lives in Skibbereen while calling the B&B's in the area; a Sheila Murphy stayed at a B&B in Glengarriff last week.'

Maeve laughed, 'Well, that's grand, Sheila, well done, we have three now to look into, that sounds like a day's work. When would you like to go?'

Sheila thought for a moment, 'I don't have much to do tomorrow--would you like to make a day trip? That would be a lovely way to spend a Saturday. Martin and I used to take drives down along the coast all the time . . . how nice it would be to take a drive with you! It'll be a bit of an adventure.'

Maeve loved the idea, 'Perfect, let's go in the morning.'

Sheila smiled, 'I'm fit for any time dear, we shall seek and we shall find. This will be joyous, it'll be an adventure I haven't had in some time--I welcome it.'

Maeve felt good; they had a plan. 'I'll see if Aelish can join us, but it's the anniversary of her da's death tomorrow.' Just then Maeve received a text from Aelish:

Can you pick me up? I need you to pick me up in 15

Maeve responded:

Of course

Sheila tilted her head, looking sad, 'Ah shame, God rest him, how long has it been? Is she doing okay?'

Maeve appreciated her concern, 'She'll be grand, it's been a year. I don't know if they'll be doing an anniversary mass tomorrow, I'll find out. I should probably go, I told her I would pick her up soon.'

Sheila stood up, 'You go, we'll see you whenever you arrive tomorrow, the morning would be good--it will end up being a long day I'm sure.' Maeve started to take the cups to the kitchen, but Sheila took them from her hands, 'Leave this to me," she said. 'How does nine in the morning sound?'

Maeve agreed, 'Nine it is, we'll see you in the morning then. Thanks so much for the tea.'

After a hug, Sheila took Maeve's hand and walked her to the door and out to her car. She put her hands on Maeve's face and said, 'You are such a special girl, Maeve, it's a pleasure getting to know you.'

Maeve smiled, 'You too, Sheila, see you in the morning.' Maeve got into her car and drove away. Sheila watched her drive down the long dirt road until she was out of sight.

Aelish walked into the house after school to find her mam, Siobhan, standing in the entryway looking beyond her, out the door.

'Where's your brother?'

'Ma, he's fine, I'm sure he'll be here any minute.'

With that, a car pulled up and Owen got out, saying, 'Thanks, see you tomorrow!'

Siobhan picked up her bag and headed towards the car before Owen was able to go inside the house. 'Right then, let's go, in the car you two.' Aelish and Owen both got into the back seat of the car. They weren't looking forward to this outing. The three of them hadn't spoken about what had happened a year ago--not much had been mentioned about their dad at all, for an entire year.

Siobhan was straightforward and had a no nonsense attitude.

'Right then, we'll go to the shops while they're still open, get your father some flowers, then head down to the cemetery today. I know it was tomorrow, but to me it was today, Friday night, this was the day a year ago, this is it and that's that. We'll go and pay our respects and be done with this year.'

Neither Aelish nor Owen said a word; they wouldn't even look at each other. It was a long drive to the shops and an even longer one to the cemetery. Siobhan handed them each a bunch of flowers. She looked at the pained looks on their faces as they sat there in the car, each holding their flowers. She didn't want to dwell on how sad or sweet they both looked. She thought for a moment how they looked younger than their years, but they'd always be her babies. 'Right, let's move on,' she said.

All Aelish could think about was how much she wanted to get out of this village and away from all of this, along with all of the bad memories. She was waiting for the year to be done; she wanted to feel like she was starting afresh with a new year, and new things to come, her new life. She wanted to leave all this pain and misery behind and start her new life right now.

They pulled into the cemetery and got out of the car, each of them walking separately, their mam in the lead. As Aelish started up the path towards her dad's gravesite, she saw a gravestone, and shook her head as she walked by, muttering, 'Jesus, seriously, how many of them are there?' Owen was right behind her and saw what she had seen: a plain gravestone with a simple engraving:

Sheila Murphy
RIP

Owen sniggered, 'Well, one less to look for.'
Siobhan overheard them, 'What are you two on about?'
They both responded, 'Nothing.' They made their way to their dad's gravesite, next to those of his parents, and two of his siblings, who had died in infancy and childhood.

Their mam had made sure he had a lovely stone.

Michael 'Mick' Flanagan
Loving husband and father
Death leaves a heartache
No one can heal
Love leaves a memory
No one can steal

He was only 49 years old. The three of them stood in front of the stone. Their mam put her flowers down and picked up some dead flowers from the ground. She stopped and looked up into the sky and all around, then looked at her two children, 'Listen, do you hear that?' she said. They both looked around; they heard it. It was a lone bagpiper playing in the distance.

Siobhan put her hand on her heart, 'Ah, that's a sign from your father, that is, God knows how he loved his bagpipes.'

Owen was unmoved, 'Yeah, the bagpipes are here every day in the cemetery, every time someone dies, they play the bloody bagpipes.'

Aelish kicked him and gave him a stern look, then turned to Siobhan and smiled, 'It's nice, Ma, it's a sign, sure it is.' They stood there in silence, listening to the bagpiper. Aelish got a chill; the hair on her neck tingled, 'Ah, do you hear what's playing? That's really eerie, Da sang that song all the time.'

Their mam knelt down and picked up some more dead flowers from the ground. She stayed kneeling, put her head down and listened to the tune, "Fields of Athenry". It brought a sudden surge of emotion within, and her eyes welled with tears. She pinched herself on her wrist with her nails to stop the tears. She'd always felt that if she started to cry, she wouldn't be able to stop; she would unravel and lose her mind. She needed to stay strong for the kids' sake. She picked up some more dead flowers around the grave and stood up, 'Right, that's it then, let's go.' Aelish and Owen were taken aback at the abruptness, but followed their mam. That's what it had been like a year ago, there was nothing more to be said.

Aelish wanted to get away; she didn't want to be with her mam or brother anymore. She missed her da terribly but she had been taught to not think about him, to brush thoughts aside; it would pass, the pain would go away. She texted Maeve to pick her up at her house in 15 minutes. She was relieved when Maeve responded that she'd be there. She felt better that she had somewhere to go, something else to do, somewhere else to be, other than where she was and who she was with.

Siobhan pulled up to their house. They all got out of the car and quietly went inside; nothing was said, the day was gone, the year had passed, they'd commemorated it and nothing more was going to be said or done.

Aelish went up to her room, changed her clothes, freshened up her face and went downstairs. By the time she reached the front door, Maeve was pulling up in front of the house. Aelish opened the door and gave her a wave and went back in towards the kitchen.

'Ma, I'm going out with Maeve,' she said, 'We'll see you later, or I may sleepover at her house, so don't wait up for me.'

Siobhan was getting used to Aelish doing her own thing, 'That's fine, Aye, if you could just send me a text and let me know, that would be grand.'

Aelish was about to walk out the door; she stood there for a moment and decided to go back into the kitchen. She walked up to her mam and gave her a hug, 'Thanks Mammy, I love you.' She surprised her mam with a kiss on the cheek.

'Well, that's sweet, Aelish, thank you, I love you too, now be safe.'

Aelish walked towards the door, 'Will do, see you later.'

She ran out to Maeve's car and threw herself in the front seat. 'Ah my God, thank you, I couldn't imagine staying in there tonight, that was horrible.'

Maeve felt bad for her, 'I'm sorry Aye, that's gotta be hard, you doing okay?'

Aelish looked out the window, 'Yeah, I'm fine, fine as I'll ever be, life goes on, right? Right. How's things? You went to Sheila's? Any news?'

Maeve was happy to tell Aelish everything, 'Let's go to my house so I can get out of this uniform, we'll have a little chat with me ma, then I thought of this brilliant idea of going to O'Neill's for a pint!'

Aelish laughed, 'How ever did you come up with such an idea? There are *so* many other things to do in this village!'

Maeve looked confused, 'Like what?'

'Like go to the other pub, The Lighthouse! They have music.'

Maeve laughed, 'O'Neill's has music as well, Aye, I just prefer O'Neill's cuz we know everyone there.'

Aelish started making kissing noises, 'I think I know your 'everyone' you're looking for, maybe a little smooching from that Yank, is he going to be in O'Neill's tonight, ha?'

Maeve interrupted her, 'No, I don't know, maybe, I don't know, he only said he was staying at the hostel, I don't know anything else.'

Aelish was really laughing at her now, 'Look at you! You're all flustered and nervous!' Maeve denied it as Aelish pushed her hand away from her twirling her hair, 'Look at you!'

Maeve pulled up to the front of her house. She said, 'Do me a favour and don't mention anything about the Yank to my parents, all right?'

Aelish shrugged, 'Fine, what's to tell? Is there something to tell?' Maeve didn't answer, she just got out of the car and walked up to the door and into the house. Something smelled really good in the house.

Maeve smiled, 'I'm starved, how about you?'

Aelish walked in and took a deep breath, 'Ah my God, I know *exactly* what that is, it's your mam's steak and stout pie! Ah Jaysus, I hope she made extra pies.'

A voice came from the kitchen, 'She *always* makes extra pies, but they're usually for me to take to work!' Aelish's face dropped as she walked into the kitchen.

Jack put his arm around her, 'Ah I was joking, there's plenty of pies, one has your name on it missus, now come in here and sit down. How's the form? Anything new?' Maeve and Aelish looked at each other and both shrugged.

'Grand. Nothing new. Ah Da, I do have a question. You know that old Sheila Murphy, Martin's widow? She was wondering if you would know of any other Sheila Murphys, she's looking for a cousin of hers.' Maeve's mam looked surprised in the kitchen but didn't say anything.

'Me? She asked you to ask *me* if I knew of another Sheila Murphy?'

Aelish interrupted, 'That auld one is asking everyone, she's looking for anyone that knows of this cousin of her husband, but she said it wasn't a big deal, she was just wondering if anyone knows of another Sheila Murphy, 'tis all.'

Jack looked a little confused, 'I can't say that I do, sorry girls. So, how was your day at school today? Did you learn anything new?'

Maeve shook her head, 'Haven't you grown tired of asking me that, Da? You've honestly asked me that every single day since I started school at the age of four.'

Jack looked at Mary, 'And I've been hearing the same answer now for the same amount of time now, haven't I hun?'

Maeve laughed, 'Ye'd think you'd've given up by now, Da.'

Jack chuckled and hit his hand on the table, 'Never! Never give up on anything! Now let's eat, it smells too good to wait another minute!'

Maeve went into the kitchen to help her mam bring things to the table. Mary put her arm around Maeve as soon as she walked in, asking her, 'How was your day sweetie?'

Maeve hugged her, 'It was fine, Ma. I went to see that Sheila Murphy again, I want you to meet her Ma, she's so like you, she's so kind and so cool.'

Mary laughed, 'I wouldn't go as far as to say I'm cool, but I am kind.'

Maeve was still holding on to her mam, 'Ma, did you find any more Sheila Murphys at work today?'

Mary looked towards the table where Jack and Aelish were sitting, 'I did, as a matter of fact. After dinner, I'll show you two what I came up with. I couldn't spend too much time on it at work today, but I found a thing or two for you girls.'

Maeve gave her another hug, 'Thanks Ma, you're the best!'

After dinner the girls cleaned up and went into the office. Mary had a large map of Ireland spread out on her desk.

'I thought this would help, it will make it easier for you girls, you can write all over the map, mark up where you need to go, or where you've been, it's yours to do with it what you want.'

Aelish laughed, 'That's great, Mary, thanks, this will work *much* better than Google maps, and it's so small and compact!'

Mary smirked, 'It'll help you see the overall picture, Aelish.'

Aelish smiled, 'I'm just messing with you, thanks so much!'

Mary took a piece of paper from her desk, 'Okay, this is what I found today, I have two more addresses for you. One is in Ballydehob, which I'll show you on the map, right here, not far from Skibbereen.'

Maeve interrupted, 'That's perfect! Sheila found one in Skibbereen!'

Mary continued, 'That's great. The other one I found is a bit further away along the coast; I found a Sheila Murphy living in Ballycotton, but that's a good three hours' drive from here.'

Maeve hurried her along, 'It's okay, Ma, we'll figure it out, thank you *so* much! I love you. We're going to get going now, come on Aye.' Maeve started to pull Aelish out of the room.

Maeve's mam looked a bit surprised, 'That's it then? Right, off you go, have a good time, be safe, see you later.'

Aelish knew why Maeve was in a hurry; but she'd promised she wouldn't say anything. She said thanks to Mary and walked outside, humming 'I'm a Yankee Doodle Dandy'. Maeve grabbed her by the arm and pulled her out the door.

'Let's go, you musical girl, maybe there'll be a singsong going on for you in the village.' Aelish wouldn't stop humming the tune, making it louder as they were going out the door, sounding like a trumpet. Maeve put her hand over Aelish's mouth and hurried her out the front door, shouting goodbye to her parents.

As soon as they got outside, Aelish broke into the words of the song at the top of her voice:

> *'I'm a Yankee Doodle Dandy!*
> *A Yankee Doodle, do or die!*
> *I'm a Yankee Doodle Dandy boy!*
> *and I'm sitting at O'Neill's*
> *waiting for my Yankee wanna be girl!'*

Maeve was getting angry, 'Get in the car!'

They both got in; Aelish was laughing, 'I wonder if your little Yank will be waiting for you at the bar!'

Maeve narrowed her eyes as she looked at Aelish, 'He's not my Yank, and he's *certainly* not waiting on me Aelish, I don't even think he was interested, he's just doing his thing, and, well, I'm doing mine. I don't care if he's there or not, to be honest.'

'Ah now missus, someone is *not* being honest here.' said Aelish, laughing.

Maeve sat in the car and snapped, 'Let's just go.'

'Yeah, let's go, you're the one driving, remember? Ha! Like your mind isn't elsewhere. This is great, I've never seen you like this. I think you're smitten, I think you're a smitten kitten and you can't wait to see this, what's his name, Paddy McCrackin?'

Maeve shook her head, 'No Aelish, it's Patrick, Patrick McGettigan.' Maeve smiled as she said his name.

'Ah my God,' she said, 'look at you! Would you look at this! I hope he's there just so I can watch this, so I can watch you make a fool of yourself, all googly-eyed and drooling over this guy, this is priceless!'

Maeve was getting annoyed, 'Aelish, seriously, don't embarrass me, please I beg of you, don't embarrass me, don't say anything, promise me. Actually, could you not utter anything at all? Let's say you've gone mute, you have a sore throat and you can't speak tonight, how does that sound?'

Aelish laughed a hearty laugh, 'Fat chance! Okay, I'll *try* to not embarrass you, but I can't make any promises. I will try though, I promise you I will try.' Maeve didn't hold out much hope of that. She parked the car and they walked into O'Neill's.

Chapter Eight

Sitting at the same stool where he'd been the night before, Patrick McGettigan turned and looked as Maeve and Aelish as they walked in. Maeve's heart skipped a beat and she felt a flutter in her stomach. She waved to him and walked to the back of the bar. She heard Aelish yelling something behind her, but she just kept walking. Her heart was pounding; she felt nervous. She went into the loo and looked at herself in the mirror. She shook her head and slowly whispered, 'What is your problem?'

Aelish walked into the loo after Maeve, 'What is your problem?'

Maeve looked worried, 'Ah Jesus, Aye, I'm asking myself that same question. I don't know, I don't feel myself, I think we should leave, I may be sick.'

Aelish stood in front of Maeve and looked at her with great concern. She put her hands on Maeve's shoulders, looked her square in the eyes and said, 'Sick me arse! Pull yourself together missus! Now then, what can I get you to drink? I'll be at the front of the bar with your choice of drink, what'll it be?' Maeve bit her lip and started twirling her hair.

Aelish hit her hand, 'Stop it, I'm getting you a Guinness, that oughta do ye having a bit of the black stuff, I'll see you up front, I'll be right next to that Mr. Patrick McCraic whenever you pull yourself together.' She left Maeve standing at the mirror.

Maeve looked in the mirror and whispered, 'Seriously, get it together.' She smoothed her hair, looked closely at her makeup, put on some fresh lip gloss and nodded, 'Okay, right,

I'm grand.' She walked up to the bar and stood between Aelish and Patrick; she picked up the glass of Guinness, took a sip, then said very confidently to Patrick as she raised her glass to him, 'Hello Patrick! *Sláinte*! Fancy seeing you here!'

Patrick half smiled, raised his eyebrows and said, 'How's my Guinness?' Maeve quickly put the pint down on the bar and looked at Aelish in shock.

Aelish tilted her head, looking at Patrick, 'Sorry, we Irish are known to occasionally check to see if tourists' drinks are okay.' She looked at Maeve, 'Was that all right then? Right, our job is done here, let's go.' She gestured towards Maeve for her to follow, 'We're going to go and fetch *our* pints now, see you in a bit.' They walked down to the sidebar where their pints were being drawn. Aelish turned and looked at Maeve, 'And you were worried about *me* embarrassing *you*? I think you're doing a good job of that on your own there, missus.'

Maeve was mortified, 'Now I really do want to leave.'

Aelish laughed and glanced down at Patrick, 'Ah stop, he probably thought it was funny, he's sipping his Guinness right now where you took a sip, probably thinking about snogging your lips.'

Maeve hit Aelish, 'Stop, he probably thinks I'm an absolute eejit.' Aelish took their drinks off the bar and started walking back up to the front.

Maeve panicked, 'Wait! Don't go back there!' Aelish laughed and kept walking.

There was a stool free next to Patrick, so Aelish sat down and put Maeve's pint in front of Patrick, 'There you go now,' she said. 'You can take a sip of hers if you like, make sure it's ok and all.'

Patrick shook his head, 'Na, that's okay, I'm happy with mine. So, how are you two doing?'

Maeve jumped in, 'Grand, I mean grrrreat, I mean sooperrr.'

Aelish's mouth was open with surprise, 'That was a great American accent there, Maeve.' She tried to cover for her friend, 'Yes Sir Yee Bob, we yall tawk with Merican accents we do, yep we do, that's just what we do!'

Patrick was looking at the two of them with a blank look on his face, 'Those were American accents?' Aelish didn't know how to get out of this and wanted to get Maeve away before she said anything more embarrassing. She hit Maeve's arm, 'Ah God, Maeve, we forgot about Michael in the back room!'

Maeve was happy to leave, saying, 'Ah yes! We forgot! I forgot too! Michael! Back room! He's there! Waiting for us! Yes!'

Aelish rolled her eyes and pulled Maeve by the arm, 'Okay, come on, get your pint, let's go, see you later Patrick, bye-bye.'

Patrick looked right at Maeve with a smile, 'I will see you again.'

Maeve started to talk like Arnold Schwarzenegger, 'We'll be back, I'll be back.'

Aelish just snapped, 'Maeve!' Maeve smiled and followed Aelish. She could feel the heat of embarrassment on her face and neck. She couldn't get to the back room fast enough. Maeve looked back at the bar to see Patrick still looking at her, smiling.

When the girls entered the back room, they saw Michael O'Malley sitting with a couple guys. Aelish started to yell 'Mo--' but she stopped herself. 'Michael, how you doing?' she said instead. She thought she'd better acknowledge the others. 'Nick, John, Mack, how's things?' They all mumbled they were fine.

Aelish didn't feel like talking to them, 'Come on Maeve, let's sit over here.' They went a couple of tables down and sat.

'Did I hear you say in an Austrian accent, "I'll be back?" You should never go back there Maeve, that was mortifying. Who *are* you? You need to stay away from him until you can act normal. Jesus Christ, that was embarrassing.'

Maeve put her head in her hands and said in the same Austrian accent, 'I won't be back.'

Aelish laughed, 'Good! Now let's let that go for now and forget that whole exchange ever happened!'

Maeve agreed, 'Hey, what are you doing tomorrow, does your mam have something planned?'

Aelish shrugged, 'Nothing, we did what we were doing today, mam said this was the day, and that was it.'

Maeve looked at Aelish, 'Sorry, Aye, you okay with everything?'

Aelish looked up to the ceiling, then to Maeve, 'I'm grand. What's going on tomorrow?'

Maeve knew when to leave things be with Aelish, 'Well, are you up for going on a little day trip to a few spots?'

Aelish shrugged again, 'Sure, searching for Sheila, I presume?'

Maeve smiled, 'Precisely! Sheila wants to join us, I told her I'd pick her up around 9 am, are you up for that?'

Aelish perked up, 'Yeah, that'll be grand! If I didn't leave my house I'd have to watch people mope around and I'd be forced to do housework I'm sure, so this is perfect.'

Owen arrived and walked into the dimly lit back room of the pub followed by a couple friends. They walked over to the area where the band was setting up their instruments. Owen and his friends sat at the small tables and chairs adjacent to the musicians. Maeve and Aelish saw the boys walk in and settle into the music area.

Aelish squinted her eyes, looking across the room, 'What's the Yank doing with my brother? How do they even know each other?' They watched as Owen pushed Patrick to sit in with the musicians. Owen and Liam sat at their table laughing. Patrick was handed a bodhrán drum blazoned with worn-out Celtic knot drawings encircling the drum. He was given the short fat drum stick and was told to sit right in the front with a microphone in front of him. Owen and Liam couldn't stop laughing.

Maeve and Aelish were watching this unfold, 'Looks like my brother is taking the piss out of the Yank.'

Maeve looked a bit worried, 'What are they doing to him? They probably told him the band needed someone to just sit and hold the drum so they stuck him in there for a laugh.'

Aelish responded sarcastically, 'D'ya reckon? This ought to be good. We should move closer.'

Maeve held her back and shook her head, 'We're close enough Aye, I don't want to draw any more attention to myself.'

The group started to play a traditional tune; everyone in the room quieted down to listen. Maeve thought how embarrassing this would be for Patrick; she also thought of how he hadn't been given a very good impression of Irish people so far. The band started with a lone fiddle. The fiddle was joined by a banjo. Patrick was sitting at the front looking at the other musicians play. He was holding the drum and not looking like he knew what he was doing, drumming along quietly as the fiddle and banjo were predominant. As the fiddle and banjo finished playing the intro, Patrick perked up and put his mouth near the microphone and belted the song,

> *'As I was goin' over*
> *The Cork and Kerry mountains,*

I met with Captain Farrell
And his money he was countin'
I first produced me pistol,
And then produced me rapier,
Saying stand and deliver,
For he were a bold deceiver'

Then everyone in the pub joined in:

'Mush-a ring dum-a do dum-a da,
Wack fall the daddy-o,
Wack fall the daddy-o,
There's whiskey in the jar!'

The musicians continued playing, with Patrick singing as he played the bodhrán drum with obvious skill.

Maeve and Aelish were shocked and laughing. Aelish looked at Maeve with her eyebrows raised, 'Not bad that one, he can hold his own, so he can. I may take him for meself!'

Maeve pushed Aelish, 'Ah stop, but look, there is something about him there is, I'm smitten, Aye.' They both joined in as loud as they could, laughing and singing:

'Mush-a ring dum-a do dum-a da,
Wack fall the daddy-o,
Wack fall the daddy-o,
There's whiskey in the jar!'

As Patrick sang, he looked around the room and caught Maeve's eye. She was clapping and waiting for the chorus to come up again--they were the only words she knew:

'Mush-a ring dum-a do dum-a da,

Wack fall the daddy-o,
Wack fall the daddy-o,
There's whiskey in the jar!'

The song ended with Patrick doing a solo on the drum. The whole room clapped when Patrick got up to leave. A man off to the side came over to the microphone to announce the guest singer, 'Let's hear it for Paddy McGettigan from America! Ah, ya fit right in here lad, you're as Irish as the Irish themselves, that was brilliant, thanks for starting us off this evening, let's hear it again for Paddy McGettigan.'

Everyone clapped; Aelish was yelling, 'One more song! One more song!' Maeve told her to stop. Patrick bypassed the boys who were looking surprised, and walked to Maeve and Aelish's table.

Maeve stood up as he approached their table, 'That was brilliant Patrick, you're very talented!'

Aelish imitated Maeve, 'That was *brilliant* Paddy! You are *so* talented! Can I have your autograph?' Maeve glared at Aelish.

Finding her confidence, she said, 'I have a better idea Aelish, why don't you go and get us all a drink? Have a seat here Patrick, she'll be back with our drinks, run along now.' Maeve waved Aelish off saying, 'Sorry about her.'

Patrick laughed, 'Don't worry about it, she's fine.'

Maeve wanted to hear everything about Patrick, 'Tell me, Patrick, or should I say Paddy? Where did you learn to play the bodhrán? I wouldn't think too many Americans would know how to play that. And your singing, that was lovely, I'm thoroughly impressed!'

Patrick was getting embarrassed, 'Thank you. Yep, my parents were really into being Irish Americans, my sisters took Irish dance, we all learned the traditional instruments, songs, and we all learned a bit of the Irish language. The McGettigans always marched in the St. Patrick's Day parade, every year, rain or shine.'

Maeve smiled, 'Well, the McGettigans must be a very proud clan.'

Patrick laughed, 'Yea, my mom was really into it, she always said that St. Patrick's Day was the most important holiday of the year, it was certainly her favourite.'

Maeve laughed, 'My ma told me when she was growing up they were made to go to church on St. Patrick's Day, that was it, it was a holy day of obligation, now it's just one big drunken party throughout the world.'

Patrick looked amused, 'Yep, we were just obligated to drink on the day. Jeez, I don't think any American has ever thought of going to church on St. Patrick's Day.'

Aelish came back with their pints. She placed them in front of Maeve and Patrick on the little table, saying, 'I'm going to leave you two.'

Maeve was surprised, 'Wait. What? You're *leaving*?'

Aelish laughed, 'I'm going to leave you two whilst I go and talk to someone up front 'tis all.'

Maeve looked curious, 'Really? Who could that be Aelish?'

Aelish started to walk away, 'Never you mind missus, I'll be up front if you're looking for me.'

Maeve watched Aelish walk out. She looked back at Patrick and smiled, 'So, how far back do the American McGettigans go to Ireland?'

Patrick said, 'My grandfather was born here, not sure where though, no one has bothered to research it.'

Maeve laughed, 'With your mam being so into St. Patrick's Day and it being the most important holiday of the year to her, you'd think she'd do a bit of research on her Irish roots.'

Patrick lifted his glass, 'I think my mom was more interested in the party, having people over, dressing up in the old green, that was it. She wasn't of Irish descent, her maiden name was Smith, she didn't know where her ancestors came from so she clung to the Irish side of my dad's I guess. It gets more difficult finding ancestors the more common the name you have.'

Maeve laughed, 'Tell me about it! Some people are like trying to find a needle in a haystack!'

Patrick looked confused, 'Why, what's your last name? Murphy?'

Maeve laughed even harder, 'Ha! I suppose that would be the Smith of Ireland, wouldn't it? That *is* the most common name around here, that's for certain! But, no, my surname is Mulligan and our clan originally hailed from way up north in Donegal, so we did. It was my grandparents that came down to County Cork, my grandad was hired at a company in Cork after my mam and her sister were born, so here we are, and here we stayed.'

Patrick smiled, 'Well, I'm glad you're here.' Maeve was relieved she wasn't acting like a nervous twit any longer. She was enjoying having a nice, normal conversation with Patrick.

Just then, Owen and Liam came over to their table. Owen sat down. Liam asked Maeve to dance, she agreed with a smile when she recognized the song. She thought he must have requested it; it was a typical Single Jig, just like the songs they'd practiced to in dance class over the years. Liam and Maeve had taken dance classes together since childhood. When they started to dance, standing next to each other with their arms down, their feet jumping and tapping, people started to join them, lining up and weaving in and out of each other. Owen felt obligated to join himself. Aelish walked into the room and joined as well; they all knew the steps and had the routine down from all the years of instruction and practice. The band was delighted; they played one jig into the next, taking no pause between songs. When everyone tired and stopped dancing, the musicians started to play the intro to 'The Fields of Athenry'.

Aelish and Owen looked at each other. Maeve held her breath, thinking how it was this night a year ago that their father had passed away. It was this night Maeve had seen their dad walking down the road near their house, when she heard him singing this very song.

Aelish and Owen had already heard this song once today, playing near their father's grave; hearing it again seemed to confirm it was a sign: it was their da's favourite song. As Aelish pulled Owen up towards the band, the lead singer guessed, accurately, that they wanted to sing, so he stepped aside. The two of them stood behind the microphone and waited to sing the song. When the intro came to an end, they both leaned in towards the microphone:

'By a lonely prison wall,
I heard a young girl calling:
Michael,'

(Owen went right into the microphone and said 'Flanagan', to the cheers of the crowded room.) They continued to sing:

'. . . they have taken you away,
For you stole Trevelyan's corn,
So the young might see the morn,
Now a prison ship lies waiting in the bay.'

Everyone in the room joined in the chorus:

'Low lie, the fields of Athenry,
Where once we watched the small free birds fly,
Our love was on the wing,
We had dreams and songs to sing.
It's so lonely round the fields of Athenry.'

Aelish and Owen continued to sing into the microphone, as most people in the room sang along,

'By a lonely prison wall,
I heard a young man calling,
Nothing matters Mary'

(Owen went very close to the microphone and sang 'Siobhan' instead of Mary)

'. . . when you're free,
Against the famine and the crown,
I rebelled, they cut me down,
Now you must raise our children with dignity'

So many people in the back room of O'Neill's knew this was the one year anniversary of Mick Flanagan's sudden death. Everyone in the room joined in the chorus again,

'Low lie, The Fields of Athenry,
Where once we watched the small free birds fly,
Our love was on the wing,
We had dreams and songs to sing.
It's so lonely round the Fields of Athenry.'

They sang it beautifully. So many people in the room had known Mick Flanagan and knew this was his favourite song as he sang it all the time. The entire room sang, slow and strong. Many had tears in their eyes.

Siobhan Flanagan was shocked when she walked into the front door of O'Neill's; the entire pub was singing her husband's favourite song. It stopped her in her tracks, the hair stood up on her neck. She heard the music coming from the back room and slowly walked back there, as she quietly sang along. She entered the back room and saw her two children singing at the microphone, arm in arm. She covered her mouth and, through tears, continued to sing along.

Maeve saw Siobhan at the doorway and jumped up from her seat, went over and put her arm around her. They sang the rest of the song together. Siobhan let the tears flow as she sang the song in memory of her husband on this night. Maeve too was crying as she sang, watching Aelish sing at the microphone. Owen had his arm around Aelish, leading the song all the way through to the end. The entire back room was singing so loudly people from the front of the bar came back to join in. Behind the bar, even Mr. O'Neill put down what he was doing and sang along.

Time seemed to stand still; there was only the song for Mick Flanagan. Everyone knew the words to 'The Fields of Athenry' and sang it proudly; it went on for nearly five minutes, but it seemed an eternity to Siobhan.

She was certain this was a sign from her husband. She felt Mick in the room, leading the song himself, as he had done so many times over the years, where her children were standing now. Maeve held on to Siobhan and continued to sing. Siobhan didn't want it to end. When the song was over, Aelish and Owen walked over to their mam and they all hugged.

Owen was convinced, 'Yeah, I'd say Da was here tonight Ma.'

Siobhan was wiping away her tears, 'I'd say so. He's been with us all along you two, he just shows himself subtly from time to time. This day it wasn't so subtle. That was brilliant. I never knew you two had such beautiful voices, well done, that was really brilliant, thank you for that. Your father loved you two so very much, my God, and he was loved by so many people.'

The regular lead singer took back the microphone and thanked everyone, 'Thank you Aelish and Owen, that was a fantastic tribute to your father. Let's everyone raise a glass to Mick Flanagan. May God rest him, bless him and keep him out of trouble.' The crowd raised their glasses saying, 'Hear, hear.'

As the night went on, people told stories of Mick Flanagan; everyone had a story to tell. The entire room was roaring in laughter over some of his antics over the years. Aelish thought, they couldn't have had a better one year anniversary celebration for their father--she loved being there, she loved how everyone knew and cared so much her da. She felt good about being right where she was.

Patrick McGettigan was moved, and he didn't even know the man. Maeve sat down next to him.

'That was great,' he said, 'He must have been a great man.'

Maeve smiled, 'Ah he was a lovely man, gone too soon, he didn't even make it to 50, no he didn't. It was sudden, a heart attack, shook us all to the core it did. Everyone in the village was gutted.'

Patrick listened to everyone telling stories about Mick. Aelish came and sat next to him.

He looked at her and said, 'You live in a great place Aelish, that was something else with everyone singing for your dad, that was so cool.'

Aelish agreed, 'Yeah, I do live in a great place, don't I? It's not so bad now, is it Maeve?'

Maeve laughed, 'It will always be here Aye, don't you worry, it will always be here if you ever want to come back.'

Chapter Nine

Maeve pulled up in front of Aelish's house, honked her horn and laughed; she had never done that before. She was amusing herself thinking of the neighbours, especially Mrs. Graham who was probably aghast in her house, wondering who would have the nerve to honk their horn like that. Maeve honked again as she giggled.

Aelish came tearing out of her house in her pyjamas, running up to the car, 'Are you mad?'

Maeve was chuckling, 'You're not even ready!'

Aelish started to walk back to the house, 'You're early! Come in and have a cup of tea and don't touch that horn again!' As she walked back up to the door, she looked across the road and saw Mrs. Graham looking out of her front window disapprovingly. Aelish waved at Mrs. Graham and laughed, thinking how it was so out of character for Maeve to do that, it was more like something she would do.

She stopped and yelled back to the car, 'You know what's happening here Maeve, you're becoming more like me, and I'm becoming more like you!'

Maeve was out of the car following Aelish into the house, 'You should be so fortunate to become like me Aye, I'm perfect in the eyes of many, you know that. You know the old saying is true, a friend's eye is a good mirror and I'm a good reflection to have.'

Aelish couldn't take it. 'Ah stop! Get into the kitchen and make us a cup of tea, I'll get ready, be down in a tick.'

Siobhan was in the kitchen as Maeve entered, 'Hi Siobhan.' She walked over and gave her a hug.

'Hiya Maeve, I just made a fresh pot, help yourself.'

Maeve got a cup from the press, milk from the fridge, poured herself a cup and sat down at the table, 'That was lovely last night Siobhan, I didn't know those two could sing so well.'

Siobhan smiled, ''Twas lovely. You know what I was thinking, everyone does memorial masses on the anniversaries. I just couldn't do it, it wasn't Mick. That was Mick last night, that couldn't have been a better memorial.'

Maeve agreed, 'It was perfect.'

Siobhan sat at the table next to Maeve, 'Come here, tell us, who was the boy you were sitting with last night? He was a fine looking fella, who is this now?'

Maeve blushed a bit, 'He's from America, he's visiting here for a few weeks. I don't know much about him, but he seems very nice.'

Owen came tearing into the room and overheard this, 'Yeah, he's nice enough all right, he's helping me out this morning, we're building something in the back garden of O'Neill's. I'm heading out Ma, gotta go and take care of the Geraghty's dog, then I'm off to O'Neill's where yer boyfriend Paddy's working for me, see yous later!' He gave his mam a kiss on the cheek and ran out the door. Maeve was surprised; it seemed Owen had become quite friendly with Patrick. Maeve liked that Patrick appeared to be so helpful. She started daydreaming about him, looking out of the window, wondering if he was awake yet. She was thinking about how they had said goodbye to each other last night, as if they were about to kiss, but neither of them had made a move. They had given each other a good, long hug goodbye.

Patrick had kissed Maeve on top of her head as they hugged, and whispered in a very matter of fact tone, 'I will see you again.' As Maeve was walking out, Patrick had slipped her a small piece of paper, "Maeve, I will see you again. Patrick." Maeve sat at the kitchen table with a smile on her face, letting her tea go cold. She snapped out of it when she heard Siobhan's voice.

'So, what are you girls up to today?'

Maeve wasn't sure if Aelish had told her mam about their search, 'We're taking that widow Sheila Murphy for a drive to Bantry, she's looking for a cousin of hers and we're helping her.'

Siobhan looked pleased, 'Ah, fair play to ye, good girl, I don't think that poor woman has a relative or friend alive.' That made Maeve feel bad for Sheila.

Aelish barged into the room just then, 'Come on then, we're going to be late with you two sitting here gossiping about everyone in the village.' Maeve and Siobhan looked at each other and smiled. Maeve got up, thanked Siobhan for the tea and started to head towards the front door.

Siobhan stopped Aelish, 'Here sweetie, take some fruit and snacks for the drive.'

Aelish looked at her mam thinking how thoughtful she always was. 'Thanks Ma, see you later.' She started to walk out the front door with Maeve leading and suddenly remembered what day it was: it was the actual date of her father's death.

She walked back into the kitchen and looked her mam in the eyes, 'You okay Ma? Do you want to come with us?'

Siobhan smiled at the gesture, 'I'm fine pet, I have loads to do today. Go and have fun, I'll see you later.' Aelish hugged her mam a little longer and tighter than she usually did. Neither of them wanted to let go.

Siobhan pulled back from Aelish to look at her, they both had tears welling up in their eyes. Siobhan brushed wisps of hair away from Aelish's watering eyes and gave her another quick hug, 'Go and have a good day you sweet thing, remember life goes on, we keep moving and we keep living. Move on and move forward, it's all we can do, and have a bit of fun along the way you.'

Aelish smiled; she'd heard move on and move forward quite a few times over the last year, 'All right Ma. I'll see you later then. I love you.'

Siobhan held Aelish's face in her hands, 'I love you so much you beautiful young lady, enjoy your day. Enjoy all of your days Aelish, be sure to capture every moment and savour it, don't be in such a rush to get to the next thing. Enjoy what's right in front of you, right now, every day. And savour it, Aye, savour the moments, seize the moments and acknowledge them, don't let them pass you by. Notice the little things in this life that have long lasting impressions on you, see if you can notice and capture special moments as they happen and make them last longer. Make them have meaning, pay attention to those moments and don't let them slip by unacknowledged. Now go enjoy every moment of your day and be safe.'

Aelish looked at her mam in a different way, thinking she was insightful and cool; she'd never thought of her mam as cool before. She thought of how much she'd been dreading this day, the one year anniversary, how it was going to be as painful as it was last year--but it wasn't; she felt relief at the calm feeling she was having today. Aelish gave her mam a kiss goodbye, 'You're sure you're all right?'

Siobhan insisted, 'Yes, yes, I really am, now you go and have fun you.' Aelish ran out to the car and jumped in the front seat, and Maeve drove off.

When they pulled up in front of Sheila's cottage, the front door was wide open. As they parked the car, they could hear Sheila singing along to loud music.

Maeve and Aelish started laughing. Aelish said, 'Well, she's having a good time this morning, isn't she? Rockin' out to Neil Diamond, I love it!' Maeve looked surprised, 'My mam loves Neil Diamond, she does this exact same thing! When she doesn't think anyone can hear her, she sings so loud along with ol' Neil.' Aelish looked wide eyed, 'Ah my God, would ye listen to her!' Maeve said, 'Let's get her out of there and on the road before the entire county hears her.'

Sheila didn't hear them knocking as she sang loudly:

'Soo, soolaimon
Soolai, soolai, soolaimon
Soo, soolaimon
Soolai, soolai, soolaimon'

The girls walked slowly into the house to find Sheila dancing around with a dusting rag, waving the rag around as she danced and sang. Maeve and Aelish started to laugh.

Startled, Sheila let out a bit of a yelp and grabbed her heart. 'Ah, ye put the heart crossways in me you did, you're early!' She reached for her stereo to turn the music down.

Aelish thought of her what her mam had said before she left, and said quickly, 'Don't turn it down!' She beckoned Maeve to join in. The two girls started to sing along and dance, pretending they were doing housework as well. They twirled, fluffed up cushions, took a broom from the corner pretending it was a microphone. They all continued,

'God of my want, want, want
Lord of my need, need, need,
Leading me on, on, on
On to the woman, she dance for the sun
God of my day

Lord of my night
Seek for the way
Taking me home'

The three of them finished the song, laughing as it ended.

Sheila was beaming, 'That was a great start to our day! Let's get on with this adventure of ours.' Turning off the music, she continued, 'Now then, where are we off to first?'

Maeve took out her mam's map and placed it on Sheila's kitchen table, 'Right, so my mam found a few Sheila Murphys from records at the bank, which of course we won't let on to anyone where we found this information: the closest one to us is in Bantry, I have an address. Sheila, you found a couple that we don't have addresses for, but they're in small enough towns and villages, so it shouldn't be a problem finding them.'

Sheila looked at Maeve and said, 'I like your mam, she sounds like a bit of a chancer she does, good woman.' She then leaned over and took a closer look at the map, 'Sure I'd say Bantry looks like the first stop, then we could drive on to Crookhaven, have either of you been to Crookhaven?' They both shook their heads. Sheila continued, 'It's lovely, that's where we could have lunch, there's a pub along the harbour, O'Sullivan's. I'm sure it's still there, it's been there for donkey's years. They always had a lovely menu; I can just about taste their chowder, it was *gorgeous*. Martin and I would often take that drive, it's a lovely part of our country, it is, you girls will enjoy this.'

Maeve folded up the map, 'Sounds like a plan, we're all set then?'

Aelish said she needed to use the loo first and started to walk towards the bedroom, saying, 'Sheila, do you mind?'

Sheila said, 'Not at all, it's on your left there, we'll be in the car.' As Aelish walked through the hallway, she noticed that the photos on the walls were all old, nothing from recent times. Sheila had been beautiful in her youth; all of the photos were of her and Martin throughout the years--and there was a large painting of Sheila and Martin with two little girls she assumed were their daughters.

Then she thought of what her mam had said, that everyone was dead in Sheila's life; she wished she'd found out more information. Aelish went towards the oil painting on the wall. It was so beautiful; it reminded her of a Rembrandt painting, with similar rich colours and style. It was like a candid photo: the four of them laughing, Sheila's head on Martin's chest as they sat on a stone bench in a garden, watching over the two girls in beautiful matching white dresses, playing on the grass beneath them. It was a stunning painting, in an old ornate frame with a little gold light at the top. The painting had Sheila's signature at the bottom. Aelish was amazed by her talent; she wanted to look at the painting longer, but she knew Sheila and Maeve were waiting for her in the car, so she reluctantly moved on.

Aelish pulled the door of the cottage behind her and yelled out, 'Shall I lock up?'

Sheila laughed, 'I'm not sure the lock works, I don't even have a key come to think of it.'

Maeve laughed, 'I don't know why we bother locking our house up, we leave the key out front for anyone to find.' She looked at Aelish in the back seat knowingly, 'Speaking of which.' She reached into the back seat and pulled the metal box out of a bag and handed it to Sheila, 'Thank you for this, but my ma ended up putting the ticket into a safety deposit box at the bank.'

Sheila took the box and looked at it, 'Ah, you can keep it if you like, keep it for little treasures you pick up along the way in your lives. It could be a time capsule of sorts, holding on to little keepsakes from special moments you'd like to remember. I have no use for it any longer, you girls keep it.'

They both smiled. Maeve said, 'All right then, we'll keep an eye on it for you.'

Sheila liked the sounds of that, 'Grand, are we all set for our adventure now?'

The girls chorused, 'Yes!' and Maeve drove off.

Maeve knew where she was going, 'First stop, Bantry, should be an hour and a quarter's drive. Has anyone thought through any sort of game plan?'

Sheila looked at Aelish in the back seat questioningly, 'I think it makes it a bit more enjoyable if we don't have a plan, let's just go up to the front door and see what happens.'

Aelish started laughing, 'That's mad! I know I'm sounding like you Maeve, but we need a plan!'

Maeve laughed, 'Oh, I don't know, I say anything goes, we just need to find out if she's the Sheila Murphy that breezed through Allihies last week throwing five million euros out of her car window, that's all!'

Sheila agreed, 'Ah, let's not worry about the details, it'll come to us. It's over an hour's drive to Bantry, let's listen to some music, shall we?' Maeve apologized that she didn't have any Neil Diamond.

Patrick was standing across the road from O'Neill's pub waiting for Owen to arrive. He saw Mr. O'Neill walk into the pub, but he hadn't seen Owen arrive yet. Just then Owen came riding up on a bicycle, leaned it against the pub wall, and gestured to Patrick to wait there, that he would be back in a minute. Patrick turned around and looked out to the sea; it was clouding over, looking like it was going to rain, and the sea was starting to look rough. He breathed in the sea air; the distinct smells brought back clear memories of him being here over the years and how much he loved Ireland.

He saw Mr. O'Neill get into his car and drive away. Owen popped his head out of the pub door and gave a whistle to Patrick to come in. Patrick walked across the road into the pub to find Owen already through the bar yelling, 'Come on man, we don't have all day!' Patrick didn't know what they were doing, but he figured he'd find out soon enough.

Owen went out the back door and stood by a pile of wood, saying, 'Okay, this is what we're going to do. Mr. O'Neill wants a place for people to sit outside back here, so we're going to build a wee bar against this wall here. This wood and scrap is what we have to work with, so you need to get on with it and I'll be back, I have another job of walking a dog, feeding some cats and watering some plants for the McGraths down the road, and then I'll be back. Now sort this out before Mr. O'Neill comes back, he said he'd be two hours and he's a punctual fella that one, you got that?'

Patrick found Owen amusing, 'Yeah, sure boss, I'll have this figured out in no time, see you later.' Owen left him and rode off on his bike.

Patrick started to pick up the wood, moving things around to see what he had to work with. He was good with his hands-- he'd taken a carpentry course and had an artistic flair. He was surprised with the array of tools he was left with; he was thinking someone must do carpentry with all of these tools. Not everyone had a circular saw, a jigsaw, a hand saw and routers, tape measure, crayons, files, everything he would need to build a good little outdoor bar. This was fun--he knew what he was doing and got started right away. As he was working, he thought to himself how easily he could live here; he was really enjoying Allihies. It was a such a beautiful village, nestled in the hills overlooking the sea, and he felt at home already. He felt he had an immediate connection to Ireland and all the people he'd encountered. He belonged here, as if he were coming home. He'd always had a strong sense of being Irish--it was hard not to, having the last name McGettigan. He laughed, thinking about all the Americans that came over to find their ancestry. He got it now, he felt it. He'd never felt like this anywhere else in the world, and he'd travelled quite a lot throughout his life. He had an overwhelming desire to stay here, to find where his family came from, and to connect with his ancestors.

He found a pair of work gloves and got started.

Maeve pulled over when they arrived in Bantry. She thought it would be fun to rely solely on the map her mam gave her. She wanted to have a look to make sure she was going in the right direction, towards the address of the Sheila Murphy of Bantry. Aelish yelled from the back seat, 'You're mad! Use your phone!' Maeve glanced at Aelish with a smirk, then said to Sheila, 'You don't mind if we just use the map now, do you, Sheila?' Sheila laughed, 'Not at all dear, it's fun doing things the old fashioned way, it's the only way Martin and I got around.' Maeve confirmed the house was right in the city centre, it wouldn't be a problem to find. The address they had was for a colourful terraced house, up the hill just off the main road. It was starting to rain so she was hoping she would find a parking spot right outside the house, and she did.

Sheila had an announcement, 'Right, I'm going to go up to the door with one of you girls, we don't want to bombard them.' Aelish offered to stay in the car.

Sheila looked at Maeve, 'All right, dear, I'm your grandmother, we are looking for my cousin, it's a family matter. Her name is Sheila Murphy and someone saw her driving in Allihies this past week. Let's just see how they respond to that much information and we'll take it from there, how does that sound?'

Maeve agreed; she was amused at Sheila's enthusiasm about the whole thing, 'Sounds good *Granny*. Let's do it.' Aelish was laughing in the back seat, thinking the whole thing was funny. She didn't think they would ever find this lottery winner and was beginning to wonder why they were even bothering. What if they went through all of this trouble and never found the Sheila Murphy that won. Or worse, what if they eventually found the woman and she didn't give them a reward. Aelish was shaking her head thinking to herself how futile this whole thing could be. She watched Sheila and Aelish knocking on the front door of the Bantry Sheila Murphy's house.

A woman that looked to be around eighty years old opened the door; Aelish couldn't hear what was being said. The woman at the door just kept shaking her head. They weren't invited in. Aelish was guessing this Sheila Murphy was dead. They weren't at the door long; both of them came back to the car and settled in.

Aelish was curious, 'So? What was that about?'

Sheila looked in the back seat, 'It seems that Sheila Murphy has been out of town for over two weeks, that was her mother, she said there was no way that was her in Allihies last week. She's been in Germany on business since the week before last and that's that, and that's all she knew. She said she never hears from her daughter, even when she's in Ireland. Shame really, she seemed a very sad woman.'

Maeve agreed, 'Ah she did, Aye, it was gut wrenching listening to her, she said when she does see her daughter as she did weeks ago, she picked up something for her trip to

Germany. She said she barely looks at her, no she doesn't, and she said she did nothing wrong, they didn't have a falling out, she just dismissed her as she got older. She said she wasn't the same girl she raised, it was sad listening to her.'

Sheila interrupted, 'That could be a lesson for you girls, never forget your mothers, they've been taking care of you for more years than you can recall. Ah, you never know though, what goes on in the four walls of one's home now, do you, I suppose it's not our business now, is it, everyone's business is their own. Right then, we can scratch that Sheila Murphy off the list anyway and head towards Crookhaven, it's about a 45 minute drive from here. I'm getting hungry for that wonderful O'Sullivan's chowder. We can ask there for the Sheila Murphy of Crookhaven, I'm sure someone at O'Sullivan's will know. How does that sound, girls?'

Both Maeve and Aelish agreed. They glanced at each other knowingly; there was something about Sheila's past that she was not willing to divulge. Maeve shrugged, thinking about what Sheila had said, that it was none of their business now, was it. She started to drive out of Bantry towards Crookhaven. Aelish was sitting in the back seat wondering if anyone else was thinking this whole search could be futile.

Aelish said, 'Okay, so that Bantry Sheila Murphy didn't work out, what if the Crookhaven Sheila Murphy doesn't pan out? Then what if the Skibbereen Sheila isn't it? Then Ballydehob Sheila's not the one, or Clonakilty or Ballydehoo or Kilarney or Kilimanjaro Sheila, how many Sheila Murphys do we plan to search for? When are we going to give up? What if this is all just a complete waste of time?' Maeve and Sheila glanced at each other in the front seat.

Sheila looked back at Aclish, 'Dear, we don't have to do anything we don't want to do in this life. There are two ways of looking at everything, one is positively, the other negatively.

I can tell you one thing I've learned in my lifetime: thinking positively about everything is much lighter and happier than thinking negatively about anything. To be honest, the outcome is usually better when you are positive. We can look at this as an adventure, a treasure hunt, a quest, however you want to look at it. If we find her, great; if we don't, well, there's no harm in having the adventure now is there, getting out and meeting new people, dear?'

Aelish agreed, 'Okay, why not. I've never been to Crookhaven anyway, carry on.'

Maeve glanced back at Aelish and said, 'Right then, you're all sorted back there? Sheila, what do you know about this Crookhaven Sheila Murphy? Anything? You mentioned she could be a distant cousin of Martin?'

Sheila laughed, 'Well, every Murphy in Cork County could be a distant cousin of Martin's, but this one very well could be one of the cousins I knew of on Martin's father's side, they had a farm on the outskirts of Crookhaven. Ah, it's worth looking into, maybe they took a drive up to Allihies last week and lost their ticket, you just never know.'

Aelish was still curious, 'What if we eventually find this winner Sheila Murphy and she doesn't give us a reward for all of the work we are doing to find her?'

Maeve looked back at Aelish, 'Who cares, Aye, what else were ye doing this weekend anyway? I think we should just do this because we want to, no matter the outcome and no matter how many Sheila Murphys we have to go through to find the rightful owner of that ticket. Let's just do it for as long as we can, for as many as we can find, and just see what happens, do you agree?'

Aelish shrugged, 'Yeah sure, I was just wondering 'tis all, I'm grand with whatever. I'm getting hungry though, how good is this chowder at O'Sullivan's you mentioned?'

Sheila smiled, 'Ah, it's plenty good, it was delicious every time I went there with Martin, anyway. I would imagine they've passed the recipe down--we can only hope. The pub has been in the same family for generations. Ah, it was always top-quality food and the friendliest people in the world, they were.' They drove along Bantry Bay, then headed south towards Crookhaven. The drive was beautiful, along the inlets of water, through farms and patchwork fields as far as they could see.

Sheila watched the scenery go by, with a warm feeling in her heart and a smile on her face. 'Tis good to be out, and so good to spend the day with you two girls, it truly is. Who cares if we find the winning Sheila Murphy, I'm glad you girls found me. It's curious how chance encounters with people can change the outcome of your days, it truly is amazing. If nothing comes of this search, I wouldn't be bothered, you girls found me, and I feel like I'm the winner here, I do indeed.'

Chapter Ten

Owen came back to O'Neill's pub and couldn't believe what Patrick had accomplished in just over an hour.

'Whoa, this is fantastic! Mr. O'Neill is going to love this! Jaysus, I'm sure he was thinking he was going to get a shoddy piece of plywood on two sticks attached to the wall outa me. Now this, this is something else with all the fancy cutting and shaping and all, look at you! Good man! Now then, let's finish up and get out of here.'

Mr. O'Neill came back earlier than expected. He surprised Owen and Patrick in the back, 'What do we have here? Jesus, how many guys did you have working on this, Owen? By the looks of it, I'd say you didn't do this on your own.'

Owen didn't care, 'Well, you said you were going to pay me for the job, no matter how I did it, so, I enlisted some help from this here Yank.'

Mr. O'Neill looked at Patrick and extended his hand, 'We've met--Paddy, is it? The name's John, although you'd swear it was 'Mister' or 'Old Man' according to this lot.' John patted Owen on the back.

Patrick shook John's hand, 'Yes sir, it's Patrick, nice to see you again. If you'd like anything else done over the next few weeks, I'd be happy to help, I don't need any money, I just like to keep busy.'

Mr. O'Neill let out a hearty laugh, 'Ha! That's how Owen got you into this is it? Did ye tell him the same thing, that you didn't want any money? A sly fox this one, a shyster businessman. He'll make it in the world doing something with his life, he will, I'm not sure if it will be above the table, but he'll make it.'

Owen interrupted and backhanded Patrick on his arm, 'Did ye hear that? I'm a sly businessman, quite a compliment, that.'

Mr. O'Neill ignored him, 'I'll tell you what lads, I'll pay you now for the job, but you'd better finish it by tomorrow. I'll pay you *both*. Thanks for doing it, it's looking great, a hell of a lot better than I was expecting. Now, see you lads later, clean up the mess now, would you?' He handed them each cash and walked back into the bar.

Owen looked at Patrick, 'This does look a hell of a lot better than I could have done myself, how'd you know how to do all this?'

Patrick offered to show Owen, 'It's basic woodworking, it's a great skill to have. You wouldn't believe the things you can build.' Owen was interested and wanted to learn. He was glad he'd asked Patrick to help, and he was happy Mr. O'Neill had given him half the funds for building it. He wasn't going to give up his half to Patrick: he did fancy himself as a sly businessman. Patrick laughed at Owen's antics; he was happy to help and teach him. Patrick didn't want to tell Owen that everything he'd learned about carpentry was from his father when he was Owen's age. He was realising how lucky he was to have had the time he did with his dad.

Maeve was wishing she didn't have to pay attention to the road so she could enjoy the scenery more. It was a beautiful drive to Crookhaven on the Kilmore Peninsula, towards Mizen Head. It felt like driving on an island--Crookhaven being on a long stretch of land, the bay on one side, the sea on the other. It wasn't difficult to find O'Sullivan's pub on the bay with the car park full of cars. It started to rain just as they pulled in to park.

Maeve looked at Sheila, 'Can you manage?'

Sheila looked humorously at Maeve. 'Ah yes, dear, I'll manage.' All three ran into the pub. Maeve was impressed with Sheila, being in her seventies. She was fit and trim and she had no problem running to the pub at the same pace as the teenaged girls.

Sheila stood inside the doorway and placed her hand on her chest.

Maeve panicked, 'Sheila, what is it? Are you okay?'

Sheila smiled, 'Ah, this pub always had a special place in my heart, it hasn't changed a bit since I was last here with my Martin. My God, I could just imagine him walking through that door this very moment.' She had a smile on her face as she looked at the interior of the pub, with the familiar photos and currency from every country in the world. Aelish had walked over to the large fireplace in the grey stone wall; there was a bench and table available right near the fire, that glowed with burning turf. Aelish gestured toward Maeve and Sheila to come and sit at the table by the window.

Maeve put her arm around Sheila, 'Let's go and sit by the fire, and get the chill off from the rain.'

Sheila followed Maeve to join Aelish. 'This is lovely, I couldn't think of a better way to spend a rainy Saturday!'

Maeve guided Sheila towards the bench; she was still in awe, looking at everything on the walls.

A waitress came over to greet them, placing menus in front of them, 'Good afternoon ladies, what can I get you to drink? Something warm perhaps?' Maeve asked for tea, Sheila said that sounded lovely, and Aelish agreed. Sheila stretched her hands towards the fire.

The waitress smiled, 'Right then, a pot of tea and three cups coming up. I'll keep that fire going, you'll be warmed up in no time.' They all thanked the waitress and looked at their menus. Aelish put her menu down and said she didn't need to look at it: the chowder had been on her mind for hours. Maeve agreed. Sheila was pleased that everyone wanted the wonderful chowder she remembered from years ago. She was thinking it had better be good after all she'd gone on about it.

Sheila was happy to be out, 'Honestly, if you girls didn't find that ticket, I never would have had the pleasure of meeting you both. I wouldn't be enjoying this moment with you right now.' Aelish agreed, 'We were lucky to have met you, Sheila, as much of a pain this is finding this woman, it's been fun with you.'

Maeve agreed, 'This is lovely, and what a cosy place by the sea to have a cup of tea by the fire, this is perfect!' They sat there chatting and sipping their tea.

The waitress came back asking if everything was okay and if they'd like to order.

Sheila spoke up, 'We'd all like to have your delicious chowder with plenty of brown bread, please.' The waitress said that was an excellent choice on the chowder and she'd bring them a whole loaf of brown bread if they'd like. She asked if they'd like anything else. Sheila answered, 'Yes dear, I'm looking for a cousin of mine that lives in Crookhaven, would you happen to know Sheila Murphy?'

The waitress shook her head, 'No, I'm afraid I don't, but that doesn't mean she doesn't live here, let me ask Donal here for you, he's the owner. He knows everyone in this area, leave it with me, I'll get back to you and I'll bring your chowder.'

Sheila said, 'Thanks a million.' She looked excited, 'I have a good feeling about this one, this could be it, girls.' The girls smiled.

Maeve shrugged, 'You never know.'

Aelish chimed in, 'For all we know, that ticket buying Sheila Murphy could have been a tourist from America and she's already gone back to the States, talk about a needle in a haystack! Hey, you should ask your new boyfriend from America if he knows Sheila Murphy!'

Maeve looked annoyed, 'Funny thing is Aelish, that American, who is *not* my boyfriend, was looking for Sheila Murphy himself! Well, he was looking for Martin Murphy, but still.'

Sheila was curious, 'Yes, the American you mentioned, you should bring him round tomorrow, Maeve.'

Maeve lit up, 'That's a grand idea, I'll see if he's available.' Aelish put her arms around Maeve and started leaning in towards her making kissing noises. Maeve pushed her away.

Sheila smiled, 'Well, now, I look forward to meeting this boy.'

Maeve got butterflies in her stomach thinking about Patrick, 'You'll meet him tomorrow then, I'll see to it.'

The waitress came back with two plates with bowls of chowder and placed them in front of Maeve and Aelish.

She was followed by Donal O'Sullivan carrying a basket of bread and a plate, which he placed in front of Sheila, 'I understand you're looking for Sheila Murphy, young lady?'

Sheila blushed, 'Why yes, I am! She may be my cousin I'm searching for; does she live in the area?'

Donal sat down on an empty stool beside Sheila, 'Yes, she lives on a farm just outside of Crookhaven. If you turn left out of the car park here,' as he pointed out of the front window overlooking the water, 'towards Gally Cove, then you make a U turn on the main road, follow that to Streek Head 'til you see the stone wall, and it's the farm on your left, the one with the gate. It's the old house on the hill, sort of an off-white, with black trim, you'll see it, you can't miss it, if you do miss it, you'll be headed right into the sea. Sheila should be there, she's there every day with those kids and the animals. You may even see her husband, but he's usually in the fields, or he's in here, if she's lucky.'

Sheila looked at the girls, 'Did we get those directions between the three of us?' The girls nodded their heads, seemingly confident.

Donal smiled and got up, 'You ladies enjoy your lunch, I'll be back to you before you leave and go over the directions again for you to be sure. Enjoy, and we'll see you in a bit.' The girls tucked into the chowder.

Sheila was looking out the window, 'This is such a lovely spot. I bet it was Donal's father that I chatted with last time I was here with Martin, he was around the age Donal is now. It just doesn't seem like that long ago. Ah, I have so many fond memories of being here with Martin.. how the years went by too quickly.' She tasted her chowder, 'Ah, this is lovely, just as I remembered it. This is just perfect.'

Donal came back as promised and went over the directions to the Murphy farm again. He said they should have no problem finding Sheila and her husband, Dermot Murphy. He assured them it was only minutes away.

They left O'Sullivan's pub and made their way to the Murphy farm. There was a bit of confusion in the car on the directions; they found themselves on a road headed down towards the sea, but they eventually found their way back to the farm.

Aelish squealed when she saw the off-white stone house with the black trim, 'I see it! Up on the hill, do you see it?'

Maeve looked ahead and agreed, 'Right, that must be it.' She pulled into the long road lined with stone walls that led up the hill to the old farm house. As they were reaching the house, three large dogs started running alongside the car, barking wildly, announcing their arrival. A heavy-set woman in her late

30's came to the front door wearing an apron; she had a bit of flour on her face.

She waved and yelled to the car, 'Hello!' Not having a clue who it was. Sheila got out of the car and walked up to the woman as she called the dogs off, shooing them with a towel.

Sheila approached the woman, 'Hello, I'm sorry to trouble you, I'm looking for a cousin of mine.' She extended her hand towards the woman.

The woman took her hand in both of her hands. 'Not at all! Come in for some tea, and I've just made some fresh brown bread. Who's in the car with you there, tell them to come in!' Sheila gestured to the girls in the car. They came out and introduced themselves and were ushered inside the farmhouse.

The girls noticed the outside of the stone farmhouse; it was a dingy white from many years needing a new coat of paint. As they entered the house they noticed the interior hadn't been done in a long time either, maybe even since the house was built in the early 1900's. It was clean inside, but very sparse and dark. The kitchen had an iron wood burning potbelly stove. The kettle was put on, cups were brought out, and the bread, still warm from the oven, all placed on the table.

Sheila told the woman they had just finished eating lunch at O'Sullivan's so they wouldn't have much room for the bread, but thanked her just the same. The woman brought butter to the table just in case. 'I have ham as well, and a pot roast in the oven that'll be done soon. Now then, tell us about this cousin you're looking for, what's the name?'

Sheila said, 'Well, it's Sheila Murphy, it's the cousin of my husband, Martin Murphy.'

The woman looked vacant, 'Now, I'm Sheila Murphy, but I don't know of any Martin Murphy, I can ask my husband though, he should be in any moment for his tea. Now what is it that you're trying to find? If there's an inheritance, we'll take it,' she said with a laugh.

Sheila wanted to get to the point. 'Sheila, is there any chance you were in Allihies this past week?'

The woman laughed, 'I wouldn't know where Allihies was if you placed a map right in front of me, or you drove me to it. Why do you ask?'

Sheila went on, 'Well, I was in Allihies last week and I saw someone that looked just like you driving by in a red car.'

The woman laughed, 'Well I certainly don't have a red car either. We do have a red tractor though'

Sheila continued, 'Yes, well it was a red car that passed me by while I was buying a lottery ticket. Do you play the lottery?'

The woman laughed, 'Heavens no, we never play the lottery.'

Dermot Murphy walked into the kitchen and spread his arms, 'What's this? A hen party? What's the occasion? I've never seen so many pretty women in my kitchen at one time! Ah, but this one is the prettiest.' He put his arm around his wife.

She shooed him off with a tea towel, 'Ah stop it, Dermot. These ladies are looking for their long-lost cousin Martin Murphy.'

Sheila corrected her, 'I was actually looking for my husband's cousin, Sheila Murphy.'

Dermot pointed to his wife, 'Well, she's Sheila Murphy, so she is. You found her. Is there an inheritance? We'll take it! We wouldn't turn anything away but we're quite happy as we are, aren't we, pet?'

'That's just what I said, ye big lug!'

Sheila continued, 'So, I take it you're not Martin Murphy's cousin then, is that it?'

The husband and wife looked at each other, and he said, 'Not sure of any Martin Murphy in the family, but we have an ancestry book in the attic, I'll go and get it.'

Sheila said quickly, 'Oh, no, please, that isn't necessary, if Sheila were the cousin I was looking for, she would certainly know Martin.' The couple insisted on helping any way they could.

Dermot took a black and white framed photo off the wall, 'Here's a photo when the family got together a few years back, would you recognize anyone here? Maybe Martin is in this photo? Now, if you look closely, you may find your long-lost cousin here. We'll get that ancestry book, it wouldn't be a bother, I know where it is in the attic.'

Sheila was insistent, 'No, no, no, I think we may find her on our next stop in Skibbereen. Thank you so much for the tea, we'd best be on our way now.'

The woman jumped up and put the bread in a tea towel, 'Take some bread with you for the drive, you never know when you'll get peckish.' Sheila told her again they had just eaten lunch. The woman insisted and pressed the bread into Sheila's hands, not taking no for an answer. Maeve and Aelish thanked them for the tea and bread and walked out to the car. The dogs started running towards the house as they exited. The girls ran for the car. Sheila waved and thanked them again and popped into the car just as the dogs arrived.

Maeve was laughing, 'We could have been stuck in there for the night.'

Aelish quipped, 'We wouldn't have gone hungry.'

Sheila said, 'Well, mission accomplished here, anyway, she was nowhere near Allihies, she doesn't have a red car, and she never plays the lottery, check that one off the list.'

Aelish looked back at the farmhouse, 'Too bad it wasn't them, they seemed so nice and well deserving of a bit of help.'

Maeve smiled, 'Yes, but how nice they seemed happy the way things are, a happy family on the old farm.' She glanced at Aelish in the back seat and smirked. Maeve continued, 'That's done, now on to Skibbereen! Do we know anything about this Sheila Murphy?'

Sheila seemed excited, 'Yes, this one could be the one, I found her while I was calling all the B&B's in the area for any Murphys that may have stayed with them last week. A B&B in Glengarriff had a Sheila Murphy from Skibbereen registered last weekend for a wedding. The woman at the B&B was surprised; she said if I were her cousin, then I should have been invited to the wedding. I told her that's precisely why I was looking for her! She couldn't give me any information other than she was from Skibbereen.'

Aelish was confused, 'Hang on, I thought your mam found a Sheila Murphy in Ballydehob Maeve, didn't she find that one at work, so we have an address for that one, right?'

Maeve remembered, 'Sorry, Yes! To Ballydehob first! Then to Skibbereen!'

Sheila was having a gas, 'I think we should have some music on this road trip!' The girls started to laugh; Aelish looked for something they could listen to. She found something her gran had given her, certain Sheila would like it. 'Do you like Dean Martin?'

Sheila gasped, 'NO! No I do not like Dean Martin, I do not like him, no I don't, I *love* him! I *love* Dean Martin!'

The girls laughed, 'Dean Martin it is then.' Aelish put on "That's Amore" and they all sang:

'In Napoli where love is king,
When boy meets girl, here's what they say . . .
When the moon hits your eye like a big pizza pie,
That's amore . . .

When the world seems to shine
Like you've had too much wine,
That's amore . . .
Bells will ring, ting-a-ling-a-ling, ting-a-ling-a-ling,
And you'll sing "Vita Bella!"
Hearts will play tippy-tippy-tay, tippy-tippy-tay,
Like a gay tarantella'

It was a half hour's drive, singing along with Dean Martin the whole way. Sheila couldn't remember the last time she'd felt so good . . . she felt happy and young.

They arrived at the address in Ballydehob. It was a new home, perched on a hill, surrounded by a low white wooden fence and lush green landscape. There were quite a few religious lawn ornaments in the front garden that made the girls laugh.

Sheila smiled, 'Now girls, not everyone has the same taste.'

Aelish wasn't sure if Sheila was religious or not, so she didn't want to knock the lawn ornaments too much, 'Jesus would be proud of his parents being represented on that lawn.'

Maeve gave her a quick look into the back seat and said to Sheila, 'Let's get on with this now, shall we do the same thing? You're my gran looking for your long-lost cousin?'

Sheila thought for a moment and nodded, 'Unless you girls can think up another idea, I'm fine sticking with that.' They agreed, and Aelish offered to stay in the car again.

A woman opened the door, just popping her head out, 'Yes, how can I help you?' Sheila spoke up, 'Hello, my name is Sheila Murphy, I am in search of a cousin of mine by the same name. Would you happen to be Sheila Murphy?' The woman looked at the two of them a bit surprised and taken aback,

'However did you find me, how did you get my address?' They detected an English accent. Maeve panicked for a moment, thinking her mam could get in trouble for giving out bank records.

Maeve spoke up, 'We just asked around town and someone told us that a Sheila Murphy lived up here.'

The woman didn't seem pleased. She narrowed her eyes a bit at Maeve, 'I find that very strange, I just moved here recently, no one knows I live here, who exactly told you? Where did you get my address?'

Sheila looked at Maeve, seeing she was getting nervous, playing with her hair. She spoke up, 'Ah dear, you know how people are in Ireland, everyone knows everyone, and people do seem to know everyone's business, much as we don't like them to at times, it's the ever-enduring quality of the Irish, wouldn't you agree? It's all perfectly harmless, really. I'm seeking a cousin of my husband, Martin Murphy, would you happen to know if you're a relative of Martin Murphy?'

The woman was having none of it, 'No, I don't know Martin Murphy, I have no relatives in Ireland, I only moved here recently and I find it strange that you, whoever you are, have my address, you know my name . . . I'm not interested in anything you are looking for.'

Sheila found the woman to be very pernickety and knew their time would be limited. She said, 'You look so familiar, were you in Allihies last week?'

The woman's face got all screwed up, 'What do you want? Why are you asking me where I was last week? Whatever you want, whatever you are seeking, I'm not interested. I don't know what you know or think you know, but I have nothing for you.' Sheila was thinking, if this is the woman who lost that winning ticket, she couldn't care less if it was returned to her with that attitude.

She half smiled at the woman, 'Right then, we are sorry to have bothered you, I don't think you are the nice cousin of my late husband, we are sorry we took up this moment of your time.' Sheila looked at Maeve, 'Let's go dear.' The two of them walked back to the car and quietly got in.

Maeve was angry, 'Why are some people so difficult and just plain rude?'

Aelish was curious, 'What happened?'

Sheila didn't seem phased, 'Some people are just miserable, dear, it has nothing to do with you. Never let people like that affect you, never take it personally. I always think people are that way due to an unhappiness within themselves, or an insecurity, or just an absolute miserable existence. Now, what if she was the winner? Because she was so rude, we'll never find out now, will we? And to be honest, we shouldn't care less, serves her right really, don't you think?'

Aelish was confused, 'What on earth did that woman say to you?'

Maeve looked into the back seat, 'She seemed very leery of us, it was odd, she couldn't understand how we got her address. She was really quite rude. I panicked thinking it could get my mam in trouble. She acted like we were wanting something, she said she wanted to have nothing to do with us or whatever we were up to. It was really quite strange, actually.'

Aelish was surprised, 'Sounds like another cow to me, Jaysus, or just a crazy Catholic! Say goodbye to Mary and Joseph, let's get the hell out of here!'

Sheila wanted to find levity in the situation, 'Never mind girls, if there's one thing in life you should learn very quickly, don't ever let anyone bring you down. Be thankful you are not like them, and keep those sorts of people at a distance.'

Aelish agreed, 'I'd say she was a holier-than-thou cow! Let's go to Skibbereen!'

Sheila agreed, 'How would you girls like some ice cream? My treat!'

Maeve said, 'That's a lovely idea! Let's go into the town of Ballydehob, I'm sure they'll have a 99 at one of their shops!'

Aelish yelled, 'Woohoo! I scream for ice cream!'

Maeve beeped her horn, 'I scream for ice cream!'

Sheila laughed, 'I scream for ice cream as well and I'll have an extra Flake in mine!'

They drove off down the road in search of ice cream, and another Sheila Murphy.

Chapter Eleven

Patrick taught Owen the basics of woodworking and carpentry; they spent a few hours finishing the table in the back area of O'Neill's and he showed Owen how to make a couple of planter boxes. A few items were needed to finish the job, that weren't available in Allihies, so Patrick offered to drive to the closest hardware store in Castletownbere.

Owen was curious, 'So Paddy, you drive on the right side of the road in the States, right? Is it a problem for you to drive on the left?'

Patrick laughed, 'You're not going to stop calling me Paddy, are you? If you're worried about my driving, don't be, I've driven on the left side of the road in a few countries and I haven't had an accident, yet.' Owen looked for some wood and touched it. Patrick laughed, 'Superstitious, are you?'

Owen shrugged, 'No, Jaysus, Paddy, I don't know why I do that, me da used to do it all the time. And ya, Paddy suits ye, you're Paddy here, you'll get used to it, you will.' They got into the car and headed along the sea towards Castletownbere.

Patrick felt bad about Owen losing his dad, 'I'm sorry about your dad, bro, that's gotta be tough.' Owen shrugged a bit, not saying anything, and looked out the window as they drove through the narrow country roads.

Owen eventually spoke, 'Ya, it was on this date last year, heart attack, in his sleep, me ma didn't hear a thing and she was right next to him. The only good thing of it was we think he didn't suffer. He had a bit of drink that night so it probably numbed the pain of it all. I don't know, I just like to think it was quick and he didn't suffer.' Patrick didn't know what to say.

    Owen hadn't talked to anyone about his father, for a whole year. He didn't know why it was easy to talk to Patrick, he didn't question it. He continued talking, looking out the window, 'They say the good ones are always the ones that are taken first. He was definitely a good one, he was the best, really. I wouldn't tell Liam this, but he was my best friend, he was, me da.' Owen stared out the window, his thoughts going to how fast his childhood had gone by and the short time he'd had with his da. For the first time, he thought that his childhood was over, he was going to be eighteen soon, his da had been gone for a whole year now, he couldn't believe it. It was quiet in the car. Owen could sense Patrick was looking at him. He looked at Patrick and said, 'You really oughta keep your eyes on the road or you'll get us both killed. Me ma wouldn't like it if I wasn't home for dinner.'

    Patrick felt the need to make Owen feel better, 'Say, we've put in a good day's work, how about we go have a pint after we pick up the stuff at the hardware store.'

    Owen was a bit gloomy, 'That sounds grand, that's something me da and I would do, but my da would say that alcohol didn't solve any problems, Paddy.' Patrick was worried, he didn't know what to say. Owen laughed, 'I'm only slagging you, he'd actually say alcohol didn't solve any problems, but neither did milk. Yeah, let's get a bit of the black stuff at McCarthy's, it's just down the road from Harrington's Hardware, I'll show you.'

    Patrick smiled as he pulled into the car park across from the hardware store in Castletownbere, 'Sounds like a plan, let's get the stuff we need to finish the job, then we'll have a pint.' Owen was curious, 'What are we getting anyway?' he asked.

Patrick said, 'We need to get sandpaper, stain and varnish to polish it all up and finish by tomorrow.'

Owen nodded, 'Sounds good.' They went into Harringtons, got the items needed to complete their project, and then went into McCarthy's bar. Owen smiled when they walked in the front door of the pub. They still had a little grocery behind the bar, where his da would always buy him a treat. The long, narrow bar hadn't changed at all over the years.

Owen smiled with the flood of memories he had, 'Me da and I came here many times, it's good to be back in here, thanks Paddy.'

Patrick looked at him, 'No problem, Owen, but, seriously, no one calls me Paddy.'

Owen laughed and patted him on the back, 'Someone does now, Paddy, haha.'

They walked past the grocery area to the back bar. Mrs. McCarthy was pouring a pint as she turned around. She had known Mick Flanagan and recognized Owen, 'Well would ye look what just came in off the road, how's the form, Owen? Look at the head on you, ah how handsome you're getting.' She reached over the bar and touched the side of his head as she shouted towards the back kitchen, 'Hun! Hide the girls!'

A grumble was heard from the kitchen, 'Jesus Mary, who is it now?'

Mrs. McCarthy was still admiring Owen, 'Would ye look at you?'

Owen smiled, 'Ah stop Mrs. McCarthy, "getting handsome" is right, I haven't gotten there yet. Hey Mrs. McCarthy, this is my friend from the States, Paddy, Paddy McGettigan, he's helping me with a building project at O'Neill's.'

Mrs. McCarthy looked at Patrick, 'Paddy McGettigan is it? Well if that's not an Irish name, I don't know what is, you sound more Irish than the Irish themselves, you do! Welcome, you're very welcome, what'll you have?'

He reached over the bar to shake her hand, 'It's Patrick, nice to meet you. I'll have a pint of Guinness please, and whatever he's having.'

Owen patted him on the back, 'Thanks Paddy, I'll have a pint of Murphy's, Mrs. McCarthy, thanks a mil, he'll have the same, it's better than Guinness, Paddy, you'll see.'

Mrs. McCarthy was pulling their pints as she continued their conversation, 'What part of the States did you say you were from there, Paddy?'

Patrick responded, 'Chicago.'

Mrs. McCarthy laughed, 'Ah, I've met some of the best people from Chicago, I have indeed. Would ye happen to know Butch McGuire's pub? Butch was a lovely man, he was, God rest him. They've had their share of Irish passing through that pub over the years, they have, they hire Irish kids to work there every summer, they do, bless them. I understand his son Bobby McGuire runs the place now, so he does, salt of the earth that one, a good man, like his father.'

Patrick smiled at Mrs. McCarthy, 'Yes, of course I know Butch McGuire's, it's an institution, I love it.'

Mrs. McCarthy looked pleased and agreed, 'Seems a small world sometimes, does it not. I think if we got right to it, we'd find we all know each other somehow and we're related to those we didn't even know we were related to if they were sitting right next to us.'

Patrick nodded, 'It does seem so, I think we're all related.'

Owen laughed heartily, 'Ah Yanks, he's a yoke isn't he Mrs. McCarthy? I think we should keep him. Me best mate is Liam McGuire, do ye reckon he's related to these Chicago McGuire's of yours?'

She placed their pints in front of them and said dryly, 'Yes of course Owen, and I'm related to every McCarthy in the world, so I am. Here ye go, lads, enjoy your stay, Paddy, you mind Owen here, he needs a little looking after he does, keep him out of mischief.'

Owen rolled his eyes, 'Ah stop, Mrs. McCarthy.' She looked at the front door as more people entered, and called out towards them, 'Ah look what just walked in, hello there lads, come in, come in, you're very welcome indeed!' Patrick and Owen smiled, clinked their glasses, and enjoyed their pints.

Maeve pulled into a shop in Ballydehob with a very large, plastic ice cream cone out front, remarking, 'I think we found our spot.' Aelish clapped in the back seat, squealing like a child.

Sheila joined in, 'I scream, you scream, we all scream for ice cream!'

Maeve parked in a spot right in front of the shop and said, 'I'll get them, 99's for everyone?'

They both said, 'Yes please!'

Maeve thought for a moment that she might make a mess trying to carry three ice cream cones at once. 'Aye, would you mind helping?' she asked. 'We'll be right back, Sheila, would you like anything else?'

Sheila smiled, 'No dear, I'm perfectly fine, thank you.' Sheila sat in the car and looked out the window, down the road to Ballydehob. It had been many years since she had been to this village with Martin. This was a trip down memory lane, and she was enjoying every moment of it. So much had changed over the years, yet so much remained the same; she had such a nice feeling, going to places where she had been with Martin. She thought of her girls for a moment, but pushed them from her mind and went back to thinking of the present day, and who she was with, and the joy she felt.

Maeve looked at Aelish as they walked towards the store, 'You know we need to keep in touch with her, even after this whole searching fiasco is over.'

Aelish agreed, 'Ah sure, she's happy out, she is. Can you imagine keeping to yourself for twenty five years?'

Maeve looked at Aelish, 'I can't imagine, I wouldn't do it. I could see you doing that, you're a bit antisocial at times.'

Aelish looked shocked and pushed Maeve into the store, saying, 'I am not! Hey, my mam mentioned Sheila didn't have any family left, and remember Sheila told us that her good friend died, and her cousin died. I wonder if she has any friends at all? No family to speak of? Not one person?'

Maeve shook her head, 'I don't know. We don't know much about her now, do we? We know she loved her husband, but she doesn't say much else.'

Aelish questioned, 'Have you seen the painting in her house, back by the loo? It looks like her and Martin and two little girls, could be their daughters. Where do you suppose those girls are?'

Maeve shrugged, 'I don't know, and we can't just ask. Like she said, what goes on in the four walls of someone's house is none of our business. Or maybe next time we're in her house we could ask, I don't know, Aye. Ask your mam if she knows anything else.' Maeve handed two ice cream cones to Aelish, paid the cashier and they walked out of the shop.

As they made their way back to the car, they could see Sheila, sitting there looking out the window at them with a smile on her face.

As they approached, Maeve smiled back at Sheila and said to Aelish, 'She's a lovely woman, isn't she, and so easy to be with, we should keep her.'

Aelish laughed, 'Haha, ya, we should adopt her.' They both laughed as they got into the car. Sheila asked what they were laughing about.

Aelish didn't hesitate, 'Maeve and I don't have grans close by, so we said we should adopt you as our granny.'

Sheila laughed a hearty laugh, 'Ah, that'd be grand, I'd be delighted! But you can still call me Sheila. Now, off to Skibbereen we go, another place I haven't been to in donkey's years. This is gas! Thanks for the ice cream--but I said I was getting it, so you must let me get them next time!'

Maeve agreed, 'This is fun. Do you mind if we stay here for a moment so I can eat my ice cream?'

Sheila thought that was good of her to think of safe driving, 'Ah heavens, not at all, take your time, we're in no rush, are we now, Aelish?'

Aelish had a mouth full of ice cream, 'Naugh aah awe.'

Sheila smiled, 'I think she said 'Not at all.' You finish your ice cream, then we'll head to Skibbereen. Now then, we're going to have to do a bit of poking around in Skibbereen, we don't have an address for this Sheila Murphy. The only information I have is that she was at a wedding in Glengarriff last weekend, and she stayed at the Island View House B&B there. You never know, there's a great possibility she went there for a wedding, then she went through Allihies and threw her lottery ticket out of her car window, this could very well be the Sheila Murphy we're looking for!' The girls laughed.

Maeve said, 'She didn't exactly *throw* the ticket out the window.'

Aelish chimed in, 'I wonder if this Sheila Murphy even knows she's a winner? That would be horrible if she knew!

Can you imagine knowing and losing your ticket? That would be the worst! Ignorance is bliss they say, I prefer to be ignorant about a lot of things, I'd especially like to be ignorant of that, I'd go mad looking for it I would.'

Maeve thought about that for a moment, 'You're right, what *if* she knows she won? Say she picked her own numbers . . . some people play the same numbers week after week for years. What if she was one of those people, she bought her ticket and her numbers won, and then she couldn't find her ticket, I'd go mad!'

Aelish agreed, 'She also could have bought a random ticket, lost it, and didn't think another thing of it, not knowing the lost ticket was a winner.' She continued, 'Or you could be right Maeve, she knows she won and lost her winning ticket, so now she's locked up in the mental hospital in Dublin and we'll never find her.'

Maeve laughed, 'I don't know which is worse, being locked up in the mental hospital, or having to live in Dublin.' Aelish reached up and shoved Maeve from the back seat.

Maeve started to get out of the car with her nearly finished ice cream cone, 'I can't finish this, I'm going to toss it, does anyone else want me to toss the rest of theirs?'

She got a resounding 'No!' from both of them.

'Very well, I'll toss my own, and we can get going.' She got back into the car and started driving towards Skibbereen, 'This should be about a half hour's drive. Should we go into the local when we get there? Does anyone know of a popular place in the town?'

Aelish laughed, 'I've never been to Skibbereen, I haven't a clue.'

Sheila thought for a moment, 'I know a cute little pub called Dinty's, but we could tuck in anywhere really, shops and storefronts, now couldn't we. Of course, this was another place

Martin and I would frequent often, Skibbereen is lovely. We just loved coming down here, it was our favourite thing to do on weekends and holidays. We stayed at so many B&B's in this area. We just had such fun over the years. You girls make sure you have fun in your lives, it's the best feeling in the world to have great memories to look back on.'

They arrived into the town of Skibbereen, driving down the main road lined with colourful buildings. Sheila didn't see anything that looked familiar. 'Ah, this is a bigger town than I remember,' she said.

Maeve said, 'Mam told me there are a couple of thousand people that live in Skibbereen.'

Sheila was surprised, 'Ah dear, I didn't realise it was that big. I'm not sure this will be easy, finding this Sheila Murphy.'

Maeve didn't seem bothered, 'We still have time before we should head back, it's nearly a two hour drive back to Allihies. I was figuring we'd head back by 7pm, is that okay with you two?' Both Aelish and Sheila nodded their heads in agreement.

Maeve kept driving down the main road. It was clean and colourful. She found a parking space and pulled into it. She said, 'I know we don't have a plan, but I thought we could get out and walk a bit, maybe pop into a few places and ask.'

Aelish was wondering, 'Are we going to do the same thing? We have our gran here looking for her long-lost cousin?'

Sheila smiled, 'Unless you can think of a better idea, dear?'

Maeve looked back at Aelish in the back seat, 'It seems to be working, Aye, do you have any other ideas?'

Aelish thought for a moment, 'I can't think of one, but what I do think is that we are never going to find this Sheila Murphy.'

Sheila looked at Aelish, 'Well dear, all we can do is try. Maybe we go into a shop or two and ask, let's just give it a go.'

Maeve agreed, 'Right then, off we go.'

They left the car and walked along the main road, each building more colourful than the next. Sheila was in awe, looking up at all the colourful buildings, 'Isn't this just a delight, these colourful buildings brighten up the dullest of days in Ireland. It wasn't like this when I was growing up you know, it was really quite drab, you know. All the buildings throughout Ireland were grey, just stone or cement colours, everywhere throughout Ireland, dull and drab, I tell you it was. I don't think people started to paint their buildings these brilliant colours until the 70's or 80's. I like it much better this way. It was a bit depressing, all those grey buildings, so it was. These colours could cheer anyone up I'd say, it was a brilliant idea, whoever took out that first can of paint to their building, perhaps Tidy Towns had something to do with it.

Maeve and Aelish knew nothing else; their village buildings were even more colourful than these and have been their entire lives. Maeve agreed, 'I would imagine it was depressing not having these bright colours, especially when...' Just then it started to pour rain. She continued shouting as she ran down the footpath, 'Especially when it rains! Let's tuck in here, quickly!' They all popped into a dress shop. There was a woman working in the front of the store.

She looked at the three rush in, 'Hello, that deluge came on quickly, are you just seeking shelter? Or are you are looking for dresses?'

Sheila spoke up, 'Hello, why *yes* we are looking for dresses, my granddaughters and I need to find three matching dresses for a family function, we always dress identical, the three of us do, don't we girls? Do you have matching dresses in our sizes?'

The woman looked a bit surprised, 'There are loads of dresses in the back, help yourselves, not sure you'll find three matching ones in your sizes, but have a go. I can order anything you like as well. Let me know if you have any questions or need any help.'

Sheila thought for a moment, 'I do have a question: would you happen to know Sheila Murphy in Skibbereen?'

The woman shook her head, 'No, I'm sorry, I don't. Let me know if you need any more help. I'll be around the shop, just holler.' Sheila thanked her and they went in the back of the shop to look at the dresses. Maeve and Aelish went along with it.

Aelish said, 'Come on Grandma, let's git you a perdy dress so we can all be our usual triplet selves.'

Sheila started looking through the racks, 'Ah look, this one is lovely! It comes in all sizes! Let's all try this one on!' The girls obliged and went into separate dressing rooms. They came out fairly quickly to laughter, seeing their identically dressed selves in the mirrors.

Maeve said, 'Oh, we need a photo of this.' She asked the shop lady to take their photo. Although a bit reluctant, she obliged. They tried on a few more dresses and modelled them for each other in the round sitting area with sofas and mirrors. Sheila sat down while the girls tried on more dresses; she could hear the rain pummelling on the roof of the shop. Aelish picked the most garish dresses for a laugh; Maeve picked beautiful, elegant dresses; with each one, Sheila thought Maeve looked stunning. Sheila looked at her in awe.

She looked at her watch, 'Ah would ye look at the time? We should be shoving off here girls, the rain's calmed down a bit. Let's get back to the business at hand and find this Skibbereen Sheila.'

As they walked to the front of the store Sheila thanked the woman, 'We couldn't find a dress the three of us could agree on, but thank you just the same, ta.'

It wasn't pouring any longer when they got outside, it was just a fine mist. Sheila looked up to the sky, 'It's a soft day, good for the complexion, it is.' She looked around the storefronts seeing a bank, a hair salon, then a larger shop. 'Let's pop into that shop across the road, looks like a second hand charity shop, I love poking around in those places.' The girls agreed and ran across the road and into the shop.

Aelish was happy, 'I like these shops as well, you never know what you'll find.' It was filled with racks of clothing and walls full of books, CD's and movies. There was an older woman in the front of the shop behind the counter, in a big chair, reading a book.

She looked up briefly, 'Hello, good day to ye. Raincoats are on the left rack and there's a bucket of umbrellas here in the front, help yourselves, they're only a euro. Let me know if you need any assistance.' Then she put her nose back into her book. The three of them looked around the shop a bit.

As Aelish and Sheila started searching through the racks of clothing, Maeve thought she'd make haste and get to the point of being there; she went back up to the front counter and asked the woman, 'Hello, excuse me, would you happen to know Sheila Murphy that lives in Skibbereen?'

The old woman had a very thoughtful look on her face. She smiled, and put her hand on her heart as she answered Maeve, 'Ah, Jesus, Mary and Joseph, ye just brought me back a hundred years, straight back to my childhood, ye did.' She put her book down, stood up and walked towards Maeve, 'I knew a Sheila Murphy. Not sure where she is now, bless her heart, if she's in Skibbereen, I'd like to know. Back in the day she lived in Allihies. I lost touch with her many moons ago. I've just moved back to Ireland recently, I did, it's been nearly sixty years since I've been back here.' Maeve started to turn around to look for Sheila, she was coming up from behind Maeve with her head cocked to the side looking intently at the woman behind the counter.

Sheila said slowly, 'My God in heaven, is that you, Catherine?'

The woman came from behind the counter, staring at Sheila with her mouth open, 'Christ alive, is that you, Sheila?' Maeve stepped aside as the women gave each other a hug.

Sheila looked shocked, 'It's been a lifetime, Catherine, I heard you moved to Australia. I haven't heard anything about you since, in, my God, nearly sixty years.'

Catherine looked shocked, 'Where have you been all these years, Sheila?'

Sheila laughed, 'Right back to where I started, on the old O'Brien farm.'

Catherine laughed, 'Ah, I remember it well, your parents' house. My God, this is bringing me back.'

Sheila glanced at Maeve and Aelish, 'Girls, this is my dear childhood friend, Catherine McGee. I'm gobsmacked, we haven't seen each other for a lifetime.' Maeve and Aelish said hello and went back to browsing through the shop. Catherine and Sheila were transfixed, continuing their conversation.

Catherine stood in front of Sheila; they held each other's hands. They were both tearing up.

Catherine looked off, 'Ah ya, they shipped me off to Australia they did, it was 1957, when I last saw you.'

Sheila gave her a hug again, 'When did you return?'

Catherine smiled, 'Not too long ago, actually, I came back just over a month ago. Jesus, Sheila, it's a coincidence I'm here only today volunteering, otherwise I wouldn't have seen you.'

Sheila was thrilled, 'My God Catherine, you look wonderful, what a pleasant surprise, do you live in Skibbereen? What brought you back?'

Catherine looked at Sheila, then looked around the shop, and back at Sheila, 'It was Michael, Sheila, my son.'

Sheila gasped, 'What? How?' She covered her mouth and tears started welling up in her eyes. Catherine beamed, then she looked at Sheila, waiting for her to say something, for her to give Catherine some kind of information about herself. Sheila was shaking her head. Catherine knew not to say another word.

'Let's get together next week,' she suggested. 'I'm going to give you my number, we must talk.' She walked behind the counter and wrote on a piece of paper, brought it back, and handed it to Sheila. 'Call me, I will see you next week, if I have to come up to Allihies myself.'

Sheila smiled, taking the paper. Looking down, she saw that Catherine had written, "Catherine and Michael" along with a telephone number. With tears in her eyes, she said, 'I want to know *everything*.'

Catherine gave her another hug, 'We will, first thing next week, the earlier, the better.' Catherine put her arm around Sheila as she walked her to the door.

Maeve and Aelish followed Sheila and Catherine to the door. Sheila held Catherine's hand, 'So good to see you again Catherine, bye-bye for now.' Sheila was thrilled; as she walked with the girls on the footpath, she said, 'That made my day even brighter. I didn't think that was possible. I never thought I'd see Catherine again, we were the best of friends growing up, from four years old to sixteen, then she was gone.'

As they walked down the road lined with shops, restaurants and pubs, Aelish was getting a little restless and felt like they needed a stronger plan for the rest of the day.

'Should we split up,' she asked, 'and go into every shop asking where the hell this Skibbereen Sheila Murphy is?'

Maeve glared at her, 'We could do, Aye.'

Sheila spoke up, 'Yes, let's go into shops and ask everyone until we find the Sheila Murphy of Skibbereen, someone is bound to know! I think she may be the winner!' Aelish looked at Sheila with her eyebrows raised; she'd heard this a few times now. Maeve nudged her and gestured to keep moving on down the footpath. The three of them went from shop to shop; no one knew of a Sheila Murphy in town. Aelish was ready to give up, she wanted to go home. Maeve and Sheila were getting a bit tired as well. They all decided to call it a day and head back to Allihies.

When they got back to the car, Maeve noticed her petrol was low, 'We'll make a stop at the petrol station, then head home.' They all agreed. Maeve filled her car up and went in to pay at the station and get some treats for the way home. She thought she'd ask one more person before they left Skibbereen. The teenage girl behind the counter at the petrol station didn't look particularly happy about working there. Maeve paid for her petrol and treats.

'That'll be forty five euro, twenty.' Maeve took out the card that her parents had given her for petrol and emergencies. She handed it to the girl behind the counter, and asked the question she'd been asking everyone all day, 'Would you happen to know a Sheila Murphy that lives in Skibbereen?'

The girl looked all snarly behind the counter, 'Yeah, that's my mam, why are you asking?'

Maeve was thrilled; she looked out to her car, so excited to tell Aelish and Sheila. She saw a red car parked outside, and asked, 'Is that your car there?'

The girl looked annoyed, 'Ya, why?'

Maeve was pretty excited, 'Sorry, I have my gran with me, she's looking for her cousin Sheila Murphy, it might be your mam she's looking for, can you give her a call? This is actually very exciting, you have no idea. Was your mam at a wedding in Glengarriff last weekend?'

The girl raised her eyebrows in surprise. 'Yeah,' she said, hesitantly.

Maeve was thrilled, 'Ah that's great! How can we get in touch with your mam?'

The girl wasn't terribly helpful, 'I don't know, she's out of town.'

'Oh,' said Maeve, deflated, 'when will she be back?'

The girl didn't seem terribly interested in helping, 'I don't know, she left with some guy she's dating, she'll be back sometime after the weekend I suppose.'

Maeve didn't know what to do, 'Would you mind if I left you my number to give to your mam? It's really very important, would you mind making sure she gets it?'

The girl lightened up a little bit, and shrugged, saying, 'Yeah, sure, I'll give it to her.'

Maeve was happy enough, 'Thanks a million, what's your name?'

The girl pulled at her nametag, 'Tina.'

Maeve smiled at the surly teen, 'Thanks so much, Tina, please give my number to your mam, it really is important.'

Tina half smiled, 'Yeah, I said I would, okay, bye.'

Maeve was a little put off by the exchange, but she was very happy about finding what they were looking for, nonetheless. She ran to her car, got in and looked at Sheila and Aelish, 'You're not going to believe this!' She handed them each a treat she purchased in the station, 'That girl you see through the window, behind the counter? Her name is Tina Murphy, and you're not going to believe who her mam is! *And,* where her mam was last weekend! *And* that's her car!' She pointed to the red car parked near the petrol station.

Sheila and Aelish were very surprised. Aelish squealed, 'You're joking! How did that happen?'

Maeve laughed, 'I thought I'd ask one last person before we left town, and that last person happened to be the daughter of Sheila Murphy! She's a surly little thing, but I gave her my number for her mam to call me, she's out of town at the moment. Isn't that brilliant?' Sheila and Aelish were happy.

Sheila said, 'Well, if that wasn't a perfect way to end this day . . . I'd say mission accomplished! I think we've found the winning Sheila Murphy!'

Aelish agreed, 'That's great, when will she be back?'

Maeve shrugged, 'She wasn't sure, it didn't seem like a good situation, she said her mam was off with some guy for the weekend, she guessed that she'd be back sometime after the weekend. Hopefully she'll call me when she returns. I told her it was important.'

Sheila smiled, 'Well done Maeve.'

Maeve was quite pleased with herself, 'Yes, a successful day, indeed.'

Aelish said, 'Yes it was.'

Sheila agreed, 'Twas a lovely way to spend a rainy Saturday with you two, I couldn't have enjoyed this day any more than I did.' Maeve started the engine, and they headed back to Allihies.

Chapter Twelve

On the way home Maeve received a text from her mam, *Made too much food for dinner, bring everyone by, see you soon.*

Maeve smiled; it was something her mam did often, last minute parties that turned into sing song sessions. Maeve looked at Sheila and Aelish in the car and said, 'Well, I hope you two don't mind, but my mam and da are expecting you both for dinner.'

Sheila smiled, 'I didn't think this day could get any better.'

Aelish, not sure, said, 'Let me text my mam.'

Maeve said, 'You must tell her and Owen to come along as well, my parents would insist! When she says she's made extra food, it means she could feed the village, you know how she is.'

Aelish shrugged, 'I'll tell them both to come, along with the village.'

Maeve looked back at her friend, 'Da must be in a mood. When he gets restless, Ma invites people over, it makes him happy. My mam thinks a crowd, a bit of drink, and a little singing solves all the problems of the world.' Aelish texted her mam for her and Owen to meet at the Mulligan house for dinner, telling her Mary was insisting. Siobhan responded to Aelish and said they would see them around 9pm. This made Maeve very happy; she knew her mam and da remembered that this was the day Mick Flanagan had died, and she wanted to do something special for them. She thought for a moment how grand it would be if Patrick was there--she actually wanted her parents to meet this American boy that she had a crush on. The drive home went by quickly. They all walked up to the Mulligan house hearing traditional music playing, and Maeve's dad, Jack, singing very loudly.

Maeve rolled her eyes, 'Ah, he's already at it; this should be good craic.'

Owen and Patrick were putting the finishing touches on the table and planters at O'Neill's. Everything was sanded, stained and varnished. They brought four stools from the bar and placed them in front of the newly built high table against the wall. Patrick was posting 'Do not touch' signs on everything. Owen was quite proud of the two planters that flanked each end of the table. He was glad they had picked up plants at the hardware store; it made it all complete. Owen received a text from his mam:

You and your friend go to Mulligan's for dinner and a sing song, see you there as soon as you can.

That was great, he thought--he was starving and dinner was just sorted. It was a good reward for his new friend for helping him. 'Paddy ol' boy,' he said, 'I've got dinner waiting for you, and me mam won't take no for an answer.'

Patrick looked surprised, 'That's great, let's clean up and we'll be good to go.' The two of them looked at what they'd accomplished that day. The table looked beautiful.

Owen was quite pleased, 'Jaysus, we're a talented pair, would ye look at this?'

Patrick smiled, 'Yep, it looks pretty good, great job, and now you know woodworking and carpentry skills.'

Owen agreed, 'Yeah, thanks, that was great. This is so much better than the ramshackle thing I would have thrown together.' He patted Patrick on the back, 'Thanks Paddy ol' boy!' Patrick shook his head; he wasn't going to fight it. Owen could call him whatever he wanted and "Paddy" was growing on him.

They exited the pub. Patrick looked at Owen, 'I'm starved. Is your mom a good cook?'

Owen laughed, 'Good God, no! Luckily, we aren't going there for dinner, we're going to the Mulligans' house, should be good craic, it always is. You'll like them. Ah I forgot, you know Maeve, it's her parents' house.' Patrick looked pleasantly surprised. He'd been hoping he would see Maeve again--he just didn't know when . . . he figured it would just happen. Now he was going to see her tonight.

As Maeve, Aelish and Sheila walked into the house, Maeve's Dad was singing 'The Boys of The Old Brigade'.

Sheila put her hand on her chest, 'My father used to sing this song, as did my Martin, they'd sing it all the time they did. Ah, this brings me back.'

Aelish laughed, 'So did me da, he'd make me, my mam and brother sing this with him all the time.'

Jack was singing:

'Oh, father why are you so sad,
On this bright Easter Morn?
When Irish men are proud and glad
Of the land where they were born?
Oh, son, I see in mem'ries too
Of far off distant days,
When being just a lad like you,
I joined the IRA.'

The three joined in the chorus as they were walking into the house:

'Where are the lads that stood with me
When history was made?

A Ghra Mo Chroi, I long to see
The boys of the old brigade!'
Jack was thrilled. He went on singing the song:

'From hills and farms the call to arms
Was heard by one and all,
And from the glen came brave young men
To answer Ireland's call.
'Twasn't long ago we faced a foe,
The old brigade and me,
And by my side they fought and died,
That Ireland might be free.'

Siobhan, Owen and Patrick walked in as they were all singing. Siobhan and Owen looked at each other and smiled. They loudly broke into the chorus:

'Where are the lads that stood with me
When history was made?
A Ghra Mo Chroi, I long to see
The boys of the old brigade!'

Jack continued to sing, thinking he was the only one that knew the words beyond the chorus, but Owen sat next to him and sang:

'And now, my boy, I've told you why
On Easter morn I sigh,
For I recall my comrades all
Of dark old days gone by.
I think of men who fought in glens,
With rifle and grenade;
May heaven keep the men who sleep,

From the ranks of the old brigade.'

Everyone joined in. Watching this gave Patrick goosebumps; he couldn't believe it. He felt as if he was watching a movie. He looked over at Maeve, who was looking at him, smiling as she sang. He thought of how he loved Ireland; he loved the people; and he definitely was falling for Maeve.

They all sang the chorus once again:

'Where are the lads, that stood with me,
When history was made?
A Ghra Mo Chroi, I long to see,
The boys of the old brigade!'

Jack led them to sing it once more:

'Where are the lads, that stood with me
When history was made?
A Ghra Mo Chroi, I long to see
The boys of the old brigade!'

Jack stood up and started clapping, 'Well, that was a good start to the evening. Welcome, everyone! Now, who might this be?'

Maeve jumped in, 'Da, this is Sheila, Sheila Murphy.'

He took both of her hands, 'Lovely to meet you, Sheila, you're very welcome indeed.'

Sheila smiled, 'Ta, nice to meet you as well.'

Maeve led Sheila over to her mam, 'Ah, mam, you haven't met Sheila yet!' She introduced them and flitted back to her dad. She glanced back and saw her mam hugging Sheila.

Maeve smiled and turning back to her dad and said, 'Da, this is Patrick, Patrick McGettigan, he's visiting from America.'

Jack shook his hand as Owen walked up and chimed in: 'He likes to be called Paddy, especially while he's here, it makes him feel like he belongs, it does.'

Patrick shook his head, 'It's Patrick, sir, nice to meet you.'

Jack laughed, 'Sir? I haven't been called sir since I was in my Headmaster's office. Call me Jack. Now, let's all have a drink!' He walked over to the bar he had set up and gestured for Patrick to follow him. 'Everything is set up here on the kitchen counter, help yourself.' He then shouted towards the ladies, 'Except for you Siobhan, what can I get you? And Sheila, what will you have? You ladies sit down, I'll bring you your drinks.'

Maeve smiled at her dad, he seemed so happy, 'I'll help you Da.' She walked up closer to Patrick as he stepped away to give them space, 'What a pleasant surprise to see you here, Patrick. Would you like a beer, or something stronger?'

Patrick looked into Maeve's eyes, 'I told you I'd see you again Maeve, it's good to see you. A beer would be nice, and maybe a shot of whiskey?'

Maeve smiled, 'Of course, we have it all, one beer and one whiskey coming up.' As she turned away, she said, 'It's good to see you as well, Patrick.'

Patrick was looking around at everyone, then asked Maeve when she returned, 'Is *everyone* in Ireland happy?'

Maeve laughed, 'Ah sure, we're as happy as other people in the world I'd say, I don't know. My da used to say to me: "When you have good thoughts, they shine out of you like sunbeams and you look more beautiful." I suppose it depends on yourself, doesn't it? Happy is as happy gets.'

Patrick smiled at Maeve, 'Yeah, it's a choice I suppose, it just seems the Irish choose it more than other that I've seen.'

Maeve shrugged, 'I don't know, it's all I know, we just live, we enjoy life, I don't think we analyse it all too much.' Patrick was enamoured with Maeve. She suddenly remembered, 'Oh, you were looking for Martin Murphy! Sheila Murphy is here, his wife! I was going to try to find you today, she's invited us to call in to her house tomorrow. She said she may have a photo or two of your grandfather!'

Patrick couldn't believe it, 'That's awesome Maeve, that's amazing, that was really the whole purpose of my trip to Ireland, that's so great you found him, or her, I should say, for me. I have something for her I can bring to her tomorrow, she'll enjoy it.'

Maeve was curiously thrilled, 'I'm sure she'll love whatever you have. Come over here, I'll introduce you.'

Sheila was talking to Mary; they were in an animated conversation.

Maeve knew they'd get along, 'Sorry to interrupt you two. Sheila, remember the boy I mentioned from America, Patrick McGettigan? This is Patrick. Patrick, this is Sheila Murphy, Martin's wife.' Maeve wasn't sure if she should say wife or widow.

Patrick shook her hand, 'Very nice to meet you. Maeve mentioned you may have a photo or two of my grandfather? That would be amazing to see them.'

Sheila was quite happy, 'You two call into my house tomorrow, I'll see what I can rummage up, say around noon, how does that suit?'

Maeve and Patrick looked at each other in agreement, Maeve responded, 'That'd be grand.' Sheila smiled, then turned back and continued her conversation with Mary.

Patrick didn't know where Sheila lived, but he knew where Maeve lived now, and said, 'I have a car, I could pick you up here tomorrow?'

Maeve loved that idea, 'Perfect, you could come here for tea first. Who knows how long this will last tonight, if it were up to me da we'd be singing all night long. He'll be bringing all the instruments out soon for whoever can play. I'd say you'll be playing the drum again this evening.'

Patrick smiled, 'I don't mind, I may do a jig as well, I've got a few tricks up my sleeve. I may need a drink or two in me before I do any dancing though.'

Maeve picked up the bottle of Redbreast whiskey and gestured towards Patrick's glass, 'There's plenty where that came from.' The music started again. 'Let's go and sit down with me da,' she said.

Patrick was pretty happy with how his trip was panning out; he hadn't expected to be invited into people's homes and to feel so welcomed. He had lost such a big part of his life when his grandmother died, and now he was excited to find out more about her and his grandfather. He watched Maeve as she walked towards her father, gesturing for Patrick to follow, then whispering something to her dad. As Patrick approached Maeve's dad, he handed Patrick a bodhrán drum. Patrick took the drum and sat next to Jack and started playing along with him while he played the banjo. He watched Maeve pick up a violin, surprised, 'I didn't know you played the violin!'

Maeve checked to see if it was tuned, 'Ah but I don't play the violin, I play the fiddle.' She started to follow along with the tune her dad was playing. Owen picked up a tin whistle and joined in. Sheila was clapping along with Mary and Aelish and they all sang, one song after another. The more they drank, the sillier the song.

Jack looked at Patrick with a twinkle in his eye. 'Do you know the song, "Some Say the Devil is Dead" ol' Paddy boy?'

Maeve was embarrassed. 'Da!' Jack started the song and everyone joined in:

'Some say the devil is dead,
The devil is dead, the devil is dead,
Some say the devil is dead
And buried in Killarney.
More say he rose again,
More say he rose again,
More say he rose again,
And joined the British army.'

They sang and drank and talked and told stories and laughed and drank some more. Jack sang a few story songs, like "Come Out You Black and Tans" and silly songs like "The Seven Drunken Nights".

At the end of the evening, Jack wanted to acknowledge his friend Mick Flanagan on this day. He held up his glass and started everyone off:

'By a lonely prison wall,
I heard a young girl calling:
Michael, they have taken you away...'

They all sang along with Jack, then raised their glasses saying, 'To Mick.' There were a few responses of; 'God rest him.' and 'Hear, hear.' They called it a night, Jack thanked everyone for coming. Maeve walked Patrick to the door; it was easy to say goodbye to him because she'd see him in the morning. 'You can come as early as you'd like, a pot of tea is always on here.'

Patrick thanked her, 'I'm going to check on our project at O'Neill's pub first thing in the morning, then I'll come over after.'

Maeve smiled, 'Look at you, you're just a regular Allihies resident, aren't ye now? Building things, checking on things. I'll see you whenever you arrive tomorrow morning.'

He put his hands on her shoulders while he said goodbye, he felt the soft curls of her hair, looked her in the eye and said, 'I will see you again.'

Maeve laughed, 'Yeah, you'll see me tomorrow, I'll be here.'

Patrick smiled, 'I will see you again, and again . . . good night, Maeve Mulligan.' Maeve laughed and said goodbye to Patrick, then Siobhan, thanking her for giving Sheila a lift home, and said goodbye to Owen and Aelish. She looked over their shoulders at Patrick getting into his car; he looked back up to the house at Maeve, smiling. She was thrilled to be spending time with him tomorrow. She was also quite chuffed that the feeling was obviously mutual. Jack and Mary walked Sheila out to the car. Sheila thanked them for including her in their gathering. She gave Mary and Jack a hug goodbye, 'Thanks a million.'

Mary and Jack assured her it was nothing: 'We'd have you over every weekend, Sheila, if you'd come.' Sheila felt heart warmed; she couldn't remember the last time she felt joy. Maeve waved goodbye to Sheila and stood there watching the car drive away until it was gone.

Chapter Thirteen

The next morning, Patrick got up and went into the village for coffee at John Terry's place. When he walked into the shop he saw John O'Neill standing near the coffee machine. Patrick got himself a cup and said hello to John.

John responded, 'Mornin' there, Paddy. I looked out back, a fine job you did on that, a fine job. How did you learn your craft?'

Patrick felt good, 'It was my dad, we used to build a lot of things together on weekends.'

John looked pleased, 'My da and I would do the same, that's where most of those tools are from, my da's workshop. Say, I have a couple of projects that need doing, you interested?'

Patrick was thrilled, 'That'd be great, I'd love to! Owen helped a lot you know, he learned a ton during that project.'

John thought that was great, 'It would do Owen a world of good to have you as a friend, Patrick. He needs projects to keep him busy once school's out. Idle hands make the devil's work with that one.' Patrick asked if everything was okay with the table and planters; he was going to go and check on them this morning.

John laughed, 'Ah no, it's all grand, checked it myself, you go on about your day.' Patrick left the shop and walked along the village road before heading over to Maeve's house.

Maeve had got up early and baked some oatmeal muffins; the house smelled delicious.

Mary came downstairs, wondering what was going on, 'I can't remember the last time you baked anything, sweetie, the only reason you ever wanted to help was so you could lick the bowl, if I'm not mistaken.'

Maeve was in a very good mood, 'Ah, I just wanted to have a little something with my tea this morning 'tis all, and I did lick the bowl, I'll have you know.'

The doorbell rang. Mary looked at Maeve, 'Expecting someone?'

Maeve smiled and jumped up, 'Yes, it's Patrick, we're going over to Sheila's house, she has photos to show him of his grandfather.'

Mary put the kettle on, 'That's lovely, have him come in for tea first.'

Maeve opened the door to a smiling Patrick holding a large bunch of colourful weeds. She tried not to laugh, 'Oh my, those are beautiful, wherever did you find them?'

Patrick handed what he thought were flowers to Maeve, 'Just in the village, on the side of the road.' Maeve and her mam gardened a lot together; Mary had taught Maeve the different varieties of flowers and weeds. She knew her mam would be amused with this offering.

Maeve looked at the bunch, 'I recognise a few of these, er flowers--let's see, you've found groundsel and fumitory and a bit of hairy bittercress, some oxalis and a little shepherd's purse, well done, that's a lovely variety, thank you.'

Patrick looked stunned, 'Wow, you know your flowers, these must be popular in Ireland.'

Maeve smiled, 'Ah yes, they're *very* popular indeed, they grow everywhere they do, like weeds.' Maeve walked into the kitchen and handed the bunch to her mam, 'Look what Patrick brought Mam, aren't they *lovely*?'

Mary raised her eyebrows and smiled, 'Ah Patrick, you shouldn't have, thank you ever so much, I'll put them in some water and keep them away from my garden.'

Patrick didn't understand what she meant, he smiled and said, 'You're welcome.' Mary gestured to the kitchen table and told Patrick to sit down and she'd get him a cup of tea. Patrick had not been a tea drinker before he came to Ireland, but he was learning to enjoy it--and he also learned to never turn it down. It was almost unheard of to turn down a cup of tea.

'How do you take your tea?'

Patrick responded. 'Just cream, thanks.' Maeve laughed, 'Our milk is like cream here so we just have milk in our tea, unless you wanted real thick proper cream?' Patrick shook his head, 'Just the creamy milk then, thanks.' Maeve placed the warm oatmeal muffins in front of him, with melting slabs of butter and homemade jam. Patrick watched Maeve and her mam working together quickly in the kitchen, putting things on the table; he could see this had been done a thousand times before. 'Thank you both, this is great, thanks so much.'

Mary asked Patrick what part of the States he came from. When Patrick told her Chicago, she listed off all of the relatives she had in Chicago, and in Minnesota, and California. Patrick was amazed to find every Irish person he spoke to had so many relatives in America. Mary told Patrick how Jack's father had nine brothers and six sisters in his family and most had emigrated; there were Mulligans running amok in America.

Patrick found it interesting that he had spent his whole life listening to people talk about how their ancestors came from Ireland. He'd never thought about it the other way around: how so many people in Ireland had lost so many family members to emigration and it still continues to this day. Everyone he spoke to had relatives who had emigrated over the years to; America,

England, Australia, Africa, Canada and countless other countries.

'I'm not sure where my grandparents were from,' he said, 'the only thing I remember anyone saying was Ireland--my grandparents were born in Ireland, never any details of which part.'

Mary looked concerned, 'You should do a bit of research, Patrick, sure you'd find you've distant relatives here, everyone does.'

Patrick did have a feeling of curiosity, 'If I was staying longer, I'd find out, I'm sure I'd find someone related to my grandparents.'

Maeve interrupted, 'Speaking of grandparents, let's go to Sheila's now and find out what she knows about your grandfather, that's a start.'

Patrick agreed and stood up, 'Sounds good! Thank you for the tea and muffins, that was great.'

Mary started to pick up the cups and plates, 'You two have a good day with Sheila, this must be an awful lot of excitement in her life all of a sudden.'

Maeve remembered to ask, 'Mam, do you know anything about Sheila? Did she have two daughters? I saw some photos at her house.'

Mary shook her head, 'I'm afraid I don't, Maeve. I had some great conversations with her last night, felt like I'd known her forever. We just talked about hobbies we both share, oil painting and gardening. All I know about her personally is that her husband died many years ago. I heard she didn't have any family and she's always kept to herself, especially after Martin died.'

Maeve was confused, 'She seems so social, I can't imagine her keeping to herself, that's so sad.'

Mary disagreed, 'Some people don't mind being on their own, sweetie, it's not necessarily sad, it could have been her choice and that's just what she prefers. Try not to pry too much, if she wants to tell you something, she will.'

Maeve and Patrick said goodbye and walked out to his car. Patrick noticed that the neighbour's garden was overgrown and unkempt. He stopped and looked at Maeve, 'Those weren't flowers I brought in, were they Maeve?'

Maeve laughed, 'Ah Patrick, they were lovely weeds, it was the thought that counts. It was a very kind gesture indeed.'

Patrick shook his head, 'I thought they were some wild Irish flowers. I got carried away when I saw them along the road overlooking the sea. I thought they were just beautiful flowers growing wild along the Wild Atlantic Way.'

Maeve laughed, 'Ah so you're taken by beauty and you get carried away, you sure you're not Irish?'

Patrick laughed, 'There's enough Irish blood in me to say yes, and I do know beauty when I see it.' He stared at Maeve for a moment and she turned scarlet. Patrick was about to open the car door for her but she opened it herself and popped in, saying, 'Now then, let's go and see what we can find out about your grandfather, this will be fun.'

Patrick agreed as he walked around to the driver's side and drove off, 'This *is* fun. So, how do you know Sheila? It seems no one really knows her.'

Maeve wasn't sure how to answer. Looking out of the window to the Atlantic Ocean, she said, 'Keep following this road towards Ballydonegan Lower, it's not far at all.' She didn't know Patrick; she wasn't going to tell him that she was in possession of a five million euro lottery ticket. 'We were looking for something ourselves, Aelish and myself, and we found Sheila, she's a lovely woman, wait 'til you talk to her for a bit, you'll see. This'll be grand. Now keep going a bit further down this road and you'll see a large rock, turn left there, just past the Fitzgerald farm, I'll show you.'

Patrick thought of his grandmother, how she would have loved to have been here, she always mentioned how much she wanted to visit Ireland, but she didn't make it. She would have been so happy that he had found someone who knew her Paddy. He couldn't help thinking that his grandmother had something to do with him meeting Maeve: someone up there must have had something to do with this--divine intervention, he supposed.

They pulled onto the long dirt road. By the time they reached Sheila's cottage, she was outside, walking towards the car to greet them with a smile on her face and her arms wide open.

Maeve looked out at Sheila and smiled, 'I love her, look at how happy she is, it's like she hasn't a care in the world, and it's contagious I tell you, just wait, you'll see.'

Patrick parked his car in front of Sheila's cottage. They both got out and gave Sheila hugs.

Sheila hugged them both, like welcoming family, 'Come in, come in, let's have some tea.' Patrick's eyes bulged: *how much tea do these people drink?* It was constant throughout the day, it seemed as if tea was served all day long in Ireland, with the intermittent coffee. Then it was replaced by alcohol in the evening.

Patrick smiled and pretended he loved tea and wanted more, 'That sounds great, I haven't had tea for...'

Maeve cut him off, 'That's grand Sheila, I've brought you some oatmeal muffins I baked this morning.'

Sheila laughed, 'Ah you shouldn't have! I baked muffins myself this morning, brilliant minds think alike.'

They all sat around Sheila's kitchen table. Patrick had a small bag that he placed on the floor beside him. Maeve helped Sheila bring the tea and cups to the table.

Sheila was excited to tell Patrick everything she knew about his grandfather, 'Now then, I managed to find a few photos of Paddy, I mean your grandfather, would you like to see them?'

Patrick looked thrilled, 'Of course! I've only seen a couple photos of him over the years, my grandmother didn't have many photos of him at all. They weren't married long before he was killed in the war, they'd only just had my dad when he was deployed, then he was gone within that year. Sad when you think about how young he was.'

Maeve was interested, 'So, your grandparents were born in Ireland, emigrated to the United States, then he enlisted in the Army?'

Patrick wasn't sure about all the details, but he knew enough, 'Yes, they both came over with their families. I actually think they met on the boat, and got to know each other really well on that long boat ride. I think he joined the army the following year, after he arrived in the States. He was around eighteen when my dad was born, my grandmother was eighteen as well, I think they were both born around 1925. They were very young, I imagine they got married because she got pregnant. No one in the family ever talked about it, I'm sure it was quite a scandal back then.'

Sheila poured them more tea, 'I would imagine so, it always was quite the scandal that. 1925 you say? That's the year my Martin was born.'

Patrick reached into the bag on the floor, 'I brought something with me that I found in my grandma's attic. It's all the letters that my grandpops sent to her while he was away at war. He wrote her so many letters. I read through them all after my grandma died. I didn't bring all of them with me, I just brought the ones that I thought your husband would be interested in, the letters he was mentioned in, you may want to read them. My grandpops spoke very highly of your husband in his letters. He mentions him so often, as you can see by the number of letters I have. They're filled with stories of the two of them and their experience in the war in North Africa, although places weren't mentioned. His letters didn't go into any details of the war, I don't think they were allowed, but he always mentioned Marty, as they called him. He seemed like an amazing man.'

Sheila smiled, 'Ah, he was.'

Patrick seemed very interested, 'I'm sure he told you what a hero he was.'

Sheila looked a bit disappointed, 'Well, that was a story that was once told, it's actually not…'

Patrick interrupted her, 'A story that was *once* told? According to my grandpops, he was a hero all the way through the war, time and time again. My grandpops said in all of his letters what a hero Marty was and how he saved so many men's lives over the course of the year they were in Africa.'

Sheila looked surprised, 'No, I didn't hear about those stories, he really wouldn't talk much of his days in the war, it was too painful, I imagine. Would you mind terribly if I held on to these letters for a day or two, so I can read them on my own?'

Patrick was happy that someone was as interested in the letters as much as he was, 'Yes, of course, take all the time you need, I'll leave them with you. You'll see the common thread is about Martin and the men he saved, he really seemed quite extraordinary.' Sheila found it very strange she hadn't heard any of this. It warmed her heart to hear such good things about her husband.

Patrick went on, 'My grandma used to say, if it weren't for Martin Murphy, she wouldn't have had any more children after my dad. My grandma was so heartbroken when she received the news that her husband, my grandpops, was killed. A few months later, my grandpops' army buddy was sent home wounded, and he went to see my grandma to make sure she was okay. That was Daniel O'Grady, who I knew my whole life as Gramps. They ended up getting married and having more kids--my aunts and uncles. Grandma said the little she got out of Daniel was that he wouldn't be alive if it weren't for Martin Murphy.'

Sheila was listening intently and said, 'These are stories I've never heard; I don't know the name Daniel O'Grady.'

Patrick shrugged, 'That's all I know. Gramps was also called Dog.'

Sheila smiled, 'I did hear about a man named Dog--who could ever forget that name? I don't remember anything Martin said about him though, other than that he knew a man in the army named Dog. Isn't this amazing, the world just got a bit smaller with these connections, I'd say.' She looked at Maeve and smiled, 'I never would have known.' Sheila got up, saying, 'I nearly forgot the photos, let me get those of your grandfather.' She left the room.

Maeve looked at Patrick, 'It's amazing, you have this information about Sheila's husband that she never knew, that he really was a hero, it's brilliant, Patrick.'

Patrick agreed, 'The sad thing is, when I looked up some things I had read, it seemed Martin was viewed as a coward, there was a newspaper article written at the time. That didn't match up with what these letters say.'

Maeve was very interested in this whole thing, 'That's what I heard, first a hero, but it was disputed that he was a hero, and he vehemently denied he was a hero.'

Patrick held up a bunch of the letters, 'Well, there's proof in all of these letters that he *was* quite a hero.'

Sheila came back with a few photos in her hands, 'Now then, according to the scribbles on the backs of these photos, it looks like we have Paddy and Dog in one photo, Paddy and Martin in these two, and the three of them in this photo. You have a look, I'm going to make another pot of tea.'

Patrick whispered to Maeve, 'I can't have any more tea. I'm going to have tea coming out of my ears!' Maeve laughed.

Sheila overheard Patrick and shouted back from the kitchen, 'May you always have walls for the winds, a roof for the rain, and tea beside the fire. Now then, would you like another cup of tea?'

Patrick couldn't refuse, 'Yes, of course.'

Sheila smiled, 'Speaking of which, there's a bit of a chill coming into the house, we should add to the fire.'

Maeve jumped up, 'I'll do it.' She started to load the fireplace up with tinder and turf that was sitting next to the fireplace.

Sheila looked at Maeve, 'We'll need some more wood from out back.'

Patrick jumped up, 'I'll go get it.'

Sheila laughed at the two of them, 'Well then, aren't you two the helpful pair. Thank you! The wood is in the small shed out back. Careful not to touch the walls, it will collapse on you like a house of cards, so it will, so mind yourself.'

Sheila brought the tea to the table. Maeve was getting a good fire going and Patrick came in with a armful of logs saying, 'You were right about that shed Sheila, a strong wind might blow that down.' Sheila agreed, 'Ah, God would be doing me a favour if that were to happen, that shed is banjaxed.' Patrick looked at Maeve confused. Maeve smiled, 'It seems it is beyond repair.' Patrick mouthed out a thank you for the translation and continued to Sheila, 'Yes, I agree, you need a new shed, that bang jacks thing is dangerous.' Sheila winced, 'I know, I'm afraid it's something I've put on the long finger.' Maeve noticed Patrick looking confused again and she laughed, 'I'm sure you'll get to it at some point Sheila.' Patrick got it and winked at Maeve with a smile. Sheila sat down at the table and looked at the pile of letters. She noticed the postmarks: January to December, 1942. 'I'd like to read these in chronological order.' As she started to sort according to postmarks on the envelopes, she said, 'It will tell quite a story, these.' She picked up the photos, 'So Patrick, you essentially had two grandfathers, one biological, grandpops did you say, and the other was your gramps, is that right?'

Patrick smiled, 'Yeah, I wish I'd known my grandpops, but my gramps was pretty great, I can't complain. But yeah, I've never seen photos of the two of them together; that's so cool that you have these.'

Sheila handed the one of Paddy and Dog to Patrick, 'I want you to have this one.'

Patrick looked at the photo, 'Are you sure?' She insisted. Patrick was very grateful, 'Thank you so much, wow, this is pretty cool. God, my grandma would have loved to have seen this, this is so awesome, thanks so much.'

Sheila started to pick up the cups and plates from the table. 'Ah, maybe your grandma had something to do with all of this Patrick.' Patrick smiled thinking that really was a possibility. Maeve got up and helped her bring the dishes to the kitchen area. Sheila leaned in a bit towards Maeve, 'Can you call in after school tomorrow? I may have a development on our search.'

Maeve looked very interested, 'Really? I have to wait until tomorrow to find out?'

Sheila smiled, 'It's not earth shattering, but it is a clue.'

Maeve nudged Sheila a bit, 'You're a regular sleuth, aren't you? I'll bring Aelish.'

Sheila nodded, 'That'd be grand, I look forward to see you tomorrow again then.'

Maeve went back to the table where Patrick was sitting, saying, 'What did you say Patrick? You'd like some more tea?'

Patrick looked panicked, 'No! No, thank you, I've had plenty of tea, thanks, no.'

Maeve laughed, 'We need to get going, I have tons of things I need to do before school tomorrow. I haven't studied for my exams nearly as much as I should have, they're coming up quicker than I'd like.'

Patrick stood up, 'Thank you so much for the tea, Sheila, and the photo. Would you like me to bring in some more wood before I leave?'

Sheila smiled at Patrick, 'No, dear, thank you for offering, that should do me through the night.' They all started to walk towards the door. Sheila put her hand on Maeve's shoulder, 'See you tomorrow, dear.' Then she looked at Patrick, 'I can return the letters to Maeve tomorrow, Patrick, thank you again for bringing them. Now drive safe and we'll see you soon.'

Patrick and Maeve drove off down the long dirt road, waving to Sheila from their open windows. Sheila stood outside the door of her cottage, waving until they were out of sight. She went back inside her cottage, threw another log on the fire and prepared to read all of the letters that Paddy McGettigan had sent to his wife in 1942. She thought back on how she and Martin would sit by the fire and talk in the evenings, sipping tiny glasses of sherry. She took a chair from the kitchen table and dragged it over to the glass cupboards. She climbed up onto the chair to the high reaches of the cabinet and took down one small, stemmed glass. She opened an old bottle of sherry from many years ago and poured herself a glass. She sat on the chair near the fire, put a blanket on her legs and started to read the letters, curious to read what was written about her Martin.

Patrick drove Maeve home, and purposely pulled up to the house next door, so he could talk to her for a moment. He thought about kissing her--he really wanted to kiss her before they said goodbye. He parked, and turned off the engine.

Maeve said, 'Thanks a million for driving. I'll see you again. I'll get those letters back for you. Thanks again.' She reached over to give Patrick a hug, then scurried out of the car, 'Thanks, see you again, thanks again.' She ran up to her house, mortified by how awkward that was: she'd said thank you a thousand times. She waved at him from her doorstep, opened the front door and tucked inside. She quickly shut the door behind her and let out a grunt, 'Aaarrrgh!'

Her dad came out from the kitchen, 'Hi pet, everything okay?'

Maeve was surprised at being overheard, 'Hi Da, yeah, everything's grand, just have a lot of school work to do, see you later.' She went upstairs and called Aelish, and told her how awkward and embarrassing it had been leaving Patrick.

Aelish calmed her down, 'Don't think another thing about it Maeve, it's all grand. I'm sure he's not thinking anything of it. Don't worry about it. You'll be brand new in the morning, see you then.'

Maeve was about to hang up the phone but she remembered Sheila, 'Hey Aelish, after school tomorrow we're going to Sheila's--she said she found some new information on a Sheila Murphy.'

Aelish was curious, 'What is it? Did she find *another* Sheila Murphy? What did she find out?' Maeve told her to not worry about it; she would see her in the morning. Aelish laughed and agreed, they said goodbye, both girls saying bye-bye five or six times each, as they usually did, then hung up.

Owen had overheard the conversation Aelish was having with Maeve. He walked into Aelish's bedroom and knocked on the door frame, 'Hey, how's things? Have you two had any luck finding that Sheila Murphy?'

Aelish was a bit annoyed, 'No Owen, why do you ask, you want to take matters into your own hands again, do ye?'

Owen shrugged and started to walk out of her room, 'Maybe I will, Aye, maybe I will.'

Aelish shouted, 'Don't you dare, Owen Michael! Mind your own feckin business ye greedy git, ye meddling pest, we don't want your sort of help!' She shut her door. Owen walked away sniggering.

Sheila sat in her comfy chair reading the letters. It was strange to read the love letters of another couple. She thought of when these letters were written, during the turbulent times of World War II, when there was such uncertainty in the world, and death and destruction existed every day in these men's lives. As she read the letters she thought of her Martin, sitting next to Paddy as he wrote the letters she held in her hands.

The first mention of Martin in the letters was brief, 'Doll, the guy I told you about, Marty, he saved another guy today, it's as if he knows when something's about to happen, it's uncanny.' He went on to write about the weather and how there was a lot he could *not* say in his letters. But he could tell her how much he missed her, and asked her to give their baby boy a kiss for him. Sheila read through quite a few letters, some very personal to their relationship. She read on, astonished, about how many men's lives Martin had saved. As she sat by the fire, sipping her sherry, she felt as if she was having a moment with her Martin, recalling how, through all those years, Martin had not spoken of the war; on the rare occasions that he had, he'd claimed he wasn't a hero--a coward, actually. She was dumbfounded to find out a completely different account of her husband, one she never would have known had Patrick not found her. Sheila was amazed at how people's lives are intertwined and connected, unbeknownst to them.

These letters were a comfort for Sheila to read; she'd always believed her Martin was a hero, in spite of what he'd said, and this just confirmed it. There were stories of him pushing men out of the way, and they survived explosions. She read how Martin called someone over to him, then the spot where the man had been standing was blown to bits. They called Martin 'Magic Marty', which Sheila had never heard before.

Sheila read some of the stories with her hand on her heart in amazement. She only got through half of the letters that Patrick had brought. Her eyes were getting tired. As she put the stack of letters down, she thought it was like reading a good book that she didn't want to end. She would savour the rest of the letters tomorrow.

Chapter Fourteen

Maeve and Aelish were walking into school; at the top of the steps they said in unison, 'Good morning Mr. O'Sullivan.' As he was saying good morning to the girls he was nearly knocked over by Owen and Liam tearing past him, yelling good morning to him as they kept running down the hallway.

Mr. O'Sullivan gave a lame attempt at discipline, 'No running in the hall, lads, save it for the field.'

Owen was running in front of Liam, telling him to hurry up, 'Leg it! We only have a few minutes, Jaysus, run faster, ye langer!' Liam was running blindly after Owen.

Liam yelled, 'The only reason I'm running slower than you is that I don't know where the hell we're going, ye git! Don't forget I outrun you every day on the field.'

Owen laughed, 'You lie! My sister runs faster than you, ye lazy arse!' As the boys arrived at Mr. O'Sullivan's office, Owen looked back at Liam quickly, 'You stay here and stand guard, just pretend you're looking at your phone. This will only take a second and we have to get out of here before Mr. O'Sullivan gets here, or worse, Sister Mary Military Skirt. If she comes, we're dead.'

Liam nodded, 'Go on then, I'm standing guard.'

Owen went into Mr. O'Sullivan's office and picked up the microphone to the school's intercom system. He put on a deep voice and spoke very loudly: 'Attention students! Pay attention to this announcement and you can win an award! If anyone knows a Sheila Murphy, go to the back yard. I repeat, if anyone knows *anyone* by the name of Sheila Murphy, go to the back yard. There's a reward if you know someone by the name of Sheila Murphy, go now! Run!' Owen was laughing as he ran out of Mr. O'Sullivan's office.

Liam was waving his hands, ushering him out of the office quickly. 'Come on! Jaysus, I'm sure the blue brigade is on the way! Get away from the door!' They both ran for a bit down the hallway. Sister Mary Margaret was walking towards them so fast, it was nearly a run. She was headed towards Mr. O'Sullivan's office. Owen and Liam started to walk, pretending they were showing each other things on their phones as the nun practically ran right into them. She pointed her finger right in Owen's face.

'Was that YOU?!'

Owen screwed up his face, 'Was *what* me?'

She was pointing up to the speakers, then pointed into Liam's face, 'Was that YOU?!'

Liam just smiled and said slowly, 'Wasn't that Mr. O'Sullivan, Sister?'

Her face scarlet, she went right up to Owen, 'I know it was you, what are you after? Why are you looking for my cousin? What are you on about?' Owen had forgotten about her cousin in rehab-- how it was a terrible family embarrassment for Sister Mary Margaret.

Owen looked truly surprised, 'Ah God, no Sister! I swear to you! Jeez, there's another Sheila Murphy right in Allihies, maybe it's about her? I don't think that was about your cousin at all for God's sake, you're paranoid!'

Sister clipped Owen on the side of his head with her hand, 'Don't take the Lord's name in vain.' She marched off down the hallway, running into Mr. O'Sullivan saying, 'For God's sake, lock your office door, we won't let that happen again.'

Owen looked back as he ran and yelled, 'Don't take the Lord's name in vain Sister!'

Maeve and Aelish both gasped when they heard the announcement.

'Ah my God, what is he *doing*?' Aelish started to run towards the back yard, 'I'll kill him, I will, I'll kill him!' They ran to the back yard to find Owen and Liam talking to a few people. Owen was passing out small pieces of paper.

Aelish ran towards him and squealed, 'What the hell are you *doing*? Are you mad, ye langer?'

Owen ignored her and made an announcement to the few kids standing there, 'Listen up people, call me about the Sheila Murphy that you know, I'll let you know if it's the cousin we're looking for and you may get a reward, here's my number, now get going and don't let Mr. O or Sister Martyr know it was me. Off you go, leg it, go on!'

Maeve looked at Aelish and shrugged, 'Not a bad idea Aye, we could step up the search a bit, I don't think we're doing everything we could be, you know.'

Aelish started to walk back into the school, shaking her head. Maeve followed her and continued, 'Let's see what he finds out, that wasn't such a bad idea he had there, sure it wasn't.'

Aelish reluctantly agreed, 'Right, you deal with him then, won't you Maeve? I don't have the patience, I'll see you at break.'

Maeve stood there and waited for Owen to finish talking to the few kids left in the back yard, 'That was ingenious of you Owen, what are you doing? I bet you're thinking there'll be some sort of a reward for you, I would imagine that's your motivation.'

Owen looked smug, 'I have a feeling that ticket is going to go to waste. I figured why not, why not try something, anything, you two don't seem to be doing much.'

Maeve didn't see the harm in letting Owen help, 'That's fine Owen, but be careful of who you tell, and watch what you say. Keep in mind I have the ticket, locked in a safe deposit box. You're going to have to go through me to get anything, just keep that in mind and don't mess with me.'

Owen was surprised at the usually meek and mild Maeve, 'Well then, yes, Ms. Maeve, I'll check with you about my every move. May I be excused to go to my first class now, Ms. Maeve?'

Maeve rolled her eyes, and shook her head, and walked away. 'Just watch yourself, Owen.'

As Owen was walking back into the school, he saw Mr. O'Sullivan and Sister Mary Margaret approaching the back yard. Owen ran towards another entrance, ran down the hallway and quickly slipped into his first class. He sighed as he sat down, feeling quite proud of himself. Everyone was settling down in the classroom; the teacher tapped on her desk for attention. There was a loud knock on the door. Owen rolled his eyes when he saw Mr. O'Sullivan and Sister Mary Margaret walking into his classroom. He looked out the window, pretending he didn't see them. The teacher loudly said, 'Mr. Flanagan, you are excused.'

Owen rolled his eyes again as he dragged his feet and took his time walking towards the door. Many classmates were laughing, 'Finally get caught have ya now, O?'

Owen raised his eyebrows and glanced towards the row of desks where the comment came from and said, 'Shut it.' He continued to walk out into the hallway, purposely walking slowly and shuffling his feet. When he approached Mr. O'Sullivan and the nun, he wouldn't look at her, he just looked at Mr. O'Sullivan and walked past them both.

Sister Mary Margaret hit him on the side of the head, 'Pick up your feet and march yourself into Mr. O'Sullivan's office immediately.'

Mr. O'Sullivan looked at the nun and said, 'I'll take it from here, Sister, thank you.'

The nun stood still in the hallway with her hands on her hips watching as they walked away, she yelled to Mr. O'Sullivan, 'That one suffers from a double dose of original sin, so he does, he's a hooligan he is!'

Mr. O'Sullivan glanced back, and repeated, 'I'll take it from here Sister.' He put his hand on Owen's shoulder as they continued down the hallway and said, 'We'll go and have a chat in my office, right ol' boy?'

Owen nodded, 'Yes sir.' Sister Mary Margaret gave a disapproving look, then she walked down the hallway towards her office. When she was out of earshot, Mr. O'Sullivan looked at Owen and said, 'Did you see the hurling match over the weekend?'

Owen grinned, 'Ya, it was brilliant.'

They walked into Mr. O'Sullivan's office, 'Have a seat, Owen.' Mr. O'Sullivan placed a small piece of paper in front of Owen that read: 'You know a Sheila Murphy? Call me, there's a reward if she's the long lost relative we are looking for – Owen at 277 2612.' Mr. O'Sullivan stood looking down at Owen, 'Care to explain so I don't have to hear it from Sister Mary Margaret? She feels you're meddling into her family life, you're looking to expose some family secret of some sort.'

Owen laughed, 'No, God no, I swear to you, it's nothing like that at all, Mr. O'Sullivan. I'm just trying to help an old lady in Allihies, her name is also Sheila Murphy, she's looking for a cousin of hers by the same name, that's all, I swear. She just happens to have the same name as the nutter cousin of Sister Mental.'

Mr. O'Sullivan interrupted, 'That's enough, Owen. I'll straighten Sister Mary Margaret out. Now you get back to your class, stay out of my office unless you're invited, don't touch that intercom again, and we'll see you at hurling practice this afternoon.'

Owen jumped up and walked quickly out of his office, 'Thanks Mr. O, see you later!' He ran down the hallway, thinking how amusing it was that he could do no wrong in Mr. O'Sullivan's eyes.

Sheila woke up to the fire still glowing from the previous night. She moved the metal screen and threw a couple of pieces of turf in the fireplace. She made herself a cup of tea and sat by the fire reading the rest of the letters that Patrick had left behind for her. She continued to find out things about her husband that she'd never known before. Her mind started to drift to when she had first met Martin. She had rarely thought about all the details of that time in her life, purposefully. She had always felt it was water under the bridge. Sheila looked forward, not back; she didn't want to get stuck in the past. But after reading all of the letters, and learning the new information about Martin, she couldn't help but think of all the details of when they first met. Sheila sat by the fire and started to daydream about Martin. She allowed herself to drift off into the past. She sat by the warm fire, sipping her tea, looking out into the fields and the soft mist outside the window.

Martin had been much older than Sheila. He was 15 years her senior, and he had experienced a lifetime before they met. Sheila sat there and recalled the stories that he told her of his life. Martin was 17 years old when he joined the Irish Army in 1942. The following year, he deserted the Irish Army and joined the British Military, which wasn't viewed favourably by the Irish government. He went off to England, was deployed to

Northern Africa, and back to England. When Martin returned to Ireland in 1945, he was disqualified from any form of state funded employment so he went to work for the Ford Motor company plant in Cork. He didn't want to get married, and he didn't want to have children. He told Sheila he hadn't met the right woman and he had always been a bit of a loner. He worked for Ford's in Cork for ten years, and in 1956 he asked to be transferred to the Ford plant in Dagenham, England.

The night before he left he was in the village saying goodbye to friends. He met Sheila walking down the long road in Allihies. Sheila had had an argument with her parents that evening, and had left the farm to walk into the village. Martin left his friend's house; hot from the fire and the crowd of people, he was carrying his overcoat. Martin saw this girl walking down the road on a chilly evening, wearing only a summer dress, and he said to her, 'You'll catch your death wearing that,' and he placed his overcoat around her shoulders. Martin was 31; Sheila was 16. They walked down the footpath, talking with ease. They chatted about the weather and different parts of the world where he had been. Martin was captivated by her beauty. Sheila loved how mature Martin was and the worldly experiences he'd had in his life. Martin asked Sheila to tuck into a pub with him to continue their conversation. Sheila felt this was bold, she knew she shouldn't, but she was very attracted to him and she didn't want to go home. They had a few drinks and talked and laughed for hours. Martin drove Sheila back to her farm, parking his car on the grass as soon as they turned into the long drive to her parents' cottage. They walked down the dirt road, through the field to the creek, sat on the rocks, and talked and laughed.

Martin had a flask and shared the whiskey with Sheila. They started to kiss on the banks of the creek. One thing led to another, Sheila couldn't help herself, and Martin persisted. It was all a bit of a blur to Sheila: she was tipsy and she was so taken by him. Neither of them had a care in the world that evening. Sheila had never been with a man before, and she had never met a man like Martin. She let herself go; they had a passionate encounter on the banks of the creek. They were laughing and chasing each other in the field, both of them drunk and happy. Martin walked Sheila through the field to her family cottage. He said goodbye to her; she knew he was moving to England in the morning. They gave each other a hug goodbye, feeling good; they'd had such a grand time, like they were giddy with love. They said goodbye. She didn't know if she would ever see him again.

 Sheila had thought about Martin constantly after that night--especially after a few months of missed cycles. She was 16 and pregnant, and she had no one she could turn to, no one to confide in, no one to whom to confess this horrible sin. In the eyes of the Catholic Church and the Irish Republic, this was a sin, and she needed to be hidden away from society and repent. Sheila sadly knew she would have to leave her home, her parents, and her village. She knew she would have to go into one of the Catholic run institutions and have her baby there. She didn't have a choice.

 She had heard horror stories of the Blessboro Home in Cork. She knew she would give birth to her baby there, then have to give the baby over to the nuns. She knew this was her fate and the fate of her baby--it was the only way--there were no other options. She was alone to handle the situation all by herself. When she went to the priest, he told her just that: it was she alone who had done this; it was her own fault that she had put herself and her family to shame. He told her exactly what she was to do and she didn't have a say. The priest picked her up the next day with barely a discussion with her parents. He drove her to the home in silence.

Sheila sat staring into the fire, drinking her tea, allowing her thoughts go to where she normally wouldn't, back to the events that had happened a lifetime ago. The priest dropped her off at the Blessborough Mother and Baby Home in Cork. She found out after a few months of being there that that she was having twins. It was a very difficult and painful birth. The nuns wouldn't give her anything for the pain and they had no sympathy towards Sheila whatsoever. The nuns didn't care about Sheila's well-being; they seemed to have no compassion for her or for the babies. The nuns felt that they were doing God's work, and what Sheila had done was a sin and a disgrace.

Sheila gave birth to twin girls; she wanted to name them Maeve and Grace. The nuns refused to put those names on the birth certificates, saying that they would be more adoptable if they had more basic, Christian names. The nuns re-named her baby girls Margaret and Catherine. Sheila was so sick, she didn't get to see her baby girls for weeks after they were born. She was allowed to see them only once a day after that. Sheila worked in the laundry facilities of the home for twelve to fourteen hours a day as her "penance". The slave labour was her punishment and atonement.

There was one photo taken of Sheila and her two baby girls when they were a few months old. She was holding them both in her arms in the garden. A representative from an adoption facility in America was at Blessboro taking photos, and left with several children that day. Sheila knew that eventually that would be the fate of her daughters.

The girls were taken from her when they were four months old. Sheila woke up one morning and they were gone; she was not allowed to say goodbye to them. She was told they were gone and to get back to work. She wasn't told what had happened to them, or where they went. She was coldly informed to get on with her life and that she should be thankful that the nuns had taken her in at all.

A few months after her girls were taken, Sheila was dismissed from her duties in the laundry facility of the institution. She left empty handed. As she was leaving, she begged the head nun to tell her any information of where her girls had gone. The nun looked, stone faced, into Sheila's eyes and told her that both of the girls had died. Sheila fell to her knees; for her to hear those words out of the nun's mouth was soul destroying; she was inconsolable. A younger nun, who had befriended Sheila, helped her up from the ground and walked with her down the gravel drive away from the cold stone building. The young nun slipped her the photo of her holding her two baby girls in the garden. Sheila took the photo and with her shaking hand, placed it on her heart, crying. She was guided out through the gates towards her father waiting on the road in his car. She was told to move on with her life, to not look back and to never set foot on these premises again. What was done, was done.

She was sixteen years old and wrecked. She had to go back to her family farm, and go back to school. She was told to tell everyone that she had been taking care of an aunt in England. That was that and nothing more. She cried for three months solid.

Sheila came back to her cup of tea, staring at the fire, nearly sixty years later, with tears streaming down her face. She rarely allowed herself to go through the details of her past. It was just torture, and there was no point; it was only upsetting to think about the past and there was nothing she could do about it. She stood up, took a deep breath, and made herself another cup of tea. She looked back at the pile of letters on the table and the mound of crumpled tissue; that was enough reminiscing for one day.

Maeve and Aelish were walking out the front door of school when Owen came running up to them, 'Say ladies, would you like to know the invaluable information I found out about a Sheila Murphy in the area?' Aelish didn't care.

Maeve looked somewhat interested, 'Yes Owen, what have you got?'

Owen looked quite proud of himself, 'Well, I found a Sheila Murphy that lives in Skibbereen! She's a cousin of Finn Murphy here in my class. They were all at a wedding there in Glengarriff last weekend, *and* she plays the lottery. Finn said everyone in their family plays the lottery. They always say if you're not in it, you can't win it. I'd say I found your Sheila Murphy for you, and I'll take that reward when you present her with her winning ticket that she purchased and lost while she was in this area, she's the one and I found her, I did.'

Aelish laughed, 'Ah, you're such a clever lad, a regular Sherlock Holmes, aren't ye, Owen? We already found that Sheila Murphy you nitwit.'

Maeve still wanted his help, 'Owen, that was great that you found out that information, any other possibilities?'

Owen looked right at Aelish, 'Ah, you and yer search can feck off.' He ran off into the car park.

Maeve looked at Aelish, 'You know, he really could be of some use to us, Aye.'

Aelish rolled her eyes, 'I don't know why he bugs me so much sometimes, drives me mad, he does.'

Maeve patted her on the back, 'Come on, let's go to Sheila's house and see what new information *she's* found.'

Aelish said, 'That's great, but let's have a cigarette first.'

Maeve shrugged, 'Fine, let's just have them in the car with the windows down.'

The girls pulled into the lane that led towards Sheila's cottage. They saw her walking in the field, stopping every once in a while, stretching her arms out, looking up to the sky, then walking some more.

Aelish looked at Maeve, 'What do you suppose she's doing?'

Maeve shrugged, 'I haven't a clue, she hasn't noticed us, that's for sure.' Sheila stopped again, putting her face towards the sky with her eyes closed, taking a deep breath and holding her arms out and open, around in a big circle, then together and down as if she were praying.

Maeve decided to finish the drive to the cottage and park her car. 'Looks like some sort of meditation to me, she'll be along soon enough when she sees us, I'm sure, or when she's finished.'

Aelish looked thoughtfully at Sheila, 'I wonder if she's all right.'

Maeve half smiled, 'Ah, I'm sure she's grand, maybe it's just something she does, my mam is always doing that sort of thing as well in our back garden.' The girls got out of the car and stood in front of the cottage.

Sheila saw them and walked towards them from the field yelling, 'Hello girls! The door's open, put the kettle on!' The girls waved and went into the cottage. It was warm and cosy as usual. The fire was glowing. They noticed the stack of letters along with a pile of crumpled up tissue like a little pyramid on the table.

Aelish was curious, 'Do you suppose she has a bad cold or do you think the letters were upsetting?'

Maeve looked over with a look of sympathy, 'Ah, I don't know, that'd be some cold with that pile of tissue. I don't want to ask. I would imagine she'll tell us if she wants.'

Aelish shook her head, 'Aren't you curious about her? I feel like there's so much she's not telling us about herself.'

Maeve didn't agree, 'Do you feel she's obligated to tell us anything for some reason?'

Aelish was getting annoyed, 'You're not the slightest bit interested? Something seems off.' Maeve shrugged. At that moment, Sheila walked into the cottage. The water was boiling in the kettle.

Sheila said, 'Ah, just in time, I'll get the tea.'

Maeve walked over to the fridge, 'I'll get the milk.'

Sheila brought a plate full of chocolate biscuits and placed it in front of Aelish sitting at the table.

Her eyes lit up, 'Ah, you're too good, thanks a million, these are all for me, right?'

Maeve came over to the table, put the milk and cups down, and moved the plate of biscuits to the centre of the table; then she sat down and inquired, 'What have you found out, Sheila?'

Sheila brought the teapot to the table and sat down, 'Well, after a bit of investigating, I've found out some very interesting information. I found out there were actually two winners that night of the lottery. One winning ticket was purchased in Ballydehob at the convenience store on the main road. The other winning ticket was purchased in Eyeries, not too far from Allihies, just north a bit. The strange thing I found out was they were sets of numbers that were chosen, not random, both times.'

Aelish wasn't following her, 'What do you mean, chosen numbers?'

Sheila continued, 'They weren't picked randomly by the lottery machine; they were specifically chosen numbers, each winning ticket. This is highly unusual--that two people would choose the same set of numbers. I just find that odd.'

Maeve was a bit disappointed; she'd thought Sheila was going to have a bit more information, another person to pursue. She said, 'Okay, so, one ticket was purchased in Ballydehob and one ticket was purchased in Eyeries. I don't know what to make of this information, Sheila.'

Aelish was annoyed, 'So, are we looking for two Sheila Murphys now? Didn't we find a Sheila Murphy in Ballydehob?'

Sheila laughed, 'No, we are not looking for *two* Sheila Murphys and yes, we did find one in Ballydehob, she was the English woman that was very rude, do you remember?' Aelish nodded.

Maeve looked curious, 'I thought that woman was so strange, she was acting as if we were after something, curious really.'

Sheila continued, 'The lottery office first declared there was only one winner, then it was on the website as two winners. I phoned the lottery office, and I was told that both winning tickets were chosen numbers, not quick mechanical picks, as is the norm. One ticket has been claimed, the other not. The Eyeries ticket has been collected. The ticket that was purchased in Ballydehob has not been declared. Each one is worth 2.5 million.

Aelish laughed, 'And here I thought we were holding on to 5 million euros, and it's just a mere 2.5 million euros? Ha!'

Maeve was thinking, 'Sheila, you say the ticket that was redeemed was purchased in Eyeries? That's just like a half hour from here, let's take a drive and see if the shop remembers who purchased the ticket!'

Sheila was shaking her head, 'Dear, that has already been redeemed, that's not the lost ticket. The lost ticket was purchased in Ballydehob.'

Maeve was still thinking, 'Let's go anyway, I'm just curious. I'll buy the ice cream cones!'

Sheila laughed, 'You girls, I feel like a girl when I'm with you! Okay, let's go.' They all got into Maeve's car.

Sheila looked around inside the car and squinted at the girls, 'Were you girls smoking in here?' Maeve looked back at Aelish, upset.

Aelish lied, 'No, why, does it smell like it? Maybe some kids broke into the car and smoked in it.'

Sheila wasn't buying it, 'I do hope it wasn't you girls smoking. If you were smoking, I hope you never do again. I had a few people close to me in my life who died young because of smoking, and that's all I'll say on that subject.'

Maeve gave a quick, knowing glance into the back seat at Aelish, then drove off to Eyeries, changing the subject, 'It should just be about a half hour drive.'

Aelish had no idea why they were going to check out anything about a different ticket, but she was up for an ice cream cone. They drove along the sea from Sheila's house, past Allihies east to the small village of Eyeries; it had one shop, and that was it.

Maeve parked in front of the shop, 'Three 99's?'

Sheila spoke up as she started to get out of the car, 'Yes dear, but I'll get them this time.' Aelish was happy to sit in the back seat of the car and look at her phone. She saw that she had a text from Owen:

Found more Sheila Murphy info if you're interested. Be at O'Neill's in an hour, see you there.

Aelish responded:

Thanks Sherlock, see you soon.

The woman behind the counter in the shop was very friendly; she talked non-stop the moment Maeve and Sheila walked in. It was all about the weather, where they were from, wondering why she had never seen them before, and what brought them to Eyeries.

Maeve's head was spinning. She said, 'I heard you had a big lottery win here at your shop.'

The woman was thrilled to talk to anyone about anything, 'Ah, 'tis big news here in Eyeries, this place was filled with balloons and things the day after that draw, so it was. We get a percentage of those winnings, you know. It's a small percentage, but a percentage just the same, it's better than a hot stick in the eye, so it is. It's not much, but, it's something we didn't have the day before that drawing, no we didn't.'

Maeve wanted to know some information, 'Did you know the winners? Are they from Eyeries? Did you see them?'

The woman went on, 'I was here the day that ticket was sold and I do remember the two girls. No, they weren't from here, not sure where they came from, Birmingham accents I'd say, or maybe they were Liverpool accents, I don't know, but they weren't from here. Not sure what they were doing here, they didn't say much at all. A blonde haired woman and a brunette, in their 20's I'd say. They've probably blown all that money by now, wasted on youth, I'd say.'

Maeve felt she was onto something, 'Did you happen to see their car?'

The woman looked out of the front window, 'No, I can't say that I did, but I'd say they'd have a new car by now, wouldn't you say?'

Maeve was still thinking, 'Do you remember them playing loud music in the car?'

The woman was thinking her questions were strange now; she was thinking this could be someone after the winners, 'I'd say I didn't see or hear their car now, is there something you're looking for now are you?'

Maeve looked at Sheila who looked a bit confused, 'We'll have three 99's please.'

As they were walking out to the car, Sheila looked at Maeve, 'You're onto something, what is it?' Maeve opened the door for Sheila, who got in and passed a cone to Aelish.

Aelish was thrilled, 'Tanks a million!'

Maeve got in the car and looked at the two of them, 'I think I may have figured this whole thing out. We may have found the winner of that lottery ticket after all.'

Chapter Fifteen

Maeve was eating her ice cream cone looking at Sheila and Aelish in the car, 'You know, we may have to make another trip down to Ballydehob to visit that rude Sheila Murphy again.'

Aelish interrupted, 'What for? That woman wasn't the slightest bit interested in talking to us, or giving us any sort of information, she seemed paranoid and delusional by the sounds of it.'

Maeve looked at Sheila, 'She did seem leery, didn't she? I think I know why, this is my guess anyway. I think that woman purchased the winning ticket in Ballydehob with her chosen numbers and she signed that ticket. That ticket was lost up here, you know, driving through Allihies, so she bought another ticket up north, using her numbers again as she probably always does.'

Sheila seemed to agree, 'That seems plausible.'

Aelish wasn't convinced, 'Although you are quite the sleuth Maeve, what makes you think all this?'

Maeve continued, 'It's pure speculation, but what else have we got? The woman in the shop said she remembered two girls buying a lottery ticket, one was blonde. Aye, do you remember the driver of that car was blonde? They were loud and singing, the lady in the shop said they were in their 20's.'

Aelish said, 'But the lady in Ballydehob was a crotchety old coot, and who's to say this shop lady remembers the right people? She remembered that the winning ticket was purchased by a blonde? Do they have CCTV?'

Maeve went on, 'I doubt that small shop would, but not many people frequent the village of Eyeries. I think 50 people live there, they remember their visitors. I don't know, I think maybe that blonde had her original ticket, lost it, and bought another ticket with the same chosen numbers, I don't know, it's just a hunch.'

Aelish looked at Sheila, 'She's lost the plot and off her rocker she is, that woman in Ballydehob didn't have blonde hair! Ah she's doing my head in, Sheila, so she is!'

Maeve squinted her eyes, looking at Aelish, 'Ah you can be a right nob so you can, Aye. Can you come up with anything better?'

Sheila interrupted, 'Let's not get carried away now girls, this is a very distinct possibility; we should go back down and talk to that Sheila Murphy in Ballydehob. Mind you, I think we should keep looking elsewhere as well, it may or may not be her. But any lead is a good lead.'

Aelish remembered Owen, 'Speaking of leads, I'm not sure if this is a good one or not, but Owen claims to have some information on another Sheila Murphy. He told us to meet him at O'Neill's.'

Maeve looked at Sheila, 'Would you like to join us, or would you like me to drop you off at your house?'

Sheila smiled, 'Oh, I'd like to join you, I haven't been to O'Neill's in ages! I'm quite enjoying this treasure hunt.'

Maeve couldn't finish her ice cream cone, 'Anyone else want me to throw out the rest of their cone?'

Aelish stopped her, 'I'll finish mine, and *then* yours, hand it over.'

Maeve gave Aelish her cone and started the car. They drove the narrow, winding roads through the rolling hills back down to Allihies. The sea was calm and the sun was hovering over the water. Maeve was cautious driving the blind turns, as the sun was directly in her eyes at every turn. She kept coming up to tractors in the road, and a few people speeding and overtaking her, 'This is a regular traffic jam in the middle of the country, I'd say.' With the sun in her eyes; she found it difficult to drive and she wanted to stop. She slowed down and started to pull over in a layby with an old stone wall overlooking the sea.

'When was the last time either one of you watched the sun set?' Both Sheila and Aelish said they couldn't remember. 'Right then, as me da always said, we are going to watch it set and listen to see if we can hear it sizzle as it sets in the water.' Sheila laughed.

Aelish rolled her eyes and yelled out, 'Ah my God, you're such a sap! I suppose it will be better than having a head-on.'

Maeve smiled, 'We can sit on this wall until the sun sets, come on, it will be gone in a few minutes.'

Sheila and Aelish were still eating their ice cream cones; Maeve took hers back from Aelish. They got out of the car and sat on the old stone wall. The three of them sat quietly overlooking the calm sea out into the distance. The waves delicately lapped the rocks below. The sun lit up a large swath of water towards the shore, the path of light danced and sparkled. It was quiet, there was no wind. There were a couple of seagulls flying around, and few sandpipers on the sandy beach below. The air was crisp and cool, with a fresh seaweed-and-salt smell.

Sheila took a deep breath and closed her eyes, 'Ah this is lovely.'

Maeve and Aelish agreed, 'Tis.' The three of them sat there silently, finishing their ice cream cones and looked out to the sea as the sun was settling closer to the horizon. They were all quiet until the sun seemed to touch the water. As the sun was setting, Sheila quietly made a sizzle sound, 'Sssssssssss.'

Aelish nearly pushed Maeve off the wall, 'Ah my God, look what you've done, you've turned Sheila into a sap. Come on, let's go to O'Neill's and see what Owen is up to.'

Sheila stopped them, 'Let's wait a moment longer. If I've noticed one thing in my life, it's the quiet moments, especially in nature, that can have the most profound effect on you. It's a form of meditation really. Just sit quietly for a moment, think of nothing but what is right in front of you. Look out into the vast sea and just take in the simple beauty of it all, the splendour of this beautiful place we live in. Then close your eyes and take a deep breath, breathe in the fresh air, notice how the smells awaken when your eyes are closed. Take another deep breath and simply be in the moment you are in right now, right here. Don't think about where you're going, or where you've been, just think about the beauty that stands before you, that's been here since the beginning of time. Picture yourself in the perspective of the world; you're sitting on this ancient wall on the Beara Peninsula with the jagged rocks of Ireland below you, you are sitting at the edge of the North Atlantic Ocean. Admire the colours and the amazing beauty of what is in front of you, right here, right now. Be aware of your breathing, take a deep breath, hold your arms out and embrace the world that's right in front of you this very moment.'

Maeve and Aelish had never done this before. They did everything Sheila said, and were both surprised at how happy it made them feel.

Sheila continued, 'Now then, I want you girls to do this same thing whenever you think of having another cigarette. I assure you the moment will pass, the urge will leave you, mark my words, and you'll never have another.'

Maeve and Aelish looked at each other, shrugged and smiled. They all looked out into the calm sea until the sun sank below the horizon.

Sheila broke the silence, 'Right, that's another day gone, let's go and enjoy the evening. Off to O'Neill's we go.'

The three jumped off the wall, got into the car and continued on down the winding road alongside the sea, until they reached Allihies. As they pulled up in front of the pub, Maeve saw Patrick McGettigan striding into the pub wearing his cowboy boots. Maeve felt a flutter in her stomach.

Aelish looked at Maeve and laughed, 'Jesus, I felt that.' Sheila was wondering what she was talking about. Aelish laughed again, 'The nerves on this girl! That was ol' Paddy from America walking into the pub. I think I heard Maeve's heart skip a beat.'

Maeve wasn't amused, 'Come on, let's go, let's do what we came here to do, and that's to find out what that Owen Flanagan knows, right? How about a cup of tea for everyone? Would everyone like tea? How does that sound? Cup of tea? I'd like tea. Would you like tea?'

Aelish raised her eyebrows, 'Okay, easy there, let's go in and have our cups of tea then, we're not nervous at all, are we now? You should consider a pint there, missus.'

Maeve, Aelish and Sheila walked into the pub.

Mr. O'Neill was behind the bar, 'Good evening ladies, how's the form?'

Maeve spoke up, 'Just grand Mr. O'Neill, we'll all be having tea. Do you know Sheila Murphy? Sheila, this is Mr. O'Neill.'

Mr. O'Neill leaned over the bar towards Sheila, holding out both of his hands, 'Ah, I do indeed, it's been a million years since I've seen the likes of you, lovely to see you Sheila.'

Sheila took both of his hands, 'Good to see you too, John. I remember my Martin loved to come here, I remember your father John, rest him. And you, such a young lad back then, I recall many fun days.'

John nodded, 'They were good days indeed, God rest their souls. I wasn't that young, mind you. I remember Martin Murphy, he was a good man, so he was. Now then, why don't you ladies find yourselves a place to sit, and I'll have someone bring your drinks out to ye.'

Sheila leaned towards John, 'I'm treating the girls, so don't take their money.'

John laughed, 'Ah, good woman, it'll be right out to you.'

Aelish walked up closer to the bar, 'Have you seen Owen, Mr. O'Neill?' He nodded and pointed towards the back room. 'He's back there with Paddy, the American.' Aelish looked in the direction of the back room, 'We'll go back there, you can bring us our drinks back there then.'

Mr. O'Neill waited for Sheila to start walking towards the back room with Maeve so she wasn't within hearing distance, He looked at Aelish, 'Jesus you've got a cheek on ya. Ye can bring your own bloody drinks back there yerself, Aelish, I'll have it ready for you just now.' Aelish rolled her eyes slightly and reluctantly stood there, knowing she couldn't carry it all.

Just then, Michael O'Malley walked into the pub. Aelish turned around and nearly called him by his nickname but then remembered their truce. 'Michael O'Malley, how's things?'

He smiled when he saw Aelish, 'Ah, just grand, Aelish Flanagan, and you? Are we being formal with each other now, is it?'

Aelish laughed, 'Nah, I just didn't want to slip back into me old habits, that's all.' Mr. O'Neill indicated to Aelish that their tea was ready to pick up. Aelish looked at Michael, 'What are you having?' Michael pointed to their cups and asked Mr. O'Neill for another. Aelish picked up two cups, left one and the pot and asked Michael to bring the rest to the back room when he got his. She skipped off into the back room.

Mr. O'Neill looked at Michael and shook his head, 'I'll get your tea in a minute, I'll be right back.' He picked up the cup and pot and brought it to the back room, finding Aelish at another table, still holding her two cups. John walked over to the table where Sheila and Maeve sat, along with Owen and Patrick.

He placed a cup and saucer in front of Sheila, 'Now then, that's on me, Sheila, your money's no good here, no it's not.' Sheila smiled and thanked him.

Aelish was at Mr. O'Neill's side as he said that, 'How come you've never uttered those words to me, ha Mr. O'Neill? How come *my* money is *always* good here?'

Mr. O'Neill looked at Aelish, 'Ah, if you only knew how many times your money wasn't good here, lassie, there've been many times throughout your lifetime, and before that, I'll have you know.'

Aelish could remember a time or two she hadn't paid for her drinks; he was very good friends with her da, 'Ta Mr. O'Neill, you're the best.'

He ignored her and looked at Sheila, 'Now, you enjoy your tea and let me know if there's anything else I can get you.'

Sheila smiled, 'Thank you, this is delightful.' Mr. O'Neill left the back room. Sheila looked around at everyone at the table; Maeve, Aelish, Owen and Patrick. She raised her cup, looking at all of them, '*Sláinte.*'

They all raised their cups and looked at Sheila. '*Sláinte.*'

Patrick clinked Sheila's cup and said, '*Sláinte chugat.*'

He then clinked Maeve's cup and said, '*Sláinte mhaith*' Everyone started to laugh.

Owen said, 'Jaysus man, you know more Irish than the Irish themselves.'

Aelish spoke up, 'Speak for yourself, I know my fair share.'

Owen laughed, 'You know just enough to get your leaving cert and get yourself out of school is all you know.'

Aelish quipped back, '*Mar dhea.*' Michael smiled at Aelish and sat down next to her with his cup of tea. Aelish was satisfied as she smiled back at Michael.

Maeve wanted to know immediately what Owen had found, but others at the table knew nothing about the lottery ticket, so she kept up their ruse, 'So, Sheila here is looking for her long-lost cousin, another Sheila Murphy. Owen, you mentioned you may have found something today?'

Owen looked around, 'Yeah, it's new information on that Sheila Murphy in Skibbereen, you know, the one that went to that wedding in Glengarriff?'

Aelish interrupted, 'We've already heard about this one a couple times ye muppet, I thought you had some new information, ye git?' Michael looked at Maeve disapprovingly as he finished his tea, 'Gotta run, see you later.' Aelish shrugged and looked back at Owen, 'Anything else, Sherlock?'

Owen ignored her and looked at Maeve, 'Well, in talking with that Sheila Murphy's cousin Finn at school, she apparently told him that she lost something while she was up in this area that weekend for that wedding, she lost something...' Both Maeve and Aelish looked surprised.

Maeve said, 'Did she now?'

Sheila thought she would interject, 'That's interesting Owen, how did you leave things with your friend Finn?'

Owen wasn't sure how to respond; he glanced at Maeve, not sure what to say, 'Er, I told him I'd talk to my sister's friend, and then I'd check in with him at school tomorrow?'

Maeve looked pleased, 'Thank you Owen, I'll talk to you about it at school tomorrow then.'

Sheila looked around the table, 'Why don't you all stop by my house after school tomorrow to discuss. I have some items to return to Patrick, so you could come as well?'

Patrick nodded, 'Yes ma'am, we can come by tomorrow, I could pick you up at school, Owen.'

Owen agreed, 'Sounds good to me.'

Sheila smiled and raised her cup again. 'Now then, I'd like to continue my toast. Here's to your health and the bright futures you all have ahead of you.' She looked at each one of them, 'Cherish the people you have in your lives today, your family and your friends, new and old, that's it then, to your health.'

They all clinked their cups again, with a 'Hear, hear.' Maeve and Patrick locked eyes and smiled at each other.

Patrick mouthed out, '*Sláinte*' to Maeve. Aelish saw this and imitated him, then looked at everyone at the table, mouthing it out, '*Sláinte, sláinte, sláinte.*' Mr. O'Neill came back and cleared a few things from their table, not saying a word, but gave a wink and a smile to Sheila and walked back out of the room.

Aelish sat there with her mouth hanging open, 'Did you see that? Did anyone else just see that? I've never seen 'auld man O'Neill smile at anyone, let alone *flirt*! That was a blatant flirt! Did you see that? He winked at Sheila!'

Sheila stopped her, 'Ah dear, it was nothing.'

Maeve was laughing, 'He did seem a bit flirtatious, Sheila, I have to say.'

Sheila insisted, 'It's nothing I assure you. Now then, I'm going to have to get going, when you're finished.'

Maeve stood up, 'Of course, no problem at all, let's go.'

Sheila stood up and looked at everyone, 'See you all at my house tomorrow after school for tea then.' Owen and Patrick agreed, and stood up to say goodbye. Maeve, Aelish and Sheila left the pub.

Maeve pulled up in front of Aelish's house and looked at her in the back seat, 'See you in the morning missus.'

Aelish opened the car door, 'Bright and early! See you in the afternoon, Sheila, bye you two.'

As Maeve drove on, she couldn't help herself; she wanted to ask Sheila a question, 'So, have you known Mr. O'Neill a long time?'

Sheila smiled, 'As you know, we live in a small village, dear. I didn't frequent O'Neill's nearly as much as Martin did, but I knew who John was. Women rarely went to pubs back then; there was a time we weren't allowed in some pubs at all. I'd see him around, though, it seems everyone knows everyone in some form or another in this area. To answer your question, yes, I've known John for quite some time, I just haven't seen him in donkey's years.

Maeve didn't want to press, 'Can I bring anything to your house tomorrow for tea?'

Sheila looked at her, 'No dear, just your lovely self, and your friends.

Maeve pulled in down the long road leading to Sheila's house. She had so many questions for her, but she didn't want to pry, 'See you tomorrow.'

Sheila gave Maeve a big hug before she left the car, 'Yes dear, see you tomorrow. Drive safely back home. Thank you for another wonderful day, it was just lovely being with all of you, truly it was, thank you.'

Maeve smiled and said, 'It was. You're welcome, see you tomorrow.' She watched Sheila walk up to her cottage. Sheila stood at the door waving goodbye to Maeve as she drove away down the long driveway, until she was no longer in sight.

The next day was uneventful for the girls; they were in their last few weeks before focusing on exams. Owen wasn't giving up his personal quest for finding the winning Sheila Murphy. He had his sights set on receiving a reward upon finding her. He was still handing out small pieces of paper to random people in the hallways, asking anyone if they knew a Sheila Murphy. He found out some new information to bring to Sheila's house after school.

At the end of the day, Maeve left her last class a bit early and walked directly out the front door of the school to an unexpected sight. A car was parked in the horseshoe drive in front of the school and Patrick McGettigan was leaning up against the car with his arms folded. He was wearing his cowboy boots, jeans, nice shirt and blazer. She had butterflies in her stomach as she walked towards him, thinking to herself what a good-looking man he was. They smiled at each other.

He thought she looked cute in her school uniform, but he was thinking how different they were from American Catholic school uniforms, 'Have the uniform skirts in Ireland always been to your ankles?'

Maeve looked down and laughed, 'Why yes, some are, aren't they lovely? They are compliments of the Irish government, run by the Catholic Church. The uniforms were designed by priests, hiding as much of us as possible.'

Patrick laughed, 'I didn't realise the country was run by the Catholic Church.'

Maeve raised her eyebrows, 'Since the time of St. Patrick I'd say, with intermittent times of English Catholic oppression. Not much has changed, it's all a bit archaic, it is. All of the schools in Ireland are run by the Catholic church, they are the free, public schools as you call them in the States. Things are slowly changing, they're beginning to separate church and state, but I doubt the uniforms will change anytime soon, they're an institution all to themselves and quite lovely, if I might say so myself.'

Patrick found it interesting, 'So, all of your public schools are *all* Catholic?'

Maeve nodded, 'Every single one. We also have private schools, they're Catholic as well, you just pay through the nose for them, some are quite posh.'

Patrick looked a bit confused, 'I had no idea.'

Maeve smiled, 'I'm sure there's a lot about our country that you have no idea about. So, you're here to pick up Owen, are you? Aelish and I will see you at Sheila's. If you can't remember how to get there, Owen can guide you, or you can follow me.'

Patrick smiled, 'I'd rather follow you.'

Maeve was trying hard to keep her cool around Patrick, 'Well then, I'll get my car and bring it round, see you in a minute.'

She went to the car park and drove her car around, parking it in front of Patrick's. There were still a few minutes before school was let out, so she got out to talk to Patrick a bit longer. 'So, are you leaving Allihies in two weeks?'

Patrick looked up as if he were thinking, 'It may be a bit longer than that, I'm seeing how things go.'

Maeve nodded, 'I see. Well, I hope things go well and you decide to stay longer.'

Patrick smiled, 'Things seem to be going well so far, but we'll see.' Just then the bells rang and the school doors opened to a stream of students pouring out.

Owen walked up to Patrick and patted him on the back, 'Hello Paddy ol' boy, let's go.'

Patrick looked at Maeve, 'I was going to follow Maeve.'

Owen laughed, 'I know where the auld one lives, and I don't want to be stuck behind this one, she drives like an auld one herself she does, let's go.' He got into Patrick's car.

Patrick smiled and shrugged, looking at Maeve, 'We'll see you over there then.' Maeve smiled and watched them drive away. She stood and waited for Aelish to exit school.

Chapter Sixteen

Sheila couldn't remember the last time she'd had people at her house prior to Maeve and Aelish coming last week. She couldn't recall the last time she'd had people in her life at all-- she had kept to herself for so long, she'd lost track. Her days were busy with the upkeep of her farm, selling her vegetables and eggs to markets in the area. She'd led a very solitary life, never feeling lonely, but she did feel *alone*. She enjoyed the quiet; she relished the peace; but she was thrilled with the girls entering her life, and loved all the excitement that they brought with them.

The letters were still sitting on the table by the fireplace. Sheila looked at them, thinking she should finish reading them before the afternoon, so that she could return them to Patrick. She put one more batch of biscuits in the oven, made herself a cup of tea, and sat by the fire. She read the remaining few letters. They were the same glowing letters of admiration from Paddy to his wife and about his friend Marty, saving lives in Northern Africa. She read the last letter, and was struck by something Paddy had written about what Martin had said: that he never wanted to get married, and didn't want to have children. Paddy had gone on to tell his wife how happy he was that he had her and their son, that he had something to think about, something to live for, and something to return to when the war was over. He mentioned to his wife that he didn't understand his friend Martin's way of thinking; he felt he simply didn't know what he was missing and he told him so.

Sheila finished the letters, sipped her tea and thought about Martin. He had made it very clear to her on their first meeting that he wasn't like the typical Irishman: he didn't want to marry, he didn't want to have children, he didn't follow any rules or social norms. Sheila went back to thinking about the predicament she was in when Martin left for England. He'd had no idea what she went through, the horrible institution she was kept in, the difficult birth, her daughters being taken away from her, and the most devastating: being told they were dead. The nuns had always made it clear that they were doing the girls a favour by keeping them in the home; they were sinners, just as bad as murderers. Sheila had constantly been told what a burden she was while she was there, and that she was the dregs of society. It was the longest and the most horrible, gut-wrenching year of her life. The echoes were still in her mind of the old nun yelling at her as she left, 'Move on, never come back, you are unwelcome.' She thought about when Martin had returned to Ireland in 1958.

There had been an unexpected knock at the door of her family home. Sheila looked at the door as she sat by the fire; she remembered that day as if it were yesterday. She was 18 years old, and had just finished school. She had no plans other than to help her parents on the farm. Sheila's father had answered the door; it was Martin. She'd heard her father asking who he was and why he wanted to see his daughter. Martin had explained to him that he'd met Sheila years ago and wanted to see her again. Her father didn't know this was the man who had caused such shame to the family.

Her father let Martin in and offered him a drink. Sheila was shocked to see him inside her house, sitting by the fire talking to her father. Sheila's mother was there as well, looking back and forth between Sheila and Martin, a knowing look on her face, assuming that it was probably the man who had caused her disgrace. Martin asked Sheila's father if he could see her again, and her da agreed, saying she was an adult woman now, she didn't need his permission. Martin said he would be back the following day to collect her for a picnic.

Sheila was torn: should she tell Martin of her pregnancy and the subsequent hell she had endured? She didn't know if she should tell him of the abuse and torture she had suffered at the hands of the nuns. She didn't want him to feel bad, or worse, to pity her.

Martin picked Sheila up the next day. Her mother set out a folded blanket and prepared a basket of food for them. To Sheila's surprise, her mother put a small bottle of poteen that her father had made, and two glasses, in the picnic basket. They drove up into the hills, spread the blanket, ate their lunch and drank the poteen. After a bit of drink, Sheila told Martin everything. He was stunned and devastated. He felt horrible that he'd had no idea of the hell she had gone through while he was gone. He wished there was a way he could take back the year and get their girls. Sheila had a difficult time telling Martin that the nasty head nun had told her the girls had died, but Sheila had never truly believed it. Martin was determined to find the truth about their girls. He told Sheila he would pick her up the next morning and they would drive to the Blessboro House in Cork to find out what had happened to their girls. She didn't want her parents to know; it was all supposed to be behind her. Nothing was ever spoken about it when she had returned from the institution.

Sheila was sitting by the fire thinking of that time, so many years ago. She made herself another cup of tea, and put another piece of turf on the fire. It amazed her to recall that time in her life with such detail, but she was thankful it wasn't as painful as those years had been. The thoughts swirled in her head; the pain started to creep in. There was a reason why she didn't think about her time at the home: she couldn't bear it. She thought about how Martin had picked her up that next day, a gloomy, rainy day, and the long, painfully quiet drive to the Blessboro House in Cork.

Martin pulled his car up in front of the large, three storey stone building. Sheila had only gone through that front door once, when she had arrived with the parish priest. She never went in or out of that front door again, only through the back door, when she'd left after being locked inside the premises for an entire year. She had a sick feeling in her stomach, being back on the grounds of the institution--the cold, damp hell with the terrifying nuns.

Martin and Sheila walked up to the large door and knocked. An old nun answered the door; Sheila looked at her with revulsion, remembering the horribly evil nuns during her time there. This was one of them; she remembered her clearly from the year prior. Martin introduced himself and asked the old nun for information on what had happened to their twins. The old nun looked at the two of them in disgust and told them very coldly that the twins had died. Sheila didn't believe her, but she gasped, thinking for a moment that it might be true. She held her heart and nearly lost the use of her legs. Regaining her strength, she looked at the nun and said, 'You don't even remember me, how can you possibly recall what happened to our twins?' Martin held on to her, saying that there must have been a mistake, that Sheila had been there with them until they were four months old, that they were healthy, but then suddenly they were gone, they were taken away.

'Surely,' he asked, 'they were adopted?' The nun stood her ground, saying nothing. Sheila was crippled with pain in her stomach. She was slightly hunched over as Martin held her steady. She looked up at the nun, into her eyes, and she quietly said, 'You lie, you're lying, they're alive, they were adopted, why don't you just tell us the truth? Where are my girls? Where are *our* girls?'

The nun looked at them with a cold and vacant stare; she raised her eyebrows and said in a monotonous, indifferent tone, 'They got sick, and they died. You were told to never come back here. I have nothing more to say.' She quickly closed the door on Sheila and Martin.

Sheila felt weak. Martin helped her back into the car and drove her home. He suggested they go to her parish and speak to the priest who had taken her to the institution. Martin told her he would never leave her again and they would find out what had happened to their girls together. He asked if he could come and collect her the next day. Sheila agreed.

Upon arriving at Sheila's parents' house, Martin had asked if he could speak to Mr. O'Brien in private. He asked permission to marry Sheila. Her father had agreed. Martin and Sheila went to speak to the parish priest. The priest confirmed what the nun had stated: their girls had got sick and died, and they needed to let it go and move on. The priest told them to leave their pain in the past and to never come asking about this subject again; their daughters were dead and that was that. He told them for their own sakes let the past be the past and never speak of this again. He discouraged the two from having a large celebration of their wedding; they were looked at as a disgrace in the eyes of the parish.

Sheila and Martin were married in a small ceremony the following week, with just her parents present. They never spoke of her experience in the institution ever again, and the girls were never mentioned again by Martin's insistence. They tried to have more children, but something had gone horribly wrong during the birth of their girls; it was impossible. Sheila's doctor confirmed that they would never have any more children.

Sheila remembered how they had acquired animals on their farm; a new one seemed to arrive every few months; it had kept them busy over the years.

It wasn't until after Martin had died that Sheila took up the hobby of oil painting. Her best work of art was a painting of her and Martin with their two angels; she had imagined what they would have looked like as toddlers. She always painted them in the only thing she had ever seen them in; matching white outfits. She painted them laughing and playing, scenes she would have given anything to have experienced. Not a day went by for nearly sixty years that Sheila didn't think of her girls. Every morning and every evening, Sheila said a little prayer for them.

She sat in her chair by the fire, looking out the window to the fields. It was time to stop dwelling on the past. She stacked the letters, wrapped the ribbon around them and tied it in a bow just as they had arrived, like a gift. She finished baking her biscuits, and arranged everything for her expected guests.

She heard a car coming down her road. She took off her apron and walked out the front door, pleased to see Maeve and Aelish. She met them at their car and gave them each a hug. They walked into the cottage and knew she had been baking.

Maeve said, 'It smells divine, Sheila.'

Sheila smiled, 'You girls help yourselves.' She heard a car coming down the road, and excused herself to greet them. Maeve tended to the tea.

Sheila turned back and said, 'Since we're expecting more, make yourselves comfortable in the sitting room.' Aelish was already in there, looking at the few photos that Sheila had in frames. Owen and Patrick came into the cottage with Sheila. Patrick was looking forward to a cup of tea--which surprised even himself. Sheila offered everyone tea and plates of biscuits and cakes. Owen asked to use the toilet.

When he returned to everyone sitting around the fire having tea, he looked at Sheila. 'I saw that painting of you, and is that your husband and your daughters? How old are they now? Do they live in the area? What are their names?' Maeve and Aelish were cringing. Leave it to Owen to pry and blurt things out. The two girls were very curious what Sheila's response was going to be.

'I painted that many years ago, yes, that is my husband Martin and our daughters, Maeve and Grace. I'm afraid they're gone, dear.'

Owen felt bad, 'Ah, I'm sorry.'

Sheila continued, 'It was many years ago, they'd be 59 next month, so they would. Now then, how about a cup of tea?'

Maeve jumped up, 'I'll get it.'

Sheila thanked Maeve and looked at Patrick while she picked up the ribbon-wrapped stack of envelopes, saying, 'Thank you so much for sharing these letters with me, Patrick, it was very moving reading what high regard everyone had for Martin, it was very heartwarming, thank you for that gift.'

Patrick smiled, 'It was my pleasure, I'm glad you got to see them, I'm only sorry Martin didn't.'

Sheila patted Patrick on the arm, 'Oh dear, Martin knew himself very well, he didn't need reminding. He was a very proud, confident man, so he was.'

They were all drinking and eating, and Sheila remembered the purpose of having them to her house, 'Owen, you said you had some valuable information about that Sheila Murphy from Skibbereen. The cousin at your school said she had lost something in this area, did you speak to him today?'

Owen looked a bit sheepish, 'Yes, I did speak to him, and yes, she did lose something and she wants Finn to go out on the main road with all of his friends and find it, there will be a reward she said.'

Maeve questioned, 'What exactly did she lose Owen?'

Owen was reluctant to answer, disappointed that he hadn't found the winner of the lottery ticket, 'It was a ring, she apparently threw it at the guy she was with, supposedly it was the guy's ring or something, I don't know, but it happened somewhere between Allihies and Glengarriff, and she wants to find it or there's going to be a problem.'

Sheila smiled, 'Oh, I'd say there's already a problem, and it's more than a lost ring.'

Aelish looked completely annoyed, 'Could you have saved us a trip, ye muppet? Obviously, she's not the one. Why didn't you just say something before, O, you're useless.' Owen looked at his sister, 'She could have lost a ring *and* something else, you don't know, Aye.'

Maeve smiled, 'Thanks Owen, good job.'

Patrick was confused, 'Can I help? This is your cousin who lost her ring? Should we go looking for it?'

Owen laughed, 'Ah Paddy, you'll get used to things around here, nothing is as it seems.'

Maeve interrupted to change the subject, 'Thank you for having us for tea Sheila, the cakes and biscuits are lovely as usual.'

Sheila was quite happy to have them, 'Not at all, you're all more than welcome here any time.' She looked surprised as she heard another car coming down her road, 'Are we expecting someone else?'

Maeve and Aelish shrugged, saying, 'No.' at the same time. Sheila walked out the front door; they all heard her say, 'Ah my Lord in heaven, what a pleasant surprise.' She looked back into the cottage and said, 'It's my dear old friend Catherine. Girls, remember the woman at the shop in

Skibbereen? What a treat!' Maeve looked at Aelish and the boys as she gestured towards the door for them all to leave.

Aelish mouthed to Owen and Patrick, 'Let's go.'

Maeve spoke up, 'Sheila we have to be going, we'll let you two catch up.'

Sheila thought that was fine, 'Don't leave before you say hello to Catherine, you girls are the reason we found each other again, do say hello.' They all went out to greet Catherine as she got out of her car. She remembered them from the shop, 'Hello, hello, good to see all of you again, I was coming up to the area so I thought I would track you down at the old farmstead, Sheila.'

Sheila gave her a big hug, 'I'm so glad you did, do come in for a cup of tea, they were just leaving.' They all said goodbye. Sheila stood with Catherine at her front door and waved as they walked to their cars. She said to Catherine, 'I think we have a lot of stories to tell each other, perhaps we should have something stronger than tea.'

Catherine smiled and put her arm around Sheila in agreement, 'We do have some catching up to do, my friend.'

Chapter Seventeen

Maeve, Aelish, Owen and Patrick were walking towards their cars in front of Sheila's cottage. Wanting to talk to Patrick alone for a moment, Maeve headed towards his car. Aelish was by the passenger side of Maeve's car; she just wanted to go home. Owen was standing next to her.

Patrick looked at Maeve, 'Can they take your car and I'll get you home?'

Maeve smiled a mischievous smile and yelled to Aelish, 'Catch! I'll come get my car later. Owen, go with your sister.'

Owen was quicker than Aelish and caught the keys mid-flight, 'I'll drive, you're a crap driver.' Aelish didn't care; she continued to get into the passenger side and buckle herself in. As Owen was turning Maeve's car around to leave, Aelish was looking at Maeve and Patrick standing next to his rental car.

Aelish noticed the sticker on the back window of Patrick's car. She yelled out her window, 'Hey Maeve, look at the sticker on the back of Paddy's window, it's the same sticker that was on the red car!' Maeve walked to the back of Patrick's car; indeed, it was. She remembered the shape and the colours. It was a discount Irish rental car with a rainbow logo. Maeve looked a bit confused as she watched Aelish and Owen drive away. She quietly said, 'A rental car, why would the winner be driving around in a rental car? Maybe she wasn't even Irish, maybe it was a tourist that's long gone and all of this searching is for naught.'

Patrick moved closer to Maeve, 'What are you saying?'

Maeve shook her head, 'Ah nothing, just talking to myself. Where would you like to go?'

Patrick smiled, 'Let's go for a drive, I haven't explored much around here, let's just see what we find.' They got into the car and drove down the road. Maeve looked back at the cottage. Sheila was still standing at her front door, talking to Catherine, waving goodbye. Maeve put her arm out the window and gave one last wave to Sheila before they were out of sight.

Sheila looked at Catherine, 'C'mere to me, tell me everything, there's an old bottle of whiskey inside that has our names on it.'

The two women walked into the cottage. Catherine stopped as soon as she entered and looked around the cottage, 'My God, this brings me back. I haven't been here since I was sixteen years old.' She helped Sheila pick up the cups and plates, 'What a lovely bunch of kids, are they relatives?'

Sheila smiled, 'Although they feel like it, they're not. They're kids that live in the village--I've just recently come to know them.'

Catherine looked curiously at Sheila, 'Did you have any children, Sheila, I mean after…'

Sheila stopped her, 'I wasn't able to, Catherine, 'twasn't in the cards.' She paused, looking out to the fields, 'Fancy a bit of whiskey? I have a few very old bottles that are probably quite smooth by now.'

Catherine smiled, 'That sounds perfect, I've all day, and we've a lifetime of catching up to do. I hope you're well stocked.'

Sheila laughed, 'Ah, I have more than enough, some of these bottles have been aging for twenty five years, come and have a look.'

Catherine looked over Sheila's shoulder into the cabinet and smiled, 'Jaysus, looks like a wine cellar of whiskey, what's all this?'

Sheila smiled, 'Ah, it was me da, then it was Martin, collecting a few bottles along the way, a bit of a hobby I suppose. I continued over the years, if I found a good one, I'd buy it and keep it, they don't go bad, I'm sure they don't.'

Catherine laughed, 'Sounds like stockpiling to me.'

Sheila laughed, 'Indeed it is.' She took out a bottle with a dusty label, and two glasses. She poured them both generous portions, handed a glass to Catherine and said, '*Sláinte* my friend, *sláinte.*'

Catherine clinked Sheila's glass, '*Sláinte*. I never thought I'd see you again.' They both took sips of the smooth Irish whiskey and smiled.

Sheila gestured to Catherine to sit down in the big comfy chair by the fireplace. She put her glass down, threw a few pieces of turf on the fire, and sat down in the other chair. They both sipped their whiskeys in silence for a moment.

Catherine spoke first, 'Sheila, what happened to you at Blessboro, after I left? What happened to the girls?'

Sheila sat there for a moment, thinking that she could burst into tears--she'd never spoken to a soul about the details, 'I continued to care for Maeve and Grace for a few months, although the nuns only referred to them as Margaret and Catherine, if you recall.'

Catherine interjected, 'My God, of course I remember, I remember everything as if it were yesterday. I remember they wouldn't let me keep my own name because there was another girl there named Catherine. To this day I still cringe when I hear the name Rebecca. I remember they wouldn't allow you to name the girls what you wanted because they weren't names from the Bible. Jesus, everything was such a load of sinful rubbish, those battleaxe nuns were pure evil, so they were.'

Sheila agreed and continued, 'I was able to see my girls when I was allowed to, as you know, for an hour a day, until they were four months old. They were happy and healthy they were. Then, one day they were suddenly gone. I wasn't allowed to say goodbye to them, they were just gone, they were. I had to work at the home for a while longer, which was even more difficult without the few moments of joy I had with my girls every day. The nuns said I would be allowed to leave when my penance was paid. When I begged to know what had happened to my girls, they told me very coldly that they had both died. It broke me to hear those words, I was devastated. But I didn't believe it, in my heart of hearts I didn't believe it, but I was destroyed just the same. I cried for months. Then I was allowed to leave, I was set free after over a year trapped in there.'

Catherine was curious, 'Where did they ship you off to?'

Sheila didn't understand, 'I came back here. Catherine, you were shipped off? That's why you were in Australia?'

Catherine looked sad, 'I wasn't given a choice, my father wouldn't have me back, he wanted to have nothing to do with me. I brought so much shame to the family, he disowned me. I was sent to a home in South Australia, St. Joseph's House. The place wasn't much different than Blessboro to be honest, same horrible nuns, same hard, long days working, making them money--it was just another workhouse, just farther away from home. Really, the only difference was the heat; it was a horrible continuation of my life at Blessboro, another jail sentence, it was. I was there for so many years, so many...'

Catherine took another sip of her whiskey. Sheila felt so sad for Catherine; her heart was aching, listening to her.

'Catherine, what happened to your Michael? You both disappeared at the same time. And however did he come back into your life?'

Catherine's eyes were filling with tears, 'They took Michael the same day they told me I was leaving. They told me a *proper* family adopted him, a respectable family, a good Catholic family. They told me I should feel very fortunate that someone would take the bastard; it was my penance, it was my fault. He was gone, I wasn't allowed to say goodbye to him. They put me on a boat, didn't even bother to tell me where I was being shipped off to--it was just horrible. The nuns told me never to speak a word about anything to anyone or my penance would be worse. So, I never did.'

Sheila looked at Catherine with tear filled eyes. 'I'm so very sorry, Catherine, I'm sorry for everything that happened to you, that happened to me, and to our children.'

Catherine looked at Sheila, 'What do you think happened to your girls, Sheila, do you think they were adopted?'

Sheila put her hand on her heart, 'I have felt every day since the day they were born that they were with me, they've never left me. I was told nothing, they were healthy one day, then I was told they were dead. It was Sister Mary Francis that told me, the horrible one, do you remember her?'

Catherine shook her head, 'How could I forget her, a right wretched one she was. Sheila, I need to use the loo, I'm hoping it's not still outside?' They both laughed.

Sheila responded, 'Yes of course.' and gestured to the back of the cottage, 'The place has been upgraded since you've been here, it's on your left.'

As Catherine was entering the loo, she glanced into Sheila's bedroom and saw the oil painting. She slowly walked towards it to have a closer look. She was confused.

Sheila walked up behind her, 'After my husband died, I painted that. I painted a few over the years, imagining what they looked like. It's been a coping mechanism for me I suppose. It's been easier for me over the years, thinking they've been alive, having a good life. They'll be 59 years old in a couple of weeks.'

Catherine put her hand on Sheila's shoulder, 'I know, pet, same as my Michael, he was 59 a few months ago.'

Sheila smiled, 'Well, let's have a toast to their birthdays. 59 years, hard to believe that.'

Catherine looked at Sheila, 'I have so much to tell you, I'll be out in a minute.'

Sheila walked back to the sitting room and poured them another glass of whiskey. She put more turf on the fire and waited for Catherine. She was hoping Catherine's life had got better; she was hoping for some good news.

Catherine sat down, picked up her glass and raised it towards Sheila. 'Here's to life, to my Michael, and to your girls.'

Sheila clinked Catherine's glass, 'Here's to you, my friend, how good it is to see you again. I'm thankful I found you in Skibbereen that day. If it wasn't for those girls . . .'

Catherine was curious, 'You said you've only come to know them recently, however did this come about?'

Sheila laughed, 'It's a long story, I will tell you. But, tell me, whatever happened to Michael, where did he go?'

Catherine smiled, 'He was adopted into a lovely family in America. I didn't know until recently, but he had been searching for me for many years. He travelled to Ireland for months at a time, looking for me, to no avail. In the meantime, he met a woman in Skibbereen, they married and had three children.'

Sheila smiled and felt so much joy for Catherine. She put her hand on her heart and said, 'Ah Catherine, you're a grandmother! That's wonderful.'

Catherine smiled, 'I am. Michael fought and eventually found records of my being shipped off to Australia. His search took him there. He spent so many months looking, and although he had such trouble getting to the truth, he eventually found me. Over the course of a couple years, he moved me to Skibbereen. I arrived only just a few months ago.'

Sheila still sat there with her hand on her heart, 'Ah Catherine, I'm so happy for you. My God, after all those years.'

Catherine smiled, 'And all of the horrible years were wiped away in a single stroke as soon as I laid my eyes on him, they were.' She continued, 'Sheila, the nuns at Blessboro told Michael that I had died. They lied. They truly are horrible human beings, so they are. Michael had heard from others how they lied and hid the truth from so many women and children. Come here, tell me, have you ever looked for your girls, did you do any searching?'

Sheila shook her head, 'Ah I searched as much as I knew how, Catherine. After the nuns told me the girls had died, I went to Father McLennan and he confirmed what Sister Mary Francis told me, that they'd passed. That was the end of the line for me. I didn't know where else to go, where else would I go but to the head of the church? I didn't think he would lie as well, I had to believe it. But, in my heart I never allowed myself to truly believe it. Over the years I searched other places, but never came up with anything. Some days I thought it was really the only way I could cope was just to think they were alive.'

Catherine looked at the photo on the table of Sheila holding her girls. 'It doesn't make any sense that they were fine one day and gone the next, I do hope they lived, Sheila.'

Sheila slowly shook her head, 'Ah Catherine, in my heart of hearts, I never truly believed they died. For 59 years now I have carried this with me, I have always felt it in my heart and soul that they're both alive on this earth. I've always held it close to myself that had they really died, I would have felt it, I would have felt it to my core, so I would.'

Catherine got up and knelt down in front of Sheila's chair and put her hand on Sheila's, 'Let's find them Sheila, let's find your girls, I'll help you.'

Sheila had tears welling up in her eyes, 'My God Catherine, I wouldn't know where to begin with the walls the nuns built, the barricade of lies they fabricated. Backed by the strength of the Catholic Church and our government hand in hand. I don't know if I have it in me to fight them. You of all people know what they're like. The Catholic Church still has a stronghold here, they keep the records under lock and key, and their lies are so tightly woven. I don't know if I have the strength to face them, let alone fight them.'

Catherine kept hold of Sheila's hands, 'You don't have to do it alone, I will be right by your side. My Michael will help you, Sheila. He's a solicitor. He's made it his life's work to find me, and now he's helping others; he's fighting the Catholic Church. He's forcing the government to come to terms with what the Church has done.'

Sheila felt a lightness in her heart, 'My God, Catherine, would he do that for me? Could he really find out what happened to them?'

Catherine got up, and smiled, 'Yes, I know for certain he'll help you, I know for a fact he will find out what happened to your girls.'

Sheila stood up and gave Catherine a hug, then looked her in the eyes, 'Thank God he found you Catherine, bless his heart.'

Owen was driving down the road away from Sheila's house, 'What was that Aye, what about the sticker on Patrick's car?'

Aelish looked at Owen, 'It was the same sticker that was on the back of the car that lost the lottery ticket. It was a rental car. I'm thinking you may have been right when you said they were probably tourists and they're long gone now and our search is futile.'

Owen was thinking, 'Not necessarily Aye, mam rented a car when hers was in the shop not too long ago, remember?'

Aelish shrugged, 'Yeah, I suppose ye'r right again, pest. Just don't get a big head now that you've been right twice in your life. I just don't know if we're ever going to find the Sheila Murphy that lost that ticket, seems a waste of time, doesn't it?'

Owen laughed, 'Listen to you, it's only been a couple of weeks and all of the possibilities haven't been exhausted. I still have a few ideas in me head, don't you worry, we'll all be getting a reward if I have anything to do with it.'

Aelish laughed, 'Listen to you; we, we, we, it's funny how you just nuzzled your way into this whole situation, isn't it, O?'

Owen laughed, 'Yep that's me, a nuzzler. You'll thank me when I find the loser, I mean winner, I'll get my due reward.'

Aelish sniggered, 'Whatever, you haven't come up with a whole lot so far.'

Owen shook his finger in the air, 'Ah, but I will, I will come up with something this week, I will.'

Aelish smirked, 'We'll see.'

Patrick was driving blindly. He looked at Maeve, 'You'll have to tell me where to go, I haven't got a clue.'

Maeve smiled, 'Ah, you're grand, keep on straight ahead. On your right, you'll see a sign that says 'Dunboy Castle,' then you'll see the large, dilapidated stone entrance, pull in there.' Patrick pulled in and drove down a narrow, winding road with eight foot tall hedges on either side. In the distance were castle ruins.

Patrick pointed, 'Is that where we're going?'

Maeve nodded, 'Keep following this road.'

Patrick drove down the rutted dirt road. The once stately, Gothic Revival structure of Puxley Mansion was up on a hill overlooking the lake below. It was dark and boarded up, looking ominous on the weed strewn hill. Patrick parked on the grass by the lake. He turned off the engine and looked at Maeve, 'I've seen you a few times now, and this is the first time we're alone, it's nice.'

Maeve smiled nervously, 'Yes, it is, now let's go and explore the ruins before the sun is gone.' She got out of the car and started to walk quickly towards the ruins.

Patrick got out of the car and followed her, 'Wait up!' She started to run. Patrick laughed, 'You're joking, I was a track star, you'll never outrun me!'

Maeve glanced back as she ran and yelled, 'The operative word is 'was' I *am* a track star! Good luck!' She was laughing as she was running and was determined to outrun him. Patrick was laughing as well, equally determined to catch her. When Maeve got closer to the ruins, she found it was barricaded with construction fencing. She slipped through a small opening, thinking that would slow Patrick down--he wouldn't fit through the opening as easily as she did. As she started to run up the hill to the abandoned building, she heard Patrick yell, 'I'm stuck!'

She looked back. Patrick was wedged between the two metal fences, one leg on either side. He was looking down, trying to free himself. Maeve came running back and bent down to help free his leg. He grabbed her as he came to her side of the fence. 'Gotcha!' He took her in his arms.

Maeve put her arms up to push him away, 'You cheat!'

Patrick put both of his hands on her face, 'I'd do anything to catch you. You are so beautiful, Maeve.' She melted into his arms as she looked up at him, and he kissed her very slowly on her lips. She felt weak in the knees, his kiss numbed her mind. She was worlds away in his arms, kissing his lips. Patrick stopped kissing her, looked at her and said, 'You wanna show me this haunted looking place now?'

Maeve felt like she needed to snap back into reality. She shook her head a bit and said, 'Right. This way.' They walked around the grounds of Puxley Mansion; the Gothic Revival structure looked even more eerie up close, with dark clouds forming in the sky.

Patrick was looking all around as he walked next to Maeve. 'This is a strange place, it looks like they started to make it into something and then they left it?'

Maeve nodded, 'They did indeed, mid-construction, up and left it, they did. It was being transformed into a beautiful five star hotel and spa overlooking the lake. It was during the Celtic Tiger economic boom in Ireland around 2005, then the recession hit, and that was that, most construction projects halted dead in their tracks, like this one, left for ruins. This old building has been sitting like this, all boarded up and fenced off since around 2008. This is one of the most expensive modern day ruins of Ireland, it is.'

Patrick was amazed, 'It's pretty cool though, it looks spooky and haunted.'

Maeve laughed, 'Ah, there are many places in Ireland that are haunted. This may be one of them, you never know.' They walked around the abandoned grounds of the mansion, peering into windows where they could. They were up on a ledge looking into a great room, both of them cupping their hands around their eyes to see inside the mansion windows. Maeve was looking at Patrick intently peering into the window.

She poked him and screamed, 'Ghost!' Patrick was startled. Maeve was laughing, 'Haha, that scared you!' He jumped down off the ledge and offered Maeve his hand to help her jump down.

When she landed on the ground next to him, he took her in his arms again and said, 'You don't scare me.'

Maeve laughed, 'Ah, but I may scare you off.'

Patrick looked her in the eyes, 'Never.'

Chapter Eighteen

Sheila and Catherine had a bit to drink and were chatting away. Catherine got a glimmer in her eye and said to Sheila, 'Do you remember starting that fire at Blessboro?'

Sheila started to laugh, 'Ah do I! How could I forget? Thank God we didn't get caught, that would have been a right beating that.'

Catherine raised her eyebrows and said in a sarcastic tone, 'You reckon? Too bad we didn't 'not' get caught every time.'

Sheila tipped her head and nodded, 'Yes, that would have been better, but trying to escape that place was worth the beatings. The fantasy alone was worth it, kept me sane, it did. Good God Catherine, as horrible as it was for both of us in that prison, I honestly don't know if I would have made it out of there alive, or sane for that matter, without you.'

Catherine agreed, 'Ah, I've thought the same many times over the years, pet. I certainly wouldn't have made it had you not been there. God knows we did nothing wrong. The God I've come to know over the years, anyway. Not the God those nuns believed in. You know Sheila, I've suppressed so much over the years, I feel free to talk to you now. You're the only other person, my only friend who went through the same torturous time. My Michael is angry he didn't find me sooner, that he didn't find out years ago about the atrocities at Blessboro and all the similar institutions. He said he would have sought justice, but most of those nuns are dead now. Michael says he would have given anything to prosecute them all for murder and aiding and abetting in torture, kidnapping and imprisonment.'

Sheila was shaking her head, 'My God, I know, Catherine. I've been keeping it all inside myself; sometimes that seems to make things worse, that does. When you keep something like that inside your head for a lifetime, it burns your soul, festers a life of its own so it does.' Catherine agreed, 'Jesus, the shame they made us feel.'

Sheila responded, 'Ah I know and we believed it, shame will keep you in prison if you allow it.'

Catherine said, 'The past is the past and there's nothing we can do about it. It's strange really, to think about how different the world is today, it's more different than people realise. Everything's out in the open now, anything goes. It was quite the opposite in our day, wasn't it, Sheila? Absolutely nothing was talked about, nothing of a personal nature anyway, nothing of a sexual nature, nothing about your body, especially a woman's body, nothing.'

Catherine looked away, thinking, as she spoke, 'Ah it's almost the complete opposite today as it was when we were growing up. We really were living in the dark ages. Remember we used to talk about how we didn't even know we were having sex? We didn't even know what a penis was, for God's sake!' They both started to laugh.

Sheila sighed, 'Ah sure, but we were told that we *did* know what we were doing. After the fact, we did. Good God, I remember how confused I was, did it once is all I did. I'd had a bit to drink. To me it was like an extension of kissing, it just happened, it just seemed so natural. I honestly didn't know I was doing anything wrong and I certainly didn't know it would be the cause of getting pregnant! It's amazing to think this now, but you know it to be true. I know it was just one time with you as well Catherine, I know it was the same situation with you, we had no idea, did we now? Thank God times have changed. I wouldn't wish those days of darkness upon anyone.

Catherine, I'm sure you remember when we both first got our periods, no one even uttered a word what that was all about either, do you remember?'

Catherine raised her eyebrows, 'Vividly. The only thing my mother said to me was: "You're a woman now." That was it. I hadn't a clue what was going on or what the hell she was talking about, or what to do for that matter. Thank God I had an older sister who just handed me supplies, and said: "Here, use these when it happens." That was it and all that she said to me. I wouldn't dare ask any questions, you just didn't, as you know. It's all a tragedy really, for all those years, all that was *never* talked about. Nothing from our parents, nothing from school, we really hadn't a clue about anything now, did we?'

Sheila shook her head, 'Thank God I had you, Catherine. Not having any sisters, I wasn't told a thing, even though you didn't tell me much either, at least you warned me that it was going to happen! My God, everything was so secretive; you couldn't speak about anything to anyone about anything! And it was all directed by the Church, all the ways to control the masses, all the ways to control women. Thank God they don't have as much of a stronghold on this country as they once did, they fecked it up right, so they did.'

Catherine howled, 'Ah, spoken like a true Irish woman!'

She raised her glass, 'Here's to the Catholic Church!'

Sheila laughed, 'God help them! C'mere Catherine, so you didn't have any contact with your family at all after Blessboro, nothing from anyone over the years?'

Catherine shook her head, 'No, my father wouldn't allow it, he was very strict, if you recall. Devout Catholic he was. He told my sisters that I was dead to them. He told them if they ever heard anything from me, or had anything to do with me, they would be cursed by God himself! Not a word was to be uttered, not a thought was to be had of me. Listening to anything that was ever said about me was considered a sin and it was to be stopped, it was all horrible, really it was. My sisters and I were very close, it tore us to shreds, but none of us had a choice.'

Sheila looked sad, 'Horribly common as well. It was ingrained in everyone's minds that we were the dregs of society, as were our children if they weren't adopted. Think of all the poor souls that were left in the orphanages, never adopted. Those poor children were forever looked at as bastards and lesser humans, and they were told their mothers were whores, and then they were worked to death in the institutions. Honestly Catherine, no one really knows what so many of us went through at the hands of those nuns, no one truly knows unless they experienced it themselves. The priests were just as much to blame, if not worse, guided by the church that was also the State, guided by greed and archaic faith, a twisted web it was. My God, the magnitude of it all, no one had a clue what was going on and who was orchestrating it all. It's almost as if everyone was brainwashed, isn't it? Thank God my parents could think for themselves, it's the only thing that saved me really. I was very lucky with my father, probably because I was his only child, his little girl. He was certain that no one knew about my predicament, other than the priest who picked me up, and the nuns. He was right that they were the only ones who knew; the Catholic Church tried to keep it that way as you know. Once we were put inside the prison walls of Blessboro, we didn't leave until *they* saw fit. I'm so fortunate that my father took me back--we know our mothers didn't have a say in anything back then. My father decided to ignore the entire situation; he stuck with his story that I was taking care of an aunt in England. I think he actually started to believe that story himself. We didn't even have any relatives in England! I remember clear as a bell the day the priest came to this house to pick me up and take me away, I remember like it was yesterday. I was scared to death, so I was. My mother was crying in the other room, she wouldn't come out to say goodbye to me, she just refused. My father put me and my suitcase into the car with the priest. He honestly said, 'Off you go, good trip, see you then, bye bye!' I think he truly made himself believe I was visiting relatives, going on a holiday! Anyway, if I promised him that I'd never utter a word about 'it' to anyone, ever, not to him, not to my mother, I would be allowed to come back after the "ordeal" was taken care of. That was that, so I agreed. I came back as if nothing had happened, then Martin returned, and we got married shortly after that.'

Catherine smiled, 'You really were very lucky. I feel I'm lucky as well. We're lucky we made it out alive--as we know, quite a few didn't. I'm thankful that we're here today, Sheila. I'm so thankful to be sitting with you here right now, this is truly wonderful.'

Sheila smiled, 'All the roads that are taken in life, lead you to exactly where you're meant to be today.'

Catherine raised her empty glass into the air, 'I'll drink to that! But I won't be able to drive.'

Sheila laughed, 'Ah nonsense, you're not driving anywhere, you're staying here tonight, I insist. I have a spare room, my old bedroom if you recall, with a very comfortable bed in it, you'll be grand. It'll bring back old memories of staying here when we were girls. My parents loved you, Catherine. Sadly, your name was off limits around here as well, part of my deal when they heard you sinned the great sin as well!'

Catherine rolled her eyes. 'Ah, it's all water under the bridge, isn't it Sheila? The past is the past.' She held up her empty glass, 'Right then, let's do something about *this* little problem.'

Sheila laughed, 'Ah, that can be easily fixed.'

Catherine watched Sheila as she went into the kitchen, 'What brought you to Skibbereen then, Sheila? I don't think we would have found each other had you not come into the shop with those girls that day. I've kept to myself so much over the years; I don't think I would have sought you out.'

Sheila came back into the room with the bottle of whiskey and filled Catherine's glass, 'I'm afraid I've been the same over the years, Catherine, I've kept very much to myself. It was what we were taught really, wasn't it. I'll never forget how many times the nuns would remind us not to say a word to anyone about anything that went on in that home, otherwise life would be worse for us than it already was, and the authorities would come after us. They put the fear of God into us, so they did. When Martin and I married and found out we couldn't have more children, we just kept to ourselves. After Martin died, I continued that way of life. I'd say I've had a very quiet, contemplative life, so I have.'

Catherine was still curious, 'So, why have you become friends with these youngsters recently, and what were you doing in Skibbereen?'

Sheila sighed, ''Tis a bit of a long story, and you mustn't repeat it to anyone.'

Catherine chuckled, 'I've kept all of your secrets close.'

Sheila smiled, 'Yes, I know, you were always true to your word and a fiercely loyal friend, even when we were kids. You were always my best friend, you know that. It's a strange thing, for all the decades we've been separated, it seems like just yesterday we were together.'

Catherine agreed, 'My God, I know. It was the same with my Michael, even though I hadn't seen him since he was a baby. He was still my baby, a six foot tall, hairy baby with a full beard, but my baby just the same. I felt as though he had been with me all along, which in my mind he always was. I want that for you, Sheila. I want you to know for certain about your girls.'

Sheila smiled, 'As do I.'

Catherine continued, 'We will sort that out just as soon as I get back and talk to Michael. Now then, back to Skibbereen, why was I so lucky to run into you that day?'

Sheila laughed, 'That *was* lucky; I'm thankful we tucked into that shop.' She went on to tell Catherine the entire story, starting with the knock on the door of her cottage with the two uniform clad girls telling their tale of the lottery ticket they had found.

Catherine loved it, 'What a great treasure hunt!'

Sheila agreed, 'Yes, it's been quite grand, actually. I really had gotten so used to being on my own for so many years, I had forgotten how good it was to have people in my life, and to feel useful.'

Catherine agreed, ''Tis grand to feel useful, isn't it? I hadn't felt useful to anyone for so many years. It's been lovely being back here. Michael needs me, I need him, and my grandkids need me as much as I need them. My life is completely different, just changed in the last few months it did; my life in Australia pales in comparison to my wonderful life now.'

Sheila looked happy, 'That's wonderful, Catherine. My life has felt very different for the last few weeks as well--that's strange--not exactly the same situation, but happiness just the same, and a different outlook on life. Renewed hope, so it is.'

Catherine assured Sheila, 'Michael will help you, it's turned into a passion of his. Ever since he found me, he realised what a profound effect it had on both of us--changed our entire lives, it did. Ever since, he's wanted to help make a difference in other people's lives. He knows the injustices that were done, he knows he can't right the wrongs, but he can help the survivors find each other.'

Sheila smiled, 'Ah, good man, fair play to him! There are thousands upon thousands of us, but sadly so many have passed.'

Catherine interjected, 'I know that, and Michael knows that; he wants to help the ones that are still alive, before they pass, before it's too late.'

Sheila looked out the window, 'I don't know if my girls are out there, Catherine. Whether they are or not, they've never left my heart.'

Catherine agreed, 'Michael never left my heart either, a child never leaves your heart, and they're embedded in your soul forever.' She looked up at the ceiling, thinking, 'Back to Skibbereen, maybe I can help with this treasure hunt. Just when I arrived, I heard someone won the lottery in West Cork. That's big news you know, local wins, it was a few million if I remember correctly.'

Sheila shrugged, 'Ah sure you could help, I don't see the harm in it, I'll talk to Maeve, though, she's leading this search.'

Catherine replied, 'If there is anything I can do to help, do let me know.'

Sheila tapped her finger on her chin thinking. 'Actually, you could help, Catherine. Could you find out the name of the person that won the lottery in your area? Could you find out without making too much of a fuss about it?'

Catherine laughed, 'You know how people are in Ireland, if it's any sort of trivial gossip, everyone knows about it. I probably wouldn't have to ask too many people. Yes, I can do that. I'll let you know in a day or two what I find out.'

Sheila smiled, 'Brilliant, that's grand, I'm sure that would be fine with Maeve. I can honestly say I don't care if they ever find the winner of that ticket, you see, so long as they keep coming back here. I've been having such gas with them, it's changed my life, so it has.'

Catherine smiled, 'Ah, change is in the air I'd say. That's it then. I will help with that; I can do it discreetly I'm sure. In the meantime, I think we should have a bit of *craic* ourselves Sheila, don't you think? I'd say we deserve it. We're only an hour and a half away from each other now, I think we should make a habit of this visiting.'

Sheila smiled, 'I couldn't agree more. Now then, I think we've both had our share of the drink, I'd say we could use some sleep.'

Catherine stood up, 'Right, that was enough of the good stuff, we must save some for another time. Goodnight my dear friend, goodnight.'

Sheila watched her friend walk to her room, 'Sleep well, let me know if you need anything, and please make yourself at home. 'Tis grand to see you again Catherine, such a blessing.'

Catherine looked back at Sheila and smiled, ''Tis.'

Maeve ran away from Patrick around to the back of the castle grounds; Patrick followed. A truck was driving slowly along the road adjacent to the ruins. Maeve quickly threw herself against the dirty old wall as if on a covert mission. She gestured to Patrick to quickly do the same. He obliged. He ran, ducking and dodging as if avoiding gunfire, and threw himself up against the wall. He stood snug with his back and his head against the wall, his arms spread as if he were holding on for dear life.

Maeve burst out laughing watching him, looked at the truck again and gasped, 'Shhhhhhh, we're not supposed to be here, that's probably security. We could be jailed for trespassing.'

Patrick was amused by her. He knew they couldn't be jailed, and he'd seen that same truck earlier, with a logo for a tree trimming service. He went along with her anyway. He whispered, 'Keep to the wall and we won't be seen. Follow me. Don't make a sound.' They crept along the side of the castle and came to an enclave. Patrick quickly pulled Maeve into the opening, 'Let's wait here until they pass.' He put his finger on her lips and quietly whispered, 'Shhhhhh.'

Patrick popped his head outside the enclave and gasped, pretending he heard something. He whispered harshly, 'Someone's coming!' Maeve's heart was pounding. Patrick put his finger to his mouth, 'Shhhhh, I'll go have a look, wait here.' He went outside the enclave just a bit, then came running back. He gestured quickly to Maeve to hide in the corner as he whispered frantically, 'Oh my God, someone's coming!' The two of them hid in the dark corner of the enclave. Patrick grabbed Maeve and held her close to him, pretending he was listening outside the enclave, 'Can you hear them? I hear footsteps.' He held her head on his chest and covered her ear so she would have trouble hearing. He lifted his hand and whispered, 'They're getting closer, don't move.'

She couldn't hear a thing; she was trying to move his hand from her ear and her head from his chest but he held her tight. She struggled a bit to look up at him and she caught a glimpse of his face and saw a bit of a smile. She quickly got out of his hold and playfully hit him on his chest, 'Go 'way ye langer, there's no one at all, is there now?!'

He laughed, 'Nope.'

Maeve ran away from him, out of the enclave and back to the grounds surrounding the ruins. She yelled back at Patrick,

'Let's go and watch the sunset down by the lake!' Patrick ran after her, down to the water's edge.

There were a few large boulders sitting by the lake; Maeve climbed up the highest one and sat down. She looked out at the wreck of a fishing boat, half submerged, and the small islands that speckled the water. The sun was setting near the mountain in the distance. It was calm, quiet and peaceful. Patrick came bounding up the rocks and sat down next to her, 'My God, this really is the most beautiful country, I don't want to leave.'

Maeve looked at him, 'Then don't.'

Patrick laughed, 'I have to go to school in the fall.'

Maeve continued to look him in the eyes and shrugged, 'Go to school here.'

Patrick sat there gazing quietly into Maeve's eyes, 'I'd give anything to do that, but I don't think it's possible.'

Maeve smiled and looked hopeful, 'Anything's possible if you really want it, you just make it happen 'tis all. Besides, if your grandparents were born in Ireland, you're an Irish citizen through birth naturalization, you could live here, you could go to school here. But you can only go to UCC, only to the University College Cork.'

Patrick looked confused, 'Really? Why? I know about the citizenship thing, but why would I only be able to attend that school?'

Maeve laughed, 'Because that's where I'm going, I hope to be anyway.'

Patrick smiled, 'Well, I wouldn't think of going anywhere else then.' He inched his way closer to Maeve, and put his arm around her as they sat on the rock, watching the sunset.

Maeve leaned her head towards him and whispered, 'This is lovely. I'm glad we met.'

Patrick kissed the top of her head, 'I'm glad we met as well, Maeve. It was meant to be, it was as if I was guided towards you.'

Maeve smiled, 'I do believe everything happens for a reason, for reasons we don't know at the time. I'd say that wise Sheila had something to do with all of this.'

Patrick held Maeve a bit closer, 'Well, if she had anything to do with us meeting, then she is a wise woman indeed.'

Maeve looked up at Patrick, 'It's odd how things happen though, how people you meet can change the course of your life, and how an accidental meeting, or a search for something else can guide you to find something entirely different, something you were looking for, yet you didn't know you were looking for it, or him…'

Patrick turned towards her and kissed her on the lips, 'You are a beautiful creature.'

Maeve smiled and kissed him back, then she jerked her head back, 'Creature? I've never been called a creature before!'

He kissed her again, 'A beautiful creature you are, I've never met anyone like you Maeve, I'm so glad we met.'

Maeve snuggled in closer. 'Me too.' They watched the sunset in silence.

Chapter Nineteen

Maeve and Aelish walked into school, saying to Mr. O'Sullivan in unison, 'Good morning Mr. O'Sullivan.'

Mr. O'Sullivan smiled and looked at his watch, 'Good morning ladies, lovely weather we're having this morning, try to be on time tomorrow morning then, off you go, have a lovely day.' The girls ignored him and continued walking into school.

Maeve looked back at Mr. O'Sullivan, 'We're not late.'

Aelish laughed, 'Yes we are Maeve, the bell's already rung. You a bit groggy this morning are ye missus? Out late last night were ye?'

Maeve shook her head, 'Not at all, but I was up late revising, are you all set for your exams, Aye?'

Aelish shrugged, 'As ready as I'll be, I've got my toughest in Physics. I need to do some more revision tonight and over the weekend.'

Maeve said, 'So you probably don't want to go to Sheila's after school then?'

Aelish shook her head, 'No, you go on without me.'

They were about to go their separate ways to their classes. Aelish stopped and looked at Maeve, 'Hey Maeve, I was thinking about what Owen was saying about that Skibbereen Sheila Murphy that lost her ring, we still didn't find out if she lost anything else, wasn't she supposed to call you? Remember you gave your number to her daughter at that petrol station? Did she ever call you?'

Maeve looked at Aelish and pulled out her phone, 'I forgot all about that, I did get a call from someone a couple days ago,

I didn't recognise the number so I didn't answer and they didn't leave a message. It was a Skibbereen number, I wonder if it was her? I'll call it back and find out.'

They started to walk their separate ways to their classes. Maeve said, 'See you at break, I'll call her then.'

Aelish waved to Maeve, 'Right, see you then.'

They met in the common area after their classes. Maeve was on her phone; Aelish came out and listened to the conversation: 'Hi, my name is Maeve Mulligan, I met your daughter last week at her work, at the Topaz Petrol station. I understand you lost something when you were up north?'

The woman on the phone was ecstatic, 'Ahhhh, did you find my ring?'

Maeve apologized, 'Ah no, sorry, I'm afraid not. Did you lose anything else that weekend?'

The woman was a bit annoyed, 'Wasn't it enough to lose my ring? What are you on about, "did I lose anything else", I lost my ring! Oh, I nearly lost my relationship, and my head, is that what you're after? Telling me I've lost me mind are ye?'

Maeve looked bug-eyed at Aelish, 'Ah, no, I'm sorry, I didn't mean anything, losing your ring was enough. We can help you look for it and give you a ring, I mean a phone call if we come up with anything. Have a lovely day. Bye-bye, bye-bye, bye-bye.' She hung up her phone and started to laugh, 'I don't think that woman lost anything else but her ring, well, and maybe her mind.'

Aelish was thinking, who's to say whoever lost the ticket is even aware of losing it? 'Maeve, what do you say we give up on this whole thing? Whoever bought and lost that ticket could be long gone, we may never find them you know, but we did try.'

Maeve looked at Aelish, 'I've thought about it Aye, I think we can keep looking, you never know. Maybe this weekend we can find some more Sheila Murphys to explore.'

Aelish said, 'I can't Maeve, my mam is planning to take Owen and me away for the weekend, to the Flanagan farm.'

Maeve smiled, 'Ah, you'll see your grandparents, that'll be grand. Tell them hello from me. I'll keep looking myself, I'm not quite ready to give up just yet. I'll have a chat with Sheila after school today and see if we can come up with anything else. I think she's quite keen to keep looking, she seems more into it than us!'

Aelish laughed, 'Ya, she's loved this whole thing! We got her out anyway, didn't we?'

Maeve smiled, 'We got her out all right, and we got to meet her, I'm pretty happy about that. I'll let you know if we come up with anything new.'

Aelish nodded, 'Sounds like a plan. I'll see you in the morning, I'll catch a lift home with Owen and Liam.' Maeve said goodbye and went on to her next class.

Chapter Twenty

Sheila was up early; she cleaned the kitchen listening to the soft music of Enya. She put the kettle on and went outside to fetch wood and turf for the fire. When she heard the whistle blowing from outside, she came running, hoping not to wake Catherine. By the time Sheila made it back into the cottage, Catherine was in the kitchen turning the kettle off and sorting out the teapot and cups.

Sheila walked into the cottage as the song, *"Marble Halls"* was playing. 'Jesus, that's a haunting tune that one, isn't it?' she said, 'Reminds me of that young nun, what was her name, Sister Evangeline, remember she was always humming or singing this song?'

Catherine looked up, 'Yes, I do remember that, and her. Sister Evie we'd call her if Mother Superior wasn't around.'

'She was the *only* nun', said Sheila, 'that seemed to have an ounce of decency and kindness in her body. She's the one who gave me this photo, the only photo I have of my girls.' She picked up the framed black and white photo of herself holding her twin girls, in matching white dresses, in the back garden of Blessboro.

Catherine took the picture frame from Sheila, 'You know, that's exactly how I pictured you over the years. Hard to believe the last time we saw each other was when we were only sixteen years old.'

Sheila smiled, 'The strange thing is, I don't feel like you've aged a bit, funny how you look the same to me.'

Catherine laughed a hearty laugh, 'Ha, funny is right, your eyesight is clearly gone! I know what you mean though, you're the same person to me as well.' She handed the picture frame back to Sheila, 'Your girls were beautiful, Sheila, they really were. But, how could they not be, with a stunner mother.'

Sheila took the picture frame, 'Ah stop. Now then, 'tis a lovely morning, how would you feel about having something to eat and a good walk before you leave?'

Catherine said, 'That sounds like a perfect plan.' They sat at the kitchen table and had their tea and muffins. Catherine, thinking about the day ahead, said, 'Sheila, how do you feel about coming down with me today, that way you could have a conversation with Michael, and you could meet my grandchildren.'

Sheila put her hand on her chest and smiled, 'My God, I haven't seen Michael since he was a baby, but I remember him as if it were yesterday. I often think of how we always had the three of them together during the visiting hour, it was always the three of them it was. It's astonishing what little time we had with them, but the memories are so vivid.'

Catherine agreed, 'Indeed, the memories never seemed to fade. It always felt like it was just yesterday that I had last seen Michael. When he first came to Australia a few months ago, it was as if I'd been with him all the time, all throughout his life.'

Sheila said, 'It's the same with you Catherine, so many years have passed, yet I feel like I was with you yesterday, strange that.'

They finished their tea and muffins. Sheila stood up to clear the dishes. 'Right, it's a beautiful sunny morning, what's left of the morning anyway, let's go out and get some fresh air and exercise. I have boots for you to wear if you like.'

Catherine smiled, 'I remember we were always the same size in everything; if that hasn't changed, that would be grand.' They got dressed, went across the field to the creek and walked along the narrow foot path.

Sheila stopped at a clearing. 'You know, I've never told a soul this, never thought I would mind you, for a lifetime I've been made to feel I couldn't utter a word about anything. I feel like I was imprisoned physically and mentally first, then it was just mentally, trapped in my mind with no one to speak to about anything, but here you are, Catherine, the only one I've ever confided in. I feel free, I feel like I can say anything to you, I can free my imprisoned mind!' She pointed to the ground by the creek, 'This is the very spot where Martin and I "did it"! And it was *fun*!'

Catherine started laughing heartily. 'I think you should yell it for the world to hear!'

Sheila laughed, 'I had SEX! Yes I did! Right here for the first time in my life! I hadn't a clue what that moment of passion would lead to! Honest to God, those wretched nuns were probably so miserable because they never had sex!'

Catherine smiled, 'Yes they were, they were probably jealous of all of us that we actually got to experience it and we had fun doing it!'

Sheila raised her eyebrows, 'Yes, but they made damn sure that we paid for it though, didn't they? Even so, I always felt I had something, I had a wonderful memory of something beautiful and natural that shouldn't have been so shamed. I always carried the memory of Martin with me. It made me feel stronger, it helped me get through the misery it did.'

Catherine was looking at Sheila, 'You were lucky you had the love Sheila, you're so fortunate that love continued throughout your life and he was beside you over the years. Mine was, as you know, just a summer fling--you remember him--Eugene. Nothing happened to him for doing the same thing I did; we both had a bit of fun, but he didn't have to pay the price as I did, he didn't suffer, he wasn't locked up, he was free, he went on to marry, have children, he wasn't imprisoned, he wasn't punished, he wasn't tortured. He did nothing to help me, or Michael for that matter.'

Sheila put her arm around Catherine, 'I know Catherine, that was such an injustice, it's sad how it was all on our shoulders, and we didn't have a say about anything.'

Catherine continued, 'I'm the lucky one today though, Michael is amazing, he's had a wonderful life. It's Eugene's loss that he never knew him, that he doesn't know him today, or me, he hasn't a clue. No fault of his own, his hands were tied just as much as mine were; he was warned not to breathe a word of it to anyone as well. We were at the mercy of the Church we were.'

Sheila was curious, 'Did you ever find out where Eugene ended up?'

Catherine shrugged, 'No, I didn't, he could be dead for all I know. It's sad really, he was the only man I was ever with--my entire life he was the only man I was ever with. I've been leading a nun's life, you could say.'

Sheila looked at the creek and yelled, 'At least had sex!'

Catherine laughed and looked around to see if anyone could hear.

Sheila laughed, 'Don't worry, no one's around for miles. I feel an awakening, Catherine, I feel like we still have some time left in this life. I think you and I should have a bit of fun. I think we can recapture a time in our lives when we were happy and free. I think we should find men to date!'

Catherine howled, 'That's preposterous! I've never thought of dating, who would want to date this auld thing?'

Sheila playfully pushed Catherine, 'Stop! There are plenty of men out there! You're a beautiful auld thing!' She hooked Catherine's arm, 'Let's keep walking. I think anything's possible, you know there's a whole world of men out there on the computer. They have dating sites for senior citizens. I think I saw a site called "senior citizens for sex dot com".'

Catherine pushed Sheila, 'Go 'way! You're lying!'

Sheila laughed, 'Okay, so I made that up, but there really are specific dating sites online; we could even go on double dates and have a bit of fun. We can do anything we want now, can't we? I think we should live a little. I think we should get into a little mischief together again, what do you say?'

Catherine laughed, 'I'd say I'm up for anything at this point, Sheila, life is short, and it's getting shorter every day.' She continued, 'All right then, let's have a bit of fun. Will you come back to Skibbereen with me today? I have two beds in my room at Michael's house, the other one is yours anytime you like.'

Sheila smiled, 'That sounds lovely. Would you mind spending the day here? I have Maeve coming over after school for tea. We could leave right after that, which may be around 3pm, how does that sound?'

Catherine said, 'That sounds grand. Let's enjoy this weather, get a good walk in, then I'll take you to lunch. I'd like to go to O'Neill's, if you're up for it.'

Sheila smiled, 'That sounds perfect, they always had good food and they do pull a good pint.'

Catherine felt very happy, 'Perfect.'

The two women walked the length of the creek, across the country road and down to the sea. They walked along the wet sand adjacent to the boulders lining the shore leading towards the village of Allihies.

Sheila stopped at the boulders, 'Let's sit down here for a moment and soak up this sun while it's out.' They sat down, closed their eyes and both put their faces towards the sun.

Sheila took a deep breath, 'Don't you love that smell?'

Catherine did the same, 'Ah yes, it's home to me, so it is, that's the smell of Ireland. I missed this sweet seaweed smell and the crisp air. It was entirely too hot for me in Australia, miserable really, I never got used to that heat, or the humidity, horrible really. This feels right.'

Sheila looked at Catherine, 'Ah, this does feel right.'

Catherine smiled, 'It's so good to be back, you have no idea. Now then, let's head to O'Neill's, I'm a bit peckish.'

Sheila was surprised, 'Oh, I didn't think we were going to go directly there, I'm a wreck, surely we should go back to my house, fix ourselves up and then drive over there?'

Catherine was taken aback, 'You look grand. Why do you care what you look like? I certainly don't! Besides, I don't know about you, but, I'm having a pint or two and the walk back would do me some good afterwards.'

Sheila shrugged, 'Okay, off we go then, should be about twenty more minutes.'

Catherine got up off the rock and stretched, 'This is a perfect day! The food better be as good as you say.'

Sheila smiled, 'Ah, I'm sure it's grand, you won't be disappointed.' They walked along the beach and up the hill to Allihies.

When they entered O'Neill's, John was behind the bar. His face lit up when the women walked in. Looking at Sheila, he said, 'Look what the Lord just graced upon my eyes.'

Catherine looked at Sheila with her eyebrows raised.

Sheila blushed, 'Hello John, this is my friend Catherine, she's visiting in from Skibbereen.'

When Catherine said hello and asked how he was doing, John looked confused, 'Now that doesn't sound like a Skibbereen accent to me.'

Catherine smiled, 'I've been away for a while, but I'm back home now.'

John said, 'Well, welcome home! Ladies, what can I get you? Please sit down and make yourselves comfortable.

Sheila gestured towards the front of the pub by the small tables by the window, 'Would that suit, Catherine?'

Catherine replied, 'Perfect.' The two of them started to walk towards the small round tables and stools. Sheila asked Catherine if she fancied a stout. Catherine smiled, 'That sounds positively divine.'

Sheila looked back at John, 'We'll have two pints of Murphy's please John, and it's my friend Catherine's treat so her money must be good here.'

John shook his head, 'We'll see about that. You just make yourselves comfortable, I'll be there in a moment.'

The women sat down. Catherine looked curious, Sheila said, 'He wouldn't take my money last time I was in.' Catherine smiled, 'Ah, I'll get it, don't be silly, with all that whiskey of yours I drank last night, it's the least I could do. I reckon there's something going on between the two of you?'

Sheila laughed, 'Ah heavens no, I've only been in here once recently, otherwise it's been years since I've been here.'

Catherine put her hand on Sheila's arm, 'Ah pet, there's a mutual attraction between you two, it was utterly obvious.'

Sheila looked surprised, 'Really? Obvious? Hummm, I didn't think it was that obvious.' They both laughed. Sheila looked over at John behind the bar, 'He is pretty handsome, wouldn't you say?'

Catherine looked over. 'He is, and a bit younger than you I'd say, but you look younger than your years my friend, I say go for it.'

Sheila laughed, 'I'm not *going* for anything and I'm not *doing* anything. If anything happens, it will be his doing, not mine, I can assure you of that.'

John walked over with the two pints and coasters, and placed them in front of them, 'Here you are, ladies, lovely day out, the rain may hold off for a couple of hours now. Will you just be having the pints, or would you like a bit to eat?'

Sheila leaned towards John, 'I think we'll have a bit of your delicious food John, whatever you recommend.'

John mentioned a few items on the menu and a couple of specials, 'I'll let you two think about that and I'll be back to you in a moment.'

Catherine watched him walk away, leaned towards Sheila and whispered, 'I'll have whatever you recommend? If anything happens it will be John's doing? I'd say you're doing something right now, you flirt!'

Sheila laughed, 'Ah, it's just a bit of chat is all, I'm sure he didn't think it was flirting. Cheers my friend.' Catherine lifted her glass, '*Sláinte*. It was flirting.'

Sheila laughed, 'Ah stop, *sláinte*.'

John came back to the table and took their order. Catherine left to use the ladies' room. John stayed at the table and talked to Sheila, 'Pleasure to see you again Sheila.'

Sheila smiled, 'Yes, 'tis good to see you as well, John.'

John started to walk away as he said, 'I'll get your lunch started.' He stopped and looked back at Sheila, 'Say, Sheila, there's a new place that opened up in Castletownbere, would you like to have lunch with me there next week?'

Sheila smiled, 'That would be lovely, John.'

John looked happy, 'Brilliant, I'll pick you up at your house Tuesday at noon, how does that suit?'

Sheila nodded, 'I think that sounds like a date, I mean a plan, that sounds like a grand plan.'

John winked at Sheila, 'Don't be mistaken love, it's a date.'

She raised her eyebrows and smiled, 'Well then, it's a date, that will be grand John, thank you.' He walked away. Sheila was beaming.

As Catherine was on her way back, she looked at John leaving the table, then at Sheila's face, 'Did something just happen?'

Sheila was scarlet, 'I'd say so, we're going on a *date* next week--he clarified that it was a *date*.'

Catherine almost squealed; she leaned over, grabbed Sheila's arm and said in a loud whisper, 'You're *joking*! I leave you for two minutes and look what happens, my God! You're going on a date! That's brilliant! Do you think he has a brother or a friend? You can't be the only one getting some action around here now!'

Sheila pushed Catherine's arm, 'Stop! I'm not getting any action! It's a lunch date, let's see how it goes before I sort anything for you! Ah God, I hope it's not weird when he comes back with our food. I feel like a nervous teenager, this is all very strange.'

Catherine laughed, 'Ah, it's gas and it's exactly what you need, and it's about time!'

Sheila raised her glass, 'I think you're right. Here's to a bit of fun and mischief, it's never too late now, is it?' They clinked glasses.

Catherine smiled, 'Ah yes indeed. Hear, hear.'

John looked from behind the bar at the happy women. He smiled and winked at them. As they lifted their glasses towards him, Sheila whispered to Catherine, 'Ah yes, I think I'm ready for a bit of fun.'

Sheila and Catherine walked back to Sheila's house a bit tipsy. Sheila took Catherine's arm and said, 'Okay, we have Maeve calling to the house for tea in half an hour, let's pretend we're not drunk.'

Catherine laughed, 'I'm not drunk! Ah, we'll be grand. She'll never suspect, and I'll be fine to drive in an hour or two, not a problem.'

Sheila continued, 'Let's not say anything to Maeve about my date with John. I'm not sure I'm ready for anyone to know my business.'

Catherine said, 'Understood, mum's the word. So, is Maeve coming over to discuss the treasure hunt? We should tell her I'm going to help.'

Sheila nodded, 'Yes, she'll appreciate the help I'm sure. If we find this Sheila Murphy, I do hope it won't stop the girls from visiting.'

Catherine looked at Sheila, 'It doesn't have to stop, it seems you've forged a friendship that's beyond this search.'

Sheila smiled, 'Indeed. Now let's go in and have some tea.'

Maeve pulled up in front of Sheila's cottage. She got out of her car and heard laughter coming from inside. She smiled and walked up to the door, 'Hello?'

Sheila called towards the door, 'Come in dear, come in. We've just put the kettle on.'

Maeve said, 'I hope I'm not interrupting?'

Sheila got up and went towards Maeve, 'Not at all dear, not at all.' She gave her a hug, 'Please sit down. You remember Catherine?'

Maeve smiled, 'Yes, good to see you again. Have you two had a good day? It's beautiful out.'

Catherine said, 'It is indeed, we had a lovely walk, down to the sea and over to O'Neill's for lunch. The food was fantastic and the company was even better.'

Maeve smiled, 'That's grand. Did you see John?'

Sheila blushed, 'Yes, he didn't have any servers so he was tending to us himself.'

Maeve laughed, 'He always has servers, I'm sure he just wanted to serve you. I think he likes you, Sheila.'

Sheila couldn't help herself; she felt like she was going to burst, 'I think he does, Maeve, he asked me to go on a date next week and he clarified that it was indeed a date.'

Maeve was thrilled, 'Ah Sheila, that's fantastic! He's a lovely man. I'm happy he got the courage to ask you out. He's been on his own for so many years since his wife died.'

Sheila shook her head, 'Ah I know, shame that. He does seem like a lovely man. Let's not spread this around though, dear, you know how people talk.'

Maeve laughed, 'Times have changed a bit, Sheila. Sure, people talk, but it's not that nasty judgmental gossip it was years ago. But I won't say anything to anyone just the same.'

Sheila smiled, 'Thank you dear, c'mere now, let's have that cup of tea. Catherine is going to help us on our little treasure hunt if you don't mind.'

Maeve looked excited, 'If I mind? I think that's brilliant! Aelish is losing interest, that's fantastic that you'd like to help. What did you have in mind?'

Sheila went to the kitchen to get their tea.

Turning to Maeve, Catherine said, 'Sheila filled me in. What I'm going to do is find out the name of the person that won the lottery in Ballydehob. Sheila said this may lead us in the right direction. She said you found out there were two tickets with the exact same numbers chosen, not random numbers? That is a bit odd. I'll let you know what I find out this week. Or, Sheila's coming back with me this evening, she'll let you know if we find out anything over the next couple of days.'

Maeve smiled, 'That's brilliant you want to help with the search. We haven't found anything solid yet, but I'm convinced that we will, thanks for helping.'

Catherine smiled, 'Not a bother.'

Sheila walked in with a tray of tea and biscuits, and placed it on the table near the sofa. 'Now then, help yourselves, I baked these treats the other day and I must say they are divine.'

They drank their tea and enjoyed the biscuits. Sheila noticed the cold coming into the cottage; she got up and went to the fireplace, 'I go through more turf and wood than the average person I'm afraid; I'm going to go and fetch some more, be back in a moment.'

Maeve spoke up, 'Can I help you?'

Sheila was already putting on her boots, 'Ah heavens no, you enjoy your tea, it'll take just a minute, I wouldn't want you going into my dilapidated wood shed anyhow, it's become quite dangerous that, could collapse at any moment. I'll be back before you finish that cup.'

Maeve and Catherine sat quietly for a moment sipping their tea and eating their biscuits.

Maeve said, 'These *are* divine.'

Catherine agreed, 'They are. Maeve, I must say something. Ever since you first stepped foot into this cottage it seems to have changed Sheila's life. She just adores you. I hope you'll remain friends with her after the treasure hunt ends.'

Maeve smiled, 'Ah, it seems to have changed my life as well, Catherine. I love her, I felt a connection to her the moment I met her. I feel like I've known Sheila my whole life.'

Catherine smiled, 'I know that feeling. I *have* known her nearly my entire life. She's a special woman, that one.'

Maeve was looking around the cottage, 'I've enjoyed coming here so much, and I've enjoyed our outings, we've had such a grand time. I don't know all that much about Sheila's life though, she seems to keep it all a bit guarded and I don't want to pry.' She looked over at the framed photo on the table, 'Catherine, I must ask, did Sheila have any more children? I understand she lost twins?'

Catherine looked at the photo sadly, 'She did indeed have those two beautiful little girls, but she was only sixteen years old at the time; she was sent to a Magdalene laundry institution. It's not quite clear what happened to her girls and she wasn't able to have any more children. I'm sure she'll tell you her whole story when she's ready, truth be told, it's a difficult story to tell.'

Maeve looked concerned, 'Ah that's so sad, she seems like she would have been such a wonderful mother. My mam has a photo that looks so much like that photo. My gran also had twins, looks about the same time. She has a photo of her holding her twins in a garden, just like that.'

Catherine smiled, 'Yes, my parents had similar photos in their house as well. Is there a family you know in Ireland that *doesn't* have twins?' Sheila was just coming back in with wood and turf in her arms.

Catherine continued, louder so Sheila could hear, 'Is there a family in Ireland that you know of that doesn't have at least one: priest, nun, or a set of twins?'

Maeve laughed, 'No, I suppose not. And an Auntie Mary, every Irish family seems to have an Auntie Mary.'

Catherine agreed, 'Yes, indeed.'

Sheila laughed and agreed as well, 'Ah, all of that may be very common, but *we* are certainly not common, we are unique, individual, beautiful, strong women. Let's have a toast to us!' She raised her cup of tea. They all laughed and were in agreement saying; 'Hear, hear!'

Catherine laughed, 'This one and her toasts, ever since we were kids she toasted when she drank water she did.'

Maeve smiled, 'I think it's lovely, I've enjoy your toasts Sheila. Well you two, I must be going. I have a bit of revision to do this evening, exams next week. Good to see you both, thank you for the tea.' She gave Catherine a hug, then Sheila.

Sheila took Maeve's hand and walked her out to her car. 'It's always a pleasure to see you, dear. Come back when your exams are finished and we'll have a little celebration.'

Maeve said, 'That sounds grand Sheila, see you soon. Enjoy your time in Skibbereen.' She got into her car and drove down the dirt road. Sheila stood in her driveway watching Maeve drive away, waving until she could see her no longer.

Sheila stood quietly in the driveway after Maeve had disappeared. It was very still outside; the sun was just going behind the trees and there was a lone mourning dove cooing. A sudden wind came up and blew the trees that surrounded the cottage. Sheila looked up and watched the trees swaying as she stood there, thinking, for a moment. Something felt different. The winds of change, she thought; something was blowing into her life; something was taking a different direction. She thought to herself: *I'm going to take whatever these changes are and embrace them. I can feel a strong sense of change about to happen.*

Catherine came out of the cottage to find Sheila looking up into the sky, holding her arms out as if catching the wind. 'Are you all right there?'

Sheila turned and smiled at Catherine, 'I couldn't be better, Catherine; I sense some things are changing in my life and it feels good.'

Catherine nodded in agreement, 'Yes, things are changing indeed--you are going to change your clothes and we are going to change our environment, and go to a change of scenery in Skibbereen.'

Sheila laughed, 'Right, I'll take that change for the moment, I'm up for a change of scenery. Let's go.'

Catherine was driving down the road away from Sheila's house. As they were about to exit on to the main road, a car was pulling in.

Sheila recognized who it was, 'That's Maeve's American friend Patrick, let's see what he's up to.' Catherine put her window down, and Sheila leaned over and shouted, 'Hello Patrick, are you lost?'

Patrick laughed, 'Hi Sheila, hello again Catherine. I was just passing by and I thought I'd pop in to see if you need anything, like any wood chopped or anything mended or anything that needs fixing around the farm. I'm running out of things to do in Allihies.'

Sheila beamed, 'Ah bless your heart good boy! I'm going away for a day or two, please help yourself. Chop wood, do anything you like. You can stay in the spare bedroom if you'd like to get out of the hostel for a day or two. Please make yourself at home, the door is open.'

Patrick still wasn't used to the very open Irish hospitality, 'Are you sure?'

Sheila laughed, 'Why wouldn't I be sure about you helping me around the farm? Now then, you go and indulge yourself, please feel free to do whatever you see fit. I'll see you when I return in a day or two. Thanks, Paddy. Bye for now!'

Catherine said goodbye and carried on driving out to the main road towards Skibbereen.

Sheila was thrilled, 'He's a fine fellow, that one. There's an interest between him and Maeve. I think they're well suited.'

Catherine smiled, 'That's grand, seems like a good lad, what's his name? You called him Patrick, then Paddy.'

Sheila laughed, 'He came from America Patrick, but he's turning into a Paddy; he's fitting in nicely, I'd say.'

Catherine said, 'Well, what a treat to come back to having a few chores done for you.'

Sheila agreed, 'It's been some time since I've had anyone help me with anything--I welcome it. Now then, what do you say we stop for a cup of coffee?'

Catherine laughed, 'We only just got on the road, I think we'll drive for a bit first. Unless you wanted to stop by O'Neill's first and see your boyfriend?'

Sheila laughed, 'He's hardly my boyfriend, but he does make a fine cup of coffee.'

Catherine shook her head, 'It's not exactly in the right direction, but we can go if you like.'

Sheila smiled, 'Perfect.'

Sheila and Catherine walked into O'Neill's pub to the delight of John O'Neill. He spread his arms when he saw the ladies walk in the front door. 'Ah, to what do I owe the pleasure of seeing you beauties again so soon?'

They both laughed, 'Just two coffees for carry out, John, we are headed to Skibbereen for a couple days.'

John started to get their coffees, 'So long as you're back in time for our date next week, Sheila.'

Sheila blushed, 'Yes John, I'll be back long before that. Say John, I have Patrick McGettigan at my house right now doing a few chores, maybe you could check in on him today or tomorrow?'

John looked happy, 'Yes of course, I'll pop over there today, Sheila, don't think another thing about it.'

Sheila took the coffees, 'Ta John, see you soon.' Catherine thanked him as well.

John smiled as the women were walking out, saying, 'Mind yourselves, now.' The women got into Catherine's car and drove along the sea, past Bantry Bay towards Skibbereen.

Catherine said, 'This shouldn't take us more than an hour and a half, or maybe two hours, but no more than that. It's delightful we live this close to each other now, isn't it, Sheila?' Sheila was looking out the window to the sea views, daydreaming of John. She didn't respond. Catherine looked at Sheila, 'Where are you? Ah sure, you're still at O'Neill's?'

Sheila smiled, 'Ah, I feel like a silly schoolgirl.'

Catherine said, 'There's nothing wrong with feeling like a silly schoolgirl there, I wouldn't mind feeling like one meself.'

Sheila looked at Catherine, 'Well, maybe we should put you on an online dating site, you'd have old geezers tripping over themselves to meet you.'

Catherine laughed, 'Ha, you wouldn't see me doing that. Besides, I have four men I'm looking after at the moment, my son and his three boys. Wait 'til you meet them, they're all *gorgeous*.'

Sheila looked at Catherine, 'I cannot wait to see Michael again, and to meet the boys, what a pleasure!'

Catherine smiled, 'Ah, you're going to love Michael; he's a lovely man. His name is Michael McConnell. He was adopted through the Catholic Church by an American family who weren't able to have children of their own. He's told me they're wonderful people. I was so pleased to hear that he had a good childhood. He had no memory of me, you know, which was easier on him, I suppose. But he did feel like he was always missing something in his life--and it was me.'

Sheila was listening to Catherine, 'I'm so happy for you, Catherine. I can't wait to meet him, and your grandchildren.'

They drove along Bantry Bay and through the countryside to Skibbereen. As they were pulling into the driveway to Michael's house, Catherine paused, 'Sheila, don't ask about Michael's wife. . he's on his own here with the kids, a bit of a separation of sorts. I'm not sure if they'll ever get back together--it's none of my business really, so I don't ask. She comes and goes every week or so; I'm not sure if you'll meet her or not.'

Sheila said, 'Ah, that's a shame any way you look at it. I won't say a word. Will Michael be home?'

Catherine smiled, 'Yes, he works from his home office mostly, he likes to be close to the kids and there for them before and after school.'

Sheila said, 'He sounds like a good boy.' Catherine laughed, 'Hardly a boy, wait 'til you see him.'

Catherine parked in front of the house.

Michael was at the door, with his arms open, 'She's back! And she's brought a friend! Welcome, welcome, come in, come in and make yourself at home.'

Catherine said, 'Michael, this is the Sheila.'

Michael walked up to her and gave her a big hug, 'I have heard only good things about you.' He noticed her bag and picked it up, 'How long will you be staying with us?'

Sheila smiled, 'Only a day or two. It's so good to see you again, Michael.'

Michael paused and looked at Sheila, 'Again, oh God, it is *again* for you, isn't it? I only wish I had a memory of you.'

Sheila looked at Michael, 'You wouldn't want too many memories from that place Michael, you're not missing a thing, I can assure you of that.'

Michael said, 'Just the same, I wish I remembered you both. But, here we are now, we can get reacquainted today.'

Catherine started to go inside, 'I'll put the kettle on.'

Michael said, 'We couldn't possibly have a conversation without a cup of tea.'

Sheila smiled, 'Ah heavens, no!'

They went into the kitchen. Sheila looked around, 'You have a lovely home Michael, how long have you been here?'

Michael looked around, 'Thank you Sheila, I did my best. The kids and I have been here just a few months now, we moved away from the town a bit, but not too far away from their friends and walking distance to school, it's all working out just fine. So, tell me Sheila, I'm sure Catherine has filled you in on what I do for a living. Have you done any searching for your girls?'

Sheila was taken aback at how quickly he got to the subject, 'You don't waste time, now do you? I've done little searching, Michael. I was told the girls had passed.'

Michael squinted his eyes a bit as he looked at Sheila, 'Do you believe they have passed, Sheila?'

Sheila looked away, 'No, I never believed it, but it was what I was told by the nuns and my parish priest, and I was told to live with it. I couldn't turn to anyone or find out any further information, because everything stayed with the nuns and the priests, things didn't go further than that. They were a blockade they were, no matter how much I tried--and tried I did. It was a closed book when I left the home. That was that, and that's where it stood and that's where it stayed.'

Michael was very interested, 'I know exactly what you're talking about Sheila, this is my life's work now, along with a couple of paying clients of course, but this is my passion. Would you allow me to help you find the absolute truth?'

Sheila put her hand to her heart, 'Yes of course, Michael--if you think you can find information that was refused to me, please do. I would welcome it and be forever grateful.'

Michael interjected, 'I'm so sorry if we find that they did pass, Sheila, but I have found that the nuns and the priests lied on numerous occasions.'

Sheila shook her head, 'I would imagine I'm not the only one they lied to, I must say though, I've prayed over the years that they did lie to me.'

Catherine put her hand on Sheila's arm, 'Yes, let's hope that they did in fact lie to you and your girls are alive. The truth is starting to unravel; people aren't staying quiet any longer and people are being united. Let Michael help you Sheila. He knows what he's doing and he finds it very satisfying. Good or bad, he will find the truth for you. We are proof right here in front of your eyes. The nuns refused to release any records of his adoption. They told him *I* was dead; but he found ways, he dug trenches and uncovered every stone to find me, thanks be to God.'

Sheila smiled, 'You two are very lucky. I knew of a few women over the years that weren't as fortunate. They lived with the lies and the shame and never had anything resolved in the end. They died never knowing the truth.'

Catherine said, 'And that's the ultimate punishment to end a lifetime of suffering. When the child seeks the mother, to find she's gone, or vice versa, to find one or the other has passed, it's horrific, really. No one should have to endure that sort of pain on top of everything else. That's why Michael wants to reunite as many people as he can before it's too late.'

Sheila smiled, 'Thank you ever so much, Michael. It's amazing that you want to do all of this for others, for me, for my girls. Fair play to you, you're a good man.'

Michael got up and put his arm around Sheila, 'It's my pleasure. I'll find out what I can, and you'll be the first to know. It may take a while, but I will find what there is to find.'

Sheila said, 'Thank you again Michael, bless your heart.'

Catherine said, 'Michael, would you mind if I showed Sheila the photo album from your life, she'd love to see it.'

Michael started to walk out of the room immediately, 'Of course! I'll get it, I'll be right back.'

Sheila looked at Catherine, 'This is quite extraordinary, does he normally get paid for doing all of this research for people?'

Catherine laughed, 'Ah, he wouldn't take your money, Sheila, besides, he's done quite well for himself; he's not terribly interested in money any longer. It's about people now, and justice; he feels the need to right a horrible wrong inflicted on so many, before it's too late.'

Sheila said, 'Ah, he's a good man, Catherine, you must be proud.'

Catherine put her arm around Sheila, 'I've had a lifetime of being proud of him. Although I didn't know a thing about him, I was always so proud of him, proud to be his mother. I never lost that, and no one could take that away from me.'

'I couldn't agree more,' said Sheila.

Chapter Twenty One

John O'Neill left his pub and was going to head home. He thought about Paddy being at Sheila's house. He got into his car and drove to what he remembered from his childhood as the O'Brien farm, then the Murphy farm when Sheila and Martin lived there after her parents passed. The last time John had set foot on the Murphy farm was twenty five years ago, when Martin fell ill and couldn't work the fields that last season. John had gone over with his father and friends to finish farming the field for Martin. The neighbouring farms brought their tractors and ploughs and they all finished ploughing the fields within a couple hours.

It was that evening, after the men had cut and rolled the hay for Martin, that they all had their final words with him. None of the men ever returned to that property after he passed. Martin was very much in love with his wife Sheila. He was a proud, yet very jealous man, with a bit of a temper when he drank. The men came into the cottage after they had finished their work to pay their respects to Martin. He was confined to his bed at this point, weak from the sickness but strong enough to take his whiskey and speak his mind. Martin knew he was dying; he knew this could be the last time he'd see any of these men. They all had a toast to everyone's health. Martin thanked each of them for helping out that evening with his final haul of hay.

John sat in his car thinking about that last night with Martin Murphy; John was in his 30's at the time. Martin had sat in his bed and looked each man in the eye; he raised his glass to toast each one individually.

'Here's to you Jack, to your health, and the friendship we've shared. When I'm gone, if you so much as look at my wife, I will come back to haunt you, as God as my witness I will.' The men didn't say anything, they just raised their eyebrows and their glasses and let him go on.

He raised his glass to the next man in his bedroom, '*Sláinte* my friend Mick, you lay a finger on my wife when I am gone and I will condemn you to hell and haunt your dreams. Curse the day you even think about her.'

Martin went on to the next man standing near his bedside. 'Here's to your health and the years we shared, James, you set foot on this property when I'm gone and so help me God you'll be struck down at the very thought of my wife! And you Padraig, I've seen the way you look at my wife when we go into the village, you keep your mitts to yourself, don't even look at my wife, she's *my* wife and she'll be my wife until the day *she* dies. I swear I'll come back and haunt you all.'

John's father told Martin to calm down and take it easy, to save his strength to greet Saint Peter. Although it was twenty five years ago, John remembered the day vividly. He shook his head and chuckled to himself, remembering how Martin had been, and how they had all worried a bit because of his strong will and determination--they thought he really could haunt them. They'd all said their goodbyes, and never saw Martin again. Rarely did anyone ever see Sheila, either, for the last twenty five years.

John drove slowly down the long dirt road to Sheila's cottage. He looked around at the unkempt fields and dilapidated stone wall lining the drive. He parked his truck in front of the cottage and walked to the back barn, where he heard Patrick chopping wood. John walked across the field. Patrick's back was turned as he methodically chopped one log after the next.

Between Patrick's strokes John called out, 'Hello!' hoping not to startle Patrick as he wielded the sharp axe.

Patrick jumped and turned around, surprised to see John, 'Hi, Mr. O'Neill, what brings you out here?'

John smiled, 'Just checking on things. What brings *you* out here, Paddy?'

Patrick shrugged, 'I'm running out of things to do; I asked Sheila if she could use a bit of help around here and she told me to do whatever I find that needs to be done.' He swung the axe one more time, wedging it in the stump, and gestured to John to follow him, 'Come here and have a look at this.' Patrick guided John towards the old wood shed where Sheila kept her firewood and turf, 'Look at the state of this, it could collapse on Sheila at any given moment.' As Patrick was showing John, he touched a bit of the structure and pieces of wood crumbled to the ground.

John backed up, 'Ah, that's horrid! I tell you what we're going to do right now, and that is remove this danger, knock this whole thing down. You know wood structures just don't do well in Ireland. Ah, I forgot, you're a Yank. It's too wet here, this old thing has been here for donkey's years and its days are gone. I reckon Sheila is using this shed because it's the closest to her house.' He stood there with his arms folded, surveying the farm, he looked towards the cottage and said, 'I think we should knock this down and build her a shed right up to the back of her house. What do you think, are you up for the task, Yank?'

Patrick smiled and stood up straight, 'Yes sir!'

John looked around and pointed across the field towards the larger barn, 'There's a pile of old stones there; we'll make a clearing by her house and build her a proper stone shed. I have some metal roofing materials at the bar I'll fetch and bring back. By the time I return you should have the entire thing built.' Patrick looked worried. John laughed, 'Ah, I'm messing with you lad, start clearing an area at the back of her house. We'll have to be quick about this, she may return tomorrow.'

Patrick was surprised, he questioned John, 'You're sure she'll be okay with us doing this?'

John laughed, 'Ah sure, she'll be grand, don't worry, I'll sort her out.'

Patrick shrugged and put on his gloves, 'Okay let's do it.'

John stood there, looking around the old farm that he hadn't seen in so many years. He watched Patrick as he cleared the dead bushes away from the cottage, 'Make sure it's large enough to hold a good amount of wood, we don't want her chopping any wood out here any longer. It should be stocked once a year, that's it.' Patrick nodded and kept pulling at the dead bushes, thinking to himself how the Irish seem to take care of each other--or did they? He wondered if John had a vested interest in Sheila.

John left the back garden and walked around the cottage to his truck. He stood out there alone looking at Sheila's cottage, noticing that it was well kept, but showed signs of its age. What a shame he hadn't come over sooner to help her with so many things that needed tending. Well, it was what it was, and he could help her now. He looked forward to surprising Sheila with the new stone shed, and seeing her next week for lunch. He smiled at the thought, got into his truck and left to retrieve supplies.

Maeve and Aelish were having lunch at school. Owen walked up, looking very self assured and chuffed with himself.

Aelish looked up at him, 'What are you on about, pest?'

Owen looked directly at Maeve, 'I have a bit of information on that Sheila Murphy that lost a little something while she was travelling through Allihies.'

Aelish interrupted, 'Ya, we know everything, Sherlock.'

Maeve stopped her and asked, 'What information did you find out, Owen?'

Owen looked happy with himself, 'Are you sure you can officially write her off your list? Her cousin Finn gave me this note, saying if you find the missing item, call this number.'

Aelish was getting annoyed, 'We know Owen, she lost a ring, we already know, this is no new information, we phoned her and she was rude, almost as rude as you!'

Owen smiled, 'Ah ya gobshite, she could have lost a lottery ticket as well as the ring now, couldn't she have? You don't know for sure now, do ye?'

Maeve looked at Aelish, 'You know, we didn't get a definitive answer on the phone, she was abrupt and rude but we didn't find out for sure, now did we, Aelish?'

Aelish shrugged, 'I don't know, I suppose she did lose that ring close to where we found the lottery ticket, maybe you're right Owen.'

Owen leaned in a bit closer to Aelish, 'Sorry, I didn't catch that, could you repeat that, did I hear you say I was *right*? Did you say, "You are right Owen." Is that what you said, is it?' Aelish rolled her eyes and shook her head muttering, 'Jaysus.'

Owen started to laugh as he handed Maeve a piece of paper, 'Here's the note Finn gave me from his cousin Sheila Murphy, it should eliminate her from your search, wouldn't you say, Maeve?'

Maeve took the piece of paper from Owen and smiled, 'Yes, that puts that one to rest for sure, thanks for your help, Owen, well done.'

Aelish screwed up her face, 'What? How can we be so sure all of a sudden?' Maeve handed the paper to Aelish with the handwritten note, "If you find my ring in Allihies, please call me at this number, thank you, Shelagh Murphy." It was the wrong spelling.

Aelish smirked at Owen, 'Oh, well done you clever lad, you're a regular Sherlock Holmes you are, why don't you run off now and find your Dr. Watson Liam.'

Owen laughed and walked away, yelling, 'You're very welcome indeed ladies!'

Aelish looked at Maeve, 'You know, he's really not that helpful at all, he's still a thieving maggot he is.'

Maeve raised her eyebrows, 'That was helpful, Aye, we can eliminate her, I'll give him that. I feel better that she's out. It's like that woman in Ballydehob, she was so rude, but we weren't able to completely eliminate that one either.'

Aelish laughed, 'We should send little Sherlock after her.'

Maeve smiled, 'Sheila is actually down there now with her friend Catherine, which reminds me, Patrick sent me a text, he's at Sheila's house doing some chores for her, would you like to call in with me after school?'

Aelish batted her eyes, 'And interrupt you two love birds? No thanks. Besides, I have to revise tonight, don't you need to as well, missus? We do have final exams coming up.'

Maeve shook her head, 'I've got it all sorted, Aye. Can you find your own way home after school then?'

Aelish grinned, 'Anything for the sake of you and your budding love life, ya, I can get a lift in Sherlock's carpool, don't worry, see you tomorrow!' They parted ways and went to their respective classrooms.

Maeve went over to Sheila's cottage after her last class. As she drove down the long dirt road, she could see Patrick's car, which gave her a twinge of excitement, but she could also see a truck. She was surprised that he had company, then realised it was Mr. O'Neill's truck. That made her smile. She parked her car and walked around the back, to find Patrick and Mr. O'Neill sweating, feverishly building a stone wall at the back of Sheila's cottage. She was surprised, 'What in the world are you two doing?'

The two men stopped working and looked at Maeve, both looking quite pleased with themselves. Patrick spoke up, 'We're building a new wood shed for Sheila!'

Maeve raised her eyebrows, hoping Sheila knew about this, 'That's lovely, did she ask you two to do this?'

John spoke up, 'She was desperate for it, Maeve, the woodshed she was using was a danger to her.'

Maeve agreed, 'She did mention it was going to be the death of her. It's really very good of you two to do this, quite an undertaking it is. Can I make you a cup of tea?' Patrick smiled and nodded.

John said, 'Ta. That'd be grand thanks, Maeve, good girl.'

Maeve walked into Sheila's cottage for the first time without Sheila being there. It was very quiet; all she could hear were the faint sounds coming from outside, of the men piling rocks. She could hear them laughing, and the scrape of the trowel slapping the cement between the stones as they built the shed at breakneck speed. Maeve put the kettle on the stove, then she quietly walked around the cottage. She peeked into Sheila's bedroom, captivated by the oil painting of Sheila, Martin and their twin girls. The girls were beautiful in their white dresses, like angels sitting in the grass at their feet. Maeve was confused, she remembered Catherine saying the babies had been taken away from Sheila when she was sixteen--yet they looked to be four or five years old in this painting.

Maeve felt as if she were being very nosy, poking around Sheila's house, but she was so curious. She looked into the spare bedroom that also seemed to be an art studio. Lying on the drawing table was a stack of unframed canvas oil paintings; the subject matters were all of Sheila's twin girls at different stages of their lives. Maeve was in awe; she wished someone was there with her to see all of the beautiful paintings. How sad it was that the girls were always wearing white dresses: were they deceased? The paintings were beautifully haunting; they nearly brought a tear to her eye. She took out her phone and started to take photos of the paintings, feeling the need to show someone, maybe Aelish, but more likely her mam.

She heard the kettle whistling in the kitchen, and quickly put down the canvas prints and left the spare room. As she walked past Sheila's room she stopped to take a photo of the large, framed oil painting. Standing in front of the painting, she thought how sad it was if all these images of Sheila's daughters were imagined; she wondered if they were alive, or if they were only living in her heart, the little angels in their white dresses. The whistle of the kettle got louder as her thoughts dissipated. She made a pot of tea and rustled up some biscuits for the men.

Maeve carried the tray out back, and placed it on an old, rickety wooden table by the barn, 'Here you are gentlemen. When you're finished with that wood shed, this table could use some attention.'

Mr. O'Neill looked surprised, 'Don't get ahead of yourself there, missus, we don't want to shock her with too much, do we now. Thanks for the tea, Maeve.'

Patrick poured himself a cup, 'Tanks a million as you say here, or tanks a mill, I should say.'

Maeve smiled at Patrick, 'Just a thanks would suffice--with that American accent it sounds as if you are just poking fun at us, Patrick.'

Patrick winked at Maeve and put on a terrible Irish accent, 'Neva lassie, neva wood I mayke fon of yer Oirish accent, no I woodn't like.'

Maeve hit Patrick on the arm, 'I must be going now, I'll leave you two to your construction project.'

Patrick finished his cup of tea, and placed it back on the tray, saying, 'I'll walk you to your car.'

Maeve smiled, 'Such a gentleman, isn't he Mr. O'Neill? If you're finished with your tea, I'll take it in.' John took a last sip of his tea and placed his cup on the tray.

Maeve picked up the tray and walked towards the cottage. Mr. O'Neill picked up his trowel and went back to work, 'Ta, Maeve.' Patrick followed Maeve into the kitchen; as she placed the tray on the counter, she could feel him behind her. She continued to clear the tray of dishes, placing them in the sink to wash. She could feel Patrick slowly getting closer to her, the heat of his breath as he smelled her hair, and pressed his chest against her back. Maeve held onto the counter, closed her eyes and felt the tingly sensation on every part of her body where he touched her. The hair stood up on the back of her neck, goosebumps rose along the length of her arms, as he slowly hugged her from behind and slid his hands down her shoulders to her hands. Patrick took Maeve's hands and wrapped them around herself and squeezed her tightly. She turned around and faced him, looking up at him with her big blue eyes, and he gently kissed her on the lips. Maeve felt herself melting into his arms.

Just then the cottage door slammed; they both jumped, and saw Mr. O'Neill standing there looking at the two of them.

He cleared his throat, 'Don't mind me, just need to use the jacks, carry on, but don't get too carried away there, now.'

Maeve felt red in the face. She scurried away from Patrick, 'I was just leaving, see you two later!' Patrick smiled at her as she ran out. She jumped into her car, still feeling flushed. Quickly driving down the dirt road, she smiled at the thought of how silly she felt that she was so taken with Patrick.

Maeve walked into her house to the dogs excitedly greeting her as usual. She bent down and said her hellos to Chancer and Larry, then she stood up and smelled something delicious cooking; she called towards the kitchen, 'What's for dinner Mam?'

It was her father who responded, 'Your favourite, lamb stew sweetie!'

Maeve smiled; she loved her dad's lamb stew, 'Where's Mam, Da?'

As she walked into the kitchen she found her mam standing next to her dad, 'If it were up to your father, we wouldn't have anything *but* lamb stew! I'm making vegetables.'

As Maeve gave them both hugs, she noticed the very large pot in which he was cooking the lamb stew, 'You're making loads. Are we expecting company?'

Her dad laughed, 'No, I'm afraid my eyes were bigger than my stomach when I started out.'

Maeve laughed, 'I'll have a fair share, I'm starved. I've just been to Sheila's, I want to show you some photos I took Mam.'

Mary smiled, 'That's grand, love, can you give us a minute to finish sorting out the dinner?'

Maeve started getting dishes out of the press, 'Of course, I'll show you at the table.'

Maeve set the table as her parents finished the dinner preparations. She sat down and started going through her photos on her phone.

Mary came up behind her and looked over her shoulder at the photos, 'Ah, that's gorgeous, Maeve, who painted that? Who are those girls?'

Maeve put the phone closer to her mam, 'Isn't it stunning? They're Sheila's twin girls. Sheila's friend, Catherine, told me Sheila had them when she was a teen. The strange thing is, Catherine told me they may have died, or they were taken away from her when she was sixteen, she's not certain of their fate, isn't that horrible? She was in one of those horrible Magdalene Laundries, Mam.'

Mary looked concerned, 'Shame, poor thing. So, she kept in contact with the adoptive family? They look different ages in the paintings.'

Maeve looked sad and shook her head, 'I'm not sure if she ever saw them at all, Mam, I'm thinking this was her imagining what they would have looked like.' She flipped through all the photos, showing her parents, 'Look at all the paintings she did over the years. The girls were always wearing white dresses in every painting--this one looks as if they have wings.'

Maeve's dad spoke up, 'The pain that woman must have gone through for a lifetime. To not know if your children were dead or alive? It's heartbreaking, that is.'

Maeve put her phone down and looked at her parents, 'Catherine told me that the nuns told Sheila the girls died and they were gone. Happy and healthy one day, then gone the next. Sheila presumed they were adopted but the nuns would never tell her the truth. The nuns and the priests told her the past was the past, and to forget about everything, not speak of it to anyone and to get on with her life, never look back and never go looking.'

Mary shook her head, 'My God, the number of times that happened in this country . . . Poor Sheila, but it seems she's held steadfast that they lived, unless it was a deep desire and wishful thinking. What I know of Sheila is that she led a very quiet life with Martin, then even a more quiet and reclusive life after he died.'

Maeve started to dish up some vegetables on to her plate, 'Tis a shame, she's such a sweet woman, to have spent most of her life keeping to herself must have been a hardship on its own, and sad.'

Jack looked disappointed, 'What I remember about Martin Murphy was that he kept her under lock and key, he did. From her parents to him, they all kept to themselves really, the O'Briens did as well. Strange thing is, talk around the village was people wondered if they all had something to hide, seems as though they did after all.' Maeve's dad left the table to fetch the lamb stew, he returned with the extra large pot, and heaved it onto the middle of the table, 'I reckon there's enough here to feed an entire ship and the cabin crew.'

Maeve and Mary laughed, 'Ah, but you love your leftovers, hun, you'll have them for weeks to come by the looks of it.'

Jack handed the ladle to Mary, 'Work away before it gets cold.' Maeve smiled looking at her parents, thinking how lucky she was. She thought of Sheila and all the years she didn't have a family to enjoy and wasn't surrounded by loved ones. Maeve smiled at her parents, feeling thankful.

Chapter Twenty Two

Michael came back into the kitchen with a large photo album. He placed it on the kitchen island in front of Catherine and Sheila, then excused himself, 'I've got a lot of ground to cover; I'll be in my office. The boys won't be home from their after school activities until around eight, late one tonight.'

Catherine smiled, 'I'll have dinner ready then, eight or eight thirty at the latest.'

Michael looked at Sheila and winked, 'She's a good mammy, this one.'

Catherine beamed, 'See you in a bit then.' Catherine and Sheila watched Michael walk out of the room.

Sheila was curious, 'What does he call you, Catherine?'

Catherine looked at Sheila with glassy eyes, 'Ah Sheila, he said to me the moment he met me in Australia: "You're my mother, and I can't imagine calling you anything else, would you mind?" I nearly fell to my knees, I never thought I'd ever hear my Michael utter those words. Even though it's "Mom"-- he was raised in America after all--sometimes it's "Mam", and lately it's been "Gran" or "Granny" for the boys.'

Sheila felt so happy for her, 'That's lovely, Catherine, heartwarming how this has all happened for you. Now, let's have a look at this photo album of Michael's.'

Catherine walked to the sink, 'Work away--I'm going to start the meal, I've got six stomachs to feed tonight. I hope you like meat and potatoes, it seems it's all they eat in this house, they eat them by the truckload they do!'

Sheila said, 'I'm not fussed, I like my meat and potatoes.'

She opened the photo album and was taken aback at the first photo on the first page. It was just as she remembered Catherine and Michael. It was a photo similar to the one she had of her holding her girls, standing in front of the hedge in the back garden at Blessboro House.

'However did Michael get this photo?' she asked.

Catherine looked over from the sink, 'Michael was adopted into a Catholic family of Irish descent in America. The nuns sent a photo of Michael and me to the family, prior to the adoption. The family wanted to know a bit about me so they'd be able to tell Michael where he came from when he was older. When he was young, they would explain to him that he was a gift from God, a gift from Ireland, and a gift from St. Patrick himself, they did.'

Sheila smiled, 'How fortunate he was, Catherine, you must have been so relieved to find out that he had a good life and he was well taken care of.'

Catherine winced a bit, 'He had a good life and he was loved and cared for, but he was denied any information about me. When his adoptive parents tried to find out any information, the nuns told them not to discuss me; the files were closed and they had no information about me. When he was older he contacted them and they told him I died, but, like you, he didn't believe it. Apparently, money was exchanged . . there were so many Americans in the 50's and 60's that bought Irish babies. Mind you, they claimed they were donations to the Catholic Church, but they were essentially paying for the babies. Information about me was found only by Michael himself, during his search and his own God given perseverance. Thanks be to God, he had the tenacity and the drive, or I wouldn't be standing in front of you this very moment.'

Michael's children came streaming into the house in usual form, running, pushing, yelling, and messing with each other. Sheila was sitting at the island peeling a pile of potatoes when she saw Catherine's face light up and open her arms to her grandchildren, 'My boys are home! My beautiful boys, c'mere to me and give me kisses, all of you. Sheila, look how *gorgeous* they are! I could just eat them up!' She grabbed each one and gave them big hugs and kisses.

The oldest was Mack; at twelve years old he was becoming a bit embarrassed by his Gran's attention. 'Gran, you just saw us yesterday!'

Catherine put her arms around Mack, 'Ah, give us a kiss, come here, give your old granny a kiss.' Mack smiled and obliged. Conor and Donal were younger; they loved their gran and had no trouble showing it. 'Hugs and kisses all around!' said Catherine, 'Show some love to my dear friend Sheila here, we've known each other since we were younger than the three of you combined.'

Mack looked at the ceiling, 'Gran, that doesn't make any sense at all.'

Catherine looked at him exhausted, 'Okay, my little genius grandson, we've known each other for a very long time. This is the intelligent gentleman of the bunch.'

Mack nodded in agreement, 'Good to meet you, Sheila.' He held out his hand to shake Sheila's.

She laughed, 'Gentleman indeed. Pleasure to meet you boys.'

Catherine started to swat them out of the kitchen, 'Go on now, wash up and be ready for dinner in thirty minutes, don't make me come after you!' The boys ran off.

Sheila looked at Catherine, 'They are gorgeous, I see you in the middle one Catherine, he looks so like you did at that age, face of a mischievous angel that one.'

Catherine agreed, 'That's my Conor, he *is* most like me, perfect in every way, that one.'

Sheila smirked, put her hand in the pot of potatoes she was peeling and flicked a bit of water towards Catherine, 'Modesty was never your strong suit.'

Michael called from his office, 'Sheila, would you mind coming in here for a moment?'

Sheila picked up a towel and dried her hands, 'Not at all, be right in.'

Catherine picked up the peeler, 'Doing your work as usual, I'll finish the potatoes, go on.'

Sheila smiled, 'I'll be back in a moment.' Sheila walked into Michael's office.

He gestured towards the chair next to his desk, 'Have a seat, Sheila.' Sheila wondered what Michael wanted. She looked at him as he stared intently at the two computer screens on his desk, 'Sheila, I've been doing some searching for your girls. I started as soon as Catherine mentioned you to me last week, I couldn't help myself, I hope you don't mind.'

Sheila interrupted, 'Not at all, I'm so thankful for your interest, Michael. Have you found something?' Sheila leaned towards the screens but the words were too small for her to make out anything. She could feel her heart pounding a bit faster. She felt a bit nauseous; she never wanted to hear anyone utter the words that her girls were confirmed dead, as the nuns had stated. She remembered when the battleaxe nun had sharply said that to her out of the blue, how it had felt like a sharp knife, cutting from her gut up through to her heart. After the initial shock of hearing those words, she wouldn't believe it and didn't ever want to hear them again. Over the years, believing that her girls were alive was the only thing that had kept her going most days. Her heart was racing as she thought to herself: *Please, for the love of God, don't tell me that my daughters are not alive, I couldn't bear it. God, please don't say it.*

Michael interrupted her thoughts, 'Sheila, as I mentioned earlier, I don't want to give you false hope, but I've exhausted every possibility and I've scrutinized every record and called every connection I have.'

Sheila's eyes were darting from Michael, to his computer screens, down to the notes he'd written on his desk. She looked worried, trying to grasp where he was going, trying to guess what he was going to say next. She felt sick to her stomach, waiting for him to get to the point.

'Michael, what is it? What have you found?'

Michael wheeled his desk chair closer to Sheila and took her hands into his. She couldn't bear it; her heart sank, thinking she was going to hear the words she dreaded the most. She was trying to remain stoic, looking at him, begging him silently not to say he'd found death records of the girls.

Michael held her hands as he looked her in the eyes, saying very thoughtfully, 'Sheila, I haven't found your girls, it's a difficult search, this.' Sheila felt ill. He continued, 'But my search isn't over. What little good news I have for you today is that I can't find any record of your girls dying; I've searched every possible place and I cannot find any death certificates. The government was very insistent with the institutions on receiving birth and death records; it was of paramount importance to the government. I can find nothing to suggest that your girls died, only that they were born.'

Sheila closed her eyes and took a deep breath. She opened her eyes, maintaining her composure, and looked at Michael, 'I never lost hope, I never believed the nuns. In my heart of hearts, I've always known they were alive, I could feel them in my soul--for all of these years I have felt them in my heart and soul. Thank you, Michael, I do appreciate all of the hard work you are doing. Now if you'll excuse me, I must use the ladies'. Thanks again.'

Sheila felt slightly weak as she rose from the chair. She walked out of Michael's office and into the loo. She held herself steady with both hands on the sink, head down, eyes closed, reliving the moments she had thought Michael was going to tell her that her girls had in fact died, confirming what the nuns had said so many years ago. She calmed herself, to hear there was no proof of their death was such a relief.

Sheila looked in the mirror, looked herself in the eyes and whispered out loud, 'My God, they are alive, thanks be to God, they're alive.' She looked up to the ceiling and took a deep breath as she held onto the sink, tears streaming down her face. A feeling of joy ran through her. She thought of her two beautiful baby girls. She thought of the mental turmoil she'd put herself through, thousands of times over the years. *Were they alive? Where did they go? Were they kept together, or were they separated? How was their childhood? Were they shipped to America? England? Did they stay in Ireland? How are they now? Did they marry? Did they have kids? What did they look like? Were they happy? Were they loved? My God, they are loved, they've always been loved by me.*

She wiped the tears from her face and stopped her mind spinning. She regained her composure, as she had many times before. She looked in the mirror and put a smile on her face, and thought to herself: *What's done is done and what will be already is, so there's no sense in fretting.* She wiped away the tears and marched into the kitchen, saying briskly, 'Right, how's this dinner coming along now?'

Catherine looked at Sheila and smiled, 'Michael told me he had some good news for you Sheila, you must be so relieved. Rest assured, your girls will be found.'

Sheila remained stoic, 'I've always thought they were alive, Catherine, but it was quite something hearing someone else say those words to me, to hear that confirmation was extraordinary. I've exhausted all possibilities in my searches over the years, I came to every wall there was to come to, so I did. I've all the confidence in the world that Michael will be able to do what I could not, and that will be to find them once and for all.'

Catherine put her arms around Sheila, 'You're not alone in this, missus, remember that, I'll be with you every step of the way, whether you like it or not.'

Sheila smiled, 'Ah bless you, my friend, it's good having you around, I think I'll keep you.'

Catherine pushed Sheila a bit, 'Come on auld girl, let's get this dinner on the table or those boys will eat us alive.'

Maeve had started to clear the dishes from the table, when her dad told her to sit down, 'Why don't you ladies relax, I'll take care of this women's work.'

Mary snapped, 'Women's work, is it? I'll show you women's work.'

Jack laughed as he cleared the table, 'Relax, Mary, I've got a bit of dessert coming out to ya, and yer cup of coffee.'

Mary smiled, 'Good man. A man's work is never done, now is it Jack?'

He yelled from the kitchen, 'I can't hear you, love.'

Mary whispered to Maeve, 'He hears everything I say.'

They heard a faint voice along with the clamour of dishes, 'That's right, that's right, a man's work is never done, you're a barrel of laughs, hun, you are. You two just relax, I'll serve me ladies, I'll cook, I'll clean and I'll do the ironing tonight. I haven't a problem with any of it, sure I don't!'

Mary sighed, 'I hope you find as good of a man as your father is someday. Not any day soon, mind you, but someday.'

Maeve smiled at her mam; she didn't want to tell her how she was falling for Patrick. She took her phone out of her pocket to show her mam the rest of the photos she'd taken at Sheila's, 'I want to show you the rest of the paintings Sheila did, Mam, just look at all of them, I took loads.'

Maeve handed her phone to her mother, who slowly looked at every photo of each painting.

Mary had a pained look on her face, 'Ah these are brilliant, Maeve. Good Lord, she's talented, they are hauntingly beautiful. I'm so curious if she found her girls, if she knows them, if they are alive. You must ask her, Maeve.'

Maeve shook her head, 'I feel that would be prying, it feels strange enough that I know the information Catherine told me.'

Mary interrupted, 'Did it feel strange, sweetie, when you were rifling through Sheila's personal belongings while she wasn't home?'

Maeve gasped, 'Mam! I saw an art table stacked with canvases! That's hardly rifling through someone's personal belongings! The photo of the framed oil painting is right near the loo, you can't help seeing it!'

Mary smiled, 'I'm joking, sweetie.' She flipped through the photos to find the large one in the frame, 'Ah, that one is stunning, look at the detail of this painting, it's flawless. The girls look absolutely beautiful--and strangely familiar.'

Maeve looked over her mam's arm, 'I thought the same thing, they look familiar to me as well.'

Hearing this, Jack walked back from the kitchen, 'They're Irish, what do you expect? We all look alike, now, don't we?'

Maeve and Mary didn't agree, 'Says who?'

Jack laughed, 'Says me, now tuck into this, I slaved over it all day, so I did.'

Mary looked closely at the dessert he placed on the table, 'Speaking of things looking alike, Jack, this looks an awful lot like a cake I saw at the bakery in Tesco.'

Jack looked surprised, 'I haven't a baldy notion what yer on about, I don't shop at Tesco.' Mary looked at Maeve, knowing he wasn't going to give it up.

'Looks brill, Da, thank you!'

Mary agreed, 'It does look delicious Jack, it would be lovely with a cup of coffee.'

Jack jumped up, 'Ah you'd be a long time waiting to get a bit of gratitude in this house.' Mary smiled at Jack as he winked at her. Maeve and Mary went back to looking at the photos of the paintings.

Mary said, 'Sheila is an incredibly talented artist, I'd say; I'd love to see these in person, to see the detail. You know the trouble I have painting faces, I'd actually like to get a helpful hint or two from Sheila, she certainly has the knack.'

Maeve nodded, 'I thought the same thing, Mam, I'd love to get her over here to paint with us, ours are horrible, we could use a lesson or two!'

Mary smiled, 'Now, speak for yourself, I wouldn't go as far as to say we're horrible artists, Maeve, it's all in the eye of the beholder. I quite like our remedial paintings. But that sounds like a splendid idea. You should invite Sheila over for a painting day next time we do it, that would be grand!'

Maeve agreed, 'I'll ask her next time I see her, she's away at the moment with her friend Catherine in Skibbereen. She should be back tomorrow, I'll let you know.'

Catherine and Sheila set the dishes and food on the table before calling the boys. Catherine warned Sheila, 'As they say in Australia: Brace yourself, Sheila.'

Sheila thwacked Catherine with a tea towel, 'You're cheeky!' Catherine laughed and called the boys for dinner. They came tearing into the kitchen, taking their usual spots at the table.

Sheila noticed how all three boys sat nicely and placed their serviettes on their laps, 'My God, the manners on you boys, it's quite remarkable, I must say.'

Conor immediately spoke up, with a serious look on his face, 'They beat us into submission, so they do.'

Mack had a smirk on his face, 'Has Gran showed you the stick she beats us with?'

Donal wanted to be part of the banter, 'If we had a dog, it'd be beat too.' Mack flipped the back of Donal's head scolding him on his bad grammar, 'It would be *beaten* as well, what's wrong with you?'

Michael walked into the room listening to this discussion, 'I will beat each of you if you don't stop this rubbish, you'll scare Sheila off. Although they were warned to behave and show respect and have manners, I'm afraid it's useless--I apologise for anything they may say or do, Sheila, I have no control over them. But overall, they aren't a bad lot, these lads.'

Sheila smiled, 'I should say not, you're all lovely and I didn't believe you for a moment that you are beaten, you can't pull the wool over my eyes.'

Catherine interjected, 'Right then, help yourselves before it gets cold now.' The boys rushed and filled their plates and ate like they were starved animals.

Mack saw Sheila looking shocked at the three of them eating feverishly, 'They starve us you know, we haven't eaten in days.'

Sheila smirked at Mack, 'I'm sure that's true, it's very obvious, you all look a bit willowy, nearly cadaverous, so you do. Take advantage of the meal, don't stop on my account.'

Mack looked surprised at the comeback and decided to give it a rest.

Donal spoke up, 'Sheila, have you come here because you are searching for yourself or searching for someone or something? Da seems to help a lot of people search for things.'

Sheila smiled and looked at Catherine and Michael, 'I suppose I am searching for a few things, Donal, and your da is helping me. I'm also enjoying the company of my dear lifelong friend, your gran. And now I get to enjoy the company of you three lads and your da as well. I suppose I'm searching for pieces of myself, I'm gathering the puzzle pieces of my life and putting them all together, and I am delighted to say that you are now part of it.'

Chapter Twenty Three

John O'Neill woke at sunrise in a panic, thinking of Sheila. If she came home today, she would find her back garden in total disarray. He sent a text to Patrick:
Need recruits to get the job done this morning, Owen should do.
Patrick woke up thinking that was great: he liked that the project was a top priority and he was trusted to see it through. His thoughts went to how much he loved being here, and getting involved with people in this village. He thought of Maeve, and how he'd like to see her again; he'd like to figure out a way to stay in Ireland and not have to leave--her or the country. He sent a text to Owen, hoping he'd be free:
Hey Owen, can you get a couple guys together this morning to help at Sheila's cottage building a shed? Let me know, thanks!
He got a response immediately:
Ya Paddy, Liam and I will be to you soon, can spare a couple of hours.
Patrick got ready quickly and drove over to Sheila's. As he pulled into the driveway, he saw that John had already arrived. He parked next to his truck, got out of his car, and started to head to the back garden.

John popped his head out of the front door of the cottage, 'Mornin! Come in for a cuppa, then we'll get started.' Patrick smiled, that was perfect, since he'd had nothing that morning.

The kettle was whistling when he walked into the cottage. Patrick had noticed where Maeve had put things, so he got the tray out and placed cups and saucers on it.

John laughed, 'Times have changed so much here in Ireland, for the good overall, I'd say. But when me da was your age, or mine for that matter, you'd never catch him in the kitchen at home, ever--he'd rather starve and die of thirst before he'd set foot in the kitchen.'

Patrick shrugged, 'Well, I'd rather not starve, so I'll rummage us up some biscuits.'

John laughed, 'You know you fit right in here nicely Yank, you're part of the furniture, so you are.'

Patrick smiled, 'I'd like to stay, you know. I'm working on getting my Irish citizenship through naturalized foreign birth or something like that.'

John looked at Patrick inquisitively, 'Through your grandparents, is it?'

Patrick replied, 'Yep, that way I could stay, live, work, go to school, make a life, do whatever I like, cuz I'd be an Irish citizen.'

John said, 'Fair play to ye Paddy, sounds like you know what ye want and yer doing it. Now then, let's get cracking on the shed and finish it up this morning. Did you ring Owen?'

Patrick was pleased with himself, 'Yes, Owen and Liam are coming for a couple of hours this morning; they should be here soon.'

John looked happy, 'That's grand, let's go and set things up and get the most out of them.'

Liam was driving down Sheila's long dirt road to her cottage. Owen told him to park the car, and not to worry about blocking the other cars, since they weren't going to stay long. He told him to stop a couple of times, 'Park here, just here, stop, over there, leave it.' Liam stopped the car, flipped the car into park, took the keys, got out, and started walking towards the cottage. Owen was sitting in the car looking at Liam as if he were mad.

He got out of the car and yelled at Liam, 'What are ye, an eejit? You could have pulled up closer to the cottage, ye dope!'

Liam just kept walking and yelled back at Owen, 'Are ya startin'? I didn't do nuttin'! You said stop, park it and leave it. I parked it and left it just as you said, ye gobshite!'

Owen walked up to Liam, 'Are you takin' the piss?'

Liam started walking faster towards the back of the cottage, 'No I'm not takin the piss ye bleedin' maggot, ye told me to leave it, so I left it, I did what ye told me to do as usual O, ya tosser.'

'You messin' ye slag? Lie down will ya? I'll turn you inside out with a kick.'

John was standing in the back garden, watching Owen and Liam as they were yelling at each other, shaking his head he yelled, 'Ladies! I understand you only have a short time here this morning so let's get crackin'. Haul those stones over here, follow Paddy's lead, I'll be back.' John left the back garden and went towards the front of the cottage.

Owen flicked the back of Liam's head as John walked away, 'Okay Mr. O'Neill, we'll get right on it!'

Liam looked at Owen and felt the back of his head with his hand where Owen had hit him. He lunged towards Owen and pushed him to the ground and said, 'Haul those stones from over there, to over here, lad.' As he was pointing, Owen jumped up and grabbed his arm and pulled him to the ground.

Patrick was watching this, shaking his head, then yelled, 'Give it a rest you two and give me a hand, would you?' He handed Owen a pair of gloves, and Liam a trowel. 'You haul, you slap the cement and stack the stones, and do it quickly.'

They all heard Mr. O'Neill yelling from the front of the cottage, 'Who's the eejit who left his car in the middle of the damned driveway?'

Liam reached into his pocket and tossed his keys to Owen, 'That's your doing, you deal with it.'

Liam shouted towards the front, 'The eejit is coming Mr. O'Neill!'

Owen caught the keys and lunged towards Liam, he punched him and ran to the front, 'Sorry Mr. O'Neill, I'll get it out of your way.' John was already walking towards his truck, grumbling something under his breath.

Sheila and Catherine woke up early. Catherine looked at Sheila and said softly, 'You can have a lie-in if you like, I'm going to help get the boys off to school.'

Sheila wasn't quite awake, 'I can help if you like.'

Catherine laughed, 'Don't be silly, I'll manage, you're a guest. They'll be gone in an hour. I'll bring you a cup of tea.'

Sheila smiled, 'Ah, good woman, thanks a million.'

As Catherine was leaving the room, she looked back at Sheila, 'What do you say we take a drive this morning to Ballydehob and visit that Sheila Murphy, I think there might be something to that, worth checking that out again I'd say.'

Sheila agreed, 'That'd be grand, Maeve would be thrilled, too bad she can't join us.'

Catherine went and woke up the boys in the usual fashion, 'Time to get up lads, you have twenty minutes.' They grumbled and groaned.

Donal sat up in his bed, rubbing his eyes, 'Gran, will Sheila be here when we get home from school?'

Catherine sat down next to Donal on his bed, 'I'm not sure, pet, I may take her back to her home today. But it's not far, we'll all see each other again very soon. Now get yourself ready for school.'

Donal was still curious, 'Are you two searching for things today? Can I go with you, can I help you?'

Catherine put her arm around him, 'If we find anything today, you'll be the first to know. You're going to school now so get yourself ready.' She went to the kitchen and put the kettle on, and put out bowls of cereal on the table for the boys. She overheard Michael in his office, talking on the phone. The conversation was stern and seemed to be about Sheila's daughters. She overheard him saying, 'Why is it that you could find the records of my adoption, yet within a few months' time of that adoption from the same facility, you can't find any record of these girls' adoption? They couldn't have just disappeared into thin air and they didn't die, so a record must exist! Now, what happened to those girls?'

Catherine made two cups of tea, and brought one into Michael's office as he tossed his phone on the desk, looking exasperated. She didn't say a word, just placed the cup of tea in front of him on the desk.

Michael looked at Catherine and smiled, 'Ah, perfect timing, I wasn't getting anywhere fast, I'd rather have a cup of tea than talk to those people again, it's maddening at times.'

Catherine walked towards the door saying, 'We all do the best we can, and that's the best that can be expected. Now, the boys are having breakfast if you'd like to join.'

Michael stood up and said, 'I'd welcome the break, been on the phone for hours going round in circles. I wonder at times if some people have a conscience at all, blatantly hiding things and flat out lying.'

Catherine tipped her head to the side saying, 'I have often found there's always one honest one in a sea of snakes.'

Michael agreed, 'Yes, someone will be honest and they'll be found, come hell or high water, those girls will be found.'

Catherine brought Sheila a cup of tea, finding her all dressed and ready to go, 'Look at you, I thought you'd have a lie-in.'

Sheila took the cup of tea, 'Thank you, dear, I've never been one to sleep late. I'll say goodbye to the boys and we can head back later today if you don't mind.'

Catherine shook her head, 'Not at all.' The boys were finishing up their breakfast and rushing out of the kitchen when Sheila and Catherine emerged.

Sheila said, 'C'mere to me, give us a hug, I'll see you lads in a few weeks' time, how does that sound?' They all gave Sheila a hug goodbye, scrambled for their belongings, and scurried out the front door. Sheila looked at Catherine, 'They are gorgeous Catherine, you're very lucky.'

Catherine smiled as she watched the boys run down the road, 'I count my blessings every day, and there are three of them right there.' She turned inside to see Michael heading back to his office, 'And there's another.'

Michael looked back, 'Another what? Another loud boy running you ragged?'

Catherine laughed, 'No, love, another blessing, a loud one indeed, but you are a blessing.'

Catherine and Sheila set out for the day. Sheila sent a text to Maeve, asking for the address of the Sheila Murphy in Ballydehob; they were going to call on her again.

Maeve was delighted:

Well done you two! Let me know if you find out anything! xx

Sheila smiled, 'She's a good girl that one, it would be nice to meet her family. You should come up again for a visit, we could have a gathering.' Catherine smiled, 'I'd be delighted.'

John came back with materials for the roof of the shed. He was impressed with Patrick and his skills, and pleased to see that he was keeping the lads in line and the job progressed quickly. 'Jaysus, I wasn't gone that long and you've nearly completed it!'

Patrick smiled, 'You said we were in a hurry in case Sheila returned today.'

Owen and Liam were working away without too much mischief other than the occasional push or shove while they passed each other. Owen said, 'We've got to leave soon for hurling, Mr. O'Neill.'

John reached into his pocket, 'Not a bother, let me give you lads a few bob for your time.'

Owen reached out for the cash, 'I'll take it for both of us.'

Liam leapt over stones and buckets and body slammed Owen away from Mr. O'Neill. 'I'll take it for both of us, he owes me for petrol.'

Owen came back and shoved Liam, 'Ya greedy git, I filled up yer tank yesterday!'

Mr. O'Neill interrupted, 'Lads, lads, you were here a couple of hours, I'll give you each a twenty and you can both feck off now. Go and take your aggression out on the field. Thanks for the help.'

Owen grabbed both twenties and shoved them into his pocket; he put his arm around Liam's head in a lock hold, 'Thanks Mr. O'Neill. I'd like to say one thing before we leave, something me gran used to always say, it's about me and my friend Liam here; there are good ships and wood ships and ships that sail the sea, but the best ships are friendships and may they always be!'

Liam pushed Owen away from him saying, 'You look like your gran--now give me my twenty! And yours!' Owen pushed him saying, 'Go'way with you, ye langer.' And he ran off towards the car and yelled back, 'See yous later! That truck of yours had better not be in our way, Mr. O'Neill!'

John shook his head and picked up a trowel to help Patrick, 'This is looking grand, Paddy, you're good with your hands, and managing people, as best as they can be managed anyway.'

Patrick smiled, 'They were great. I do enjoy it; I'm happiest when I'm working.'

John raised his eyebrows, 'I have plenty of work to keep you busy if you want to stay. I have a spare room above the pub if you're interested.'

Patrick looked surprised, 'Good to know, thanks, that would be awesome.'

John felt satisfied, 'Right, let's finish this up and put the roof on. I reckon we can finish this up in a couple of hours, what do you think?'

Patrick nodded, 'I think we can if we don't have any more interruptions.'

John glanced towards the front of the cottage, 'Ah, they were good for something, I'm glad they hauled all the rocks over here, I didn't want to do that job with my back.'

Patrick agreed, 'They were fast workers, in between their bickering.'

John smiled, 'Ya, lots of energy those two, I suppose I had that as well at eighteen.'

Patrick smiled, 'Yeah, those were the days.'

John laughed, 'What are ye, a year older than them?'

Patrick looked cross, 'No! I think I'm three years older than them and I'm *much* wiser.'

John smirked, 'Ah yes, wise beyond your years, I'd say. Okay, let's get this shed finished.'

As Catherine and Sheila left the house, they discussed how Maeve could have been right in her assertion about the Ballydehob Sheila possibly being the winner, but there was only one way to find out, and that was from the horse's mouth.

Catherine was driving down the road to the Sheila Murphy's house in Ballydehob.

Sheila recognised the house from being there with Maeve and Aelish. 'It's the one on the right there on the hill with the religious lawn ornaments. Should we both go up?'

Catherine sighed, 'Of course we should both go up, we'll get to the bottom of this. Now then, we are going in with the assumption that she is the winner. I couldn't find out who won in Ballydehob, it hasn't been claimed yet. So, let's go on Maeve's hunch that she's the winner, we'll find out soon enough, come on then. I have an umbrella in the boot, the weather looks like it could turn with the look of that cloud.' Sheila put her hood up and went back to the boot with Catherine. She told Catherine this woman was very curt and rude; when they'd called on her last time, they found she wasn't willing to give them any information, and she'd displayed very peculiar behaviour.

Sheila remembered feeling as if this woman had something to hide, 'I hope this isn't as difficult as it was the last time, she was really quite rude. She's from England, you know.'

Catherine laughed, 'She probably won't even remember you, the English never remember.'

Sheila laughed, 'Ah, but the Irish never forget.'

Catherine was determined, 'I think I may have something here, let me do the talking. She'll warm up to me; I'll put on a thick Australian accent--perhaps she'll like me better being from one of their colonies.'

Sheila laughed, 'Don't be daft, come on then, let's see what we can find out.'

Catherine rang the doorbell. Sheila Murphy came to the door, but wouldn't open it all the way, saying, 'Yes?'

Catherine huddled under the umbrella pretending she was getting more wet than she was, to ensure she would be let in,

'Yes, hello, might we have a word with you regarding your lottery win? Rest assured, we are not after any funds, just a puzzle that needs to be solved, which may be in your best interest.'

Sheila Murphy looked very annoyed, 'I'm not interested. I'm sure you're not looking for any money, you and everyone else that has come out of the woodwork, they were also *not* looking for any money.'

Sheila noted her sarcastic tone and spoke up, 'We honestly have a mystery that needs to be solved, we believe you may have the answer.'

Sheila Murphy looked somewhat interested, 'Very well then, you two look harmless enough, come in.'

Catherine laughed, 'I've never been described as harmless before but thank you just the same.' She collapsed the umbrella, shook it off and left it inside the front door.

The woman asked Sheila and Catherine, 'Would you like a cup of tea?'

Sheila followed in after Catherine, 'That would be lovely, thank you.'

Sheila Murphy walked towards the kitchen, 'Please make yourselves comfortable, I'll be back in a moment.' The two women sat in the sitting room in silence for a few moments.

Catherine looked at Sheila and whispered, 'Well, we got this far, I'm sure we can get the information we need without giving away too much.'

Sheila looked around the sparse sitting room and whispered, 'This doesn't look like the house of someone who won the lottery.'

Catherine whispered back, 'Jaysus, it was just a few weeks ago, would you have had it all spent by now would you? Good thing it wasn't you.' Sheila laughed, then stopped herself as

Sheila Murphy walked back into the room carrying a tray of tea and scones.

The English woman placed the tray on the large round ottoman in front of the ladies, 'Please help yourself.'

Catherine poured herself a cup of tea, 'This is lovely, thank you. Now, I'll get straight to the point, when you won the lottery, where did you purchase your ticket?'

Sheila Murphy narrowed her eyes, 'I beg your pardon, but before you ask any questions, I'd like to know why you're here, and why you have any questions at all regarding anything about my lottery ticket and where I purchased it, let alone how you found out that I'd won at all.'

Catherine wanted to press on, but knew she must tread delicately. 'Did you purchase a ticket in the small village up north in Eyeries? Did you drive through Allihies?'

The woman shook her head, 'You're not telling me why you are asking.'

Sheila quietly interrupted, 'Sheila, do you know anyone that's been to that area in the last few weeks?'

Still looking annoyed, the woman relented, 'My niece was in, visiting from England; she and a friend were up there tootling around.'

Sheila could sense her annoyance and wanted to get quickly to the point before the woman asked them to leave for being evasive, 'Did your niece happen to rent a car while she was visiting?' The woman nodded. Sheila continued, 'Was it a red rental car?'

The woman looked stern. 'Now, however would you know this information about my niece? I am starting to get agitated, please get to your point at once.'

Catherine smiled, looking at Sheila, knowing that Maeve's hunch was right on. 'Bear with us for a moment as we put this unusual puzzle together. Did your niece happen to have your lottery ticket in her car?'

The woman raised her eyebrows, 'Yes, as a matter of fact she did, we purchased them the day before she left, and I had forgotten it in her car. I reminded her to not lose my lottery ticket that was in the back seat.'

Catherine pressed on, 'Did you happen to have a habit of signing your lottery tickets?'

The woman nodded, 'Yes, always.'

Catherine smiled, 'So, the ticket that your niece brought back to you, it wasn't signed, was it?'

Sheila Murphy raised her eyebrows and smiled; she was satisfied, 'I'd say you two found the ticket my niece lost, now didn't you? What do you want from me?'

Now Catherine got annoyed, 'My good woman, we want nothing at all from you. There are two girls in Allihies that have been doing everything in their power to find you. Maeve and Aelish found your signed missing ticket. Had they not found your ticket, it would have been lost in the sea or succumbed by rainfall. The only thing they wanted to do was to find the rightful owner, and it seems we have. We want nothing in return, and nor do they, I can assure you of that.'

The woman softened her tone a bit, 'Forgive me, but I've had nothing but trouble since I won. From my niece, to other family members, to neighbours and perfect strangers relentlessly expecting a handout. It's been nothing but pure begging from everyone and I'm quite tired of it.'

Catherine looked chuffed, 'Well then, you should be quite pleased to find out that your winnings have just doubled.'

Sheila interrupted, saying to the woman, 'I'm afraid to say that we don't have your ticket with us at the moment, it's in a safety deposit box at a bank in Castletownbere.'

The woman sighed, 'This is quite unexpected actually, my niece told me it blew out of the window somewhere along the sea, then it rained, so she assumed it was gone forever. Obviously at the time she didn't know it was a winning ticket, it was just my ticket that was lost with my weekly numbers, so she used my pick sheet and bought me another set, not thinking much of it at the time. Sadly, she felt the newly purchased ticket was hers, and now expects most of the winnings, in spite of the fact that she halved my winnings by losing my original ticket. Apparently, she's taking me to court. It's awful really, and very upsetting, and shameful on her part, really.'

Sheila looked concerned for the woman, 'I'm sorry you're going through this, I hope it doesn't ruin your relationship with your niece. I hope you two can work things out.'

The woman shook her head, 'I'm not sure, it's times like these that bring out the best and the worst of people.'

Catherine said, 'What's done is done and tomorrow is another day. Here's my number, give us a call and we'll get you your ticket. I think our work is done here. I must get this one home and get myself back for my grandkids before they get home. Thank you for the tea, we'll be in touch.' They all stood up.

The woman thanked them sincerely, 'I apologise for coming on strong earlier, I'm sure you understand.'

Sheila was quick to say, 'Not a bother. We'll be in touch with you next week. I'm glad we found you and our puzzle is solved, we found the missing Sheila Murphy we were searching for. It's been a wonderful journey finding you, that's for certain. Maeve and Aelish will be so thrilled to hear you've been found, it's all they've been doing for weeks.'

The woman showed them to the door, thanking them again. 'Thank you both very much, I appreciate it beyond measure. I'll speak to you next week.'

Chapter Twenty Four

Patrick and John were putting the finishing touches on the stone shed with a sturdy, sloped, corrugated metal roof. John was cleaning up as Patrick was up the ladder securing the last bit of the roof.

John shouted up to him, 'Well done, lad, this has turned out better than I expected.'

Patrick smiled, 'Not bad eh? I think Sheila will love it!'

John grimaced, 'Let's hope she does, she needed it and I'm not taking it down.'

Patrick laughed, 'I'm sure it'll be grand, as you say.'

John was looking at Patrick, admiring the work he had done and how he kept things neat and tidy along the way, 'You're a good craftsman, lad, well done. How about a cuppa, eh? I'll go and make us a pot.' He walked towards the front of the cottage.

Patrick shouted from up on the ladder, 'That'll be grand, tanks a lot!' He laughed at himself putting on an Irish accent. He leaned to see if John was still there and he lost his balance. The ladder gave way; he fell from the roof, hitting his head on a heavy pipe, and landed face down into the prickly bushes below. Patrick gave out a yell as his head hit the pipe; then there was silence..

John heard something as he was walking inside the cottage; he looked towards the back window but reckoned it was nothing. He continued putting a tray of tea together for the two of them. He noticed that the hammering outside had stopped; it was quiet. He put the kettle on the stove and walked back outside, around the cottage to the back garden, expecting to see

Patrick where he'd left him, up on the ladder, securing the last bits of the roof. He first saw the ladder lying on the grass; his heart starting to beat faster as he rounded the corner. The silence worried him; he shouted, 'Paddy?' As John came closer, his fear was realised. Patrick was lying face down on the thorny bushes, not moving. 'Ah, Christ on a bike! Jesus, Mary and Joseph, lad, what have you done to yourself?' He slowly pulled Patrick off the bushes; he knelt down and carefully laid the young man on the grass, he touched his bloodied face and trying to assess if he was okay, 'Ah look at the state of ye, lad. Paddy, can you hear me?' There was silence. Then finally Patrick moaned. John felt it was safe to leave him for a moment, 'Don't move lad, I'll be right back.'

John ran to get towels from the cottage, he could hear the kettle screaming in the kitchen as he rounded to the front. Just then Sheila and Catherine were pulling into the long driveway. John flagged them down to come quicker. Sheila could sense there was something wrong by the look on John's face. As soon as Catherine pulled the car over, Sheila jumped out.

'John what is it? What's going on?'

John looked panic stricken as he continued running into the cottage, 'I need wet towels. Paddy's fallen off a ladder into thorny bushes in the back, he's all bloodied. He was knocked out, but he seems to be coming to.'

Catherine got out of her car and immediately started running towards the back, 'I'll see to him!' Sheila ran past John into the cottage and went straight to the hob to stop the loud whistling kettle. She scurried about getting towels and wetting one.. She handed John a tea towel and asked him to fill it with ice. Sheila ran out of the cottage to the back garden. Catherine was down on the grass, holding Patrick's head on her lap. Patrick's eyes were opening and closing as Catherine reassured him that all would be well.

'You've had a fall pet, stay still, we'll sort you out.'

Sheila knelt down next to Catherine with a wet towel and started to gently wipe Patrick's face, 'Looks like just surface wounds here, ah you'll be grand Paddy. Do you know where you are lad, do you know who we are?'

He sleepily looked at Catherine, then to Sheila, as his eyes looked towards the shed, 'Your house, look what we did, I hope you like it.'

Sheila glanced at the shed, 'Well look what you did indeed, that's brilliant, Paddy.' Sheila looked at Catherine bewildered. John rounded the corner to Sheila's glare, 'What's all this?'

John was flummoxed, 'That old shed was going to be the death of you Sheila, so we built you a new one.'

Sheila had a blank look on her face, 'It seems the new shed could have been the death of Paddy, John.'

Patrick opened his eyes, looked at John and smiled a bit.

John said, 'Ah, he's grand, look at him, just a fall is all, and a bit of a bloody mess. Like you said, just surface wounds, nothing else.' Catherine and Sheila continued to clean up Patrick's face.

Sheila shook her head at John, 'Let's get him inside where he'll be more comfortable. Paddy, are you okay if we move you?' Patrick nodded in agreement.

John stepped in, 'All right lad, up you go, nice and easy, let's get you inside. Are you feeling okay?'

Patrick nodded, 'Yeah, just a bit dizzy, I think I'm okay.'

Sheila helped steady him, 'We'll put you on the sofa, you've got a nasty bump on your head there, we'll have to keep an eye on you and cool down the swelling. No sleeping for you until we're certain you don't have concussion.'

Catherine picked up the towels and followed them into the cottage. They laid Patrick on the sofa. Sheila looked at John,

'I'll get some extra pillows, he must be sitting, not lying, for at least a couple of hours.'

As Sheila left the room, John looked at Patrick. 'You heard her, sit up straight, put your shoulders back.'

Catherine swatted John with a tea towel, 'Stop, you don't need to sit up straight, just propped up a bit, let's put some ice on that head of yours.'

Patrick rolled his eyes, 'I'm fine, really, it's no big deal, you don't need to fuss over me.'

Sheila came in with extra pillows, 'We can fuss over you all we want, it's what we do best. Now, I've sent a text to Maeve, she's on her way.'

Patrick's eyes widened, 'What? Why? That wasn't necessary, seriously, I'm fine!' He started to get up and immediately grabbed his head and fell back onto the pillows.

John jumped towards him, 'Steady there lad, you're not going anywhere. I think he's going to need some paracetamol or a good shot of whiskey, or both.'

Sheila placed the towel of ice back on Patrick's head, 'Whiskey would do him well, Catherine, would you mind?'

Catherine walked into the kitchen, 'Not at all, shall I pour three extra glasses?'

Sheila smiled, 'Yes, that should do us all some good.'

Catherine came back with a small tray and four glasses, holding the tray towards Patrick first, 'Here's to the one that needs it the most, down the hatch, bottoms up, it's medicinal, you know. Heals all ailments and wounds it does, *sláinte*.'

Patrick took a glass, 'Thanks, cheers.' He drank the whiskey down and put the glass back on the tray, then he leaned back, grimaced and held the ice pack on his head.

Catherine presented the tray to Sheila and John, then took her glass and held it up, '*Sláinte* my friends.'

Sheila raised her glass, 'Ah just a wee bit cures everything, it'll get your strength back Paddy, you'll be grand.'

John held up his glass, 'And on the eighth day, God created whiskey to keep the Irish from taking over the world.'

Catherine shook her head and took the tray of glasses back to the kitchen, 'Right, I think you lot are sorted, I must push off and get back for the boys.'

Sheila walked Catherine out to her car, 'Thanks for everything, my dear friend.'

Catherine gave her a hug, 'We'll see you soon.'

Sheila looked at her and said, 'Please God. Drive safe.'

As Catherine was getting into her car, Maeve was driving down the road towards them rather quickly. She parked her car, yelled hello to Sheila and waved to Catherine, and ran towards the cottage yelling, 'Is he okay?'

Sheila smiled, 'Ah, he's grand, dear, see for yourself.' Sheila waved Catherine off and watched as she drove away. She stood alone in the quiet and thought about her visit with Catherine, and how lovely it was to see her son Michael and to meet her grandsons. Then she turned to her cottage; how wonderful it was to have these people in her life now . . . they felt like family.

John came to the door looking for Sheila, 'Would you like a cup of tea hun? I've just made a pot.' Sheila smiled and nodded, wondering if she had just heard him correctly calling her a pet name.

She smiled, 'Thank you John, I'll be there in a tick.' She went around to the back of her cottage to look at the new shed. She couldn't believe they'd built it in a day, and without her knowledge. As she rounded the corner she smiled; it was just perfect. She walked in and couldn't believe the size of it, and how well it was constructed. She smiled and said out loud to herself, 'How lovely,' She came out and looked around at the back garden; the old shed was a collapsed pile of wood. She looked beyond the old barn and into the fields. Her thoughts went to the many years she'd spent on this farm, alone, lost in her solitude and pain. She had an overwhelming feeling of shift: things were changing, she wasn't clear what, but something felt different. She felt hope, she felt open to anything. Sheila wondered what this feeling had to do with, was it John? Was it her girls? She didn't know and didn't want to question it. *Just go with it, feel happy and hopeful. What will be will be.*

Sheila continued to look at the shed and the tools strewn about. How good of John to go to all of this trouble; he did seem like such a lovely man. She walked around the back garden and heard John's voice,

'Come on girl, your cuppa's ready'

Sheila chuckled to herself: how familiar he seemed, and how natural it felt. She called back, 'Coming!'

She walked into her home; it felt warm, more of a home filled with these people that she had grown quite fond of. She asked, 'How's the patient doing?'

Patrick spoke up, 'I'm fine, just a headache.'

Maeve was sitting on the sofa acting the nursemaid. She stood up, 'Sheila, do you have any paracetamol?'

Sheila looked towards her bedroom, 'Should do, I'll have a look.' John was pouring a cup of tea for everyone. Sheila went to her bedroom to fetch painkillers for Patrick. As she walked past the guest bedroom, she noticed the stack of canvas paintings were spread out. When she returned to the sitting room she asked the three of them, 'Did someone stay here while I was away? I just noticed my paintings are all strewn about in my spare room.'

Maeve jumped up, 'Ah Sheila, I'm so sorry, I was having a peek, I couldn't help myself--they are so beautiful! I feel terrible, I hope you don't mind. I was admiring them and wanted to show them to my mam; she and I paint together. Sorry, I didn't mean to snoop.'

Sheila half smiled, 'It's okay, dear, no harm done. Let's have that cup of tea, thank you, John.' They all sat drinking their tea.

Sheila spoke up again, 'Thank you for the addition to my house you two, that was quite an undertaking, and such a surprise! It seems everyone is taking liberties around here, eh?'

John spoke up, 'Well, I wasn't the one rummaging through your house, but you know damn well that wood shed would have killed you, it collapsed with a light push it did. Paddy and I will finish up and fill your new shed with enough wood and turf to take you straight into next year, just as soon as he recuperates.'

Maeve was standing there with her eyebrows raised at John's comment. 'Well, I didn't put an unauthorised addition onto your house, I was merely admiring your talent.'

Patrick interrupted, 'Okay, I'm feeling much better, I'm going to get going now.' He stood up and winced. He couldn't open his eyes from the pain.

Maeve helped him back down onto the sofa, 'You're *obviously* not okay and you're *not* going anywhere. I'll get you some water to take your paracetamol.' Sheila followed Maeve into the kitchen. Maeve looked at Sheila as she was filling up a water glass, 'I am sorry for snooping Sheila, I couldn't help myself, you really are so talented. My mam and I were wondering if you'd come over to our makeshift studio and give us some helpful hints sometime.'

Sheila smiled, 'It's quite all right dear, thank you for the compliment, I'd be happy to call in anytime you like.'

Maeve smiled, 'That'll be grand, I'll ask my mam.'

John finished his tea and put on his overcoat, 'I'm going out there to finish the job meself, someone has to work around here.' He smiled, winked at Patrick and told him to stay put.

Sheila heard John leave, and went after him out to the back garden, 'It's brilliant, although it was a surprise, it's grand.'

John looked at the shed, 'Ah sure, look it, it needed to be done and it's done. I'll just finish up here and get these tools out of your way. Are we still on for lunch on Tuesday then?'

Sheila smiled, 'Yes, of course, here, let me give you a hand.' She picked up a few items and followed John to his truck. John took the trowel from Sheila and touched her hand. She felt a spark and looked into his eyes and smiled.

John touched the side of Sheila's bare arm, 'You'll catch your death wearing that, why don't you go in, I'll finish up.'

She agreed and smiled at him, 'Thank you John.'

Sheila went back into the cottage to find Maeve holding an ice pack on Patrick's head. He lay there with his eyes closed.

Maeve mouthed out to Sheila, 'He's asleep, is that okay?' Sheila nodded and gestured for Maeve to go into the kitchen. She slowly got up, trying not to wake Patrick.

Maeve whispered to Sheila in the kitchen, 'Should we be worried about concussion?'

Sheila shook her head, 'Ah no, he'll be grand. It's been a few hours now, he seems fit. I'll keep him here overnight, no sense in sending him back to the hostel. Besides, I can keep an eye on him if he's here.'

Maeve smiled, 'Ah, you're too good. I have to go to school tomorrow but I'll come by straight after. Let me know if I can bring anything, won't you?'

Sheila responded, 'Yes, of course, dear, I'm sure we'll manage.'

Maeve started to walk back into the sitting room and looked back at Sheila, whispering, 'I'm going to go now, we'll let him sleep.'

Sheila whispered back, 'I'll walk you out, dear.' They quietly walked through the the sitting room and out the door, careful not to wake Patrick. When they got outside near Maeve's car, Sheila slapped her head, 'My God Maeve, with all the excitement with Patrick's accident, I completely forgot to tell you!'

Maeve's eyes widened, 'You forgot to tell me what?'

Sheila continued, 'Ah Maeve, you're not going to believe this, the puzzle is solved, the treasure hunt is over, the search for Sheila is done. It was the snarky woman from England! There were two tickets purchased from the same card of chosen numbers, just as you thought. It was that Sheila Murphy's niece visiting from England, she and a girlfriend lost the original ticket so they purchased another! Well done, you must congratulate Aelish as well for all of the hard work searching, poking and prodding you two did, well done! Isn't that brilliant?'

Maeve gave Sheila a big hug, 'That's fantastic! I can't believe it! I'll tell Aye, she'll be thrilled!'

Sheila laughed, kissed Maeve's cheek and said, 'Drive safe now, God bless, see you tomorrow.' Maeve got into her car, smiled and waved at Sheila. As she drove down the long dirt road, she could see Sheila in her rearview mirror, watching until she disappeared. Maeve gave a last wave out her window before she reached the main road. As she drove, she smiled and felt a sense of satisfaction. What a grand little adventure that was, she thought to herself. She couldn't believe the search was over.

Chapter Twenty Five

Mary heard Maeve come in the front door. So did the dogs, who came running, excitedly greeting her.

'Hello Chancer, hello Larry, ah, you're good boys now, aren't you?'

Mary came to the front door and gave Maeve a kiss hello, 'Hi Sweetie, I've made a roast, should be done in a few minutes if you like.'

Maeve breathed in, 'Yes, it smells divine Mam, thanks.' She gave her mam a hug then led the way to the kitchen, 'I've just come from Sheila's, I mentioned to her about coming here to give us some helpful hints on oil painting and she loved the idea. I'm going back tomorrow to check on Patrick. What day would work for you for her to call in for a painting day?'

Mary looked curious, 'You're going to Sheila's to check on Patrick, what's this about?'

Maeve chuckled, 'Ah, it's a long story, I'll tell you at dinner. Which day would work for you so we can set that up?'

Mary smiled at Maeve's enthusiasm, 'Well, I'm a bit busy at the moment with work and planning the birthday celebration in a fortnight.'

Maeve's face lit up, 'Ah I forgot about the birthday party! We will of course be inviting Sheila, and Patrick, right? And now you must invite Mr. O'Neill because he's interested in Sheila--oh, I wasn't supposed to say anything about that to anyone. You must also invite Catherine, Sheila's long-lost friend who came back to Ireland just recently.'

Mary stopped Maeve, 'Our house is only so big, sweetie, let's make a list and we'll see what we can manage. In the meantime, if you could set the table and say hello to your father, that would be great.'

Jack was sitting in his chair reading the paper. Maeve came up behind him and gave him a kiss on the cheek, 'I said hello to you when I walked in the room!'

Jack pointed to his cheek for another kiss, 'No you didn't.'

'Ah Da, I did!' She kissed him again.

They all sat down for dinner and Maeve went through the the series of events that had happened at Sheila's cottage. Mary and Jack were surprised by a few details.

Jack was curious, 'So, here's this Sheila Murphy that we've heard nothing from for twenty five years, and all of a sudden she has all these friends and a new love interest? John O'Neill no less? What's this world coming to? It was nice and quiet, now it's all run amok, all of these scandals are coming about. I'd say you had something to do with all of this!'

Maeve cocked her head to the side, 'Da, stop!'

Jack continued, 'Tis true though, isn't it? And we have to invite all of these people to the birthday party? I'd better start cooking now!'

Mary knew Jack was joking, 'You have plenty of time.'

Maeve was getting excited about the party, 'Gran will be coming into the village then, won't she?'

Mary smiled, 'Yes, of course she is, sweetie, she'll be staying at the B&B as usual. I'm not sure why she doesn't stay here, I think it might be the dogs.' She looked at Jack while she was saying that.

Jack smiled, 'Yes, of course it's the dogs. Let's see your plates, I'll dish up this lovely looking roast for you ladies.'

Maeve smiled, looking at her mam as she passed her plate to her dad, 'I'll help you with whatever you need, Mam, just let me know.'

Mary handed her plate to Jack, 'Thank you, sweetie, I'll let you know, now let's tuck in before this gets cold.'

Maeve excitedly continued, 'I nearly forgot the biggest news of the day, we found the Sheila Murphy that won the lottery! We should invite her to the party as well! You'll need to get the ticket from the bank, Mam!'

Mary was thrilled, 'Ah Maeve, that's great news! You found her? Your search is over, then is it?' Jack joined in on the praise, 'Your mam told me about your search, Maeve, I was sworn to secrecy, but now that it's out in the open, well done you! Just in time for you to concentrate on your final exams I'd say.' Mary smiled at Jack and gestured to Maeve to eat her dinner.

After dinner Maeve excused herself to go and study.

Maeve woke up thinking about Patrick; she hoped that he'd had a good night's sleep on that sofa. She looked at the time on her phone and panicked: she was running late to pick up Aelish. She got herself ready and tore out the door.

When she pulled up in front of Aelish's house she saw Aelish standing in front of her house holding her hands up in the air questioning where she'd been.

Maeve put the window down, yelling, 'Sorry!'

Aelish got in the car, 'Jesus woman, we can't be late!'

Maeve sneered, 'Yes of course, you don't want to get detention now, do you Aye? You've never had *that* before.'

Aelish looked at Maeve. 'Well now, we're late *and* snarky.' Maeve pulled away and sped down the road, filling Aelish in on all the latest news.

Aelish was thrilled, 'My God, a lot happened at Sheila's house yesterday! I'm glad Paddy's okay. That's great, the real Sheila Murphy was found, wasn't that the bitch that wouldn't let us into her house?'

Maeve looked at Aelish disapprovingly, 'Yes, it was the English woman.'

Aelish chided, 'Isn't that what I said?'

Maeve shook her head disapprovingly, 'Apparently she had good reason for not being terribly friendly. It's her niece that's after her winnings, it's sad really. I think we'll invite her up for my mam's and aunt's birthday party.'

Aelish questioned, 'Do we get to meet the loud obnoxious niece as well?'

Maeve shook her head, 'No, we won't extend the invitation. But if this Sheila Murphy doesn't come up, we're going to have to go down to deliver her ticket. Mam is getting it out of her safety deposit box at the bank.'

Aelish thought for a moment, 'Jesus, that's odd how that all played out, isn't it Maeve? I can't believe she was found, I didn't think we'd ever find her to be honest.'

Maeve laughed, 'You made that quite clear a *few* times that you didn't think we'd find her, Aye!'

Aelish looked quite chuffed, 'Mystery solved, was there any mention of a reward?'

Maeve shook her head, 'It wasn't asked Aye, and it's not expected.'

Aelish rebuked, 'Ha! Speak for yourself! That's what I expected all along!'

Maeve shook her head as she pulled into a parking space at school, 'I look at it as we did a good deed and we had fun doing it, wouldn't you say?'

Aelish rolled her eyes, 'Whatever, it would be grand if we were compensated for our fun good deed.'

Maeve didn't pay any attention to Aelish, 'See you later. You can go with me to Sheila's after school if you'd like to check on Patrick.'

Aelish laughed, 'I'll pass, I'll get a lift home with Owen.'

Maeve waved, 'Right, see you in the morning then, bye!'

Maeve pulled into Sheila's drive and smiled when she saw Patrick's car. Mr. O'Neill's truck was there as well.

Sheila came out to greet her, 'Just in time, dear, we were just having a cup of tea.' They gave each other a hug and walked arm in arm towards the door. They walked into the cottage to find John and Patrick sitting having tea.

Sheila announced, 'Nurse Mulligan is here to check on the patient.'

Maeve laughed, 'How are you getting on Patrick, are you better today?'

Patrick smiled at Maeve, 'Yep, much better, my head's not pounding as much.'

John chimed in, 'He's fit to work, and set to stay.'

Maeve smiled, then paused, looking at everyone's faces, 'What are you on about, Mr. O'Neill? Why are you all looking at me so strangely?'

Sheila smiled, 'Well, dear, we've had a long and productive day of discussions and planning. You tell her, Paddy.'

Patrick was smiling like a Cheshire Cat, 'Well, they helped me organise my Irish citizenship, John's hired me at the pub, he's given me a place to live, and I'm taking a few classes at UCC in the fall.'

Maeve looked very surprised, and said very slowly, 'Really? Wow! This is a lot of news, this! That's great, and crazy, and--wow!' Maeve's head was spinning, she didn't know what to make of this new information. She was happy and bewildered at the same time. She drank her tea, but felt she needed to leave.

'I mustn't stay, I have so much revision to do before my exams. I'm glad to see you're doing all right, Patrick. Thanks for the tea, Sheila, see you, Mr. O'Neill.' She started to walk towards the door.

John felt awkward, 'I'm going to finish up the shed. If you fancy a bit of work now, Yank, you could help me clean up.' Patrick looked at John, then back to Maeve, and then at Sheila, not knowing what had just happened.

'Okay, ya, I'll help you.' There was an awkward moment at the door when all three tried to walk out.

Sheila stopped Maeve, 'Can I have a word, dear?'

Maeve turned back, 'Of course.' They let John and Patrick leave to finish the shed.

Sheila looked at Maeve, concerned, 'Why don't you sit down for a moment, dear.' Maeve sat down feeling a bit overwhelmed.

Sheila sat next to her on the sofa, 'Was that a sudden bit of information you weren't ready for? Did you think it was just a summer crush and he'd be gone?'

Maeve was nodding her head, 'I wasn't sure, I like him, I'm just surprised, 'tis all. I'm off to school, everything is changing.'

Sheila reassured Maeve, 'You just stay on your track dear. He's not staying because of you, and you're not responsible for him, or the decision he's made. He'd thought about staying prior to meeting you.'

Maeve looked relieved, 'That's good to know, I wouldn't want to be in that position, he must be doing it because it's what he wants for his life, not for me.'

Sheila put her hand on Maeve's, 'It is what he wants and his future is here, just carry on as you were, let the chips fall where they may.'

Maeve felt calmer, 'You're right, I didn't act horribly when I heard that news, did I?'

Sheila winced a bit, 'You looked like a deer in the headlights, so you did, but I wouldn't worry. If I were you, I'd go to the back garden, admire the shed they've built, and say a proper goodbye. It's completely understandable, your reaction, but don't think for a moment it's a bad thing, just a new direction 'tis all. It's up to you where this thing goes, if it goes anywhere at all.'

Maeve gave Sheila a hug, 'You're amazing, you know that? You truly are.'

Sheila smiled and stood up, 'Now then, you come and see my lovely new shed.' Maeve followed Sheila to the back garden.

As they walked to the back garden, John was chopping wood and Patrick was stacking it inside the new shed.

Maeve smiled at Patrick and looked at the stone shed, 'Ah, it's lovely! A far cry from that dilapidated death trap over there.' As she was speaking, and gesturing over towards where the old shed had been, she could feel Patrick staring at her. She felt nervous again. 'I really must be getting to my studies, well done you two. I'll see you all soon.'

Patrick spoke up, 'I'll walk you to your car.'

Maeve laughed, 'Because it's broad daylight and someone may attack me on Sheila's farm?'

Patrick smiled, 'No, I just want to make sure you leave, now come on.'

Sheila and John laughed; John said, 'He fits right in here, he does.'

Sheila agreed, 'Like a piece of the furniture.'

John laughed, 'Ha, that's what I said. Brilliant minds think alike, ha Sheila?' She smiled as he put his arm around her.

Patrick took Maeve by the hand and walked towards her car. 'I was going to tell you on my own that, I hope you're not worried about anything. I'm doing this because I want to, Maeve. We can take things slowly, or not at all if you'd like.'

Maeve smiled at Patrick, 'I'm thrilled you're staying, Patrick, don't get me wrong, I was just surprised is all.'

Patrick felt her unease, 'Let's just take things as they come and see what happens. I'm going to be very busy at O'Neill's pub, and doing construction jobs for John. I'd like to take you out when you're finished with your exams, we could celebrate.'

Maeve smiled, 'That sounds grand. You're more than welcome to come to my mam's and aunt's birthday party, in a fortnight.' Patrick looked confused. Maeve laughed, 'It's not this weekend, but next, you must go! Oh, I forgot to tell Sheila and John about it, I must tell them before I leave.' She turned away to head back to the back garden.

Patrick grabbed her arm and turned her around, bringing her closer to him, 'There's no pressure for anything, and things shouldn't change between us just because I'm staying, okay?'

Maeve looked up at him as he held her against his chest, 'No, nothing is different, it's just a change of thought that you're staying now, 'tis all, you're not leaving, I'm just taking it all in and imagining what it will be like.'

Patrick put his hands on either side of her head and looked at her in the eyes, 'Don't overthink anything, just enjoy.' He kissed her on the lips.

Maeve pulled away, 'I think I'm going to have a think, and think about this, because I don't know what I think right now. I'll talk to you after I have a think.' Patrick shook his head and smiled as he watched her run to the back garden.

Maeve rounded the corner to find Sheila and John in an embrace. She stopped dead in her tracks and said, 'Oh, I'm sorry!'

They parted and laughed, Sheila saying, 'Not a bother, dear, what is it?'

Maeve felt her embarrassment in her face. 'I forgot to mention: both of you are invited to my mam's and aunt's birthday party in a fortnight. I hope we'll see you both there?'

Sheila and John looked at each other and shrugged, nodding, 'Yes, sure, of course we'll be there.'

Maeve said, 'Grand!' She gave them both quick hugs and ran back to her car.

Patrick was standing by her driver's side door, 'When will I see you again Maeve?'

Maeve was scrambling inside her head for an answer, 'My mam's and aunt's birthday party?'

Patrick seemed put out, 'Okay, can I call you?'

Maeve stammered, 'It's final exams coming up, I'm afraid I'd say I'm going to be quite busy until the party.'

Patrick retreated. 'That's okay, call me if you'd like. Good luck with your exams, I'll see you again.' He started walking towards the back garden.

Maeve called out after him, 'Plan to be at the party, okay?' Patrick smiled and waved to Maeve as he walked away. She got into her car and drove down the long dirt road, noticing that no one was there in her rearview mirror waving goodbye to her. She was confused about how she was feeling; she just wanted to be home in her bed to have a think.

When she got home, she had the usual greeting from the dogs and her mam and dad calling hello from the kitchen.

She responded, 'Hi Ma, hi Da, I'm going to study. I've eaten, so I'll see you later, good night!' She heard footsteps so she quickly went up the stairs.

Mary came out from the kitchen, 'Hang on, everything okay, Maeve?'

Maeve looked down from the stairs to her mam, 'Everything's grand, Mam, just a lot of revision to do for my exams, and I'm going to have a bath. I'll see you later, g'night, love you.'

Mary was looking up the stairs after her daughter, 'Love you too, sweetie, let me know if you need anything, okay?' Mary heard a muffled, 'Okay, thanks, g'night Mammy.' She smiled; she hadn't heard that in a while. Mary thought she would wake her up in the morning with a cup of tea and maybe have a conversation with her then. Mary always taught Maeve to think quietly with her thoughts to sort out any problems. A bath and sleep always did wonders.

Mary brought Maeve a cup of tea and toast, placed it on her bedside table, and sat on her bed. She gently stroked Maeve's hair and whispered, 'It's time to get up, sweetie.'

Maeve sleepily replied, 'Morning Mammy.'

Mary looked at her . . . her little girl, her youngest, was going to be gone soon, sooner than she'd like. She felt tears welling up in her eyes, thinking about her baby no longer being in the house. She shook her head and stopped herself thinking about it. She continued, 'Sweetie, I've brought you tea and toast. I wanted to make sure that you were okay before I left for work.'

Maeve smiled and looked at her, 'Thanks Mam, I'm fine.'

Mary didn't want to give up, 'You didn't seem yourself last night, did something happen?'

Maeve didn't know where to begin and didn't want to get into details. 'Everything's grand Mam, just exams is all. I hope you don't mind, I've invited Sheila and John and Patrick to your birthday party.'

Mary smiled and got up, 'That's fine, sweetie, I suppose the more the merrier.'

Chapter Twenty Six

Final exams were complete; the students streamed into the church for mass. The first few pews were reserved for the graduates. Maeve and Aelish walked arm in arm together down the aisle of the church.

Maeve whispered to Aelish, 'I can't believe it's over, Aye.'

Aelish laughed and whispered loudly, 'Christ, thank God, Jesus, Mary and Joseph it's over! Well, it's not over until this fecking useless boring mass is over.'

Maeve elbowed Aelish and whispered harshly, 'Shhhhh stop! Jaysus, Aye, we're in church!' As they walked to their seats, they saw their families lined up behind the empty pews reserved for the students in the front of the church. Maeve smiled at her mam and dad and Siobhan and Owen. Further down the pew she saw Sheila, Mr. O'Neill and Patrick. She caught Patrick's eye and smiled even more.

Aelish was surprised; she whispered to Maeve, 'I thought it was just parents and siblings that were supposed to be here.'

Maeve shrugged, 'I'm special.'

Aelish laughed, 'You're special all right. Now let's hope this doesn't take long, I'm sure we're going to have to listen to the drivel of how we've been in a cocoon for all of these years, and now we're butterflies, free to fly and blah blah blah, it's going to be an hour of pure shite, analogies of birds, bees and bullshit.'

Maeve looked crossly at Aelish, 'Ah stop, keep your voice down, Aye, it's true though, it's exactly what you said, we *are* free now, free to do whatever we like with our lives, it's time. We're no longer under the guidance of our parents.' Maeve looked back at her mam and dad sitting in the pew behind her; Mary and Jack were whispering to each other and giggling.

As she watched her parents interact with each other, Maeve felt she wasn't the centre of their universe any longer. She smiled, 'It's all different now, isn't it Aye, everything's going to change now, and it's all okay, change is good.'

Aelish raised her eyebrows, 'Listen to you, Miss Mature, you sound better than usual lately, I wonder what's brought this on?' She peered around Maeve and looked at the pews behind, 'Hmmm, let me see if I can see him back there, let me see if I can see the reason for this change of heart, where is he sitting now?'

Maeve hit Aelish in the arm, 'Stop, turn around, shush, we're in church for God's sake, quit talking.' They both looked at each other and laughed.

Aelish continued, 'Here comes the shite, I guarantee he says something about some cocoon we were trapped in here and now we're free from this hellish school!' Maeve smiled but elbowed Aelish to be quiet.

Mr. O'Sullivan walked up to the podium at the side of the altar. He adjusted the microphone, tapped it lightly, cleared his throat and said, 'Good morning, ladies and gentlemen. Before Father O'Shaughnessy comes out, I would like to say a few words to our graduates. I have a poem I'm going to read to you that poignantly wraps up your time spent here with us. Words by the Irish poet, Sophie McGee, in her poem, *'Le Farfalle'*.

Aelish burst out laughing, whispering loudly to Maeve, 'Ah stop! That's butterflies in Italian, I knew it! What did I tell you? We were trapped in a cocoon and now we're free, please save me. Jaysus get me out of here!' Maeve grabbed her arm and shushed her, but she started laughing as well. The two of them were shaking with laughter, trying to stifle it, but they couldn't stop.

Maeve reached into her bag and pulled out two tissues and handed one to Aelish whispering, 'Pretend you're crying.'

Mr. O'Sullivan continued as the girls tried to control themselves. He cleared his throat; looking down at the podium, he spoke softly and closely into the microphone.

'We came cocooned in seasons past,
the memories fill our minds.
The years flew by, not to last,
breaking free from endless binds.
Blossomed and bloomed
we grew together,
Ah, the happy days we had.

The world is ours to seek and find,
our memories we will create.
In our hearts and in our minds,
fly free now, allowing fate.

Soar now, sing your song,
spread your wings with hope and glee.
We say goodbye, but not for long,
bound forever,
yet we are free.'

Mr. O'Sullivan went on, closer to the microphone. 'Words well spoken by Sophie McGee, who was in your shoes not too long ago. We all go through these passages of time; some occasions are marked with pomp and circumstance. But there will be monumental occasions in your life that will not be marked with any celebration or acknowledgement at all, except for your own self praise and gratitude that you achieved a personal goal.

'Be proud of yourselves for all the milestones you reach, and for all the strides you make in your lives. Pat yourselves on the back when you achieve something, anything at all, big or small; be very proud of yourselves. This is your journey you're about to embark on, this is your life. It's time for you to blossom; you were buds, slowly opening over the years. It's time for you to flourish and bloom and show your brilliance.

'It's time for you to leave this cocoon, as comfortable as it was for you, or as stifling as it may have been; it's time to break free, let loose, and fly away. You will become the beautiful butterfly that you create, that you design, that you orchestrate. It is your life now to do with what you will. Go forward with love in your hearts, and fear cast aside. Be forever grateful for what you have, and do not pine for what you want or don't have. As you embark on your individual journeys, always remember where you came from, and in turn, we will never forget you.

'Goodbye, see you soon, return often, in your minds and in your hearts, come back to where you came from. Allihies will always be here and will forever be your home. If you go further, Ireland will remain for your return. When you love something, set it free and it will flourish. You are all now free; find your passions, pursue your dreams. Don't forget where you came from and don't leave us behind for long.

'Goodbye to you all, it was an honour knowing you, teaching you, learning from you and watching you grow. God speed.'

There was a moment of silence. Both Maeve and Aelish were crying; the sounds of sniffles and nose blowing echoed in the church. Father O'Shaughnessy came out to assure everyone in a very dry tone, 'You will all survive this day, and many more to come, God willing. Now please stand to join us in the Lord's Prayer.'

On the front steps of the church, John O'Neill announced to Maeve and Aelish that everyone was going to O'Neill's pub; drinks were on him.

Jack Mulligan looked at his watch, 'Bit early for that now, isn't it, John?'

John laughed, 'Ah now, It's never too early to celebrate.'

Mary nudged Jack, 'Come on you old stick in the mud, our last baby is leaving, we can celebrate a little.'

Jack looked at Mary sideways, 'We are doing plenty of celebrating with your birthday party tomorrow, Mary.'

Mary put her arm around Jack and led him to the car, 'This is for Maeve.'

Maeve was standing next to Patrick, laughing.

Mary said, 'Look at her, Jack, she's a young woman now.'

Jack looked concerned, 'Am I going to have to have a word with that Yank?'

Mary tilted her head and smiled, 'No hun, I think your daughter can hold her own.'

Jack smiled, 'Indeed she can. Now let's go and have that celebratory drink. I may have a word with him anyway.' Mary smiled and shook her head.

O'Neill's pub filled up quickly. John scanned the crowd for Sheila; he saw her flitting from one group to another, he was surprised at how sociable she was. She came up to John and ordered all sorts of drinks.

'Can I help you pour?' she asked.

John smiled, 'No Sheila, you're not here to work, just enjoy yourself.'

Sheila smirked at him, 'Maybe this *is* enjoyable for me, I'll take three pints of Guinness, two pints of Carlsberg and a glass Bulmers, please.'

John shook his head, 'As you wish.' Then he looked around for Patrick, caught his eye and gestured behind the bar, 'Fancy a bit of work, Yank?'

Patrick smiled as he quickly walked around to the back of the bar, saying, 'You got it!' John and Patrick served everyone, then John looked around to see if he could think of anyone that was missing. He figured everyone was there that was going to be there, so he put a handwritten note on the front door: "In back, fetch us for yer pint".

He yelled to everyone, 'Who's up for a session in the back room? Instruments are along the wall, first come, first served.'

Jack's face lit up; he looked at Mary, 'Now, aren't you glad we came?'

Mary smiled, 'Of course, dear.' Everyone settled in the back room to play, sing, and listen to the music.

Sheila watched John as he took the lead at the small microphone, playing a tin whistle. Jack joined John, picking up a banjo, and Patrick picked up a drum. They all played around with whatever tune came to them. Owen joined in with another tin whistle. Everyone sat enjoying the jigs and reels.

Aelish came into the back room, walked over to the table where Maeve was sitting with her parents, and beckoned her onto the dance floor. Maeve was a bit reluctant. Aelish took her by the hand and pulled her onto the small, wooden dance floor.

The two girls stood next to each other with their arms by their sides, and began to dance in their school uniforms. They looked at each other, smiling. They'd done this routine countless times before on the small plank of a dance floor; a flash of memories came to Maeve as she danced. A few others joined in, and everyone clapped along. Maeve tripped, and Aelish laughed.

'Ah Jesus, you'd think you'd know this by now, we've been doing this since we were four years old, for Christ's sake, pay attention, Maeve, would ye.'

Maeve smirked at Aelish while she continued dancing, 'Not everyone can be as perfect as you, Aye.' Aelish laughed and pushed her. Maeve danced to the other side of the dance floor, away from Aelish, and continued dancing with a smile on her face.

When the dance was over, Maeve sat back down with her mam. 'Are you planning to have the party outside tomorrow?'

Mary looked annoyed, 'I suppose it depends on the weather, why, how many more people have you invited, Maeve?'

Maeve laughed, 'Not that many, but a few. I'll set the tables and chairs up in the back garden, the weather's meant to be good tomorrow Mam.' Mary shook her head while Maeve continued, 'I think that Sheila Murphy is coming up to collect her ticket, did you get it from work?'

Mary nodded, 'Yes, sweetie, I'll have it for her. Who else is coming?'

Maeve grinned, 'Not that many more, you may not even notice them, maybe six more people? Maybe eight. As you always say, "The more the merrier", right?'

Mary looked at Maeve and put her hand on her daughter's knee, 'It's fine, Maeve, you know your father, there'll be plenty of food and drink, we'll manage. I'm sure it'll be grand and we'll have a lovely day.'

Chapter Twenty Seven

Jack and Mary were up early, cleaning the house, getting ready for the party.

Jack was sweeping the floor, 'Mary, something has to be done about these dogs, look at this fur I've swept up, we could make another dog with all this shedding.'

Mary looked at the large pile of golden yellow fur, 'Yes dear, would you like a third dog to add to the two other dogs that *you* brought home?'

Jack smiled, 'Maybe they could just use a good brushing, that's it, that's all, come on boys, let's go outside and give you a good brushing and get you all spiffied up for the party.'

Mary said, 'While you're out there, would you mind setting up the back tables and chairs for guests? We're expecting more people, according to Maeve.'

Jack agreed, 'Come on, lads, out you go!'

Maeve came downstairs looking for her father, calling, 'Da? Da?'

Mary responded, 'He's out back with the dogs. If you could help him quickly, then go to the shops for me, that would be a grand Maeve. Your gran will be here soon; you know how she is, we won't get much done when she arrives, it'll be all talk.' Maeve went back and offered to help move the patio furniture.

She looked at Jack, 'Da, Patrick is coming over today, can I ask you a favour and please not embarrass me in front of him?'

Jack howled with laughter, 'What are you on about? When have I ever embarrassed you?'

Maeve raised her eyebrows, 'All the time, Da, every chance you get. Please don't mention anything about him going to CCU.'

Jack looked shocked, 'He's what? What? He's going to CCU? How? Since when?'

Maeve rolled her eyes, 'I've already told you, he's decided he's staying and taking classes, it's nothing to do with me.'

Jack chuckled, 'Ah, my heart of hearts, it has nothing to do with you my eye. I will say what I please, and I will do my best to not embarrass you, not in front of you anyway, you have my word.' Maeve shook her head, unsatisfied. She knew he would say something; she would just have to warn Patrick.

The house filled up, people were streaming in for hours.

When Patrick arrived, Maeve made a beeline towards him, but she was cut off by her father, 'Maeve love, would you please go and help your mam in the kitchen? She was just calling for help.'

Maeve looked mortified, 'Da, she was calling for *you*!'

Jack smiled, 'Ah, be a pet and go and help your mother, I'll get your friend Paddy here a drink. Hello Paddy!'

Patrick looked confused, 'Hello Mr. Mulligan, hi Maeve.' Jack put his arm around Patrick and guided him away towards the sitting room.

Maeve shook her head in disbelief; she looked at Patrick and mouthed out, 'Sorry!' with a half smile. Patrick just shrugged and didn't seem bothered.

Jack looked at Patrick, 'What can I get you, Paddy?'

Patrick looked around, 'A beer would be great, thanks.'

Jack continued, 'Are you a whiskey man?'

Patrick wasn't sure how to respond, 'At times, sure.'

Jack patted him on the back, 'Let's get you a whiskey then, sit down here and we'll have a chat, eh?' Patrick sat there looking confused, wondering what this was about.

Jack quickly returned with drinks in hand, 'I understand you've decided to take some classes at UCC in the fall, that came up pretty unexpectedly now, didn't it? And I understand you've decided to stay and make a life for yourself here, is it?'

Patrick drank the shot of whiskey that was handed to him and responded, 'Yes sir.' He didn't feel the need to elaborate.

Jack pressed, 'C'mere Paddy, did this decision have anything to do with Maeve, is she part of your plan, lad? What are your intentions, young man?'

Patrick shook his head, looking surprised, 'Mr. Mulligan, I was hoping to find a way to stay in Ireland before I met Maeve. I've found my way, with a job, a place to live, and a few classes I signed up for in Cork, at the community college. I do like your daughter and I would like to see her, if that's okay with you, sir.'

Jack laughed as he patted Patrick on the back, 'You two are adults, you can do what you like, I was just messing with you. But I will be keeping my eye on you.' Jack gestured with his two fingers to his own eyes, then towards Patrick's eyes, and back again. He made this gesture a few times back and forth, staring at Patrick while he did it, then he left the room. Patrick sat there for a moment with a surprised look on his face.

Maeve came running into the room, 'Sorry about me da, did he say anything incredibly embarrassing to you?'

Patrick laughed, 'Oh, he's fine, he didn't say anything, well, except that he's going to be watching me.' Patrick imitated what her dad did with two fingers to his eyes, then to her eyes and back.

Maeve grimaced, 'Ah God sorry, he's so embarrassing!'

Sheila and John were laughing, talking to Catherine and the other Sheila Murphy, who had driven up with her to the party.

Maeve walked by and reintroduced herself to the English Sheila Murphy, 'I'm so thrilled we found you! Thank you for coming. My mam has your ticket ready for you anytime you like.' Sheila Murphy smiled as she took Maeve's hand, 'Thank you, I'd like to thank both you and Aelish. You two did me a great service searching and finding me, I can't thank you enough.' Maeve smiled, 'Not a bother, we're glad we found you and we had such fun doing it! Can I get everyone a drink?'

Sheila answered, 'No dear, don't you worry about us, we can fend for ourselves.' She nudged John to fetch them drinks.

Maeve flitted around to say hello to everyone. She went to the back garden to say hello to her aunt and gran. She gave them both big hugs, 'Hi Granny! Happy birthday, Auntie Kate, it's been ages! So good to see you both. What can I get you?'

Maeve's gran spoke up, 'Not a thing, dear, we're all set, but you can sit and talk to us for a moment. We understand you have a love interest, a Yank no less, tell us! Don't leave out a single detail.'

Maeve laughed, 'Ah Gran, it's nothing like that, oh, here he comes now, I'll introduce you. Patrick, come and meet my gran and aunt.' Patrick walked over just as Mary called out to Maeve, needing help in the kitchen.

'Sorry, I'll be back,' she said. Patrick took Maeve's chair.

Gran pushed him for more information, 'Tell us Patrick, are you and Maeve "an item"? How did you meet? Tell us everything, don't leave out a thing. I want to know if there is a future with this or is it just a fling?'

Patrick looked at the two women, 'Are you messing with me?' They both looked confused.

Aunt Kate said, 'Now, whatever do you mean? We're looking for details, now come on, tell us the story.'

Patrick didn't know what to say. 'Well, it's a long story.'
Gran interrupted, 'We have time, pet.'
Patrick continued, 'Well, my grandfather was in World War II.'
Aunt Kate interrupted, 'Ah Jaysus, we're going back *that* far? This is going to be a long one, I'm going to need a drink.'
Patrick continued, 'My grandfather wrote to my grandmother just about every day. He wrote so many things about a man in Allihies named Martin Murphy. I really wanted to meet him, so I came to Ireland in search of him, and while I was looking I found Maeve.'
Maeve came back out and called for Patrick to come inside. She looked at her gran and aunt swooning over him.
Her gran said, 'He's *lovely* Maeve, a fine fellow, leave him with us, dear.'
Maeve walked over, took Patrick's hand, and pulled him off his chair, saying to her gran and aunt, 'You two can come in and see him in the sitting room, or I'll come back to you in a minute.'
She pulled Patrick saying, 'Come on, my da asked for you to help liven up the place with a bit of music.' Patrick obliged.
Sheila came outside with Catherine. Maeve shouted over Patrick's shoulder, 'Gran and Aunt Kate, these are my friends, Sheila and Catherine. That's my gran, Esther, and Aunt Kate, go and sit with them, I'll be right back. Come on Patrick!'
Sheila and Catherine sat down next to Maeve's grandmother. Sheila smiled at Maeve's gran, 'Good to meet you, your granddaughter is such a lovely girl.'
Esther said, 'She is indeed. We just found out Maeve and Patrick met looking for his grandfather?'
Sheila winced, 'Well, not exactly. Patrick was searching for his grandfather's friend. Maeve was searching for something entirely different.'

Just then, the other Sheila Murphy came outside with Mary.

Sheila continued, 'Maeve was actually looking for that woman with Mary--we met through that search.' Esther and Kate looked thoroughly confused as Mary came over, introducing everyone.

'Jack is having a bit of a music session, everyone please come in.'

Catherine said as she walked back into the house, 'I may have to help them out.' The English Sheila Murphy and Mary went back inside. Sheila sat down with Maeve's gran and aunt.

Sheila looked at Maeve's aunt, 'This is a lovely party, Kate. Happy birthday to you, is it your actual birthday today?'

Kate responded as she stood up to leave, 'Thank you, no, our birthday is actually July 2nd. I'm going to go in to listen to the music, if you'll excuse me.' Sheila felt faint; she steadied herself on her chair.

Esther looked at her, concerned, 'Are you okay? You don't look well; can I get you something?'

Sheila put her hand to her heart, 'I'm okay, perhaps a drop of water would do me good.' There was a jug of water and glasses on the table beside them. Esther jumped up and poured Sheila a glass. As she handed the glass to Sheila, she noticed that Sheila was shaking.

'Are you sure you're okay? Should I get help?'

Sheila tried to snap out of it, 'No, no, please, I'm fine, just a little bit of a dizzy spell is all, I'm grand.'

Esther still looked concerned, 'You're sure?'

'I'll manage. I'm just going to go inside for a moment and freshen up, I'll be grand.'

Sheila stood up, not feeling sure of her footing. Everything sounded like an echo; it felt as if everything was closing in on her. She slowly walked into the house and headed for the loo.

As she walked through the house, she could hear the music but it was echoing in her head; her mind was spinning, but everything seemed to be moving around her in slow motion.

Maeve came around the corner of the kitchen, nearly running into Sheila, 'Oh! Didn't see you there!' She gave Sheila a hug. She held on to Maeve feeling a rush of emotion, her heart swelled. Sheila could feel tears welling up in her eyes; she closed her eyes as she hugged Maeve and asked God for strength. *Don't cry, think clearly, don't say anything.* Then she said, 'Sorry dear, I was just on my way to the loo.'

Maeve let her go, 'Of course! Then come in and listen to the music, we never know how long these things will last.'

Sheila smiled, 'I'll be back in a tick.'

She continued down the hallway towards the loo, where she ran into Kate, followed by Mary, who said to her, 'Come and listen to the music, Sheila.' It was as if Mary was speaking in slow motion. Sheila looked into her eyes, then at Kate, who was saying, 'Yes, come in and help us sing!' Kate also seemed to be speaking very slowly. Sheila looked into Kate's eyes and felt as if she was going to faint.

She mustered the strength to say, 'Be right there.' She guided herself into the loo and sat on the closed toilet with her head in her hands.

'My God,' she said out loud. 'Why didn't I see it, why didn't I know the first time I laid eyes on them? July the 2nd. Is it them? My God, is it them? Could it be them, do they know?' She sat still, trying to absorb this information. *What are the chances they're my girls? They must be. What kind of coincidence would that be, the same day, the same year? The familiarity of them? Especially Maeve, my God, Maeve. I felt love for Maeve immediately upon meeting her, that explains that. Their eyes, I saw a familiarity in both of their eyes, My God in heaven, are these my girls?*

Sheila's head was spinning: so many thoughts about so many things over a lifetime swirled in her head. She could barely fathom the possibility that her girls had lived their entire lives not far from her own house. She could scarcely comprehend any of it. She looked at herself in the mirror and regained her composure. There was only one way to find out. She took a deep breath and went back outside to talk to Maeve's grandmother. But Esther was gone.

Sheila walked back into the house, looking at everything deliberately and slowly. Everything looked different. Her head was swirling, thoughts racing..

As she entered the sitting room, they were playing the song "Hard Times Come Again No More", Patrick on the drum, Owen playing the tin whistle and Jack playing the banjo. John was leading the song; while he sang, he looked at Sheila standing in the doorway. He sensed by the look on her face, there was something troubling her. He fixed his eyes on her and sang softly.

Let us pause in life's pleasures, and count its many tears,
While we all sup sorrow with the poor.
There's a song that will linger forever in our ears,
Oh, hard times come again no more.
'Tis the song, the sigh of the weary,
Hard times, hard times, come again no more.
Many days you have lingered around my cottage door,
Oh, hard times, come again no more.
While we seek mirth and beauty, and music light and gay
There are frail forms fainting at the door.
Though their voices are silent, their pleading looks will say
Oh, hard times, come again no more.

Sheila saw everyone in the room in a different light. All of these people she had just got to know over the last few weeks, they felt like family, they *were* family.

John continued to sing the words that resonated with Sheila:

'Tis the song, the sigh of the weary,
Hard times, come again no more.
Many days you have lingered by my cottage door,
Oh, hard times, come again no more.
'Tis a sigh that is wafted across the troubled wave,
'Tis a wail that is heard upon the shore,
'Tis a dirge that is murmured around the lowly grave,
Oh, hard times, come again no more.'

Sheila was the first to start clapping, then the entire room erupted. Sheila left the room and dabbed her eyes as she walked back into the kitchen. She found the English Sheila Murphy at the island in the kitchen, writing something. As Sheila got closer, she noticed Sheila Murphy was writing checks: one was written out to Maeve, the other to Aelish.

Sheila said to the English woman, 'Ah, Sheila, that's awfully kind of you.'

The woman looked at Sheila, 'I wish I could give more, but I'm afraid it's all tied up in the courts at the moment. But I wouldn't have half of it if it weren't for those girls.' She showed Sheila the winning ticket.

Sheila slowly looked around the room and softly said, 'I wouldn't have any of this if it wasn't for those girls.' The woman had no idea what she was talking about; she continued writing the checks and putting them in envelopes for the girls. Sheila glanced down and was shocked at the amounts: fifty thousand euros each, one hundred thousand in total.

In awe, but preoccupied with her own thoughts, she merely said, 'Good woman.' She patted her on the back and walked outside to the back garden and sat down. At that moment, she saw Maeve's grandmother walk back into the garden by herself.

Esther pulled up a chair next to Sheila.

Esther looked down at Sheila before she sat down with a concerned look, 'Are you feeling better? You don't look as pale as you did.'

Sheila nodded, 'Esther, I must ask you a personal question.'

Esther looked surprised, 'Whatever could that be?'

Sheila leaned towards Esther; quietly and deliberately, she asked, 'Esther, did you adopt your girls from the Blessboro House in Cork?'

Esther looked shocked, then looked fiercely at Sheila, whispering loudly, 'What in God's name are you on about? Did I adopt my girls? What kind of preposterous question is that? Why on earth would you ask me such a question? Have you asked anyone else this absurd question?'

Sheila was taken aback--she didn't think the conversation would turn this way. She was confused. How could she have been so wrong?

'No, heavens no, I wouldn't say anything to anyone. I'm terribly sorry, I beg your pardon. My God, it was unbelievable wishful thinking on my part I suppose. I've upset you and I apologise. I hope you understand: when I heard your girls were born on the 2nd of July, the same day and the same year my twin girls were born when I was sixteen, I just thought . . . I've yearned for them and mourned them every single day of my life since. I'm sorry I've upset you asking that question. I suppose it was preposterous of me to ask you that, I apologise, I hope you understand.'

Esther was still bothered, 'I'm certain there are twins born every day in Ireland and probably plenty more on that day throughout the country.'

Sheila gave Esther a weak smile as she excused herself, she got up and went back inside the house looking for John; she just wanted to leave. She felt sick and sad. Esther remained in her seat, expressionless.

John saw Sheila coming into the house, and he walked towards her. As he looked into Sheila's eyes, he could see them filling with tears. He put his arms around her, saying, 'Come on auld girl, let's get you out of here before you cause a scene.'

Sheila shied away from him, 'I've never caused a scene in my life. I'm grand, I'm always grand. Have you seen Catherine?'

John replied, 'She's in the sitting room, you ok? Can I get you anything?'

Sheila partially smiled, 'I'm okay, thanks John, I'll be back.'

She found Catherine fiddling around with an accordion. Sheila sat next to her and whispered, 'Catherine, I've just discovered the birthday party we are at, Maeve's mother and aunt, these twin girls, they were born on the 2nd of July, Catherine, in 1956.

Catherine put the accordion down, pulled her head back in shock, 'Are you *serious*? Are you sure?' Catherine sat speechless.

Sheila looked serious and nervous, 'I confronted the grandmother in the back garden, she vehemently denied she adopted them. I feel a fool for asking, she seemed quite upset that I asked if she'd adopted her girls from the Blessboro House.'

Catherine raised her eyebrows, 'That doesn't surprise me: the children of wayward mothers were the dregs of society as well; many hid the fact they were adopted. Jaysus Sheila, what do you think?'

Sheila looked worried, 'My God, Catherine, I thought if I ever saw my girls, I would recognise them in a split second, but I didn't. But then after hearing that birth date, I looked at Mary and Kate and I saw something in their eyes. I look at Maeve and I see even more. I don't know, but my gut tells me they're my girls.'

Catherine shook her head, 'Ah sure look it, it's very possible indeed, don't be hard on yourself--or daft--you'd hardly expect to recognise children that you haven't seen since they were babies, after fifty nine years no less, no one would.'

Sheila wasn't convinced, 'When I first came to this house, I should have known Mary was my daughter, if in fact she is.' And Maeve, I should have known *immediately* that she was my granddaughter, if in fact she is?'

Catherine reassured her, 'That's neither here nor there, the question is what to do now.'

Sheila thought for a moment, 'Put yourself in her shoes, Esther, the mother, if those *are* my girls and she kept that fact hidden from them and the rest of the world, it's not my place to tell them, it's hers.'

Catherine looked out the door towards the kitchen, 'Let's go back and socialise a bit more, I'll think of something.'

Sheila wasn't sure what to do; she was still a bit shaken up, 'I think I'll have a drink.'

Catherine led the way, looked back at Sheila and whispered, 'I'll have a drink as well, for I have new eyes now and it will help me see a bit more clearly.'

Sheila tapped her back and whispered loudly, 'Say nothing at all.'

Esther was in the kitchen, talking to the English Sheila Murphy as she stood there holding two envelopes with Maeve and Aelish's names on them.

Esther gestured towards Maeve, 'There's Maeve now, you can give her both of your cards.'

Sheila Murphy shook her head, 'That's okay, I'll be giving them these notes when I leave, but thank you.' Esther shrugged and looked across the island at Catherine staring at her. Esther looked away; then she saw Sheila talking to Maeve, and thought she saw pain in Sheila's eyes. Esther wandered back outside and sat at the table by herself. She sat quietly, deep in thought.

Esther had a sense of apprehension. She had known this day would come. She had dreaded it, and tried to avoid thinking of it over the years, but now it had come to a head and it must be dealt with. She came to the conclusion that it had better be her, not Sheila, nor anyone else, to say anything at all to her daughters.

Esther went back inside and looked around for Mary and Kate. She asked them both to step into the spare bedroom with her; told them to get themselves a drink first, that she needed to have a word with them both in private. She poured herself a whiskey and walked into the room. The two sisters followed.

Esther looked pained, 'Sit down you two, drink your drinks, I have something that may come as a bit of a shock to you both.' Mary and Kate looked at each other, not having a clue what was going on.

'What is it, Mam?'

Esther took a breath, 'Times are very different today than they were when you two were born and growing up.' They were sitting on the day bed intently waiting to hear what their mam was getting at. Esther pulled up a chair and sat in front of her girls. 'As you remember, your father was very strict; he was as stubborn as stubborn gets, he was, and he was a very private man, God rest his soul.' Mary and Kate had no idea where this conversation was headed.

Esther continued, 'The truth became blurred over the years, after time, it didn't seem possible to tell you girls the truth-- your father forbade it. I was going to tell you when he died, but the years simply passed.'

Mary looked very concerned, 'Mam, what is it? What are you saying?'

Esther continued, 'It was the church as well, it was the priests and the nuns, they actually forbade it as well.'

Kate was getting annoyed, 'Forbade what? What are you on about Mam?'

Esther was having a difficult time finding words, she was quiet for a moment. She spoke slowly, 'I never wanted you girls to be upset, I never wanted you to feel different or ashamed.'

Mary was looking wide eyed at her mam and shaking her head, 'What is it Mam, what is going on?'

Esther looked at her daughters, she leaned over and took their hands into her own, 'I've always loved you two, from the moment I laid eyes on you both, I loved you with all of my heart. The first moment I laid eyes on you was in a photo . . . Mary, have you that photo of me holding you girls in front of a bush, where is it?'

Mary stood up, 'It's right here, Ma.' She walked over and picked up the framed photo off the shelf, brought it back and handed it to her mother.

Esther took the photo and touched it, 'There's another photo that looks just like this; it's the first photo I ever saw of you girls.' She paused and took a breath, then slowly said, 'A photo of you being held by your sixteen year old birth mother, who had to give you up for adoption.' There was silence. Mary and Kate looked at each other with their eyebrows raised, dumbfounded. They looked back at their mam, completely taken aback.

Kate began looking so confused, 'What the..?'

Mary looked concerned; she slowly said to her mam, 'What are you saying Mam? Kate and I were *adopted*? From where? From who?

Kate still looking shocked, 'I don't understand. Where did we come from? Why are you telling us this now? I don't know what to say, or think, or feel.'

Esther was crying, 'It's been such a burden hiding this, you two have no idea, the guilt ate at my gut daily but I had to get used to it. Your father and I weren't able to have children. You two have no idea what a different world we used to live in back then, you have no idea the stigma, the power of the church, the stronghold they had on us.' Esther was looking down at the framed photo on her lap, tears streaming down her face. 'We waited years for you two. Oh, how your da wanted children. He came home one day with a photo that looked just like this, it was given to him by a nun, a nun at Blessboro House in Cork. They had two girls we could adopt, it was all very quick and quiet, nothing was to be spoken of it. We had to move from our village up north and pretend you were our own after the adoption, it was the only way it could be done. You were our girls and we never spoke of it again, that was that.' Esther was sobbing, 'It's just the way things were done.'

Mary and Kate saw their mother's anguish as they held her hands. Mary spoke up, 'It doesn't matter now, does it? You're our mam, and we love you, and we loved Da.'

Kate agreed, 'This is a lot of new information to wrap our heads around, but ya, Mam, you're our Mammy.' Esther looked at the two of them, 'I've loved you with all of my heart I have, and your father did too.'

Mary prodded, 'It's strange you're telling us now Ma, all of a sudden at our birthday party, why now?' Kate was curious as well, 'What brought this on Mam? Why now?'

Esther looked at both of them, 'I'm telling you girls now because it's time, and, well, because your birth mother is here.' They both slowly looked around the room and at each other. Kate and Mary looked stunned. Their eyes wide and their mouths hanging open, shocked. Mary stood up then sat back down feeling uneasy, 'What? Who? She's *here*?' Kate pressed, 'Who is she, where is she?'

Esther continued, 'To my surprise, she is here. I didn't expect this to happen today, I never thought this day would ever come to be honest, but, here it is and it's the right thing. It's been a difficult road for your birth mother, she's missed you terribly all of these years. She didn't have a choice, you know, they never did back then. She was put in an institution, she had you at sixteen and you were ripped from her arms-- that's how it was done back then.'

Mary was aghast, 'My God! Who is she, Ma? She's here?'

Kate pressed, 'Ma, who is she? Why is she here?'

Esther looked towards the door, 'She's in the kitchen. You may want to take her aside, tell her yourselves in private; she doesn't know for sure, but she has an idea. I was speaking to her earlier, when she heard your birth date, she wondered if you were her girls. I was taken aback so I said no. That's not fair though, as you can imagine, she has a right to know.'

Mary asked slowly, 'Ma, who is she?'

Esther responded, 'Mary, she's already in your lives, she and Maeve have made a connection recently.'

Mary shook her head and put her hand over her mouth, 'My God, it's Sheila.' She sat back silently and started to cry.

Kate looked curious, 'Sheila? On the farm? Maeve told me about her, she loves her, how could that be? Sheila is our birth mother?' Kate sat there in disbelief.

Esther continued, 'Go to her and tell her yourselves, tell Sheila you are her girls, both of you, do that now, would you? She has a right to know and it would be best to come from you two. Go on now.' Mary and Kate stood up not quite sure how to handle this. Mary looked at her mam, 'You'll always be our mam.' Kate agreed, 'Yes, Mam.' Esther smiled, 'I know, we can't change that or the life we've had together. But, you wouldn't be here if it weren't for her. Take her aside, tell her alone.' They each gave their mam a hug. Mary gestured to Kate to follow her down the hallway into the kitchen.

Sheila was standing by the island with Catherine.

Mary said, 'Sheila, can I have a word with you outside?'

Sheila looked at Mary, 'Of course.' They started to walk out to the back garden, and Sheila noticed Kate was coming as well. Sheila wasn't exactly sure what was going on. They all reached the table and chairs; Mary gestured for Sheila to sit down. Mary and Kate sat on either side of her. Sheila sat down not taking her eyes off the two women.

Mary said, 'Sheila, our mother just told us some earth moving news that we had no idea of, until just a few moments ago.' Time stood still. There was a heavy silence. Sheila knew what was coming; she looked back and forth between the two women sitting on either side of her. She couldn't say a word. She was frozen with the realisation of what was about to be said. Closing her eyes for a moment, reaching out with both of her hands, she took Kate's in her left hand and Mary's in her right, holding on to both of them very tightly. Now she looked at both of them slowly, tears welling up in her eyes. As if in slow motion, she heard the words Mary spoke, seeming to echo in Sheila's head but going right through to her chest, piercing her heart. Sheila was looking at Mary's lips as she spoke; they looked like Martin's lips. She looked at Mary's eyes, *Her eyes, my God her eyes, it's as if I'm looking into my own eyes and a reflection of my mother's; she has her eyes.*

Mary said slowly and deliberately, 'Sheila, our mam just told us that you were our birth mother.'

Sheila closed her eyes, gripping onto her girls' hands, tears falling down her cheeks, 'My God, sweet Jesus, my God, it's true. Oh, my God.' She was shaking.

Kate started to cry, 'It's true, we had no idea.' The three of them sat silent for a moment, looking at each other in disbelief, and quietly crying. Sheila got to her feet; she bent over to hug Mary, who stood up and held her tight. Kate stood up as well, and hugged the two of them as they all wept together.

Sheila held her two girls as close as she could, saying, 'My babies, my God, my babies, my girls. I have thought of you two every single day of my life since the moment you were born. You have been with me your whole lives.'

Mary was crying, 'I wish we'd known, I wish we'd been told.' Sheila looked at Mary and touched her face. *Oh, to touch her skin again, her soft skin that I haven't touched since she was four months old.*

She took Kate's hand and looked into her eyes as tears streamed down her face.

Kate said, 'I wish we'd known.'

Sheila looked at Kate and saw Martin in her eyes; she saw her father; she saw herself in Kate as well. She looked back at Mary and took her hand, and she said to both of them, 'Don't wish away this moment. I feel like my heart is going to swell and burst from my chest. Thank God, thanks be to God we've found each other.' Then she paused, looked at her girls standing in front of her, and she gestured towards the chairs, saying softly, 'C'mere to me.'